To Jasmir
L euR12 7c mnn) JoU

Malice, Matrimony, and Murder

A Limited-Edition Collection of 25 Wedding Cozy Mystery and Crime Fiction Stories

Joslyn Chase, Charlotte Morganti, P.M. Raymond, Paige Sleuth, Teresa Inge, Sally Milliken, Rebecca Olmstead, Nikki Knight, Shari Held, Barbara Howard, Ashley-Ruth M. Bernier, KD Sherrinford, Stephen D. Rogers, Elaine Togneri, Lynn Hesse, Margaret S. Hamilton, Stella Oni, Robert Petyo, Pamela Kyel, Karen McCullough, Wil A. Emerson, Jack Bates, J. Aquino, Sharyn Kolberg, Becky Clark

Bechs on 7Hr Banch
h n sh...

17 | 8 | 2024

Project coordination, interior formatting, and cover design credit to Marla Bradeen.
Ebook ISBN: 979-8223878360
Paperback ISBN: 979-8223154907

Table of Contents

About the Anthology

Marla Bradeen (aka Paige Sleuth) has coordinated a handful of limited-edition anthologies over the years and always found the process to be highly enjoyable. However, *Malice, Matrimony, and Murder* is a bit different in several respects. This time, she wanted to 1) include more authors, 2) offer a print edition, and 3) start off the project as a Kickstarter campaign.

The Kickstarter campaign launched on May 23, 2023 and was successfully funded within twelve hours, making it possible for us to produce both a print edition of *Malice, Matrimony, and Murder* and to pursue some paid advertising. We are hugely grateful to everyone who believed in this collection from the beginning and backed us on Kickstarter. This is the result of your support!

It should be noted that authors from the United States, Canada, and the United Kingdom have contributed to this collection. For this reason, you may notice a slight variation in spelling and punctuation between the different stories.

We hope our stories provide you with some entertainment, insight, and enjoyment no matter what is going on with your life at the moment. And for those of you who enjoy being the sleuth, we've weaved a special overarching mystery into our anthology. Read on to learn more about the Wedding Whodunit and how you can collect a bonus ebook for solving the crime. Happy reading and sleuthing!

OUR STORIES:

"The Groom's Club" by Joslyn Chase. Mystery novelist, Cathryn Harcourt, attends an April wedding, anticipating only a lovely ceremony and a sumptuous lunch, but is instead surprised by a series of unexpected twists as murder mars the day and the groom becomes the prime suspect.

"A Wedding Planner's Nightmare: A Persimmon Worthing Mystery" by Charlotte Morganti. Ask what could go wrong at the first ever triple wedding in Blossom City, and Persimmon Worthing will tell you, "Anything and everything, because this is Blossom City where something untoward happens at every event."

"Cinderella at Midnight" by P.M. Raymond. It's a race against the clock for Lyla, a six-year-old demon detective, to help Andrina, the bride-to-be, locate her missing dog, Walter, and the enchanted rings around his collar and avert catastrophe before the clock strikes midnight.

"Ring Robbery: A Cozy Cat Caper Mystery Short" by Paige Sleuth. Cherry Hills amateur sleuth Imogene Little must locate a bride's stolen heirloom ring or risk a wedding being canceled.

"What's a Little Murder Between Friends" by Teresa Inge. When Rhiannon Cassidy unwillingly becomes the unofficial wedding planner for her best friend Maggie May's wedding; she encounters a flooded venue, unsigned prenup agreement, missing marriage license, and drama between a bridesmaid and the groom.

"Icing on the Cake" by Sally Milliken. Carrie and her team the Ice Witches gather each year for an annual pond hockey tournament but when the ex-husband of teammate Ashley arrives, the action moves off the ice.

"Love and Death in Madison, Georgia" by Rebecca Olmstead. It's 1957, and Violet Davenport's nurse, Mama Bea, says the good Lord has a way of working things out, but when the groom drops dead at the reception, it appears someone took matters into their own hands.

"Second Chances Are...Murder: A Vermont Radio Mystery" by Nikki Knight. At a beautiful Vermont inn, the wedding of 103-year-old Grandpa Seymour and 92-year-old Aunt Patsy is interrupted by moose...and murder.

"Wedding Vows & Vipers" by Shari Held. Maid of honor Casey Kelly employs her sleuthing skills to infiltrate the den of vipers that make up the wedding party and save a bride accused of murdering her groom from a possible prison sentence.

"The Bride Wore Death" by Barbara Howard. Candace, a nervous bride on her big day, receives a handmade necklace from her young niece and later collapses at the reception from poison.

"Chill: A Naomi Sinclair Short Story" by Ashley-Ruth M. Bernier. When restaurant sabotage prevents a fellow bridesmaid from joining a Bridesmaids Day on the pristine waters of Magens Bay, St. Thomian food journalist Naomi Sinclair must trade chilling in the sun for solving the case.

"A Bit of a Do" by KD Sherrinford. Rookie detective Liv's sleuthing skills are sorely tested when she attends her cousin Rachel's pre-wedding dinner.

"Goes Around" by Stephen D. Rogers. Hearts aren't the only things that get stolen.

"Jilted" by Elaine Togneri. A jilted bridegroom chases down his former bride-to-be, discovering the secrets she's been hiding without revealing his own.

"Sabotage and a Murder Mystery" by Lynn Hesse. A meddlesome mother-in-law-to-be and a stunning ex-fiancée sabotage the wedding plans, making Sissy, the bride and mystery buff, wonder if it's all worth it—until a body winds up in the church pantry.

"Til Death Do Us Part" by Margaret S. Hamilton. When custom cake baker Poppy learns someone has sabotaged her magnificent wedding cake, she plunges into an investigation.

"A Wedding Most Bitter: A Lara's Detective Agency Series" by Stella Oni. Lara Thompson, ex-agent turned PI, navigates high-society intrigue and deadly secrets at a lavish Lagos wedding turned murder scene.

"Better Late Than Murdered" by Robert Petyo. Rita, while attending a pre-wedding party, tells her date she is convinced that her cousin's previous fiancée was murdered.

"Charm City Wedding" by Pamela Kyel. Special Agent Laci Duvall, Air Force OSI, thought she was just the last-minute stand-in for the wedding of her boyfriend, Baltimore Police Detective Antonio Desio's brother, but a bullet to the wedding coordinator quickly unravels a web of blackmail.

"The Other Wedding Crasher" by Karen McCullough. A wedding crasher's secret mission may be compromised when she realizes that she's not the only one.

"Marriage, Neighbors and Best Friends: A Wally and Ollie Series" by Wil A. Emerson. Walter Mason's new wife and best friend are at odds so it's up to Wally to resolve the problem.

"The Wedding Dress in the Middle of the Road" by Jack Bates. A private detective uncovers a murder when she is hired to find a missing wedding gown.

"Death, the Unwanted Wedding Guest" by J. Aquino. When a wedding guest is murdered, bridesmaid Jenny and maid of honor Lynn, also government agents, take the initiative to solve the murder.

"We Haven't Had Cake" by Sharyn Kolberg. A wedding goes viral for all the wrong reasons when a soap star's character is killed off and she and her daughter are desperate to get back into the spotlight.

"To Have and To Scold" by Becky Clark. The "mandatory activities" for the wedding set forth by the bride's mother did not include Charlee and AmyJo investigating a mystery.

Wedding Whodunit

NOSY NEWS NETWORK
Official Press Release
For Immediate Publication

● ● ●

Buckle up for a wedding you won't forget! International bestselling author and prominent social media influencer Virginia Leah, aka Lady V, has finally decided to settle down. Whispered rumors first began over the holidays, when the tall and elegant forty-seven-year-old was spotted wearing a killer red dress and a diamond ring the size of a lobster tail during an intimate dinner with self-made business billionaire Buddy Bill Corey. Paparazzi tracked the elusive power couple for months, hoping to get the inside scoop. However, both Lady V and Buddy always managed to deflect questions about their relationship, and nobody was ever able to definitively confirm whether the two were indeed romantically involved.

But that all changed two nights ago when Lady V was photographed with wedding dress designer to the stars, Dessy D'Amato. Dessy wasn't talking but an unnamed source at her boutique did. And, it turns out, the wedding is happening today. Surprise!

It's been a whirlwind twenty-four hours as media outlets around the world, including those of us here at Nosy News Network, scrambled to be on the scene. Every A-list celebrity has been clamoring for a last-minute invitation, but Lady V and Buddy have chosen to keep their ceremony small and intimate. They've limited those in attendance mostly to close family and friends, all of whom have been sworn to secrecy about the whole event. Somehow, the couple has gotten their wish to keep the guest list hush-hush—until now.

That's right! Those of us here at Nosy News Network managed to secure a copy of the guest list mere minutes ago, a scant half hour before the big event is scheduled to begin. And, dear readers, without further ado, here it is:

GUESTS OF THE BRIDE

1. Nancy Jean. It's no secret Lady V credits her success to her beloved mother, a woman she's publicly praised in almost every interview she's done. Lady V claims she's done her best to use the traits and gifts her mother has bestowed upon her to the fullest, and that's why she is where she is today. A masterful cake decorator who loved to sew in her younger years before the shoulder and back issues of age derailed those hobbies, Nancy Jean raised Lady V and her brother to recognize right from wrong and to always do what's right no matter the personal sacrifice. Sadly, Lady V's brother died years ago—a fact that still pains Nancy Jean—but Lady V knows he's at this wedding in spirit and would be so proud of how his children and their youngsters have thrived under Nancy Jean's love and care. Nancy Jean might not always understand the kids of today, but she's always happy to help them see the world through fresh eyes and stands by her belief that everyone has a right to make their own mistakes. In fact, it seems Nancy Jean might believe Lady V's marriage to Buddy is one of those life mistakes. She's been caught frowning in the groom's direction several times this afternoon. Does she disapprove of her daughter's man, or is she, a woman who generally shies away from the spotlight, merely uncomfortable attending such a high-profile event?

2. Tammy Barker. One of Lady V's first fans turned close friend might be pushing senior citizen age with her full head of gray hair, but her age didn't stop Tammy from giving up her boring auditor job to become Lady V's public relations agent when the social media personality first started developing a sizable

following. Then again, Tammy has never been one to shy away from a challenge. Her hobbies are quite eclectic and her creativity knows no boundaries. From home repairs and refurbishing vintage furniture, to woodworking, cooking, classical piano, and crafts of all shapes and sizes, Tammy has done it all. Tammy describes herself as HOPS—or Happy, Overweight, Productive, and Sassy. While she struggles with small talk, she has no problem performing in front of large crowds, often keeping them in stitches with her stories and antics. She can be very wordy, loves to quote movies, is a fan of Christmas, and will try any food—as long as she's not warned beforehand that she's about to ingest something as stomach-churning as organ meat or cicadas. Tammy is also a budding writer herself. Indeed, it's rumored the PR agent is working on a mystery novel when she's not marketing Lady V's books. Could it be she's secretly hoping to find some fodder for her work-in-progress at today's event?

3. Jason, aka JJ. Lady V's six-foot-two, half Kiwi, smart and handsome ex-boyfriend boasts he "knew her when." One of three siblings raised by two accountant parents who both died of cancer, JJ ran away from home at a young age to join the circus. Now in his fifties, JJ is a ringmaster and occasional performer who loves what he does. He's also an environmentalist and drag queen who goes by the name Bunni. When he's not performing, you might find him engrossed in *Doctor Who* or the latest science fiction offering. JJ dated Lady V years before she built up a sizable social media following or published her first international bestseller, back before he went bald and sported the salt-and-pepper beard that now complements his hazel eyes behind those reading glasses. While the kind and generous JJ adores his two young nephews—both under the age of ten—and has considered starting a family of his own, his hectic life has prompted him to stay mostly single over the years. JJ and Lady V have remained friends since their break-up, but lately JJ seems

a bit melancholy. Could he regret letting his ex get away before she hit it big?

4. Steven Smith. Lady V met Steven in college while she was studying for her Masters in creative writing and he was pursuing a PhD in Anglo-Irish literature and history. Born in Stevenston, Ayrshire, Scotland, to a coal mine supervisor named Robert David Orr Smith, Steven has done quite a bit of genealogical research into the origins of the "David Orr" name, which has been passed down through the generations of his family since 1720, when an ancestor married into the Orr family. Professionally, Steven works for the British Museum and is responsible for the King's Library located in the East Wing. In fact, Steven is only one of three people with keys to the rare book room's locked displays. It's rumored that raised voices were heard coming from Steven's basement office when Lady V paid him a visit not too long ago. Steven's secretary hinted the argument concerned Buddy rather than the messy state of Steven's office, a sign he was busy arranging a new exhibit, but nobody here at Nosy News Network has been able to confirm. Does Lady V's longtime friend not approve of her husband-to-be?

5. Carly Redmund. Lady V's five-foot-nine, thirty-something distant cousin works for The Warner County Police Department in Mobile, Alabama. She hesitated to attend this wedding at all, as she has been busy prepping for the sergeant's test and trying to help her abused kid sister get her life back on track. But her rich new love interest encouraged her not to miss out on such a prestigious event. Carly seems rather bored now that she's here though, almost as if she would rather be at home reading her favorite book, *The Feminine Mystique* by Betty Friedan—or wishing she were on duty with a crime to solve.

6. Scarlett Jade. Three years ago, Lady V's long-time psychic advisor—a formidable brunette with a penchant for flashy

jewelry and colorful caftans—warned her most prominent client about a doomed romance on the horizon. That didn't stop Lady V from adding the woman to her guest list though. Granted, Scarlett Jade's insights were spoken so cryptically no human could possibly decipher them. However, with skeptical customers fleeing toward more reputable fortunetellers by the droves, it's clear Scarlett Jade is getting desperate to have one of her predictions come true. Could it finally be this one?

GUESTS OF THE GROOM

7. Joyce Corey. The groom's mother endured fifty hours of painful labor while giving birth to Buddy and his big head, a fact she's quick to tell everyone who will listen. With her Jersey accent and ready laugh, the sixty-something likes to tell everyone she has more energy than three twenty-year-olds combined. Joyce treats every day as a new adventure—and a new excuse to change her hair color. At the moment her short locks are copper, a color that nicely complements her green eyes and freckles. The former school crossing guard takes full credit for both of her sons—and all of the town's children, to boot—making it to adulthood. After all, she was the one who taught them to stop at the "red rectangle" before crossing the street. Only three children have ever failed to stop on these "truncated domes and detectible warning pavers," incidents that sent Joyce racing into traffic to save them. No child has ever been injured on Joyce's watch, but she still flinches at the sound of screeching brakes. Her reaction is understandable, considering that Buddy was one of the three disobedient children. Joyce insists no other woman will ever sacrifice as much as she did for the self-made billionaire and reminds him of that fact whenever she gets a chance. It's no secret that Joyce believes Buddy should be doing more for her financially and resents him legally binding himself—and his fortunes—to a wife.

8. Kirk Corey. The only brother of Buddy has been extremely jealous of his sibling ever since Buddy made his debut in the business world. That's no surprise as Buddy's net worth is nine digits longer than Kirk's. Only a year older than Buddy, Kirk is a burly pool-playing addict with a gold tooth and a quick-fuse temper whose drinking habit keeps him drowning in loans. He may have only accepted this wedding invite for the free booze.

9. Kelly Corey. Buddy's ex-wife has remained close to him despite their divorce four years ago. In fact, she's confessed in several interviews that she still loves her ex and the only reason they broke up was because she'd had enough of his overbearing mother. She doesn't seem happy about this wedding, but who would be when the love of their life is about to walk down the aisle with someone else?

10. Preston Corey. At first glance, the groom's son appears to be a typical, sullen sixteen-year-old boy. He's clearly only at this wedding at his mother Kelly's insistence and seems eager for the ceremony to be over so he can go back to playing video games on his cell phone. Apparently Preston is quite skilled with weapons—at least digital ones.

11. Rob Archer. The blue-eyed restaurant owner and part-time DJ is married to Buddy's good friend Tim, who backed out of attending this wedding at the last minute due to a work emergency. The tall, skinny, brown-haired man seems rather low-key, but could that cool exterior be concealing a hidden jealousy at Buddy's friendly relationship with his husband?

12. Walton Herringford. Buddy's septuagenarian butler is slowing down in his old age, but that didn't stop him from attending today's nuptials. Then again, Walton probably didn't have a choice if he wants to keep his job. But his job may be in jeopardy regardless. Lady V doesn't have any history with

the elderly butler and may not have any qualms about letting him go in favor of hiring a more ambitious manservant after she becomes the lady of the house.

13. Riley Forte. The concert pianist hired by Buddy for pre-reception entertainment was apparently invited to attend the ceremony as well. Her presence here seems awfully suspicious to those of us at Nosy News Network though. Rumor has it Riley might be an undercover security expert biding her time until she's called out on her next international mission. So what is she doing at this wedding?

14. Tiger Corey. Buddy's thirteen-year-old brown mackerel tabby was adopted from the Furry Friends Foster Families rescue organization in Cherry Hills, Washington, ten years ago and doesn't seem particularly happy about his owner's impending nuptials. Or maybe he's merely upset that his dinner has been forgotten about in the excitement of the big day. The fractious feline insists the groom refuses to feed him an adequate amount of treats, and loudly proclaims on a daily basis that one day his human will get what's coming to him after subjecting Tiger to a lifetime of starvation.

And, folks, you wouldn't believe this incredible venue. Lady V and Buddy rented out the entire Happy Homicide Hotel for today's celebration. Boasting the most prestigious accommodations you'll find within a hundred-mile radius, Happy Homicide Hotel is known for unmatched customer service, five-star dining, and an elegance that will leave you breathless. The entire property has been decked out for this event. We're talking red pillow hearts hanging from ceiling tiles, a full orchestra playing on the front lawn, and so many white roses they'll leave you blinded.

Wait a minute. We're receiving unconfirmed reports that Buddy has been found dead in his dressing room. Could this be true? It is! The emergency vehicles have just begun pouring onto the scene.

Oh, my. The general consensus is that this wasn't an accidental death, but a homicide. The authorities aren't revealing how the forty-three-year-old died though. Was he stabbed? Shot? Strangled? Hit on the head with a blunt object? Or did the glass of Macallan 25 in his hand contain something more sinister than expensive scotch? Through a little bit of eavesdropping and a lot of speculation, Nosy News Network has managed to narrow down the possible murder weapons to the following:

1. Knife. A pocket knife with a sterling silver blade was discovered in the hallway outside of Buddy's dressing room. An inside source recognized it as belonging to Steven Smith. The knife was a gift from Steven's father and is one of Steven's most prized possessions, perhaps second only to the signed first edition of *Erewhon* given to him by Holmes and written by his favorite author, Samuel Butler. But how did the knife end up so close to the scene of the crime?

2. Gun. A six-chamber revolver was recovered from underneath the settee in Buddy's dressing room. Nobody knows who it belongs to or how it got there.

3. Poker. Hotel management insists there were five fireplace pokers located beside the dressing room fireplace before the wedding party's arrival. Only four remain.

4. Poison. A small, empty vial was discovered in one corner of the dressing room floor. It's unknown what the vial held, but imaginations are working overtime.

5. Chisel. A common tool for furniture makers, a bench chisel with a five-inch blade was spied in a garbage can just outside the hotel lobby. Nobody seems to have an explanation for what this particular item would be doing at this venue though. Could the killer have brought it?

Lady V, who was seen by several witnesses consulting with Dessy

D'Amato on last-minute dress alterations at the time of the murder, is frantic with grief. It's clear neither woman could have had anything to do with Buddy's death. But who did?

Unfortunately, the local police department's lone detective is currently on a cruise around the world and will be unavailable for the next six months. As an employee of The Warner County Police Department, Carly Redmund volunteered to help, but this case is way outside her jurisdiction. Besides, she's a prime suspect and not to be trusted. Buddy's dressing room didn't have any cameras installed inside. So how does one even begin to identify Buddy's killer?

We're hoping one of you savvy readers can assist. We've been talking to those in attendance, obtaining copies of the venue's security footage, and sniffing out evidence ourselves. We've managed to gather up quite a few clues, but none of us here at Nosy News Network are able to make sense of them. Can you help?

We desperately want justice to be served, and not only because Buddy often took out many costly advertisements in our publication. We're offering a reward to anyone who can solve Buddy's murder before December 31, 2025 by identifying the killer and determining which weapon was used.

First, collect the clues scattered throughout the anthology. Stories may have more than one clue included or none at all. Some clues will be embedded within the story narrative as one-sentence statements written on the back of wedding invitations, business cards, scraps of paper, or the like. Others will be planted within the pages between diamond symbols as follows: ◊ Wedding Whodunit Clue ◊

Example Clue: If Buddy's killer is his cat, the knife was used.

Second, organize all of the clues and compare them to the guest list and possible weapons to rule out certain suspects and murder method combinations.

Finally, once you know who the killer is and what weapon they used, input the answer in the format of "Killer/Weapon" (ex. "Tiger Corey/ knife") on this webpage: https://marlabradeen.blogspot.com/p/ malice.html In exchange, you'll receive a free ebook download filled with fun extras such as recipes, alternative endings, character profiles, author

13

interviews, bonus stories, and more!

A huge heartfelt thank-you from all of us here at Nosy News Network for taking on the case. Happy sleuthing!

The Groom's Club
Joslyn Chase

Cathryn Harcourt took Jordan Porter's hand as he helped her from his old maroon Mercedes. Stepping from the car, she caught her breath in delight, assailed by the uplifting fragrance of many blossoms fluttering in the light April breeze. Wordsworth's "Lines Written in Early Spring" flowed into her mind and she spoke them aloud:

> "Through primrose tufts, in that green bower,
> The periwinkle trailed its wreaths;
> And 'tis my faith that every flower
> Enjoys the air it breathes."

Her companion looked at her, his eyebrows raised questioningly.

"It's poetry," Cathryn said. "Really, Jordan, you sincerely ought to read more."

"I read all your books promptly and with pleasure," he said gallantly.

"Yes, you do," Cathryn agreed. "And for that, I am humbly grateful. I think you'll really enjoy the next one. It's set on the high seas."

"Indeed? I look forward to it."

Cathryn thought with satisfaction about the mystery novel she'd just submitted to her editor for a final review. She'd had such fun with the research and writing but felt in need of a break. When Jordan had invited her to drive up from their little town in southern Virginia to attend his niece's wedding in Manassas, she'd accepted without hesitation. Jordan was a good friend and an April wedding seemed just the thing to refresh and prepare her for writing the next book.

The dogwoods and cherry trees were in glorious bloom, pink and white blossoms thronging their branches, perfuming the air with sweetness. Cathryn walked along beside Jordan, her heels sinking into the soft earth beneath the lush green of the grass, aerating it as well as any tool designed for the job. If a tubful of barefooted women could produce a fine wine, why not put them in high heels and turn them loose on the lawn? Cathryn smiled as she thought about suggesting the method to her gardener.

Jordan's sister, Abigail Ellis, lived with her husband and their daughter in a gorgeous sprawling house large enough to host a convention of investment brokers, and likely had, since that is how Winston Ellis had made his fortune. As Cathryn and Jordan moved past the many cars parked along the lane, the sound of strident shouting arose and they watched two men in dark suits and sunglasses escort a struggling young woman to the edge of the property.

"I won't stop digging into this!" the woman shouted. "I'll expose it all. Are you people afraid of the truth?"

Shaking the men off her, the woman took a defiant step back and snapped a few photos with her cell phone. The men ignored her and returned to their posts as she pulled a ballpoint pen from behind her ear and scrawled something into a notebook before tucking the pen back into her nest of curls and stalking off further down the road. Cathryn watched her go, intrigued by the way the woman's wild red hair bounced with every furious step.

"What was that about?" Jordan asked.

"I'm certainly interested to know," Cathryn replied.

"Come on. I'll introduce you to Abigail and Winston. And I can't wait for you to meet the bride, my favorite niece, Tamara. And her soon-to-be husband, Andre."

"Do you have any lesser-favored nieces?"

"No."

On the expansive lawn beside the house, a huge white pavilion had been erected and a small orchestra played, setting the strains of Beethoven free on the gentle breeze. Jordan hailed a slender woman in pale yellow silk and she waved back, affection showing through the strain on her face.

Mother of the bride.

"Cathryn," Jordan said, taking her elbow. "This is my sister, Abigail."

"I'm so happy to meet you," Cathryn said. "And congratulations on Tamara's marriage." She glanced over the surroundings. "What a lovely venue, too. You have a beautiful home."

"Thank you."

"Sis, we saw your, er...bouncers eject a woman off the property," Jordan said. "She was yelling about exposing the truth. What's she talking about?"

A wave of annoyance washed over Abigail's face. "Just what we need today," she grumbled. "Some tabloid reporter has been harassing us, digging for a headline story. She's cooked up a theory that the whole family is involved in a smuggling ring, selling Mayan artifacts on the black market."

Jordan's brow wrinkled. "Ridiculous! And she draws that conclusion simply because Andre and his friends dabble in amateur archeology and collect fine replicas?"

"Hare-brained, right? Tabloids." She let out a long breath and brushed the air with her hands as if dismissing the topic. She gave Cathryn an apologetic smile. "Do you mind if I borrow Jordan for a moment, Cathryn? We've got a spot of family business to attend to. It won't take long."

"Of course."

As Jordan disappeared into the house with his sister, Cathryn wandered toward the gift table piled high with brightly decked boxes and bows. When she'd asked Jordan why he wasn't bringing along a beribboned package, he'd sent her a secret smile and said his gift was the sort that couldn't be gift-wrapped, refusing to say more about it except that she'd find out soon.

Stopping beside a brick-lined bed of multi-colored tulips, Cathryn watched two young men in tuxedos approach the gift table. She guessed she was looking at the groom and perhaps his best man. They shared a conspiratorial grin as the best man lifted a long rectangular box from the table and gave it a little shake.

"Bet you can guess what this is," he said, his voice low and just audible to Cathryn from where she stood.

"From Professor Huggins?" the groom replied. "I hope I can. He knows I've been wanting that Macuahuitl club for ages."

"And this box is just about the right dimension."

"I was thinking the same."

The two men slapped a high-five and wandered off to chat with a knot of guests. But as Cathryn watched from the corner of her eye, the groom returned to the table a moment later. Tucking the oblong box beneath his arm, he walked with brisk steps to a side door of the house and vanished inside.

Jordan appeared at her elbow. "You've got a flower petal in your hair," he said, brushing it away. "Come inside. I want you to meet Tamara."

The house had an impressive entry with marble floor and a sweeping staircase. Jordan led her up the stairs and along a pale green plush-carpeted corridor. "I'm taking you to the bride's dressing room," he said. Gesturing at a mirror-image corridor on the opposite side of the wide gallery, he added, "The groom's dressing room is down there."

He knocked and was invited to enter. Cathryn stepped into a room filled with brilliant natural light, thanks to a row of tall, narrow cathedral windows. The bride, turning in a swirl of white satin and caught in the pool of sunbeams, looked radiant.

"My dear," Jordan said, embracing her, "you are beautiful beyond words. I'm so happy for you."

"Oh, Uncle Jordan, thank you." She gave him a meaningful look and a peck on the cheek, pressing a small, folded slip of paper into his hand. He opened and read it while Cathryn stole a glimpse over his shoulder. *Contraba*—was printed in neat handwriting but Jordan's thumb covered the rest of the message. He refolded the paper and tucked it into his pocket.

Cathryn guessed the word on the paper was *contraband*—a term for smuggled goods—and felt a moment of anxiety. Remembering the ousted reporter, she wondered if her friend was involved in something illegal. Dangerous, even. It would surprise her greatly, being completely unlike the Jordan Porter she knew.

"Cathryn," he said, pulling her into a circle with him and his niece. "This is Tamara, and I'm so pleased the two of you could meet on this happiest of days."

Cathryn expressed her best wishes and listened while the two of them chatted, Tamara clearly nervous as brides tend to be in the hours before the wedding.

After a moment, Jordan glanced at his watch. "It's time, my dear. We'll leave you now." He hugged her and stepped back. "See you on the other side," he said.

Back on the lawn, under the enormous, tented pavilion, she and Jordan found their seats as the orchestra finished "Pachelbel's Canon" and moved into the "Wedding March." Winston Ellis escorted his daughter down the aisle, followed by a string of little girls in pastel chiffon scattering tiny flowers in their wake.

The groom stood at the end of the aisle watching Tamara's approach, his face poignant with adoration. The best man and maids of honor occupied the front row, alongside Tamara's mother, Abigail.

As the minister began his remarks, Jordan surprised Cathryn by excusing himself with a murmured, "Be back in a moment." He was gone for nearly ten minutes, returning just in time for the vows.

"You almost missed it," Cathryn said, frowning.

"Couldn't be helped," he replied.

The minister pronounced the couple husband and wife and they kissed as the orchestra swelled with the harmonies of Mendelssohn. With a whoop of joy, Tamara grabbed Andre's hand and they ran down the aisle to the cheers of their guests. Tamara tossed her bouquet and it hit an astonished octogenarian, falling into her lap amid laughter and applause.

The couple didn't stop when they reached the end of the pavilion. They kept running, Tamara's skirts clutched in her hand, and disappeared around the corner of the house. Winston Ellis stood up, chuckling as he went to the microphone.

"My daughter and her new husband, ladies and gentlemen," he said, raising another round of cheers. He let a beat pass, then made his appeal to the absent couple, trusting they were still within the sound of his voice. "Let's have Tamara and Andre up to the front here," he boomed into the mic. "I'm sure they'd like to thank our guests and say a few words."

He waited, but the couple didn't appear. Cathryn saw him turn to one of the men she'd seen earlier in suit and sunglasses. Winston uttered a terse command and gestured toward the house. The man trotted off. Winston stepped away from the mic to speak to Abigail, and Cathryn watched in amazement as the same determined red-haired reporter appeared from a fringe of shrubbery and rushed the unattended microphone.

"Members of this family," she sputtered into the mic, "are stealing precious cultural artifacts belonging to the countries of Mexico, Guatemala, and Belize. They've tried to silence me, but I will be heard!" she shouted, punching her fist into the air.

The remaining man on security detail wrestled her away from the mic, but before Cathryn could see what happened next, Jordan grabbed her hand and pulled her from her chair.

"Come on, Cathryn. We have to go. Now."

He led her, not down the lane to where he'd earlier parked, but around the house and past a redbrick outbuilding. Through its open door, Cathryn saw a sprawl of instrument cases and realized the orchestra was using it as a staging area. Following Jordan, she squeezed through a gap in a hedge of evergreens and saw his car, now hidden there behind the bushes.

"What on earth is going on, Jordan?" Cathryn demanded, really starting to worry about what he might be involved in. And what he might be dragging her into.

"No time to explain now, Cathryn. Just get in!"

HESITATING FOR A FRACTION of a second, Cathryn wondered how much confidence she could honestly place in her friend. Jordan threw open the driver's door and tumbled into the seat, firing the engine. He gestured frantically for her to join him, and Cathryn decided she trusted him to the hilt.

Scrambling into the passenger seat, she barely had time to pull her skirts in and slam the door before they were speeding across the back lawn, bumping over uneven ground like a motorboat cutting across the wake, accompanied by the sound of laughter.

Turning, Cathryn saw Tamara and Andre in the back seat, gleeful and giddy, no longer dressed in their wedding finery. Jordan laughed with them, and Cathryn found herself caught in the contagion as she began to have an inkling about what was going on.

"This is my wedding present, Cathryn," Jordan said, grinning wide. "My brother-in-law is a good guy at heart, but he tends to be a bit..."

"Domineering," Tamara finished for him.

"And not just a little bit," Andre added. "He steamrolled right over everything Tamara wanted for this wedding."

"He got the wedding his way," Tamara said. "But thanks to Uncle Jordan, I'm getting the honeymoon *I* want."

Jordan reached into his breast pocket and handed a sheaf of papers over the seat to Tamara. "Your tickets and itinerary, my dear. We're headed straight to the airport. Your bags are in the trunk."

"My heartfelt thanks," Tamara said, reaching out to squeeze Jordan's shoulder.

Sitting sideways in her seat, Cathryn watched the three of them, feeling bemused. Jordan grinned across at her. "I hope you're enjoying this, Cathryn. I'm sure you must have picked up on some of my clues."

"Oh, yes. I knew something was going on beneath the surface, but I'm pleasantly surprised to know this is it." She didn't mention the direction her suspicions had actually pointed.

"Let me guess," she continued, "the note Tamara passed you said *contrabass*, as in double bass. And that's why you excused yourself during the wedding. You hid a change of clothes in the double bass case. It's sufficiently roomy, and unambiguous since there's only one bass in the orchestra."

"Right you are," Jordan confirmed. "Winston's had those two goons of his watching Tamara like a hawk on steroids. I moved the car around back to maximize our chances of getting away without being seen. I think we did it!" he said, smiling at Tamara in the rear-view mirror.

As Jordan merged into a river of traffic on I-95, his cell phone jangled in his pocket, signaling a notification. Fishing it out, he handed it to Cathryn.

"Read that message for me, will you?"

Cathryn peered at the screen. "It's from Abigail. She says: 'Where are you? I need help. Everything's gone haywire.'"

Jordan chuckled. "I imagine things are in a flurry there. I hate to put my sister through that, but I think she'll understand and forgive me."

"I'm sure of it, Uncle Jordan."

The phone jangled again, and Cathryn read the new message. "Tamara's gone. Lee Collins is dead. And Andre is wanted for murder."

The atmosphere in the car turned instantly cold. As shocked as the others, Cathryn stared at the phone, wondering if she'd read it wrong.

"Is this a joke?" Jordan sputtered, a wave of red rising up from his neckline to cover his face.

"Mom wouldn't joke like that," Tamara insisted. "But it can't be true!"

"This is impossible," Andre said. "I didn't kill anyone."

"You certainly didn't," Tamara agreed. "You were with me every second."

"Who is Lee Collins?" Cathryn asked.

"He's one of the goons my uncle mentioned earlier."

"We need to turn back," Cathryn urged. "Your best option is to cooperate with the police."

"But I ran," Andre said. "That makes me look guilty. It doesn't matter that I ran for a completely unrelated reason. The damage is already done."

"Hold on," Cathryn said. She texted Abigail, asking for more information. The reply came back: "Lee was found in Andre's dressing room, clobbered over the head with a Mayan club."

Andre looked dazed. "My coveted Macuahuitl war club." He pounded his fist on the back of the seat. "I just couldn't wait," he said, grimacing in self-disgust. "I knew the gift from my old professor had to be a replica of the Macuahuitl with obsidian blades. It was the star of my thesis paper, after all, and that's what brought Tamara and I together. Huggins would have thought it an eminently appropriate wedding gift."

Slouching back in the seat, he clenched his hands, pressing both fists against his forehead. "I've wanted it for so long. I just couldn't wait until we got back from the honeymoon to open the professor's gift. I had to see if I was right. I took out the club and wielded it like a warrior. My fingerprints are all over it and in all the wrong places, as if I really had used it to club someone." He groaned. "I'm doomed."

Tamara's face was as white as the dogwood blossoms. "And you argued with Lee this morning," she said in a faint hopeless tone. "People witnessed the fight. It got pretty heated."

"I didn't like the way he was always staring at you."

"My father paid him to stare at me."

"Your father would have fired him on the spot if he'd caught Lee ogling you like that."

"Let's not get into a squabble about it," Jordan warned. Looking at Cathryn, he said, "We can't let them arrest Andre. Why don't the kids lay low while you figure out who really killed Lee Collins."

Cathryn stared at him. "Me?"

"Of course, you. You solve crimes all day long, Cathryn."

"On paper!"

He shook his head, lips pressed together in grim determination. "On paper, and beyond," he said. "You don't think I've heard about your exploits in England? In Brazil?"

"Please, Cathryn," Tamara pleaded.

Andre placed his hand on the console between the front seats, as if on a Bible at the stand. "If you don't solve the murder in 24 hours, I'll turn myself in. I swear."

Jordan exited the freeway and pulled into the parking lot of a strip mall, rolling up in front of a Hertz rental car outlet. "I'm afraid we're not going to the airport," he said. "It would look doubly bad if you fled the country, Andre. You kids take my car and head down to my house. I keep a spare key in the—"

"No good, Jordan," Cathryn said. "Your house is the first place the police will look. They need somewhere a step removed from any family member."

After a brief struggle with her conscience, Cathryn said, "Take the car to my place. I'll tell you where I hide my spare key."

WHEN CATHRYN AND JORDAN arrived back at the Ellis home, less than an hour after their hasty departure, the lane was still lined with guests' cars, now interspersed with patrol vehicles. Uniformed officers stood talking with small groups of wedding attendees, and Cathryn knew the types of questions they'd be asking. When did you last see the victim?

When did you last see the groom, Andre Chavez? Did you notice anything unusual or out of place?

The golden aura of spring that had so delighted Cathryn earlier in the day seemed tarnished now and dimming, though the fragrance of the many flowers was as sweet. She and Jordan passed through the sentries and entered the house, arriving in time to find Winston and Abigail being questioned by a plainclothes detective.

"I sent Collins to bring Tamara and Andre back," Winston was saying. "They should have come back to thank the minister and their guests. I can't believe they just ran off like that."

"What happened after that, Mr. Ellis?"

"That crazy woman came out of nowhere and grabbed the mic, accusing our family of being mixed up with Mexican antiquities and smuggling rings. Like we didn't have enough drama already."

"Why would she crash the wedding and make such claims?"

"How should I know? Find her, ask her."

"We will, I assure you." The detective paused, making a note on an electronic memo device. "When did you discover the body?" he asked.

"When Collins didn't return with Tamara, I searched him out and found him dead on the floor of Andre's dressing room."

"And how much time had passed from the end of the ceremony to the time you found the body?"

"I don't know." He looked at Abigail. "Fifteen minutes, maybe?" She nodded in agreement.

"Just enough time for Andre to get to the dressing room, bludgeon your security man, and flee the scene."

"Now, wait just a minute—" Jordan said, stepping forward.

The detective held up a cautioning hand. "Please, tell me who you are," he said, including Cathryn in his gesture.

"Jordan Porter, uncle of the bride. Abigail is my sister. And this is Cathryn Harcourt, my friend who is very versed in the art of murder. She can contribute a lot to your investigation, if you'll let her."

Cathryn felt her face go hot as the detective turned to stare, one eyebrow lifted enquiringly. "What he means," she said, "is that I write mystery novels. I do a lot of research. So—theoretically speaking—I know a bit about criminal investigation."

"Is that right?" The detective offered his hand. "Alfonso Mills," he said. "Homicide. And my experience goes beyond the theoretical, I'm sorry to say." He turned back to Winston. "I'm also sorry to say that Andre is our prime suspect and it's our first priority to find him."

Jordan spoke again. "What would be his motive?"

Mills shrugged. "I don't know yet, but I'm sure to turn up something." He paused. "How about this? Maybe Collins found Andre and his bride in the dressing room and overstepped his bounds, got a little too forceful. The victim has a long, narrow scratch across his wrist that could have been made by a woman's fingernail. Maybe while he was grappling with the bride, Andre picked up the club and slugged him in the head. They got scared and ran. Sounds plausible, doesn't it?"

Before anyone could reply, a uniformed officer interrupted. "You'll want to see this, sir. One of the guests must have recorded the ceremony and posted the footage."

He placed an iPad on the coffee table and pressed a button. Along with everyone else gathered around the screen, Cathryn watched the video of the end of the wedding. It captured the couple's escape, the zealous reporter's accusations, and the hue and cry that went up at the discovery of the murder. Sensationalistic stuff, already gone viral.

Something in the recording niggled at Cathryn, a mental tickle, but she couldn't place what was bothering her. She'd find it online and watch it again later.

Another officer brought in three evidence bags, showing them to Mills. "Ah," the detective said, holding up the first one. "A napkin, found in the victim's jacket pocket and stained with a smear of his blood. No doubt he used it to wipe the scratch on his wrist."

The second bag contained a heavy square of cardstock embossed with a purple lily and "If Buddy's killer is his sibling, poison was used" scrawled across the back.

Cathryn saw the final bag contained strands of curly red hair.

"I believe you'll find that those hairs belong to our fanatical reporter," she said.

"I'll buy that." Mills nodded to his man. "Go pick her up. And get samples from underneath her fingernails," he added.

Cathryn held up a finger. "May I make a suggestion?"

Mills made a rolling motion with his hands. "Make it quick."

"I noticed the reporter keeps a fancy ballpoint pen behind her ear. That scratch could have been made by the tip of that pen. Why not check it for traces of the victim's skin and examine the victim's scratch for traces of ink?"

"A sound theoretical suggestion, Mrs. Harcourt." He sent the officer away to see it done.

"Any fingerprints on the murder weapon?" Cathryn asked, afraid to hear the answer but needing to know. It looked to her as if someone was attempting to frame Andre for the murder, so she was not prepared for the detective's response.

"None," he said. "The club had been wiped clean."

A killer seeking to lay the blame on Andre wouldn't have wiped away his fingerprints, would he? Or she? It didn't make sense.

Mills tossed out a few more questions, then wandered off to attend to other business. Abigail sighed. "We may as well eat," she said, "we've got six tables covered with wedding fare just going to waste."

Many of the guests were still on the premises. They flocked around Winston and Abigail, offering their sympathies, and were invited to stay and partake in the feast. Some of them did, including the maids of honor and Andre's best man who joined them at their table.

"I've known Andre for a long time, Mrs. Ellis," he said to Abigail. "And I know he couldn't have killed that man."

"Thank you. I couldn't agree more."

He bit into a caviar-topped hors d'oeuvre and tipped his head at Cathryn. "We haven't met," he said. "I'm Kent Bell."

"The best man."

"Well, Andre thought so, I guess." He smiled modestly.

"Cathryn Harcourt."

His handshake was firm but his palm slightly sweaty. Cathryn discreetly wiped her fingers with the edge of the tablecloth. "I understand you and Andre worked dig sites together in Mexico and Belize with one of your college professors. That must have been very interesting."

"It was," he assured her. "But we're just amateurs, enthusiastic students.

We didn't really get to handle any of the important artifacts."

"Nevertheless, I'm sure it was fulfilling."

"Oh, absolutely."

Detective Mills approached the table. "I thought you might like to know that the reporter—her name is Regina Goodwin—has been arrested. Preliminary lab results indicate the hairs we pulled off the victim belong to her, the blood on the napkin matches Collins's, and there is indeed ink in the scratch and skin in the pen, Mrs. Harcourt."

He gave her a curt nod before continuing. "It looks like Ms. Goodwin got into the house and Collins found her there. They struggled, she scratched him and at some point, grabbed the club and hit him over the head. She's refusing to make a statement, but the evidence is stacking up. It looks as if we'll wrap this one up in short order."

"The only question now is where are Tamara and Andre?" Abigail said. "And why don't they return home?"

"I have another question," Jordan said. "What's her motive? Why would the reporter kill Collins?"

"To get what she's getting," Kent Bell said. "Fame. Notoriety. She's a nut, like that guy who tried to kill the president to impress Jodie Foster."

"Perhaps," Mills conceded. "We'll know more once we get her to open up."

"With the case all but cracked, I guess there's nothing left for us to do," Cathryn said. "I'd like to go home and sleep in my own bed tonight, if that's all right." She looked at Mills.

"Sure," he said. "We know where to find you."

Cathryn and Jordan said their goodbyes and headed south on the interstate.

"We'd better hurry," Cathryn said. "We need to get home and make some new arrangements for Tamara and Andre. The cops are going to be closing in on our little town very soon."

Jordan's brow furrowed. "What for? You heard the detective. Case closed, they caught their killer."

"Regina Goodwin did not murder Lee Collins."

"How do you figure?"

"A number of different ways," Cathryn said. "But how's this for starters?

Collins had a napkin in his pocket, stained with smears of his blood. Picture the scenario—he discovers Regina in Andre's dressing room and tries to remove her. They struggle and she scratches him with her pen in the process. She picks up the club and bludgeons him to death. Then he grabs a napkin, wipes the blood from his wrist, and places it in his pocket. See anything wrong with that?"

Jordan gave a rueful chuckle. "Now that you point it out," he said, "I guess I do."

A HAZY LINE OF PINK and lavender streaked along the western horizon as Cathryn and Jordan loaded bags of groceries into the trunk of Cathryn's car, parked outside her local Farm Fresh. Upon returning from Manassas, they'd hustled Tamara and Andre to a neighbor's house. Sally Farnham and her husband were on an eight-day Caribbean cruise and Cathryn, agreeing to water their plants, had the key to their house and took advantage of that, feeling Sally would approve when she heard all about it later.

That done, she thought it best to resume her normal activities and Jordan had insisted on staying with her. As she turned onto her street, she noticed an unfamiliar car parked two doors down from her house, the faint silhouette of a head visible through the driver's window.

"Even sooner than I expected," she said, pulling into the driveway. "Don't look now, Jordan, but we've got company."

"We moved the kids just in time," he replied.

No sooner had they carried the groceries in from the car when the doorbell chimed. Cathryn opened the door to Detective Mills and a pair of uniformed officers. Mills greeted her by holding up a sheet of paper.

"We have a warrant to search your house, Mrs. Harcourt," he said.

"Whatever for, Detective? I thought you'd arrested the killer."

Mills motioned for his officers to get busy. As they scurried off, Cathryn invited Mills to have a seat in the living room.

"The reporter, Regina Goodwin, started talking. She told a very interesting story, one which I find credible. She's convinced the Ellis family is involved in stealing cultural artifacts out of—"

Jordan leaned forward, chopping the air with his hand. "Absolutely absurd!"

"Perhaps," Mills said, "but *she's* convinced it's happening and that's why she persisted in intruding on the wedding. She says she got as far as the gift table when a man wearing a dark suit and sunglasses assaulted her and attempted to frogmarch her off the property."

"Collins?" Cathryn asked.

"Correct. She says she broke free and grabbed her trusty..." He consulted his notes. "Her trusty abalone seashell gold plated ballpoint pen costing one hundred and sixty dollars and struck out, catching the man on the wrist and raking the pen across his skin."

"Impressive," Jordan said.

"The man cursed at her," Mills continued, "and grabbed a napkin off a nearby table. As he dabbed at the blood on his wrist, another man she referred to as his 'infernal twin' arrived and the two of them forcibly ejected her from the Ellis property."

"Yes," Cathryn said. "I believe we witnessed that moment."

"But she didn't go away," Mills said. "She went around to the back of the property and crept in from that angle. She says she watched from the bushes as a man parked a car and moved stealthily into a redbrick building, carrying a bag. He emerged a moment later, empty-handed, and walked around to where the wedding ceremony was taking place."

Cathryn studiously avoided looking at Jordan as the detective went on.

"She waited for her moment, seized the mic to get everyone's attention while she pled her case, and was once more thrown out, protesting loudly." He paused. "Here's what I find particularly interesting. She clearly described the creeping man she saw with her reporter's keen eye and was able to identify him from photos taken at the wedding. That man," the detective said, looking at Jordan, "was you, Mr. Porter."

Jordan stared back, deadpan. Then he rose from the sofa and held his hands in front of him, wrists together. "I confess," he said, "to the murder of Lee Collins. Arrest me, Mills."

Cathryn gasped. "It's not true, Detective. Don't you believe it."

Mills gave her a withering glance. "I don't. Not for a moment. But I must warn both of you that Andre Chavez is once again our prime suspect and I believe you are harboring him. I advise you to give us any information you have as to his whereabouts."

Cathryn gazed at him mutely. Jordan did the same.

The two uniformed officers returned, having finished their search. Both shook their heads to indicate they'd found nothing. Mills rose from his seat and moved toward the front door.

"Have it your way," he said. Stepping out, he turned on the porch and added, "But it's a decision you may regret."

"DID YOU REALLY THINK Mills would arrest you?" Cathryn asked as they watched the detective stride down the front walk.

"I guess not," Jordan said. "I was just trying to buy you a little more time. Are you any closer to figuring out what happened?"

Cathryn tapped her lips, staring off into the distance while she tossed bits and pieces of the case in her mind. "Maybe," she said. "I'd like to take another look at that wedding video we saw at Abigail's."

It wasn't hard to find online and soon she and Jordan were watching again as the camera panned across the wedding party seated in the front row. The photographer had captured the exchange of vows, the couple running down the aisle, Winston's request for their return and his subsequent dispatch of Collins. It ended with Regina Goodwin's dramatic claims at the microphone and her humiliating removal.

Cathryn hit the repeat button and watched it again as the thing that had been bothering her rose to the surface of her brain and focused her attention. She realized the key, the piece of information she'd been searching for, lay not in what was there on the video, but on what was *not*.

Jordan stood at the living room window, peering out through the curtains. "You are aware that we're under surveillance, aren't you, Cathryn?" Jordan said.

She laughed. "Of course we are. And you've given me an idea." Pulling her cell phone from her purse, she looked at it doubtfully. "Do you suppose they've put a wiretap on our phones, too?"

"I think we should assume they have."

"Hmmm. What's your sister's number, Jordan? I want to call her."

"Okay. Just be careful what you say."

"Oh, I will," Cathryn assured him. "I'll be very careful."

When Abigail answered, Cathryn said, "How are you holding up? Jordan and I are concerned about you."

She heard the strain in Abigail's voice as she replied. "We've had better days. The police are after Andre again. The reporter's arrest fizzled out."

"Yes, we heard. I'm so sorry, Abigail." She paused, then asked, "Is Kent Bell still there, by chance?"

"I saw him just a moment ago. Did you want to speak to him?"

"Yes, please."

A moment passed, then the best man spoke into the phone. "This is Kent Bell."

"Hello, Kent," Cathryn said. "I don't know if you remember me. We met—"

"Of course, I remember, Mrs. Harcourt. What can I do for you?"

"I have a message for you." She lowered her voice. "From Andre."

"What? Did you say—"

"Shhh! Yes, please don't say his name. Someone there may hear you."

"What's the message?"

"Andre says he found evidence that there really is a smuggling operation. He's frightened. He doesn't know who he can trust, and he needs help." She paused. "You're an old friend, his best man. Can he trust you, Kent?"

"Yes. Of course. Where is he, Mrs. Harcourt?"

"I can't tell you that. But come to my house and I'll take you to him."

She gave her address and ended the call. Jordan stared at her, his eyes wide, his face going slightly green around the mouth.

"What have you done?" he moaned.

THE SKY WAS FULL DARK with a risen moon by the time Kent's car rolled up on the verge next to Cathryn's house. She and Jordan had taken turns watching for it over the past half hour.

"He must have welded the gas pedal to the floor," Jordan said. "I've made the trip from here to Abigail's house a hundred times and never come close to his speed record."

"He's feeling squeezed."

"So am I."

The doorbell rang and Cathryn shooed Jordan into the kitchen. "I want him to think I'm alone," she said. "You'll scare him off."

"Darn right," Jordan grumbled. "That's my intention."

"And a good one," Cathryn told him. "But save it for later."

She opened the door and Kent burst into the living room. "I got here as fast as I could. Where's Andre?"

"He's safe, and somewhere nearby, Kent."

"What about Tamara? Is she with him?"

"Yes, Tamara too. I can walk you over there right now."

Outside, the moon was a crescent in the sky. The wisp of a night breeze lifted the tails of Cathryn's blouse, fluttering it like a flag as she stepped from the shelter of the hedge onto the street. Together, she and Kent walked along the pavement, their steps keeping time with the chirp of cricket song.

They turned the corner and entered the Farnhams' yard. Cathryn used her key to let them into the house. "Don't worry," she called out. "It's just me, and I've brought someone to help you."

The fugitives crept out from the hallway. Andre's face broke into a grin when he saw his best man. They embraced. "Thanks for coming," Andre said. "We could use some company."

Kent nodded. "Sure thing. Now, what about that evidence you found?" he asked. "Dude, show me."

Andre's brow wrinkled. He looked at Tamara but she only shrugged.

"What are you talking about?" Andre said.

Kent's eyes narrowed as he glared accusingly at Cathryn. "Mrs. Harcourt told me you found evidence of a smuggling operation."

"I'm sorry, Kent," Cathryn said. "I'm afraid I lied to you. It was the only way I could think of to get you to reveal your motive for killing Lee Collins."

Kent sputtered. "You're crazy!"

"There's no way—" Andre began before puttering off into uncertain silence.

"You are surely mistaken," Tamara said.

"I don't think so," Cathryn answered. "You see, when I watched the video that was shot during the time of the murder, I noticed a few things missing. Lee Collins was missing—the victim. Andre and Tamara were missing—the patsy and his bride. And someone else was missing from the wedding party. You—Kent—the murderer.

"I determined you had the means and the opportunity for killing Mr. Collins, but I couldn't fathom why you would have. At first, I thought you might be in love with Tamara. Murdering Collins and framing Andre for the crime could open the way for you to support Tamara in her grief and distress and perhaps worm your way into her affections."

"This is absurd," Kent said. "Tamara's a nice girl, but I have no interest in stealing her away from my best friend."

"So I came to realize," Cathryn said, "when the police found the weapon, with all the fingerprints Andre had so obligingly left behind, wiped clean. Which put me back at square one. Until it dawned on me that Andre collects replicas of Mayan artifacts."

"So?" Kent said.

"Very high-quality replicas with the appearance of authenticity, but replicas, nonetheless. While smugglers would only be interested in the genuine article." Cathryn turned to Tamara. "What were your father's plans for your honeymoon?"

She frowned. "My father doesn't understand the purpose of a honeymoon," she said, her tone dry. "He booked a private jet. He was flying the entire wedding party to a big beach house in the Bahamas."

"Including your wedding gifts?" Cathryn asked.

"Yes, we were supposed to open the gifts at the beach house."

"Here's what I think happened," Cathryn said. "The gift from Professor Huggins contained an authentic Mayan war club, bought on the black market and destined for a buyer in the Bahamas. Customs clearance on a private jet—especially one carrying a wedding party—is a lot more relaxed than a commercial flight. Once on the island, Kent planned to trade the genuine piece for a very well-made replica. The copy would go to Andre and the authentic club to someone paying a good deal of money."

The three of them stared at her, each with a different expression. She continued.

"When Kent saw the two of you run down the aisle and disappear around the corner of the house, he suspected you were ruining his scheme. Maybe he'd even picked up on some of the planning you tried to keep so secret," she said to Tamara. "He ran to Andre's dressing room to try to stop you, not realizing you had clothing and transport waiting for you elsewhere.

"Andre wasn't in the room, but the club was. Just lying there in the open—an authentic and very valuable artifact. Kent couldn't just leave it like that. He probably had the replica in his luggage, ready to be loaded on the jet for the honeymoon trip. He got it and was in the process of swapping them when Lee Collins arrived, looking for Andre. Instead, he put two and two together—you with the duplicate clubs and the reporter's claims of smuggling—and instantly became a danger to the operation."

Tamara and Andre were giving her their full attention, utterly absorbed in her account. But Cathryn thought Kent was getting restive. And desperate. She worried he might do something foolish.

"I doubt Kent had time to think it through. He simply picked up the club and dispatched the threat to his enterprise. By accident or design, he'd used the authentic club—the one with Andre's fingerprints. So he left the replica in its place, taking care to first wipe his own prints from the weapon. He knew that, even without fingerprints, it would implicate his friend and focus police attention away from the suspicion of smuggling."

"Are you finished?" Kent said, taking a step toward her. His eyes bored into Cathryn's, stone-hard and unwavering. "Because I think you are. Finished."

His hand went into his pocket, but before he could pull it free, Jordan was on him from behind, whipping his hands behind his back. Mills stepped forward and snapped a pair of handcuffs over Kent's wrists. He extracted a pistol from Kent's jacket pocket, removed the bullets, and shoved it in the waistband of his pants.

"I think you're the one who's finished, Mr. Bell," Mills said. "I guess you weren't the best man, after all."

Mills and his two men escorted Kent to the back of a patrol car. Cathryn watched from the porch as they placed him inside and slammed the door. Before climbing into his own car, Mills looked up and saw her watching. He smiled and shook his head as if struggling to believe what he'd just witnessed.

"That was some nice detective work," he called out. "In theory."

Cathryn laughed. "Goodbye, Detective Mills."

Inside the house, Jordan and his niece were sharing a hug. "I'm taking you home to your mother," he told her.

"Thank you. And thanks to you, Cathryn. You both have done more than we can ever repay."

"I know how you can begin making it up to me," Jordan said.

Andre squeezed Tamara's hand. "Name it."

"I'm changing your tickets, and day after tomorrow I want you on that plane," Jordan said. "You owe me a boatload of honeymoon pictures."

They all laughed, and it felt good, though Cathryn's bones were beginning to ache with exhaustion. As she left the Farnham house with her friends and walked back along the moon-striped pavement, Cathryn breathed in the sweet, blossomy air of the April night and remembered how the day had begun. She'd stepped out of Jordan's car into the light of spring, expecting only a lovely wedding and a sumptuous lunch. How much had changed in a very short space of time!

Single to married. Living to dead. Suspected to vindicated. Clueless to case cracked.

And she knew of one more thing she longed to change before many more minutes passed.

She wanted to go from awake to deep, dreamless slumber.

FOR MORE INFORMATION about the author, please visit Joslyn Chase's website: https://joslynchase.com/

A Wedding Planner's Nightmare: A Persimmon Worthing Mystery

Charlotte Morganti

Weddings are popular in Blossom City. Our small town's event planners are booked solid from late spring to early fall, the time when most brides-to-be have confidence that rain or snow won't fall on their parade.

This year, in a stroke of genius, the owner of Weddings to Die For hit on a strategy to increase his business during the off-season. Paolo Strada promoted World Marriage Day, which happens on the second Sunday of February. He offered package deals for three-quarters of his usual fee. Within days, sixteen clients had taken advantage of his offer.

Frankly, I'm surprised Paolo didn't anticipate what was bound to happen on the big day. He's lived here long enough that he should have taken Blossom City's history into account. Something untoward is guaranteed to occur at events in our town and the celebration of World Marriage Day was no exception.

Let me tell you what happened:

Among Paolo's sixteen new wedding clients were three young women—Selena, Jody and Maria. I didn't know these brides-to-be personally, but certainly I knew of them and knew they had been BFFs, as their generation says, since grade school. Apparently, a triple wedding on World Marriage Day was their collective dream wedding.

As you might expect, news of the upcoming triple wedding made its way around town faster than my Porsche. Everyone loves a wedding—not only for the chance to witness a happy couple exchange vows, but also for the opportunity to critique the attire of the bridal parties and the guests, to take note of who brought whom as their plus one, and to consume copious amounts of food. And to be able to say, "Well, I knew that was coming," when a guest inevitably developed a fondness for the complimentary red wine and challenged the bridal couple to a limbo contest.

Blossom City's triple wedding offered three times the opportunities for that special form of entertainment.

Since I didn't know any of the brides or grooms personally, worries that I might miss out on the weddings of the year had set in by late January. But then my friend Milton Courgette, a sergeant in the Blossom City Police Department, phoned me. "Persimmon, I must ask a favor. Our desk sergeant's son is getting married. In fact, his wedding is part of that triple affair everyone is talking about. I have been invited and wonder if you'd come with me?"

Although my heart rate picked up when I realized I would be able to attend the event, I was momentarily perplexed. Sergeant Courgette was sweet on my cousin, Cleo Branch. Had something happened to that budding romance? "May I ask why you are asking me?"

Courgette sputtered. "Err, emm." Then he sighed.

"Cleo is busy that day?" I asked.

"*Oui*," he said. "Not that you are second choice, by any means, Persimmon."

A pause. Then, "However I must be truthful and admit I did ask Cleo first. So I suppose in actuality you could say you are second."

"I see."

I was about to say I would be happy to accompany him, when he continued. "And it would harm my stature in town if I went alone. People will see me as a hopeless unwanted bachelor rather than the well-respected pillar of the community I am."

Courgette had a knack of stepping into doggy doo-doo without even smelling the danger.

"Ahh," I said. "So, better me than no one?"

"Er, *oui*?" He paused and then sucked in a breath. "Wait! *Non*! You are better than so many others."

Another pause and a long sigh. "*Désolé*. Sorry. It is hard to find the right words with my foot in my mouth. I would be pleased and very grateful if you could attend with me."

You have no doubt noticed Sergeant Courgette loves to sprinkle the occasional French word into a conversation. While he manages to pronounce "*oui*" and "*non*" correctly, he mangles almost every other French expression. The truth is Courgette is as Anglo as most of us in Blossom City. However, because of his family name, he believes Frenchness is in his blood. I don't have the heart to tell him that a facility with the French language is not.

When Courgette mentioned his foot-in-mouth disease, I laughed. "Relax, Milton. Of course I will go with you. I love weddings and I have a new outfit I'm dying to wear."

An added bonus to my day was a telephone call from my niece, Violet. She told me Harry Lovely, one of Courgette's young constables, had invited her to the wedding. "I'm taking a few days away from university then, if I can stay with you, Aunt Persie?"

I love hosting Violet. We both have a fascination with the way human lives intertwine and spread—often secretly—like a grapevine. Violet's mother, my younger stick-in-the-mud sister Jasmine, would rather I refrained from involving Violet in what she calls the "unseemly habit of sticking one's nose into everyone's business." Jasmine inherited all the prudish genes in my family.

I looked forward eagerly to the upcoming celebration. February in Blossom City can be dull, and a triple wedding was sure to liven things up. As they say, "famous last words."

WORLD MARRIAGE DAY in Blossom City was sunny and warm for mid-February. I took that as a good omen for the sixteen weddings scheduled for the day and suggested to Courgette that I could drive us to the wedding. "We can put the top down on my Porsche," I said. "What do you say?"

"*Non*! I am a sergeant of the police. If I ride with you I will be seen as condoning the crime of breaking the speed limit."

When Sergeant Courgette arrived in his sedate Volvo sedan to collect me for the short trip to the church, he looked uncomfortable out of uniform. I studied his dark suit and said, "You look smashing. But to be honest, I expected you to be in your dress uniform."

He tugged at the sleeves of his suit jacket. "I acquired my dress uniform when I was a mere beat officer, too many years ago to count. It is sadly in need of updating."

That, of course, was code for "I can't get into my dress blues anymore." When I first met him a few years ago during the investigation of the death of an avid gardener who had been zonked on the head with a beribboned zucchini, Sergeant Courgette was middle-aged and perhaps ten pounds past what we would call trim. Once I introduced him to La Patisserie, a short block away from the police station, he began leaving his uniform jacket unbuttoned. Last year when Courgette discovered Dough Vinci, my cousin Cleo's bakery and café, he developed a crush on her and became addicted to her sourdough waffles. Or it could be the addiction preceded the crush. Whatever the chronology, Courgette is now a middle-aged man on a first-name basis with the owner of Blossom City Discreet Alterations.

I liked the old Courgette, but I favor the current Courgette—he is happier and it shows in the smile that creases his chubby cheeks most of his waking hours.

But, I digress.

Courgette and I arrived at the church hosting the triple wedding just as Paolo Strada, the event planner, bounded down the stairs, clipboard in hand.

"Paolo," I said, "how did you manage to plan this gorgeous weather as well as sixteen weddings?"

He chuckled. "I wish I could say the sun was part of my package deals, but no."

"How did you manage, really?"

He leaned toward me and whispered, "Cookie cutters are wonderful tools, not only in the kitchen but also in the world of weddings. One menu, one caterer, one dressmaker, one tailor, one florist, and set music."

"Don't your clients want to put their own touches on their weddings?"

Paolo waved my concern aside. "I gave them all a significant fee reduction. So to make it work for me, I streamlined the planning. But not to worry, each client chose their color scheme, the venue, and officiant." He gave us a jaunty wave and hurried away.

When Courgette and I entered the church the colorful bouquets of iris, tulips, and freesia, affixed to the end of each pew with honey-colored organza bows, surprised me. So did the two foot-tall vases of pink and white peonies at the front of the church. I'd been to several events organized by Paolo and knew he was a fan of heavily perfumed stargazer lilies.

Not long after we settled in a pew, my niece Violet and Constable Lovely (looking dashing and trim in his dress blues) joined us. "Gorgeous spring flowers," I said to Violet. "Such a refreshing change from those headache-inducing lilies Paolo usually chooses."

"That's because he delegated the décor at the church and the reception to Abby," Violet said.

Violet was referring to Abby Johnson, Paolo's assistant. She and Violet had met at last summer's accordion festival and had become good friends.

"Abby's so good at planning events," Violet said. "Less than a year after graduation and she's already gaining a reputation for fresh ideas and creative touches. Don't tell Paolo, but she plans to open her own business in the next year."

"Mum's the word," I said, even though this was Blossom City and that secret was probably already making the rounds.

The officiant, along with three grooms and their assorted groomsmen, entered the nave from a door beside the sanctuary. Courgette pointed to two of the men who wore police dress uniforms. "The tall bearded one is Greg Alsoli, the groom who invited us."

As the officiant directed the men where to stand, Violet said, "Abby told me all the women are wearing the same dress—a bouffant-skirted, floor length, taffeta ball gown. The brides will be in white, but the bridesmaids will be in a variety of gem colors. The rainbow of shimmering gowns at the front of the church will be spectacular."

The organist played the opening notes of the Bridal March, and the first bride and her attendant walked down the aisle. Courgette said, "That's

Maria, Greg's fiancée."

Maria's long blond hair and crystal-adorned white gown swung with every step. A broad smile graced her face; a sparkle lit up her blue eyes. The bridesmaid wore a matching grin and an amethyst gown.

Once the two cheerful women took their places beside Greg and his best man, the second bridal procession began. As Jody and her lone attendant strode past us, I asked Violet, "What gem color do you think the bridesmaid is wearing? Jade? Peridot?"

"Avocado?" Violet said.

"Not a gem, but I think you've nailed it."

On better days the attendant's skin probably appeared creamy. Today, however, the guacamole green of her gown turned her pale skin a cadaverous beige. Has there ever been a wedding where at least one bridesmaid did not look like a reject from budget fashion school?

The faces of Selena, the last bride, and her two attendants were thunderous. The bridal gown would have looked fabulous on a tall woman. However, Selena barely topped five feet, and trod on her gown's hem at least twice as she stomped down the aisle.

One of Selena's attendants wore sapphire blue, the other rose quartz. Although the dresses complemented the attendants' coloring, again there were hem issues. Like Selena, the shorter attendant struggled not to trip on her skirt. The taller bridesmaid's gown ended mid-calf. If I didn't know better, I would have said they were wearing each other's dress.

"Whatever is going on with those gowns?" I said.

Violet shrugged. "Abby thought Paolo made a mistake using only one dressmaker. Apparently, the woman was so overwhelmed with sixteen weddings that some fittings didn't happen. I'm guessing there was no time left to fix these dresses."

The three bridal parties arranged themselves in front of the officiant. Instead of a kaleidoscope of prom dresses, we gazed at a scene from *What Not to Wear.*

Despite the wardrobe mishaps, the wedding ceremony itself was flawless. No lost rings, no fumbled vows, no objections from the crowd. After the signing of the register, the officiant addressed the crowd. "Today these happy couples have made history—the first triple wedding in

Blossom City. You are all invited to the reception, which I'm sure will be absolute perfection."

I said, "Oooh, tempting fate is never a good thing."

Violet shushed me. "Aunt Persie, you know that's just a superstition."

True, but this was Blossom City and those of you who are familiar with my small town know it doesn't take much to derail the best laid plans. Most of us long-time locals do our best to avoid statements that invite disaster.

ABBY, PAOLO'S ASSISTANT, had transformed the reception room at our community hall from uninspired and utilitarian to whimsical and romantic. The floral and organza theme of the church décor repeated itself—vases of spring flowers graced each table, napkins were rolled and tied with organza bows, and garlands of peonies decorated the bridal parties' tables. I breathed in the sweet aroma of the peonies, once more grateful for the absence of stargazer lilies. I'd have to keep Abby in mind for my next dinner party.

When the three bridal parties arrived at the reception, the wardrobe malfunctions had been rectified. A neat line of staples glinted along the shortened hems of once too-long gowns. Jody's pale-skinned bridesmaid had added a scarlet pashmina that counteracted her guacamole dress and gave her face a rosy glow.

Tiny alarm bells, the result of the officiant's prediction of perfection, still tinkled in my head during the reception. However, because the food was mouth-watering and the speeches blessedly short, I decided my worry about tempting fate was unfounded.

After we devoured the dessert—white chocolate mousse topped with liqueur-soaked berries—Greg Alsoli, Courgette's constable, stood and offered a toast. "To all of our friends and families joining us in the celebration of our weddings, and to the beautiful brides, especially my true love, Maria."

Maria didn't even glance at the crowd as Greg offered the toast. Instead, she focused on her hands and forearms, inspecting them. She patted her face a few times before pulling on Greg's jacket sleeve. When he turned his attention to her, his mouth dropped. He put his wine glass down, fumbled in his pocket, and then offered her a small cylinder. Maria grabbed it, stabbed herself in the thigh, and leaned back in her chair, breathing deeply.

I pointed out the drama to Courgette. "Something's happening with Greg and Maria."

We hurried over to their table. "Is everything alright?" Courgette asked.

Greg glanced at Maria and then nodded. "Maria had an allergic reaction to something. She used her EpiPen so she should be fine. But..." He gestured at his bride.

Maria's skin, which had been unblemished and glowing with happiness at the church, was now blotchy. Red welts appeared on her cheeks, neck, and forearms. An angry rash spread across her upper chest. "I'm going to look a fright for days," she said. "But the worst part is the itchiness."

"What are you allergic to?" I asked.

"Vanilla beans. The caterer must have used them in the dessert. I don't understand how that could happen. Paolo Strada, the planner, asked us to list our allergies. I specifically told him the caterer should avoid vanilla or use artificial flavoring. So I thought everything would be safe."

"It's fortunate Greg had that EpiPen," I said.

Greg said, "Maria always keeps one nearby. Today I carried it because I was the one with pockets." He turned his attention to Maria. "I think we should go to the hospital to have you checked out, just to be safe."

After Greg and Maria left, the band began tuning up. Courgette said, "I'm afraid we will need to leave as well, Persimmon. I have an early day tomorrow. A police sergeant's life is never calm."

Between you and me, I think fear of embarrassment was the real reason Courgette wanted to leave before I could invite him to jive. He is left-footed, and I suspect he did not want his junior officers to see his ineptitude on the dance floor.

"That was much better than I feared it would be," Courgette said as we walked toward his car.

"Oh?"

"*Oui.* I have learned how events in this town have a way of going very wrong. Fortunately, no one died."

I agreed. In Blossom City we've come to mark that outcome as evidence of an event's success.

ON THE MONDAY AFTER the triple wedding, when I mentioned I was going to Dough Vinci, my cousin Cleo's bakery and café, for an afternoon coffee and gab session, Violet asked to join us.

"Just one small issue," Violet said. "Harry's coaching baseball today at the high school and invited me to watch. It should be over by three."

For a relative newcomer to town, Constable Harry Lovely, who had been Violet's date at the weddings, was doing a wonderful job of working his way into Blossom City's various social circles. He coached the high school boys' basketball and baseball teams. He belonged to the mountain biking club and the local search and rescue team. According to Courgette, Harry had enrolled in Italian cooking classes. He also was an avid square dancer and had made it his mission to teach Violet its intricacies (I suspect because it gave him yet another reason to spend time with my niece).

I agreed to collect Violet from the baseball practice on my way to Dough Vinci. Because it was winter and the ball diamond lay under several inches of snow, I knew the practice was being held in the school gym. When I arrived at the school half an hour early, I decided to join Violet inside. I wiped my boots carefully so as not to track grit onto the polished hardwood floor before entering the gym. When I spotted Violet sitting on the bleachers on the far side, I made my way over.

Harry Lovely threw hardballs to a group of teenage boys. The sharp smack of the ball hitting their gloves told me there was power behind his pitches. Another group of boys ran sprints at the far end of the gym. The man encouraging their efforts took me by surprise. "Is that Paolo Strada?"

Violet nodded. "Yep. He's focusing on quick starts from a standing position. Teaching them base stealing, do you think?"

I laughed. "Oh Violet, what I know about baseball strategy could be written on a wine cork. But your theory sounds plausible."

When the practice ended Harry and Paolo approached us.

"Have you recovered from the World Marriage Day?" I asked Paolo.

He shot me a look and his face reddened. "What do you mean?"

I detected a note of sharpness in his words but had no idea why my comment would have upset him. "Well, sixteen weddings in one day is an enormous undertaking. I'm surprised you have the energy to then come here and coach baseball."

"Oh. Yes, right," Paolo said. The redness left his face. "It's actually relaxing to coach, because it's such a change from my day job."

Harry said, "In addition to coaching base-running, Paolo helps the boys with batting. If they can manage to hit one of Paolo's rocket-speed pitches, I know they are ready for league play."

Paolo chucked Harry on the shoulder. "Hah. I don't know about rocket-speed. Maybe in college, but not now. I blame it all on age."

"The weddings yesterday were lovely," I said. "I thought the décor and flowers at the triple wedding were magnificent."

"Thank you. The entire day was successful, overall. It's all about managing details."

Violet and I said our goodbyes and jumped into the Porsche for the quick trip to Dough Vinci. Judging from her clenched jaw, I knew Violet had also noticed that Paolo took credit for Abby's work.

At Dough Vinci, Violet and I ordered Americanos and two of Cleo's sinful cinnamon buns, and then chose a table beside the window. We'd devoured half of our treats when there was a momentary lull in customers and Cleo sat down with us.

"Well!" she said. "Based on what I witnessed this morning, yesterday's triple wedding must have been quite the event! What exactly went on?"

I took a sip of my coffee. "You mean the allergic reaction that Maria, one of the brides, had to the dessert? If her husband Greg had not had an EpiPen handy, things could have been dire."

"And what about the dresses?"

"Yes. A few bridesmaids wore outfits that looked like they belonged on someone else."

Violet said, "Plus one attendant's gown was completely the wrong color for her. It amazes me what happens to women's sense of fashion when they plan a wedding."

Cleo nodded. "It has something to do with endorphins or serotonin or one of those things. When I married Logan, rest his soul, I had my attendants wear scarlet caftans. One size fits all."

Violet made a poor attempt at hiding her horror. I said, "When we walked down the aisle in front of Cleo it looked like a procession of Cardinals."

Cleo laughed. "Back to the triple affair. What about Selena's sprained ankle? Did that happen the way she said it did?"

"What sprained ankle?" I asked.

When two women entered the bakery, Cleo raised a finger in a "hold that thought" motion, pushed back her chair, and rushed to the counter to serve them. Violet took the opportunity to check her phone for messages. I played idly with a coaster on the tabletop, wondering who had scrawled "Buddy's killer's first name does not start with the same letter as the murder weapon" on the back.

When Cleo rejoined us, I said, "So, how is it you know more about the weddings than I do? Did Sergeant Courgette have breakfast here and fill you in?"

Cleo shook her head. "No, he did not. He may have been in here for his usual waffles but I had an appointment so I would have missed him in any event." She wriggled in her wooden chair and sighed. "Honestly, I must replace these chairs. Get some that are…"

"Bigger? More space for one's bottom?"

She frowned at me. "You better be teasing. I would hate to ban you from Dough Vinci."

Even though we were alone in the café Cleo glanced around the space. Then she leaned forward, resting her elbows on the table.

"As I said, I had an appointment. I met with Paolo Strada at his office to pitch my baking for his event planning."

"Excellent idea!" I said.

"I took my portfolio along so Paolo could flip through it to see what I can do. Not long after I arrived however, Greg and Maria showed up and interrupted our meeting. I must say Maria looked a fright—a walking welt, covered in pink anti-itch lotion. They wanted to know how real vanilla got into the dessert when Maria had specifically mentioned her allergy to him. Paolo said he had no idea, unless Abby had forgotten to pass on the information to Diana Hopper."

"Oh, that wouldn't be good," I said.

Violet sucked in her breath. "No way Abby would forget."

Cleo went on. "And get this: When he mentioned Diana's name, Maria shrieked at him and said, 'She was the caterer? Why didn't you tell me?'"

Cleo leaned back and took a breath. "Did you know Diana Hopper was once Greg Alsoli's girlfriend?"

"No!" I said.

"Yes. And apparently, she blamed Maria for their breakup."

I said, "So Maria thought Diana deliberately put real vanilla in the dessert?"

"Correct. After Greg and Maria left, Paolo told me Abby had obviously messed up. 'It's typical of her,' he said. 'Too young for a responsible job like this.'"

"That's ridiculous," Violet said. "Abby is more responsible than anyone I know."

"Hmmm. There's more," Cleo said.

"More?" I said. "Oh yes, the sprained ankle."

Cleo nodded. "Right. Paolo and I had almost wrapped up our discussion about what services I could offer when Selena and Jody, the other two brides, burst into the office. Well, Jody burst in. Selena limped in with the help of a cane. They wanted a refund because of the mix-up with the dresses. Somehow the dressmaker had switched the colors for the attendants' dresses. Jody's attendant ought to have been in blue, and one of Selena's bridesmaids in green. Plus, the dressmaker got the measurements confused, resulting in either too-long or too-short gowns. Last, the women said Paolo forced them to use a dressmaker who hated them and had done so ever since grade school."

"Who was the dressmaker?" I asked.

"Sally Pincher."

Ah yes, I remembered the stories a teacher friend told me. "Bullied terribly by Selena and Jody in school, is what I heard. You know, Cleo, it would serve them right if Sally *had* sabotaged their wardrobes. But that would harm her reputation as a dressmaker. Would she deliberately ruin her business for revenge?"

Cleo shrugged. "Who knows?" She blew out a breath. "Those two women were very angry. Selena said the staples she'd used to shorten her dress had come loose, causing her to trip and sprain her ankle. She wielded her cane like a weapon. It had a knob on the top almost the size of a billiard ball. She shook it at Paolo, saying, 'My honeymoon is ruined. For two cents, I'd bean you with this.' Honestly, Persie, at that point I did my best to disappear into the background."

"So, what happened in the end?"

"Paolo offered a partial refund and promised to look into the mix-up. He said Abby had been in charge of instructing the dressmaker. 'If she messed up, I might fire her,' Paolo said. At that point Selena said, 'You should do more than fire her. I'd throw her under a bus.' And then the women left."

"Quite the meeting you had!"

"You know, I had thought of pitching my services to Abby as well, because I'd heard she was opening her own business. But after what Paolo said about her irresponsibility, I don't think I will."

Violet put her coffee cup down with a bang. "This is so unfair. None of that is true. My guess is that Paolo was the one who messed up and wants to blame it all on Abby. I'm going to call her and fill her in. She has to stop these rumors fast."

ON TUESDAY MORNING, Violet left for a walk to Dough Vinci where she planned to meet with Abby. She'd been gone from the house about half an hour when she phoned me in a panic. "Aunt Persie, Abby's hurt! I found her in Blossom Park. I called an ambulance. Can you drive me to the hospital?"

I jumped into the Porsche and sped over to the park. I presumed Violet had found Abby as she walked by the park on the way to Dough Vinci.

When I arrived at Blossom Park, paramedics were attending to Abby, who lay at the bottom of the wooden staircase that ran down the hillside from the main street into the park. The stairs could be slippery when it snowed or rained, but we'd had a spell of unusually dry weather so I didn't think Abby would have slipped.

"Do you know what happened?" I asked Violet.

"No. She's unconscious. The paramedics think she fell down the stairs. One of her shoelaces is undone, so they believe she tripped. And there's a bit of a depression on her skull. Apparently, they found a small rock beside her head, so perhaps she hit her head on it when she landed."

"Is she bleeding?"

"I don't think so," Violet said. "I hope she comes out of it okay."

After the ambulance took off with Abby, siren blaring, I gave Violet a lift to the hospital. In the car she said, "Abby phoned me this morning and said her plans had changed."

"Oh? Changed how?"

"I don't know. She said she'd tell me at coffee. Her voice was shaking though, so I think she was still angry after our conversation last night."

"You mean when you told her about what Cleo overheard?"

"Yes. I said Paolo had blamed her for the mishaps at the triple wedding. Abby was incensed about it and planned to confront him."

"And did she?"

Violet thought for a moment. "I don't know. I assumed so. But maybe when she said her plans had changed, she meant she'd changed her mind about confronting him."

"Tell me honestly, Violet. Do you think Abby could have made the mistakes as Paolo alleges?"

"What?" Violet said, her voice rising. "Abby wouldn't lie to me. She is the most honest, truthful person I know. Plus, she writes everything down and has people sign off on instructions. She is meticulous about checking things off her list. I can't believe she would have messed up."

I parked outside the hospital emergency department and told Violet to check on Abby. "See if they will let you see her. If not, we'll go home."

Five minutes later, Violet returned. She slipped into the passenger seat. "Abby's still unconscious. No visitors allowed."

OVER A DINNER OF SPAGHETTI and meatballs, Violet raised the

topic of the wedding mishaps again. "Abby told me she was in charge of the venues," she said. "Not the wardrobes or catering. She would have told me if she had a bigger role to play, because gaining all that experience was important to her."

Violet broke off a piece of Italian bread and dunked it in the oil and vinegar mix. "You want my theory? Paolo lied about who messed up and wanted to blame it all on Abby. She told me taking on sixteen weddings for World Marriage Day had stressed him out."

"Hmm. If the brides were as angry as Cleo said when they met with Paolo, I can see why he'd want to deflect them and try to pass off the blame. Especially when Selena threatened to smack him with her cane."

I thought about the angry brides, and how they believed Abby was responsible for the things that went wrong at the weddings. "I wonder if one of the brides decided to get back at Abby for messing up her day?"

Violet sucked in her breath. "You mean maybe she didn't fall?"

I nodded. "Maybe she was pushed? Or maybe someone had words with her and swung a cane?"

I mulled things over a bit more. Then I said, "I think we should invite Sergeant Courgette and Constable Lovely for breakfast tomorrow at Dough Vinci. And hopefully convince them to look into Abby's suspicious fall."

Violet grinned and shook her head. "Aunt Persie, waffles and maple syrup may work to convince Sergeant Courgette to do your bidding. I know how often you trade pastries for favors from him. But Harry isn't so weak. He isn't susceptible to offers of sweets."

I nodded. "Oh, I know, dear. But Harry Lovely is smitten with you. And I am sure he may be interested in taking on an investigation if you believe it's necessary."

WEDNESDAY MORNING VIOLET and I met Courgette and Lovely at Dough Vinci. Cleo gave us a table in a corner, well away from other diners so that we could speak in privacy.

Courgette said, "How nice of you to invite us for breakfast,

Persimmon. What's the occasion?"

"We haven't had a chance to chat for ages it seems, Milton. And Violet will be returning to university in a few days. So, we thought a get-together before she leaves was a good idea."

Harry glanced at me and raised his eyebrows. "Didn't you and Sergeant Courgette manage to chat at the weddings?"

I smiled at him. Smart man, Harry. He had his doubts about my motives and suspected I was up to something. "We chatted," I said. "But not about anything that matters."

I waited until Cleo delivered her famous sourdough waffles to the table and placed a large carafe of genuine Quebec maple syrup in front of Courgette. I waited while he arranged his waffle just so on his plate, while he lifted the carafe of warmed maple syrup and breathed in the aroma, while he said 'ahh, genuine Quebec maple syrup, nectar for my soul,' and while he poured the liquid in an amber stream over his waffle, ensuring that each small depression filled to its brim. I waited until he completed the ritual by gazing lovingly at his waffle swimming in its syrup bath before carving a piece, precisely an inch-square, and lifting it to his mouth.

As soon as Courgette's lips closed around that syrup-drenched square of sourdough waffle, I said, "Violet and I have been talking about Abby's unfortunate fall down the park staircase. Has your team looked at the case, Milton?"

He choked, then swallowed and wiped his mouth with his napkin. "*Non, non.* It is not a case, as you put it Persimmon. A mere accident."

He cut another square of waffle.

"I wonder whether that's true," I said, "On Monday I learned that Paolo blamed Abby for the mistakes at the triple wedding. Apparently, the brides were very angry with her. Don't you think it's possible one of them pushed her?"

Courgette put his knife and fork down. "Persimmon." The sigh he emitted was worthy of Broadway. "Why do you always look for a mystery where there is probably none?"

I stayed silent, as if pondering his question. He dissected the waffle once more and forked the piece into his mouth quickly.

"Probably is not the same as absolutely," I said.

Milton chewed slowly. His go-to strategy to discourage conversation.

Harry's police instincts took over. He said, "Do you have any evidence that someone would want to hurt Abby?"

You would not believe how glad I was that he asked.

"First," I said, "Selena's dress was too long, and she tripped on the hem, resulting in a sprained ankle. She is walking now with the aid of a cane. One that has a knob on top, by the way."

Harry nodded. "So?"

"So, Paolo told Selena that Abby was in charge of instructing the dressmaker and hinted she may have mixed up the measurements. I think Selena blamed Abby for her sprained ankle."

Violet leaned forward and stared directly into Harry's eyes. "Plus, Jody and Selena discovered the dressmaker was a grade school classmate who had a grudge against them. She could have deliberately sabotaged the dresses."

"And that would be another motive to hurt Abby?" Harry's eyebrows rose with skepticism.

"Perhaps, if they believed Abby had hired the dressmaker," Violet said.

"Next," I added, "there's Maria who had a near-fatal reaction to the vanilla in the dessert. Again, Paolo told Maria that Abby had instructed the caterer. And, in case Greg Alsoli didn't tell either of you, the caterer was his former girlfriend. The word around town is she blamed Maria for the break-up of her romance with Greg. So perhaps the caterer deliberately spiked the dessert."

Harry said, "And of course Maria believed Abby had hired the caterer?"

I have to admit that as Harry asked his questions, I became doubtful that any of the brides had deliberately set out to hurt Abby. The motives seemed childish. But then, we were dealing with at least two women who had been bullies in grade school. Perhaps they had not changed their ways.

"None of this is evidence," Courgette said. "It is only supposition."

"True," I said. "But it is supposition based on what we know about the women involved. Milton, you have lived here only a decade. And Harry, what is it—a little over a year now?"

The men nodded.

"In Blossom City terms, you two are raw rookies. I've lived here all my life, if you ignore those unfortunate years at finishing school. You can't be expected to know the town and its residents the way I do. Hopefully you will give my intuition some credit. Indulge me and take a look at the case?"

Violet placed her hand atop Harry's. "It would mean a lot to me if you could help put my mind at ease over what happened to Abby. She's still unconscious and can't tell us anything. Suppose she's still in danger from someone?"

Frankly, I don't know if it was my plea for indulgence or Violet's hand on Harry's that did the trick, but Courgette and Lovely agreed to look into things.

"Don't get your hopes up," Courgette said. "It's bound to be an accident. Didn't you say she had loose shoelaces?"

When Violet nodded, Courgette said, "*Voilà*. There you go. She tripped."

THE NEXT DAY COURGETTE invited Violet and me to meet him at La Patisserie, the café near the police station. When we arrived, one minute late, Courgette and Lovely were already seated at a table in the back corner. A French press of coffee and a silver platter heaped with pastries sat on the tabletop.

"Ahh, here you are at last," Courgette said. He glanced at his wristwatch. "I was afraid Harry and I would have to start without you."

I bit back a smile. Courgette was not afraid at all. He'd been hopeful.

Courgette studied the pastry tray, hovering his hand over a croissant, then a crème caramel, then a slice of gâteau St. Honoré. Finally, he selected one of each.

After he poured coffees for each of us, Courgette said, "We do not know if any of the brides could have pushed or hit Abby. All three say they were somewhere else that morning. So far, only Maria is in the clear because Greg vouched for her."

"Is there any hint at all of what happened to Abby?" Violet asked.

Courgette blew out a breath. "Not much. Untied shoelaces, which could have caused her to trip. A small rock that she could have hit her head on."

"However," Harry said, "according to the doctor I spoke with, the depression in her skull doesn't match that rock. He said the depression was more spherical."

"Like the knob on Selena's cane?" I said. "Cleo mentioned it was about the size of a billiard ball."

Violet jerked in her chair. "Oh! Could it be a baseball?"

"Why?" Harry asked.

"Because I saw one in the park. When I was on the phone calling the ambulance, I paced around. I saw a ball lying under a bush not far from Abby. Maybe some dog left it there."

My mind flashed back to the baseball practice in the high school gym. "Suppose someone pitched it at her?"

Harry took a mere second to make the connection. "Like someone who used to pitch in college?"

"Exactly. Abby told Violet she planned to confront Paolo about blaming her for the mishaps at the wedding. I don't think he'd like people to know he made the mistakes and lied about it. And suppose he knew Abby was going to become his competition for event planning?"

Courgette slurped his coffee. He said, "So, we have Selena, Jody and Paolo who we have not cleared of suspicion."

Violet said, "But how can we prove if any of them hurt Abby?"

"We could set a trap," I said.

Courgette shuddered and pushed the remains of his croissant away. "I was afraid you would say that. Goodbye appetite."

WE PUT OUR PLAN INTO action that same day. Violet attended the afternoon baseball practice at the high school, and then dropped by the hair salon where Selena and Jody both worked.

Later, Violet told me, "I managed to find a way to let all of them know that, although Abby was still unconscious, she was showing signs of coming around, and that the doctor believed she'd be fully conscious by tomorrow morning."

That evening, I donned my pink hospital auxiliary smock and sat at the information booth in the hospital where I could watch who entered the building. I had my cell phone at the ready in order to text Courgette whenever I saw one of our suspects arrive.

Courgette was on the ward, dressed in scrubs, a surgical mask and cap, and playing the role of a doctor. Harry Lovely donned a wig and snuggled into a hospital bed, pretending to be Abby.

I had been at my station perhaps fifteen minutes when I noticed Maria and Jody enter the hospital, carrying flowers. Even though Harry had said Maria was not a suspect, I quickly texted Courgette.

As soon as I put my phone down Selena showed up. She limped past me, heading toward the elevator. I called after her: "Hello, Selena, can I help you with directions?"

She stopped and leaned on her cane. "No need, I know my way."

"Oh? Visiting a patient?"

"No." She gestured at her ankle. "X-ray," she said, and then walked to the elevator bank.

I watched the elevator display after the car's doors closed, and when I saw that Selena's elevator was heading down instead of up to the wards, I relaxed.

Courgette texted me then. "Brides brought flowers for Abby. All good."

His text arrived at the same time as the elevator doors opened. Jody and Maria stepped into the hospital lobby and headed to the exit.

An hour dragged by.

I had almost concluded our trap would not yield results when Paolo Strada entered the hospital, carrying a bouquet. I waved at him and said, "Paolo, can I help with directions?"

"Yes, thanks. I heard Abby was improving. What's her room number?"

I gave him the number of the room in which Harry Lovely was playing patient. "Abby isn't conscious yet, but we are all very hopeful."

The minute Paolo headed for the elevator, I texted Courgette to alert him.

Then I abandoned the information booth and climbed the stairs to the second floor. That gave me a week's worth of cardio in five minutes. Exercise is over-rated.

When I arrived at the ward, I secreted myself in the alcove by the stairs.

Paolo was speaking with Courgette. If I hadn't known who was beneath those scrubs and mask, I never would have guessed it was the sergeant.

Fake Dr. Courgette said, "Can I help you, sir?"

Paolo asked after Abby.

"I'm afraid she is still unconscious and we're not allowing visitors," Courgette said. "However, if you would like to leave your flowers with me I will make sure she gets them."

Paolo handed the flowers to Courgette. "I'm pulling for her and hope she recovers quickly."

Courgette nodded and walked into the staff room carrying the flowers. The minute Courgette was out of sight, Paolo headed straight for the room he believed was Abby's.

I texted Courgette: "Hurry."

Courgette and I arrived at the room in time to see Harry Lovely wrestling Paolo to the floor.

After Harry handcuffed Paolo he said, "This man tried to smother the patient. What a shock it must have been when, instead of a weakened young woman, the patient was a fit police officer."

Courgette telephoned me early the next morning. "Good news," he said. "Abby has regained consciousness and is doing well. And Paolo confessed to attacking her."

"Did he say why?"

"Your theory was correct. Abby told Paolo she was going to tell everyone he had lied about who caused the wedding mishaps. He also knew she was going into competition with him and said it would ruin him."

"So he hit her with the baseball?"

"*Oui.* Paolo said he pitched a perfect strike at Abby's head, but she suddenly bent over her shoe, I suspect to tie her laces. In any event, the ball glanced off her head. When she tumbled down the stairs Paolo hoped that if his pitch hadn't killed her, the fall would. And if not, he was certain everyone would think it had been an accident."

"Well, almost everyone," I said.

THE NEXT DAY, AS VIOLET was packing her suitcase to return to university, Abby stopped by.

"You look recovered," Violet said to her.

"I am," Abby said. "You'll never guess what's happened. Selena, Jody and Maria have hired me to plan their first anniversary party!"

"An entire year in advance?" I said.

Abby shook her head and grinned. "No, their first *month* anniversary. They want a destination event, perhaps a weekend ski trip. It's short notice but I'm sure I can manage it. It's going to be absolute perfection."

Violet and I exchanged a look.

"Abby," Violet said, "this is Blossom City. You should know better than to tempt fate with predictions like that."

FOR MORE INFORMATION about the author, please visit Charlotte Morganti's website: https://charlottemorganti.com/

Cinderella at Midnight
P.M. Raymond

11 **:05 PM**
The problem wasn't a wedding under cover of night. Lyla knew starry evenings of celebration were a nice problem for humans to have. No, this problem was much bigger. Walter was missing and only Lyla, a little pint-sized demon with all the cunning and cleverness of a regular-sized demon, could solve it. At least that's how she saw things as she peered through the crack in the door.

11:07 PM
Lyla grabbed the doorknob and leaned stealthily just inside the bridal suite watching the drama play out like a bad community theatre production. Her normally squeaky patent leather shoes were library quiet as she stood still, absorbing the unfolding confusion.

Blooming roses on scrolling vines accented the wallpaper that covered every wall of the room. The décor was a controlled chaos of heavy wood and overstuffed furniture. It gave Lyla the feeling of being suffocated by a Victorian grandmother's pillows.

The weeping bride was huddled by a curvaceous older woman in a subdued pink two-piece satin suit with a matching veiled hat and a pair of white gloves in her hand, a step beyond her Sunday best. Another woman closer in age to the bride hovered next to her in a pale blue flowing halter dress, presumably the bridesmaid.

Lyla observed varying degrees of panic around the room. This was fertile ground for her to do what she does best.

"Who would want to snatch a defenseless miniature pinscher?" Andrina Brownstone, socialite and bride-to-be, examined the note. The felt tip block letters expanded, soaking up her tears. She fluffed the crinolines of her wedding gown with her free hand as she dipped to retrieve the red and green plaid blanket that Walter used as his resting pallet. The tartan-style fabric dangled in her shaking hands.

The groom, Vincent Booker, leaned against the armoire near the sliding glass door. "This is a joke, right? Only a psycho would hurt a dog." He strode over to the cluster of frantic women and eased the note from Andrina's hand. Vincent attempted to comfort her.

Andrina gave her well-meaning but socially brash husband-to-be a slight frown. What Andrina had in New Orleans pedigree, Vincent matched in wealth, but his money wasn't spent on etiquette lessons.

"My Cinderella fairytale is practically sliding into the Mississippi." She sniffed.

Her eyes glistened with a fresh trickle of tears as she pressed the blanket to her cheeks like the soft weave harbored clues.

Andrina's midnight nuptials, an elaborate spectacle that spent the last twenty years gestating in her mind, would commence in just under an hour. Guests bustled just beyond the suite's glass sliding door, none of them aware that a precarious situation was unfolding.

Wagging the cloth in Vincent's face, Andrina bawled, "I can still smell the lavender shampoo from his special bridal bubble bath! For heaven's sake, where is *he!*"

Walter's disappearance could very well bring this wedding to a screeching halt but before Lyla could intervene, she wanted to hear more.

Vincent massaged Andrina's back as the wails leaped and dipped like a rollercoaster of grief. "Walter probably got lost," he said anxiously. "He's pretty resourceful, though. Remember that time he got stuck in the fence at Mama Garrett's house? He wiggled out of that just fine."

Andrina was having none of Vincent's Pollyanna nonsense.

"Don't you get it?" she snapped, stomping her satin heels. "The rings? They were around his collar!" She snatched the paper from Vincent's hand.

"Whoever has him doesn't *need* him anymore. They have the..." Andrina pointed to a still trembling ring finger.

Vincent swallowed hard to steady his nerves. He assessed where on the spectrum Andrina's emotional state might lie at that moment—anywhere from fragile to homicidal. "The note doesn't exactly say he was taken. He still could have wandered off."

Lyla was so laser-focused on the verbal tussle inside the room that she did not detect a pair of soft orthopedic shoes approaching. The booming voice that accompanied the footwear made up for that.

"What in the world are you doing?" Lyla jumped at the accusing voice. Aunt Sylvie observed Lyla with a stern stare. "Get out of grown folks' business," she barked.

"I wasn't in anybody's business," Lyla mumbled. "I can't help it if they're carrying on so loud." She swayed her neck with the response. The coiled afro puffs on each side of her head bounced outrageously.

Aunt Sylvie didn't appreciate what old-timers would refer to as "back talk" from a sassy six-year-old. "Hmm." She crossed her arms and pursed her lips. "Go find your...I thought this was a child-free wedding. Who are you here with at this time of night?"

Lyla's face pinched in protest to the question. "But I wasn't doing anything," she asserted, fists clenched at the sides of her white cotton dress.

Aunt Sylvie settled a perplexed glance on Lyla. "Go find your family, please." The elder sashayed into the room, the sleeve of her crepe ensemble grazing Lyla's cheek. The woman promptly got to work providing her matriarch version of comfort. "Oh, sweet Andrina, you mustn't worry. Everyone is searching. Marion, be a dear and grab her a Kleenex."

Before the door could close, Lyla slipped in.

11:12 PM

She made her way to the other side of the bridal suite. The open sliding glass door invited the humid night air to waft in and mingle in the air-conditioned space. Lyla stared out at the manicured grounds of St. Edgewood Country Club, one of New Orleans's most exclusive playgrounds of the rich and richest in the area.

"Just under an hour to find this scrappy little hound," she murmured. The heirloom rings that adorned Walter's collar were as important as the sun rising in the East. *Le Conseil des Démons* tapped her as a background observer, demon eyes on the ground, to confirm this union took place. She was one of their most senior operatives with an extensive knowledge of human behavior, having over 200 years of experience. The world would change in the most unholy way, and it was Lyla's mission to preserve humanity until *Le Conseil des Démons* was ready to take control 32 years from now.

Lyla noticed Bea sitting on the edge of a puffed armchair near her destination. As Lyla walked up, Bea placed an empty champagne glass on the tray next to the sliding door.

"Where've you been? You were supposed to relieve me 30 minutes ago," she huffed in a low tone. "I'm on my third champagne holding down the fort here."

The young woman looked impossibly fresh and cool in a teal shimmery slip dress with sheer sleeves that maximized her athletic brown frame. Bea was Lyla's mortal guide assigned to her late last year.

"Haven't you noticed we have a problem?" Lyla tilted her head toward Andrina and the gaggle of fixers talking but not personally doing anything to find Walter.

"A problem? I thought you said this was an 'easy peasy' walk down the aisle," Bea whispered.

Lyla grew restless with the young woman's unhelpful observation. "Walter is missing along with the rings. Those rings are everything, so we need to find that scrappy dog."

Lyla let out a hiss that turned into a sneeze. Lyla wiped her nose with the back of her hand. There were still aspects of humanity that irritated her. One of them was pollen. Lavender and hibiscus were in full bloom in the Louisiana nighttime heat and doing a number on Lyla's nose. Bea pulled a tissue from her small clutch purse and handed it to the little girl.

The Brownstone rings, engraved with 'things are as they should be,' were the key to the power that the Brownstone women would manifest in the future, not that Andrina or any newlywed before her was aware. An unbroken line of inheritance to each eligible bride, one per generation, was the Lego block to the plans the *Démons* had set in motion.

"Can't you use your power to open a black portal and find the dog that way?" Bea casually patted her tight curls pushed back with a pearl headband.

Lyla wondered if Bea, with her unbothered attitude and killer fashion sense, was the real demon.

"The portal isn't a party trick," Lyla grumbled. "It can find people most of the time but not animals. Not reliably anyway."

Bea tightened her lips in recognition of the implication of the hole but remained unfazed by the current events. "Okay, where do we start."

Lyla waved her hands in a hush motion and said, "I need quiet so I can think."

She glanced outside as guests and waitstaff wove in and around the ceremonial area located about half a football field away. Lyla had to admit the setup was quite a sight. Poles lined the length of the perimeter on each side with lights draped and crisscrossed everywhere forming a twinkling canopy.

The sounds of "Waterfalls" by TLC began on the heels of "Gin and Juice," ending Snoop Dogg's reign over the DJ's speakers. Lyla shimmied to the musical earworm floating her way, the fabric of her dress airy like cotton candy on her honey-colored skin. Over the decades Lyla had done the bidding for the *Démons* organization, she was enjoying the 1990s the most.

Early arrivals were beginning to occupy ivory satin-covered chairs fitted with lush aubergine-colored bows. Champagne, poured and served by wordless servers in white jackets, lubricated their idle hands. Lyla wondered which guests would be bold enough to snatch their gift back from the table inside if this wedding didn't come to fruition.

◊ If Buddy's killer's first name starts with R, the fireplace poker is not the murder weapon. ◊

11:17 PM

Lyla felt a tap on her shoulder. It was Aunt Sylvie. "Excuse me, little biscuit, if you insist on being in this room, you should stay out of the way. Us old gals need some fresh air." Lyla politely retreated to allow the women to exit through the sliding glass door. Aunt Sylvie slid the door closed and, with a darting glance, dared Lyla to open the door again.

Didn't matter. Lyla had the ability to rummage through any human for words spoken and unspoken. This combined with her ability to mesmerize entire rooms of people into a shared reality made her a legend in the halls of the *Démons*. She had a 90% successful conversion rate, after all. What Lyla did back in 1969 with the moon landing was basically a game changer.

She watched as the women walked over the freshly cut grass to a bush at the side of the clubhouse. The exterior lights at the corner where they convened shone down like an interrogation spotlight.

"That silly girl wanting a dog in her wedding. Absurd. Just one more thing that can go wrong if you ask me," Aunt Sylvie said.

Lyla closed her eyes. Prisms of color floated inside her lids as words tend to do when she tapped into conversations or crawled through other minds.

"I warned Andrina against marrying into the Booker family. They are just terrible luck." Aunt Sylvie shook her head in disapproval as she said the words. "But she is set on it, so I am going to support it." She kneaded the back of her neck as if a tight crick was forming at the base of it. "He'll certainly keep Andrina in the style of living she's accustomed to and she does seem to be sweet on him."

Miss Marion, a woman known for her silver hair and salty tongue, responded, "Hmm, hmm, hmm," and nodded in the negative. "But if you think it's worth it...remember the last time the Brownstones and the Bookers joined together?" The woman rolled her eyes. "Even a snake has enough common sense to avoid this union."

As the matriarchs of their respective families, Aunt Sylvie and Miss Marion had seen a thing or two over the years. So had Lyla and she knew exactly what they were referring to.

Miss Marion confided as she removed a white glove, "Andrina has lived such a charmed life so far, maybe a little adversity would do her some good." She scratched her hand furiously. "Well, Corky had her chance to make some magic with Vincent," she said with resignation.

Aunt Sylvie paused then gave her old friend a wicked look. "If I didn't know you any better, I'd think you were stirring something up by recommending Corky to Andrina."

"Oh, now that is foolish talk, Sylvie. Foolish. If Vincent was thinking twice about options, we'd all know it. He can't hide much of anything he's thinking." A fresh round of scratching overtook Miss Marion.

"You okay, cher?" Aunt Sylvie asked as she pulled a small bottle of Gold Bond from her pocketbook.

Her friend kindly waved it away, then concluded her musings with a chuckle. "Who'd a thought one missing dog could bring the whole house of cards tumbling down? Besides, Walter is the only one coming between those two, right?" The silence from Aunt Sylvie caused Miss Marion to look away.

11:21 PM

Within minutes of the older women reentering the room to begin their subtle coercion to get Andrina down the aisle, the bridal suite door swung open with a flourish.

A blunt twenty-something in a vivid yellow suit and black sensible flat shoes burst through the suite door barking orders. "Okay, everyone! Small hiccup in the run of show, but we are staying the course. Chop, chop!" She swung her planning notebook in her right hand like an axe.

"The bumble bee? That's Corky," Lyla whispered to her companion. "The wedding planner."

Corky swung her head toward the fair-haired, gangly man, about the same age, who entered with her. An errant box braid flew within an inch of his face, nearly taking his eye out. His reflexes were quick, avoiding the braided missile.

Lyla sighed and informed Bea, "And that's her lackey, Braden."

Aunt Sylvie held up her hand in an effort to slow Corky's roll. "Corky, I know you have a job to do but there is a pressing matter of finding those rings."

"And Walter!" Andrina howled.

"Yes, and Walter," Aunt Sylvie said as she stroked Andrina's back. Vincent took a few steps back like distancing himself from his bride's emotions would inoculate him from catching any feelings about the situation.

Lyla took in this latest dramatic scene.

"What are you thinking?" Bea asked.

"Not sure yet but..." Lyla ceased talking in order to concentrate on Corky. The planner's expression intrigued her. Lyla inhaled deeply, absorbing the vibes Corky was emitting. Her ears began to tingle. She massaged them like a radio dial.

Corky took Braden's elbow and moved him towards the door to put some space between them and the others in the room.

But Lyla was now tuned into Corky's mental frequency and the words she spoke. The other tidbits inside Corky's mind flowed into Lyla's like a torrent of lava.

She loved it.

"Can you believe this bride is going to allow a non-essential canine to derail her wedding? She really lacks imagination, that one," Corky said softly but with a bite at the end. She gently tilted her head into a slow roll as if to loosen her neck. A slight grimace curled her lips.

Corky's strong personality and heightened anxiety created color swirls streaming before Lyla like a fire hose. Lyla wondered what Corky was anxious about.

"Walter is so cute," a fidgety Braden commented. His personality was the equivalent of human tapioca, his words like drying paint to Lyla's senses. His fingers bounced between straightening his tie knot and tugging the collar of his shirt.

"Besides," Braden continued, "the rings are sort of important, don't you—"

"But she doesn't need the rings to seal the deal with Vincent." Corky slapped her notebook in her hand as if this was the definitive word in the discussion. She stepped over to Andrina, muscling in between Aunt Sylvie and Miss Marion. The women did not appreciate the interruption.

"All right, let's divide and conquer," Corky announced to the room. "Braden will search the ceremony area." She turned to the older women,

"And maybe you two can check the common areas? Vincent and I will check the—"

"Umm, not so fast." Lyla breezed into the center of the bridal suite.

"Can I help you?" Andrina's voice rose in a singsong confused pitch.

Andrina was being very resistant to Lyla's mesmerizing and mind-trolling techniques. What Lyla would call a 10-percenter given that 10 percent of humans take a bit longer to be swayed by her tactics. The fact that Andrina would challenge Lyla troubled her but she brushed it off.

Fake it till you make it, girl. You got this.

Bea hung back as Lyla launched into her interrogation.

"We are just as concerned about Walter as you," Lyla stated with a serious demeanor well beyond her years. "So, I'm just going to jump in." Andrina's confused stare worried Lyla so she strode across the room to put distance between the two of them and mentally regroup.

Andrina trailed behind her.

Great! This woman is following me around like a stain on my soul. If I had one.

Lyla climbed into the tufted chair next to the dressing table and faced the bride with her best, mesmerized stare, and continued, "Where did you last see the pup?"

"What?" Andrina cocked her head as if in disbelief that a child would be bold enough to insert herself into an adult situation and be up past her bedtime.

But Lyla could see the tide shifting. The telltale sign that she was wiggling her way in.

Andrina rubbed her neck.

When mesmerizing takes hold, it pinches the nerves just above the collarbone. Lyla knew she was back in business.

"Where was Walter last seen? Who was tending to him?" Lyla's legs dangled over the chair's edge. She clasped her hands in her lap. "I see the crate in this room so..." She stopped and leaned forward, her hand in front of her nose, a sneeze coming but then retreating. She shook her head and continued, "Why wasn't he in it?"

Corky slouched on the sofa, sucking her teeth and checking her nails like this was none of her business.

Andrina said, "Well, for your information, little girl, that is what everyone is trying to find out." She stopped and tilted her head to the left in a good stretch.

Lyla could feel a previously suppressed memory of Andrina's barrel to the forefront. Or that could be wishful thinking on her part. She wasn't entirely sure.

"Walter was supposed to be on his potty run with Vincent. Yes." Andrina's eyes cast a dark look on Vincent as he idled by the sofa, a little too close to Corky.

"Vincent," Andrina pointed her French manicured finger in his direction, "said he put him back in the room but..." She was about to zero in on Vincent just as her bridesmaid, Emily, spoke up from the other side of the room.

"I didn't see Vincent. And I was here the whole time." The bridesmaid with short natural hair colored an unnatural platinum blonde fidgeted with her dress as she took up space on the loveseat.

"Ugghh, Vincent, where did you—" Andrina spun to her left as if her eyes needed her body to be in motion to see better.

"Where is Vincent?" she exclaimed.

Everyone gazed around at each other with bewilderment. While everyone was distracted by the Emily and Andrina show, Vincent had quietly exited the room without anyone noticing.

Lyla could kick herself. She hadn't planned on Andrina's mind being Teflon to her mental coercion. Or on Vincent being a runner.

Lyla cleared her throat to grab everyone's attention and get things back on track. "So, there is a gap in the time between Vincent picking Walter up for his poop run and when he should have been returned when no one saw either of them."

"Yeah, that's right, Tiny Sherlock." Andrina planted herself at the dressing table.

Lyla slid down out of the chair next to the table for her next announcement. "Talk amongst yourselves. We'll," she pointed to herself and Bea, "get Vincent and bring him back."

11:30 PM

Lyla crossed her arms and mentally reviewed what she had learned but hesitated to share it with Bea lest she had to divulge how powerful her mesmerizing really is. But after careful consideration of what was at stake, she decided to give Bea the Cliff Notes version of the older women's conversation.

"If Aunt Sylvie is second-guessing Miss Marion's motives, maybe we should?" Bea squinted like an original thought was coming to her. "I've been wondering...why does that council need Andrina and Vincent to get married?" Bea was full of questions tonight which was unusual for her.

Lyla decided she would answer this one. "Simple. Andrina and Vincent will have a daughter they'll name Lucille. Lucille needs to be born so that she can inherit the rings. If Walter isn't found in the next," she looked at her Tweety Bird watch, "the next 15 minutes, give or take, it will shift things. That could be very bad."

"How bad?"

"Black portal goes berserk bad." Lyla waved her hand like a magician's assistant.

Bea raised an eyebrow. "That bad?" She had an idea of what the portal was capable of. "Let's find Vincent."

11:33 PM

The duo found him alone in the groom's suite. It was a mirror image of the bridal version with a few exceptions—the sofa along the wall to the left, the loveseat placed to form an L shape, and the end table between them remained the same. But, instead of a heavy armoire, there was a substantial credenza near the sliding glass door and the dressing table was replaced with a fully stocked wet bar with a box of cigars for good measure. Because gender roles were reinforced like prison barbed wire in the South.

He faced the sliding glass door peering out at the twinkling canopy that may or may not host a wedding, the dog strap meant for Walter in his hands.

Vincent waved in a 'don't come closer' motion. "This is a private area. You can't be in here." He looked from Bea back to Lyla. "Aren't you a little young to be up this late?"

Lyla was beginning to see that Brownstones and Bookers, Andrina and Vincent, in particular, had slippery minds that did not take well to mesmerizing.

She shook it off and continued her advance toward Vincent until she climbed into the chaise lounge next to the bar across from him. With tiny fingers steepled under her chin, she started her questioning.

"Thank you for your concern about my bedtime." Lyla nodded. Before Vincent could respond, she launched in with, "Where is Walter? Really."

Vincent threw the leash to the ground. Frustration flashed in his eyes but flamed out when he realized it was only a child sitting in front of him. A child who could take care of herself just fine, but he didn't know that. Vincent put his head in his hands. "I wish I knew. I swear I opened Andrina's door and dropped him off in there."

Lyla looked Vincent up and down, way down to his shoes. Things looked suspicious.

"If you walked him for poo time, then why don't your shoes have dirt on them?"

Vincent took a few steps back, bumping the credenza next to the glass door behind him. Just as Lyla was about to go trolling in Vincent's head, he said, "Okay, I didn't walk Walter." He crumbled under Lyla's discerning gaze like a schoolyard snitch.

"Ah, ha! I knew it!" Lyla yelled as if she was destined to wear a deerstalker hat and a pipe cocked between her lips. Or an oversized trench coat.

Lyla puffed her pom-pom hair in delight and satisfaction that she didn't have to crawl inside his head, not that she would find much.

Bea sighed under her breath and smiled.

"I asked Braden, Corky's assistant, to take care of walking him for his, you know, business." 'Business' was in air quotes. Vincent clasped his hands and scrunched his face. "I didn't want to pick up after Walter and get my suit messy." He shrugged and concluded, "There. I said it." He sat against the credenza, hands in his pockets, eyes practically boring a hole in the carpet. "What's it to you anyways, little slice?" His voice was soft with shame.

"It matters a whole lot to me that you make it down the aisle. On time." She tapped her watch. "Don't you think it matters?"

"Yeah, of course, I do. More than you know." Vincent's tone was contemplative and somber.

Lyla felt for the man. "Save the 'I do' for your bride." She slipped down from the chair. "We're all going back to the bridal suite. And you need to face Andrina."

Vincent looked as if he would rather swallow thumbtacks but agreed.

As the group made their way down the corridor, Lyla exercised her considerable gifts to reach Corky and Braden and send them back to the suite as well.

Lyla's little face was stone cold as she anticipated her confrontation with Braden. She was curious to pick through his mind to determine why she didn't see this turn of events shuffling around in his pudding brain. *Is Braden a 10 percenter*, she wondered.

11:45 PM

Vincent walked in as Corky and Andrina kicked off their dueling accusations. Bea and Lyla were right on his heels.

"How could you lose the dog *aaaannd* the rings? You had one job!" Andrina seethed.

"I beg to differ with you, Andrina. This isn't on me. Vincent was responsible for Walter when he went missing."

"That's not exactly true." Vincent's interjection startled everyone in the room.

"That's one way to make an entrance," Lyla whispered to Bea with more than a bit of joviality in her voice.

Vincent craned his head to look around and spotted Braden.

Braden attempted to fade into the background. His knees buckled as he crouched behind Emily's statuesque frame near the loveseat and end table.

Andrina gave Vincent a glare that could melt stone. "Really? Then tell us all what happened, Houdini!" She sat at the dressing table, arms crossed, legs crossed, complementing her cross attitude. Vincent drew in a deep breath and stood next to her. He rested his hand on her bare shoulder and surprisingly, she didn't push it away.

"Okay, I deserved that," Vincent said sheepishly. With the requisite amount of guilt, he recounted handing off Walter to Braden for the tiny pup's call of nature.

Andrina nearly shoved Vincent out of the way to get to Braden who, in turn, slinked even closer to the back wall. "What did you do with him!" she yelled, arms outstretched in Braden's direction as Vincent held her at the waist.

"Okay, fine! I should have said something before," he exclaimed. "I took him for the potty run," he finally admitted.

Lyla slowed down to respond, "You still didn't answer the question."

Everyone turned to gawk at Lyla.

Although she appeared like a spunky child, Lyla was far older than human form would suggest but still young enough in demon years to still be fascinated by making adults uncomfortable.

"Can you stop asking me questions?" Braden raised his hands in an exasperated motion and addressed Bea. "Can you get her to stop it? It's freaking me out, man!"

Bea answered succinctly, "No."

A bit annoyed, Lyla said, "You've been all over the venue this evening, privy to all the comings and goings. It's not so farfetched that you could put Walter in a service vehicle and ship him off. He'd fit pretty nicely in a box." She waved her arms in an upward motion, the signal for Bea to come over and lift her up. Bea set her on the end table. Lyla felt that being closer to eye level with a suspect gave her leverage given the nature of her size.

With a confused look, Braden finished with, "That's your opinion. Which, I have to say, it's pretty dark for a kid."

"Not so much." Lyla cocked her head and leaned in. "I am a demon," she mouthed.

"Ohhhkayy??" Braden's sideways glance at Bea broke into a crooked smile.

Lyla's surprise at Braden's sudden cheekiness discombobulated her balance. She listed like a Regency heroine in the midst of a fainting spell and plopped into Bea's waiting arms. A few murmurs of "My goodness" peppered the room. Bea softly settled Lyla on the floor.

"I'm fine, nothing to see here." Lyla smoothed out her dress all the while peering at Braden.

He ignored Lyla's impenetrable stare and answered, "Well, for the record, I cracked the door open, and he scooted inside but I didn't put him in the crate. I didn't even open the door wide enough to see if anyone was in the room."

In an effort to deflect any culpability by proxy to Braden, Corky added, "I had no idea about this." She scowled at her second in command who immediately found his shoes and the floor more interesting, and finished with, "Anyways, that doesn't explain the note at all."

Andrina slumped cross-legged to the floor, blankets of satin spilling from her waist all around her. She pulled the folded piece of paper from her décolletage, her off-the-shoulder neckline dipping dangerously low. "I know," she said dimly. "But why," Andrina kept repeating. She uncrumpled the note, portions of it still damp from her tears, to reveal its vile words and read it aloud. "*Bookers and Brownstones will be the death of the world. Walk away from this marriage or Walter will not.*"

Lyla climbed back into the same tufted chair from the previous detecting session and continued to hold court by turning her attention to Corky. And a side eye to Braden. "Did you have a bone to pick with the bride?"

Corky gasped with indignant fury. "Whatever do you mean?"

"You know what I mean. You have a history with Vincent, do you not?"

Now it was Andrina's turn to gasp. "What?" Her eyes squinted in anger at Corky. "Is that why Miss Marion lobbied for you as my wedding planner? So you could muck about with *my* big day?"

"Night, actually," Lyla piped in.

Andrina slowly rose to her feet, silent like a Trappist monk, ready to remove her satin pumps. That could only mean one thing in New Orleans. Andrina was preparing to go medieval on her wedding planner nemesis.

As much as Lyla delighted in Andrina getting flat-footed and ready for a fight, she intervened. "Corky, you tried to date Vincent in the past, but he was never interested, right?"

Corky lashed out defending her good name for what it was worth. "Truth be told, I never had designs on Vincent. I'm a friend of Miss Marion's family," she said smugly. "That's how I made his acquaintance." She turned her high cheekbones upward and looked at the ceiling. "And he, yes, may have escorted me to a few debutante soirees during carnival season, back," Corky did her internal math, "in 1993 or 1994 when we were at university."

Then Corky pivoted to face Andrina. "It's been three years since that happened. I would hardly say I had *designs* on him at this point." She fidgeted with her black velvet choker, diverting her eyes again. "Besides, he made his choice when he met you," and added, "Obviously."

Lyla noticed that the onlookers in the room rubbernecking during this exchange were highly engaged in the outcome. Except one.

Emily, the bridesmaid.

Lyla observed the young woman, distracted and agitated, but not by the bickering. Then she saw it like a homing beacon, clear as day. Dark, damp stains clung to the blue satin fishtail hem of this fishy bridesmaid.

"Emily—" Lyla began. Her small voice drew everyone's attention away from Andrina and Corky and to the new matter at hand.

"That's Miss Emily, young lady," Andrina interrupted in a chastising tone.

Lyla folded her arms indignantly and then did as she pleased.

"Emily...why is your dress hem so filthy?" Lyla hurled the question like an accusation.

Before she could whip the fishtail behind her, everyone got an unobstructed view of the dirty hem. Andrina's eyes flashed hot with displeasure. "Your dress is ruined! This is yet ANOTHER disaster! How could you?"

Corky flew into wedding planner mode. "I'll find some club soda. It'll be fine." She sprinted from the room in search of carbonated sanctuary, nearly pushing Braden into the loveseat.

"I guess you're in the frying pan now." Lyla tapped her tiny fingers on the winged chair's arms, her stony glare on Emily. "Well? What were you doing out in the dirt? Pushing Walter out into the wild?"

"Who is this kid?" Emily spat. "I went outside..." She paused.

Lyla crawled around in Emily's mind seeking answers.

Emily rubbed her temples and moved downward, right above her collarbone. "Fine," she blurted out. "I was chatting up Rev. Howard's son by the reception site. That's probably how my dress got dirty." Taken aback by her own outburst, she rushed to her friend. She stuttered, "You were getting poured into your dress in the bedroom, so I thought I had a few minutes." The look on Emily's face was hesitant.

Andrina looked her friend squarely in the eyes and demanded, "Did you see Walter come back into the room?"

Emily sighed, still massaging her neck. "Okay, yes and no."

A collective gasp reverberated off the rosy walls and chintz furniture.

"No, I did not see Walter walk back into the room. Yes, I did see Walter. Out in the ceremony area." She moved over to the sofa and flopped into the same spot Corky had vacated.

"Who was he with?" Andrina and Lyla asked at the same time.

"Well, no one. He was wandering by himself, and, at the time, I didn't know there was anything wrong with that." Emily's eyes pleaded. "Please don't be mad. I didn't know!" She snapped her fingers as she remembered one more thing and followed up with, "But guests were feeding him. That, I know. Saw one of them give Walter some water. Poured it into a cup and laid it on the ground for him. I thought he was fine."

Braden crossed his arms and walked to face Andrina, his expression growing with haughtiness. "See? Based on what I just heard, someone took him when the room was empty for those few minutes when Ms. Lovesick was talking to the reverend's son."

Emily, ready to storm into Braden, took two steps in his direction but Lyla intervened.

"Emily, make yourself useful and ask the guests what they know and meet us back here. You have 10 minutes," Lyla said.

Emily stomped her foot and waved a fist at Braden, lips curled, ready to speak her mind. The words bursting in Emily's mind made even a demon like Lyla blush. Lyla quieted the angry woman's thoughts.

Emily lowered her arm, and a faint smile came across her lips. "Yes, I'll go talk to the guests."

As the door shut behind Emily, Lyla turned to Aunt Sylvie and Miss Marion and stated, "Something has been eating at me."

11:50 PM

Lyla's ears prickled with the sensation of veiled emotions throughout the room.

Miss Marion was a tougher nut to crack. Her strong will made it difficult to keep her mesmerized over a long period of time. Right about now, Miss Marion was getting annoyed with Lyla and that could cause a metric ton more problems for the pint-size detective.

"You sure are a busybody, little girl," Miss Marion said with a frown on her face. She winced as she rubbed her right hand. Her white-gloved hand.

"Am I?" Lyla asked.

"Why I never!" Miss Marion bent over to get nose level with Lyla. The stretch of the woman's crepe jacket over her ample hips flattered the older woman's figure, but the stare in her eyes was most unbecoming, Lyla had to admit.

"You listen here, you little rascal." Miss Marion rubbed her temples. "Keep your little heinie out of this!" Miss Marion grabbed Lyla by the arm and began to scoot her toward the door just as Corky returned with soda water and a cloth.

"Let go of me!" Lyla protested. The woman released her little arm. "I think I know what happened to Walter," Lyla replied as she rubbed the place where Miss Marion's fingers had grabbed her.

"What is wrong with all of you!" Andrina shouted. "You should all be out searching high and low for Walter but yet," she threw up her arms, "I have a carnival happening in here with a six-year-old ringleader."

Lyla sneezed. Her eyes widened and a cheeky grin came over her lips. "I know what happened to Walter. Most of it anyway."

Stares circled the room.

"Why are you itching?" Lyla squinched her eyes and pointed to Miss Marion's gloved hands. "Are you allergic to something?"

Miss Marion straightened up and smoothed her pink jacket out with a tug at the hem. "I don't have to answer you!"

Aunt Sylvie crossed her arms and took two steps towards the door where Lyla stood. Her bottom lip turned into a frown and the words that followed matched. "This is not a game for your amusement. This is a serious matter." She clapped her hands once to signal this charade was done. "Go on, now. Get to the garden so things can get started." Aunt Sylvie turned her attention to Andrina. "And you, young lady, are going to grab your bouquet and start walking down the aisle. Dog or no dog."

"I will do no such thing," Andrina shouted, tears spilling down her cheeks. "Where is my Walter?"

Lyla tilted her head and cleared her throat. "I know how and why it happened," then she paused for maximum effect. "But there is only ONE of you who knows exactly where he is."

Silence coated the room like a parishioner about to give confession.

Lyla walked through the room, her arms parting the adults like Moses parting the Red Sea, and climbed into the same wingback chair where the investigation started and now would end.

With her hands gently placed on the armrest, she began. "Andrina, the note stated you had to choose between Walter or a wedding, correct?"

The bride with her swollen, curious eyes nodded her head. "Yes, I guess that is correct."

"So, who had skin in the game for this wedding TO happen?" Lyla pointed to Aunt Sylvie.

The room turned to Aunt Sylvie with suspicion.

"Vincent might not be your first choice for Andrina as a partner, but you support Andrina. And Vincent's bank account."

"How dare you!" Aunt Sylvie squawked.

"Be that as it may but it is true," Lyla countered.

Andrina held up her hand to prevent Aunt Sylvie from taking a closer step toward the little girl. "Aunt Sylvie, you know it's true. But I love Vincent and those things don't matter to me as much as they do to you." She turned to Corky. "This must be your doing. Where is my dog?" she asked with a growl.

Corky flushed with anger. "You're pointing in the wrong direction,

Miss I-Have-It-All," her words a tightrope of tension.

"Ha, you've never gotten over not getting Vincent!" Andrina slid out of her pumps, easy as you please. Vincent noticed this and darted between the two.

"Sweetheart," he said to Andrina, "you know I belong only to you." He pulled her in for a hug. She accepted it, limp and exhausted.

Lyla watched as this all unfolded hoping for a bigger showdown but when Vincent defused it pretty quickly, she continued. "No, it was not Corky although I can see why you would think so."

Corky shot Lyla a nasty look. Lyla shot Corky a look that made goosebumps rise on her skin.

"The real culprit here is...Miss Marion!" Lyla stated emphatically.

Andrina extricated herself from Vincent and stormed to the older woman and demanded, "Why would you do this? Why are you trying to ruin my big day?"

"YOUR big day? Isn't EVERY day, your big day?" Miss Marion sat in the chair adjacent to the dressing table, a shimmer of fury illuminating her face. "You never get tired of being the queen bee do ya?"

Aunt Sylvie stared at her old friend with sadness and resentment. "Why would you begrudge young love like this? In such a hateful manner?" Her scorn hit each syllable.

"How did you know?" Andrina asked Lyla.

"The lavender. See how Miss Marion is scratching her hands? How she wears gloves on such a hot evening? She's breaking out in hives from the lavender. She's allergic."

"I don't get it," Vincent said.

"Of course, you don't. Let me break it down. Walter had a lavender bath to start the day. When Miss Marion handled him, the contact with the flower residue triggered the reaction."

"But that doesn't explain why she did it," stated Aunt Sylvie.

"The reason is Corky. Because Corky is like family to her. Miss Marion always wanted Corky to 'do well for herself' by marrying upward," Lyla directed the next statement to Corky, "without realizing that the successful wedding planning business Corky nurtured is, in fact, 'doing well for herself.'"

Corky nodded as she walked to Miss Marion and took her gloved hand. "I'm doing fine. And Vincent and I," she looked at him and acknowledged, "were never going to be more than friends."

Lyla climbed from the chair and stood next to Miss Marion. She said, "Why don't you show us where Walter is."

Miss Marion pointed to the armoire in the corner.

"I saw Walter with the guest right after Emily probably did. He must have left through the sliding glass door after Braden brought him back," Miss Marion said.

"It was like a freezer in here, so I kept the door open. I forgot to make sure it was closed again," Andrina realized.

"I scooped him up," she explained, "and I thought, let's make lemonade out of lemons for Corky. So, I hid him away." Awkwardly she looked at Corky. "I only wanted you to have what I thought you deserved. Turns out you do."

Andrina had already swung the armoire doors open and squealed with delight.

Walter lay curled up on a tuft of white towels, sleeping. Pebbles of dry dog food rolled on the floor of the cabinet. Water from a plastic bowl sloshed onto the floor as Andrina retrieved him.

"Walter!" Andrina lifted the sleepy dog into her arms. "I missed you so much."

"Are the rings still on his collar?" Vincent asked. Andrina gave him an exasperated glance.

"Oh, okay, I see them." Vincent's inquiry was ill-timed, but Andrina quickly forgave him with a hug.

"You're so tired, my little guy." Andrina stroked his sleek black coat.

Emily ran into the room, winded but excited. "The guest, the one who gave him water, said a woman—" She stopped as soon as she saw Walter in Andrina's arms. Once she assessed the situation, she responded a bit deflated, "Oh, I guess you found him."

"You've had a long day. And night." Andrina raised Walter's little head and kissed him. "That's okay. We'll carry you down the aisle, won't we?"

Vincent smiled. "Of course."

Lyla clapped her hands, and everyone turned. "Isn't it time for a wedding?" She pointed to the sliding glass door. "Out there?" She gave the adults a look of 'duh' and then the commotion began.

12 MIDNIGHT

Andrina's Cinderella at Midnight wedding was happening on time, just like it was supposed to.

As Lyla and Bea stood at the back of the garden watching Andrina glide down the aisle toward the man of her dreams, Lyla wondered. Could the bride ever fathom the nightmare that will be made possible all because this wedding, this union, has come to pass?

"Beautiful ceremony," Lyla mused.

Bea asked, "How does that thing you do in their heads work?"

Any truthful explanation would open an endless cyclone of more fantastical questions that would eventually break Bea's brain. Even Lyla didn't want to purposefully wreak that kind of havoc.

She skirted the question by responding, "I guess I didn't really *need* to go on a fishing expedition in their heads, but sometimes it's fun to do it just for kicks."

"Hmm, interesting." Bea gave Lyla an unsettled smile. "Guess we should skedaddle." She took Lyla's hand and walked away from the ceremony and out to the immaculate grounds surrounding the club. In the darkness, a black hole opened.

Braden yelled out, "Lyla!"

She turned around to see him strolling up behind her and Bea.

Lyla turned to look at the black hole and then back at Braden. "You can see that?" she asked.

"Yes, actually, I can," he said with a tinge of fear in his voice. "You know that's not a party trick."

Lyla rolled her eyes.

Braden extended his hand. "You did good, kid. Well, maybe not 'kid' but you get it."

Lyla shook his hand. "Yeah, I get it, and thanks. But who are you, anyway?"

Braden rubbed his chin like he was weighing his options then spoke. "I'm just like Bea, a mortal guide." He chuckled. "I gotta tell ya, seeing your work in action was a real treat. The legend about 1969, whew, you are a hero."

"Thanks, I guess."

"Sure, well, I have to get back to the reception." With a tip of his head, he offered a short salute and said, "Maybe we'll run into each other again."

With that, Braden grinned and shuffled off.

Lyla, with a startled expression on her face, said, "That was a first. A mortal guide observing me."

"I wonder whom he guides," Bea said.

Lyla had a few ideas but answered, "Who knows."

The little girl shook her head, afro puffs bouncing with the weight of a job well done.

FOR MORE INFORMATION about the author, please visit P.M. Raymond's website: http://www.pmraymond.com/

Ring Robbery: A Cozy Cat Caper Mystery Short

Paige Sleuth

Imogene Little beamed as she slid into the pew next to Kenny Davenport. "What a beautiful venue."

The inside of the Cherry Hills Community Church had been transformed into a wedding wonderland. Soft classical music piped through hidden speakers, and flower garlands adorned the wood-stained walls. Sunlight streamed through the stained-glass windows abutting the high ceilings, creating a breathtaking collage of intermingling colors as the light landed all along the white fabric runner that stretched down the main aisle. The scene looked like something straight out of a movie.

Kenny, however, didn't look nearly as awestruck. "Can't imagine why anyone in their right mind would get hitched in the middle of winter," he grumbled. "Took me a good twenty minutes to chisel all the ice off my windshield this afternoon. My fingers are frozen solid."

Imogene rolled her eyes. "Maybe Martina and Doug are so in love they didn't want to wait until spring just so you wouldn't have to brave the cold for one day. Or maybe they wanted to be the first couple in Cherry Hills, Washington, to marry in the new millennium."

"I don't reckon that's anything to brag 'bout. So it's the year 2000 now. So what?"

She twisted in her seat to face him better. "What are you so grumpy about?"

"Dunno." Kenny sighed. "The lack of sunshine must be getting to me."

Imogene could understand that. January days were short in Central Washington, and this winter in particular had felt unusually long.

Of course, that might have had something to do with all of the crimes Imogene had found herself involved in these past couple of months. Between being held at gunpoint, attempted murders, and actual murders, she was more than ready for spring to arrive.

She shook the memories away. Today was a day to forget about her troubles and to focus on the positive.

"Have you ever seen so many roses?" Imogene asked. "And they're such a gorgeous array of colors. Why, I didn't even know green roses existed before today."

Kenny scrunched up his nose. "Green, red, white. Who gives a fig?"

Imogene smacked his arm. He winced, but Imogene was pretty sure it was only for show. As big and burly as Kenny was, she doubted her slap had registered as little more than a mosquito bite.

But just because they were physically mismatched didn't mean she had to put up with his sour attitude. "I don't know why you even came today if your plan was to just sit there and complain all afternoon," she said.

"You didn't give me a choice. If I recall correctly, you threatened to dissolve our friendship and never bake me another batch of cookies ever again if I refused to be your plus-one."

Imogene couldn't remember issuing such an ultimatum, but he was probably right. Although she had been single for most of her forty years and liked to think of herself as independent, one thing she hated attending solo was weddings.

"How do you know the bride anyway?" Kenny asked.

"Martina adopted one of the cats I rescued." Imogene smiled at the memory of how quickly the brown-and-black tortoiseshell had taken to Martina when the two had been introduced three years ago. It had been love at first sight, for both human and feline. "Chopin's the ring bearer, you know."

"Who's Chopin?"

"Martina's cat, the one I saved."

Kenny's brow furrowed. "The ring bearer is a *cat*?"

"What's so strange about that?"

"Uh, let me count the ways. First, last I checked, most ring bearers actually have the ability to carry rings."

"They'll be tied to a pillow strapped to Chopin's back. All she has to do is walk down the aisle."

Kenny snorted. "Oh, this oughta be good. I've seen some of your rescue cats, and not one of those little devils ever did a single thing they were told."

Cats did tend to have minds of their own. Imogene couldn't deny that. But given how close Martina and Chopin were, was it any surprise the bride wanted her beloved feline companion to serve a prominent role in her special day?

"Kenny Davenport!"

The shout came from behind them. The church had started to fill with more people, forcing Imogene to crane her neck as she sought out the culprit. She spied a trim dark-haired man waving in their direction from the aisle.

"Adam? Adam DiRico?" Kenny rose to his feet as the man approached. "Good grief. It's been a minute, hasn't it?"

Adam halted next to their pew. "Tell me about it. When's the last time we saw each other?"

"It's gotta be high school graduation." Kenny grabbed Adam's outstretched hand and gave it a hearty pump. "What've you been up to since then?"

"This and that. College in Boston, then an accounting job kept me there for a bit longer. I only moved back to Cherry Hills a year ago."

"Accounting, huh?" Kenny laughed. "How 'bout that? Never woulda pegged you as the paper-pushing type."

"We all have to earn a living somehow. Unless we're lucky enough to marry rich, that is." Adam gave Imogene a wink.

She reared back. Did Adam think she was rich? She might look decent today, dressed in a peach pantsuit with her auburn hair hanging loose, but most days she wore ponytails and T-shirts covered in animal fur.

"You haven't tied the knot yet?" Kenny asked Adam.

Adam shook his head. "Still looking for the one. What about you?"

"Also single, though I got close once."

"That sounds like a story worth telling."

Kenny chuckled. "Maybe, but not today."

"And how are you paying the bills these days?"

"I'm a police officer on the Cherry Hills force."

Adam leaned against the side of the pew. "Well, isn't that a surprise?" He paused, then said, "Our little town doesn't get much crime though. Don't you get bored?"

"Nah, we've got plenty to keep ourselves occupied."

Kenny slid a glance toward Imogene. She wondered if he too was remembering how criminally busy her winter had been.

Preferring not to dwell on that, Imogene forced a smile on her face as she turned toward Adam. "Hi. I'm Kenny's friend, Imogene Little. I grew up here too, but I'm not sure we've met before."

Adam shook her outstretched hand. "If we had, I certainly would have remembered. But until recently, I only lived here my senior year of high school."

"That explains how we managed to avoid each other," Imogene said. "I graduated a couple years before Kenny—and presumably before you, too."

"Imogene's the reason I'm here," Kenny put in.

Imogene wasn't sure if the statement was meant as a rebuke or an explanation. She chose to interpret it as the latter. "The bride adopted one of my cats a few years ago," she told Adam. "That's what I do in my spare time, rescue homeless animals."

"Oh, cool." Adam nodded his approval. "I've always been quite fond of cats myself."

"Well, then you're gonna love this wedding," Kenny said. "The bride's cat is today's ring bearer."

"That must be why I saw Chopin wearing a white satin collar." The corners of Adam's lips twitched. "How'd Martina convince kitty to take on that role?"

"Dunno, but it sounds like a disaster in the making to me," Kenny said.

Imogene was on the verge of defending Martina's decision again when a scream rang out from the back of the church.

Everyone in attendance whipped their heads around. Imogene spied Martina standing near the exit. The thirty-seven-year-old looked gorgeous with her brown hair freshly curled and highlighted, and a long, flowing white dress hugging her trim figure.

But the agonized expression on Martina's face stopped Imogene from admiring her beauty for long. She squeezed past Kenny and hurried down the aisle.

"Martina," she said. "What's wrong?"

"Oh, Imogene." Martina choked on a sob. "There's been a horrible, terrible tragedy. I'm afraid the wedding is off."

IMOGENE'S HEART SKIPPED a beat at Martina's pronouncement. "The wedding is off? You mean canceled? What on earth for?"

She expected Martina to tell her how she had caught her fiancé Doug kissing one of the bridesmaids or that the priest officiating today's service had been rushed to the hospital with a medical emergency.

But all Martina said was, "My ring is gone."

Imogene stood there for a second as she processed her friend's words. "Your ring? That's it?"

"That's it?" Martina gaped at her. "We're talking about my grandmother's—my great-grandmother's—heirloom ring! It's been passed down between the women in my family for four generations. That ring is priceless. And blessed. Nobody who's tied the knot with it has ever gotten divorced." She folded her arms across her chest and jutted out her lower lip, reminding Imogene of a recalcitrant child. "I can't get married without it."

Imogene could see why Martina was upset. Still, canceling a wedding over a missing ring struck her as a bit extreme.

"Someone must have stolen it," Martina said. Her narrowed eyes assessed the guests gathered around them one by one.

"Or it could have been misplaced," Imogene proposed. "Where did you see it last?"

"Tied to Chopin's pillow."

"And is Chopin currently wearing the pillow?"

Martina managed a nod as tears sprang to her eyes.

Imogene patted her arm. "Well, there you go then. Chopin was probably walking around and the ring got snagged on something. All we need to do is retrace her steps. Where is she now?"

Martina swallowed hard. "In my dressing room. She's been there all afternoon."

"Then let's go."

Martina lifted up the hem of her dress and spun on one of her low, white heels. She headed for a short hallway located near the rear of the church, Imogene trailing right behind her.

The first two doors on either side of the corridor led to the men's and women's restrooms. Martina blew past those to an unlocked, closed door on the right.

"Chopin!" she called out as she swept over the threshold. She clucked her tongue. "Chopin, where are you, precious?"

The room was small but nicely furnished. Two bright yellow armchairs faced a full-length mirror set up in the center of the room. The freestanding clothes tree next to it held a long lace veil, a black winter coat, and the street clothes Martina must have worn to the church. A table near the lone window overlooking the side lawn overflowed with makeup and other beauty supplies. A small litter box and water dish had been placed on the floor on either side of the table. Imogene guessed the room's color scheme—light blue for the walls, and lemonade yellow for the furniture—had been selected with the intention of calming nervous brides as they prepared for their big day.

But Martina looked anything but calm. She pulled at a loose strand of hair with so much force Imogene thought it might rip from her scalp. "Chopin!" she yelled. "Come out, kitty!"

Chopin must have decided there was no point in hiding. The tortoiseshell peeked out from behind one of the armchairs. Her beautiful bi-color coat came with a face split down the center into a mostly light brown side and a mostly black side. A fawn-colored patch of fur located above the left edge of her mouth made it look as if the feline's lips were perpetually quirked in annoyance.

Or maybe Chopin truly was annoyed, Imogene considered as the cat let out a petulant meow.

"Chopin! There you are." Martina shuffled over to the animal and scooped her into her arms.

Imogene took in the white bow tie collar circling Chopin's neck and the red heart-shaped pillow tied to her back. A simple gold band bobbed atop the pillow, held there by a blue ribbon.

A second, pink ribbon lay beside it. That one was conspicuously empty, its ends dangling uselessly down the pillow's sides.

"Grandmama's ring should be right here," Martina said, fingering the pink ribbon.

"It probably wasn't tied tightly enough," Imogene surmised.

"That's impossible. I secured it there myself using a double knot. Somebody had to have untied it."

"We should search the room, just in case."

Before Martina could protest, Imogene walked purposefully to one side of the room and began sifting through the items scattered atop the makeup table. She was glad when she spied Martina setting Chopin on one of the armchairs so she too could join in the search.

But their efforts didn't turn up anything other than a dusty scrap of paper with "If Buddy's killer's first name starts with S, the chisel was not used" scribbled on the back. The room wasn't large by any means, and five minutes later they had checked every possible nook and cranny.

"I'm telling you," Martina said, "it's not here. Somebody took it."

"Martina!" An attractive, muscular forty-something stormed through the doorway, his short brown hair looking noticeably disheveled. He strode over to Martina with nary a glance in Imogene's direction. "Mar, what's this about our wedding being canceled? One of the guests said he overheard you screeching such nonsense in the church just now. I would have dismissed it as crazy talk, except two more guests confirmed it."

"Doug, you can't go in there!"

A blonde wearing the most hideous poofy turquoise dress Imogene had ever seen burst through the door. She looked too similar to Martina to be anything but a close blood relative.

"Mar," she said, "I'm so sorry. I told Doug he couldn't come in here, that you were already dressed and it was bad luck for him to see you in your gown before the ceremony. But he—"

"You're assuming there will even be a ceremony!" Doug interjected. He swiveled toward Martina. "Why does everyone think our wedding is canceled?"

"Because it is!" Martina shouted.

The blonde gasped. "What?"

Martina faced her. "It's true, Carmen. Our grandmother's ring has been stolen."

Carmen's face paled. "Stolen?"

Martina looked to be on the verge of tears. Her voice wobbled when she said, "Somebody must have snuck in here and taken it when I went looking for you."

"You were looking for me?" Carmen said. "When was this?"

"Maybe fifteen minutes ago. I—I had to go to the bathroom."

Imogene eyed Martina's dress. With its tight bodice held together by an army of tiny buttons marching up the back, the abundance of tulle billowing below the waistline, and the six-inch train trailing behind, she wasn't surprised Martina would need another person's assistance to free herself from it.

Doug scoffed as he crossed his arms over his chest. "You mean our wedding is off all because you couldn't use the toilet by yourself?"

Martina wiped away the tears that had started to fall down her cheeks. "I didn't know the ring would be stolen. I only left the room for a minute."

Doug didn't seem to be affected by her show of emotion. "You couldn't have taken the ring with you?" he said. "For Pete's sake, Martina. How careless could you be? You know that ring is worth a fortune."

Carmen blinked at him. "And it's a family heirloom."

"Right, right, that too." But Doug didn't really seem to be listening. "How much is it insured for?"

"There is no insurance," Martina said.

"What?" Doug looked ready to combust. "How can that be?"

Imogene studied him. Could Doug have taken the ring hoping to cash in on the insurance money? Maybe he planned to return the ring later, after the check had been cashed, never expecting that Martina wouldn't go through the ceremony without it.

"We've never needed insurance," Martina said. "It's never been gone before."

"In that case," Doug said, "you'd better hope Chopin ate it and it's just a matter of time before it shows up in a pile of cat litter."

"Don't be silly," Martina said. "Chopin wouldn't eat a *ring*."

"How do you know? I once knew a dog who ate a rock."

"Chopin is a cat, not a dog."

"So? One is just as dumb as the other."

Chopin had clearly listened to enough. The tortoiseshell hopped off the armchair, marched over to Doug, and proceeded to pee on one of his leather loafers.

Doug yelped as he jerked his foot away.

"Chopin!" Martina clapped her hands. "You are a bad, bad cat!"

Chopin didn't look the least bit repentant. In fact, with her head held high and her tail twitching, she appeared to be quite proud of herself.

Doug's nostrils flared. "That beast better learn to treat me with some respect after we're married, or I'm carting it off to the pound."

"I thought the wedding was off," Carmen said.

Martina shot her a dirty look. "It will be back on if I can find the ring in time. Speaking of which, *you* haven't seen it, have you?"

Carmen jammed her hands on her hips, the oversized sleeves of her blue dress billowing around her shoulders in a manner that reminded Imogene of a balloon animal. "What are you asking me for?"

"It was just a question."

"It didn't sound like 'just a question' to me. No, I daresay you were accusing me of something."

"Maybe that's your guilty conscience speaking," Martina suggested.

Imogene glanced between the two women. "Why would Carmen take the ring?" she asked Martina.

Martina swiveled toward Imogene, fire flashing in her eyes. "Jealousy. Entitlement. Greed. Take your pick. My beloved sister here thinks that, being the older sibling, the ring should sit around and be saved for her own wedding."

"It should," Carmen said.

"That's not what Mom put in her will."

"Mom's wrong. Family tradition says the oldest sister gets the ring."

"That's assuming they marry first. Need I remind you that you currently have *zero* romantic prospects on the horizon, and it's questionable at this point whether you'll ever find a man willing to put up with you for more than five minutes?"

Carmen winced. "That's low, even for you, Mar."

"You're right." Martina drew in a deep breath. "I'm sor—"

"Regardless," Carmen interrupted, flicking her wrist as if she were uninterested in her sister's apology. "I wouldn't stoop to stealing the ring, even if I do think it should be mine."

Doug threw his hands up. "Well, somebody stole it. And if we don't find out who soon, I'm afraid we're going to have a lot of disappointed guests out there."

Imogene's stomach sank. At least that was one thing they could all agree on.

THE AIR WAS RIPE WITH tension when Imogene left Martina's dressing room. She excused herself with the promise to discuss the missing ring with Kenny. Assuming it really had been stolen, maybe, as a police officer, he had some ideas on how they could encourage the thief to come forward before the ceremony was scheduled to begin.

She found Kenny where she had left him, sitting alongside Adam. The two men were in the middle of a conversation, but they both quieted when Imogene slipped into the end of the pew.

"Is everything okay?" Adam asked.

"Not really," Imogene said. "Something has come up."

Kenny raised one eyebrow. "Oh?" They apparently hadn't been close enough to hear Martina's shrieks about canceling the wedding.

"Martina's ring is missing. And she's adamant that the wedding can't proceed without it."

"I suppose she knows best," Adam said.

Imogene hadn't expected that. "You think she should call off the wedding?"

Adam shrugged. "This could be a sign. Perhaps the universe is trying to tell her that Doug is not the right man."

"Is that what you think? That Doug isn't right for her?"

"Maybe."

Kenny and Imogene exchanged looks. He appeared to be just as curious about Adam's pronouncement as Imogene.

"All I'm saying," Adam continued, "is that sometimes these things happen for a reason."

"Do you not like Doug?" Imogene asked.

"Do *you*?" Adam shot back.

"I don't know him well enough to have an opinion."

But as Imogene said the words, she replayed how Chopin had acted in the dressing room, going so far as to soil Doug's shoes. She wholeheartedly believed animals had a sixth sense about people. Maybe Adam was right not to care for the groom.

"How well do *you* know him?" Kenny asked Adam.

"Not very," Adam said. "But I've talked to him a couple times when he's come into the office to take Martina out to lunch."

"You work with Martina?" Imogene asked.

"That's how we became friends." Adam's gaze slid toward the back of the church. "She looked really distraught when she was talking to you earlier. Perhaps I should see if there's anything I can do for her."

"She's in her dressing room," Imogene told Adam as he stood up. She angled her legs aside so he could pass by her more easily. "It's located down that corridor over there, second door on the right."

Adam gave her a nod of acknowledgment before making a beeline for the back of the church.

As soon as Adam was out of earshot, Kenny said, "He fancies her."

Imogene looked at him. "I'm sorry?"

"Adam. He likes Martina. As more than a friend and coworker, I mean."

"How do you figure that?"

"C'mon." Kenny snorted. "It's written all over the guy's face in big, bold letters. He's smitten as a kitten."

Could Kenny be right? And, if so, was Adam somehow involved in the disappearance of Martina's ring? Maybe he'd pilfered it knowing she wouldn't marry Doug without it.

She was still pondering over that possibility when a dark blur sped down the aisle and the second scream of the afternoon rang through the church.

KENNY WAS ON HIS FEET in an instant. His stiff stance and heightened alertness made it clear he'd transitioned into cop mode.

"Chopin!" Martina called out from the back of the church.

Imogene set a steadying palm on Kenny's arm. "Martina's cat must have gotten out." That had to have been the blur she'd seen.

And the scream had to have originated from the woman seated in the pew behind them. She looked as white as a sheet, her finger aimed toward the front of the church as she spoke in low tones to another woman beside her. The tortoiseshell had undoubtedly startled her when she'd gone racing by like a feline possessed.

Imogene went to join Martina. "Did Chopin slip out when Adam went to talk to you?"

Martina frowned. "Adam DiRico?"

"He went to find you just now."

"I must have missed him. I didn't even know he was here. What did he want?"

"Just to see if he could comfort you."

Martina flapped her hand. "Well, I'll have to catch up with him later. Right now, I need to find Chopin before she causes any more chaos. Have you seen her?"

"I did, actually." Imogene pointed toward the altar. "I believe she went that way."

Martina lifted up the hem of her dress and started hotfooting it down the aisle. "Thank you."

Imogene hurried after her. "Did Chopin do something?"

Martina grimaced. "That's putting it mildly. She shredded my veil, then proceeded to use the mess as her makeshift litter box."

Imogene had to slap one palm over her mouth to keep the giggle rising in her throat from escaping past her lips. "Oh my."

Martina didn't appear to see the humor in the situation. Her lips were pursed as she surveyed the area in search of her runaway cat. "I'm telling you, Imogene, I'm starting to seriously regret involving Chopin in this ceremony. It's almost like she's determined to ruin this day for me."

"I thought you decided she had nothing to do with your ring disappearing."

"I'm not blaming her for the ring. No, I still think somebody must have taken that. But between my veil and Doug's shoes, she's turned into a destructive little terror."

"She doesn't seem to care much for Doug."

"Unfortunately, he doesn't care much for her either." Martina stopped hunting for Chopin, a sigh deflating her shoulders as she looked at Imogene. "But they're both a part of my life now, so they're just going to have to learn to get along. The last thing I want is to turn into Carmen."

"What's wrong with Carmen?"

"She's forty and still searching for love. How sad is that?"

Imogene felt her cheeks heat. "Some of us do just fine on our own."

Martina's eyes widened. "Oh, Imogene. I wasn't talking about *you*. I mean, you have your rescue animals."

Imogene bit her tongue, reminding herself that Martina didn't mean the comment as an insult. Besides, Martina was right. Imogene *did* love her rescue work and valued its role in her life much more than she did any man's.

"But Carmen is different than you," Martina went on. "She's always wanted a husband and children—lots of children. And with her being almost too old now to have them, I think she's starting to realize her fantasy life might not happen. And that's making her bitter."

"Wanting to avoid becoming bitter is hardly a good reason to marry the wrong man," Imogene said.

Martina regarded Imogene, the sheen of unshed tears making her eyes shine. "Do you think Doug is the wrong man?"

"Only you can answer that."

Chopin chose that moment to slip out from underneath one of the pews near the front of the church. As if she sensed her human could use some comfort, she strode over to Martina, sat down by her feet, and meowed.

"Chopin!" Martina lifted the cat into her arms. "Where have you been?

You've been a very naughty girl, you know."

Between all of the petting and kisses, Chopin didn't seem to realize she was being scolded. She rubbed the top of her head against Martina's chin and started to purr.

A small smile broke through Martina's sad countenance as she angled her head to stare into Chopin's big yellow eyes. "You really are a pill, you know that?"

Chopin trilled in happy agreement.

"What happened to her pillow?" Imogene asked.

"I took it off. She didn't like wearing it."

Chopin hissed as if to emphasize the point.

Martina attempted to soothe the cat with slow strokes. "If I had just waited to tie it to her until right before the ceremony, this entire day might have turned out differently. I would have my ring with me right now, and the wedding would still be on."

"You can't blame yourself for that," Imogene said.

"I have to blame somebody."

Chopin meowed. Imogene wondered if the tortoiseshell knew who the true culprit was. She must, given that the thief had literally taken the ring off her back.

Martina hugged Chopin closer. "I know, baby. No more pillows—or bow tie collars either for that matter."

"You took her collar off too." Imogene hadn't realized that immediately. She stared at the cat, something niggling at the back of her mind. "When did you affix that collar to her?"

"The same time I put on the pillow, maybe half an hour before my ring went missing. I thought that would be about the right length of time for her to get used to wearing them without me scrambling to get them on in time for the ceremony."

"And she never left your dressing room after you put them on?"

"No, why?" Martina squinted at Imogene. "What are you getting at?"

Imogene waved her hand in the air with a nonchalance she didn't feel. "Oh, nothing."

That wasn't true though. Imogene was starting to develop a theory. And if she were right, she knew who had taken Martina's ring.

But she needed proof before she got her friend's hopes up.

She took a step backward. "Martina, if you'll excuse me, I need to go find someone."

Before Martina could protest, Imogene scurried away, her heart pounding hard.

IMOGENE FOUND HER TARGET heading for the restroom. She wasn't quick enough to intercept him before he could slip inside, so she marched right in after him, tapping him on the shoulder before he had time to duck into a stall.

"You took Martina's ring," she said.

Adam stumbled backward, bumping into a garbage can. "What are you doing in here? This is the men's room."

"Never mind that. I want to know why you stole Martina's ring."

Adam looked around, perhaps searching for support. But they were the only ones in here.

He faced Imogene again with obvious reluctance. "Why do you think I took her ring?"

"Because of what you said earlier, when you were talking to Kenny and me. When he mentioned that today's ring bearer is a cat, you said something about Chopin's white satin collar."

"So?"

"So, there wasn't any way you could have seen that collar unless you had been inside Martina's dressing room. Except, she claims she hasn't talked to you yet today." Imogene tilted her head. "So my question is, if you weren't in there to talk to Martina, what were you doing there?"

"I did go there to talk to Martina." Adam worked his jaw back and forth a few times before his shoulders slumped in defeat. "But you're right. She wasn't there."

"So you took her ring instead?"

Adam nodded once, a simple acknowledgment of guilt.

Imogene frowned. "But why?"

"Because Doug isn't the right man for her."

Imogene regarded him, realizing that Kenny had been right. "You're in love with her."

Adam lifted one shoulder. He didn't say anything, but he didn't need to. Imogene could see the answer in his eyes.

"You've never told her how you feel?" she asked.

He shook his head. "I thought it would be awkward if she didn't feel the same way, with us working together. And then she met Doug, and well, I guess you could say I'd waited too long and missed my chance."

The bathroom door opened. A man started to enter, then he spotted Imogene. He froze for a second before doing an about-face and scurrying back into the hallway.

Imogene shifted her attention back to Adam. "If it makes you feel better, I'm not so sure Doug is the right man for her either."

Adam brightened, his spirits clearly buoyed by her support. "It's obvious, right? The guy is such a boor. Martina is so sensitive and sweet, and he isn't like that at all. All he cares about is money. I truly don't know what she sees in him."

"That still doesn't make what you did right."

"I know. But I never planned to keep the ring."

"What was your plan?"

"I didn't really have one. I didn't think that far ahead. Taking it was kind of an impulse decision." Adam scrubbed one hand down his face. "I originally went to Mar's dressing room to talk to her. I'd decided I needed to tell her how Doug was all wrong for her, before she set herself up for a miserable life by marrying him."

Imogene's stomach tightened. "Oh, dear."

"I never got the chance to say anything though. When I set off to find her, she was exiting the room, looking preoccupied by something."

"She went to look for her sister." Imogene left off the part about Martina needing help in order to use the restroom.

Adam nodded. "That makes sense."

"What happened then?"

"The door to her room was unlocked, so I let myself inside. I figured I could wait for her there."

"But before she came back, you spied Chopin and the rings," Imogene guessed.

"Yes. Chopin came right up to me, wanting to be petted." He gave Imogene a rueful smile. "Cats have always liked me."

"Animals can sense kindness."

"Maybe, but apparently they're not very good at judging character." Adam exhaled. "When I saw the rings there, I got the bright idea to take Martina's. She's talked about it often enough that I know how much it means to her. So I untied it, slipped it into my pocket, and ran back into the church."

"That must have been when you found me and Kenny," Imogene said.

"It was." Adam's lips slanted. "I must say, learning that Kenny had become a cop threw me off guard. When he told me that, I thought I might faint right there on the spot."

"What were you hoping to accomplish by stealing Martina's ring anyway?"

"I didn't think that far ahead. All I could focus on was how wrong Doug is for her. The times he visited the office he was so haughty, always talking down to her. The only time I ever heard him even mention Mar's ring was to remark on how much it must be worth. He doesn't seem to care at all about its sentimental value or the fact that it's been in her family for generations."

Imogene couldn't argue with that. Adam's observation jibed with Doug's reaction when he'd first learned the ring was missing.

Adam raked his fingers through his hair. "Did you know I almost didn't come to this wedding? I mean, who wants to watch the woman they love marry someone else?"

"But you did come," Imogene said.

"Yeah, I did. And now look what's happened. I've made a mess of things. Martina will never be able to forgive me for this."

"I don't know about that," Imogene said. "Perhaps, in time, she'll realize your heart was in the right place."

Adam straightened. "You really think so? You don't think I've completely destroyed our friendship?"

"I have no idea. All I know for sure is you must return her ring right away. She's frantic about it being gone, you know."

"I know." Adam reached into his pants pocket and emerged with what had to be the ring in question. He turned it around in his fingers, studying the gold band and diamond setting, before looking back up at Imogene. "Well, I guess there's no point in delaying the inevitable."

Imogene gave Adam an encouraging smile as he walked past her. He really did seem like a good man, one who had made a bad decision in the heat of the moment, maybe, but a good man nonetheless.

She kept her fingers crossed that Martina would be able to see that too.

"I WONDER WHAT ADAM is telling Martina right now," Imogene said as she and Kenny stepped outside of the church.

Kenny shoved his hands deeper into his coat pockets. "Can't say I envy the guy."

Imogene pulled her own coat tighter. She had come out here for some fresh air but had forgotten how cold it was. "Martina should be happy to get her ring back at least." On the other hand, she wasn't sure how Martina would react to the news that her trusted colleague had been the one to take it.

"Chopin!"

Imogene turned around in time to see the tortoiseshell cat zipping out of the church's front doors and into the snow. Martina raced after her, her progress impeded by her wedding attire.

Imogene held her arms out to the cat. "Here, kitty!"

Chopin headed straight for her. As soon as Imogene picked her up, Chopin snuggled against her chest, seeming relieved to have somewhere to warm her paws. Like Imogene, the cat probably hadn't realized how cold it was out here until it was too late.

Martina hurried over to them. Frost misted the air in front of her mouth as she worked to catch her breath. "Thank you, Imogene. I don't know what's gotten into Chopin today, but she sure is a handful."

"She's probably afraid you're going to make her wear that pillow again," Imogene replied, handing the cat over.

Martina looked pained as she adjusted Chopin in her arms. "Well, she won't have to worry about that for a long while, maybe never."

"Oh? Did Adam find you, perchance?" Imogene had left Adam on good faith, trusting that he'd do the right thing and return the ring. Was it possible she had misjudged him?

But Martina allayed her concerns when she said, "Yes, he gave me back my ring. He said you'd figured out that he'd taken it and urged him to confess."

Imogene relaxed. "Good."

Martina smiled at her. "Thank you for that, Imogene. You don't know how relieved I am to have my grandmama's ring back in my possession."

"But you're still going through with canceling the wedding?"

"I am." Martina petted the cat with gentle strokes, but it was clear from her flashing eyes that she was upset. "Do you know what Doug said to me when I told him the ring had been returned?"

"What's that?" Imogene asked.

"He said thank goodness, that now that I had my—and I quote—'stupid ring' back, we could hurry up and get on with the ceremony."

Imogene fingered the collar of her blouse. "Oh my."

"Apparently his biggest concern was that all of the money we spent on this wedding would be wasted if I canceled. He didn't care one whit about the emotional distress this whole ordeal has caused me. In fact, not once this afternoon did he ever even attempt to comfort me."

"I'm sorry," Imogene said.

"Don't get me wrong, he was thrilled to have the ring back—because of how much it's worth. Never mind what it means to me personally." Martina sighed. "Anyway, I'm pretty sure things are over between us. I've had my suspicions for a while now that we aren't on the same page. Today merely confirmed that."

Chopin started purring, her eyes slipping shut in contentment.

Martina planted a kiss between the cat's ears. "Yes, precious, I know you've never liked him. And I should have viewed your contempt as a red flag." She shifted her attention back to Imogene. "I've decided to give the ring to Carmen."

"Really?"

"I know, it's quite a change of heart. But she really wants it, and I feel like maybe it's cursed now—for me at least."

"I can definitely see why you'd feel that way," Imogene said.

"Plus, maybe this will go a ways toward repairing our relationship." Martina's shoulders drooped. "She never did like Doug. I figured she was just jealous that I had someone and she didn't, but now I realize I've had blinders on this whole time and that Doug himself was the problem."

"At least you realized you weren't compatible before you married him."

"Thank goodness." Martina paused, then asked, "So, you and Adam are friends?"

"I only met him today." Imogene gestured toward Kenny. "Kenny here knows him though."

"Adam's all right in my book," Kenny put in. "Then again, today's the first time I've laid eyes on the guy since high school."

"You're a cop, right?" Martina said to Kenny.

Kenny offered her a little bow. "Guilty as charged."

"Imogene mentioned something about her plus-one being on the force when I told her about my ring being stolen." Martina focused on smoothing out a patch of Chopin's fur, not meeting either of their eyes. "So, do you get the sense that stealing is something Adam does regularly?"

Kenny spread his hands. "All I can say for sure is we've never booked him at CHPD headquarters."

It was hardly a glowing endorsement. Still, Kenny's statement elicited a grin from Martina.

Imogene studied the woman across from her. "Martina, do you like Adam?"

"Oh." She averted her gaze, a faint pink creeping into her cheeks. "I don't know. I was just talking."

"Well, I believe he's rather fond of you."

Martina peeked at her from beneath lowered lashes. "You do?"

Imogene debated for a moment as to whether it was her place to say anything before relenting. "He practically told me as much earlier. And, while I can't condone the course of action he chose, I do believe he had your best interests in mind when he took that ring."

Martina cocked her head to one side. "He did stop me from making a huge mistake. I suppose I owe him for that, even if his methods were rather unorthodox. And Chopin seems to like him. She went right over to him and rubbed against his ankles when he came to talk to me."

That was certainly a more pleasant greeting than the one she'd given Doug and his footwear, Imogene thought.

"Oh, what am I saying?" Martina squared her shoulders. "I just broke off an engagement. It's too soon for me to be thinking about another relationship."

"If the person's right, it's never too soon," Imogene said.

Martina chewed on her lower lip as she appeared to consider that.

Imogene patted her hand. "But you take all the time you need."

"Thank you, Imogene." Martina gazed at the church. "Well, I suppose I ought to go tell everyone that the wedding is officially off."

"Good luck," Imogene said. "With everything."

"Thanks." Martina firmed her grip on Chopin, throwing Imogene and Kenny a smile as she started back toward the church.

"Welp," Kenny said, clapping his hands together. "I reckon there's no point in us hanging around here any longer."

"No, I don't think there is," Imogene agreed.

She watched Martina's retreating figure while she and Kenny headed for the parking lot. Martina looked resplendent in her white dress against the backdrop of fresh snow, Chopin peeking over her shoulder. Imogene couldn't be certain, but she thought that, underneath that discolored patch of fur above her left lip, the cat might be smiling.

Imogene smiled back. The afternoon hadn't ended the way she'd expected, but perhaps it had ended exactly as it should have. And, in her mind, that was ample cause for celebration.

FOR MORE INFORMATION about the author, please visit Paige Sleuth's website: https://www.marlabradeen.com/

What's a Little Murder Between Friends
Teresa Inge

R hiannon Cassidy trudged through the crowded Trio Wine bar. Her lanyard swayed back and forth, while her purse slid down her shoulder. She approached the future bride-to-be and her bridesmaid. "Sorry, I'm late, Fridays are crazy at work. How's it going?"

"I'm in a crisis mode." Maggie May, the bride put her fingers in quotes.

Rhiannon eased into the booth next to bridesmaid Carla Maxwell and sat opposite Maggie May. She pulled her lanyard over her head and stuffed it into her bag. "What's wrong?"

"First of all, some of the wedding venue is flooded from the storm yesterday. My shoes are wet from sloshing through the parking lot," Maggie May said.

"What do you mean by some of the venue?"

"There's water damage to the wedding room and the back deck where I had planned to have a cocktail hour overlooking the beach."

A waiter approached the table. "Would you like to try a wine flight this evening?"

"I'll take the rosé trio," Rhiannon said.

The others nodded in agreement.

"These are offered with a charcuterie board of artisan cheeses, cured meats, and accompaniments."

"Perfect," the women said in unison.

"I'll have your wine flights out soon." The waiter headed to the bar.

"What are you going to do about it? The venue I mean," Rhiannon asked Maggie May.

"The OBX Wedding Chapel assured me they will do their best to repair the damage before my wedding."

The OBX was the local vernacular referring to the Outer Banks, a string of barrier islands off the east coast of North Carolina and a mecca for beach vacationers.

"But that's two weeks away," Rhiannon said.

"I don't know how they can do all the repairs in that time, but they are working on it," Maggie May said.

"It's a sign," Carla said.

"What do you mean?" Rhiannon asked.

"She doesn't trust Jonathan." Maggie May referred to her fiancé Jonathan Carson.

"Why?" Rhiannon said.

"Because he's the biggest player in OBX and has been married twice. In my opinion, third time is not a charm. Plus, I'm very protective of Maggie May," Carla said.

Rhiannon closed her eyes for a beat and thoughts of Carla's short, disastrous fling with Jonathan danced in her head. Brushing off ancient history, she glared at Carla.

The waiter placed the wine trios on the table. "Charcuterie boards will be out shortly."

Maggie May grabbed the first of her three glasses and took a sip. "It's true that Jonathan had back luck with girlfriends and marriages, but that's in the past."

Sensing Maggie May's frustration, Rhiannon changed the subject. "What does Jonathan think about the repairs?"

"I'm not speaking to him right now."

"Why?" Rhiannon tasted the first of the rosé wines.

"Because there's something else I need to tell you," Maggie May offered.

Rhiannon's eyebrows knitted together. "What's that?"

"He refuses to sign the prenup."

Rhiannon's mouth flew open. "I thought that was taken care of months ago?"

"That's why I don't trust him," Carla said.

The waiter approached with the charcuterie boards. "Here we are, ladies." He placed them on the table with plates. "I'll check on y'all shortly." He headed to another table of guests.

The women grabbed the plates and filled them with dried fruits, olives, nuts, salami, and various cheeses.

"Is there anything that I can do to help?" Rhiannon asked.

Maggie May added a few grapes to her plate. "Actually...can you talk to Jonathan about the prenup?"

"Why me?" Rhiannon touched her chest. "Why not Carla?"

"Because you're my maid of honor, best friend, and you know how much I would lose if he doesn't sign it."

Rhiannon grabbed another glass of wine from the flight. She took a long sip while glancing at the women waiting on her response. She'd already assisted with the wedding invitations, venue, catering, marriage license, and more. Somehow she'd become the unofficial wedding planner for her childhood friend. Despite surviving skinned knees and puberty together, the two had a special bond since both of their mothers had named them for characters in popular rock songs. Plus, Maggie May's wealthy family would never allow her to marry Jonathan without a prenup. Rhiannon's head told her to stay out of their marital rift, but her heart told her to help her friend. She set the glass on the table. "Okay. I'll talk to him but there's no guarantee."

After finishing the last glass of wine and saying goodnight to the women, Rhiannon drove her 1955 Torch Red Thunderbird along North Croatan Highway. Ten minutes later she pulled into the driveway of her beach cottage in Nags Heads, a small town on the thin strip of the barrier island. Rhiannon yawned. It had been a long week at the financial firm she'd worked at for twenty years. Before she could exit the car her phone rang.

"Hi, Jonathan." Her voice was upbeat even though she wasn't.

"Have you seen Maggie May?"

"She's at the wine bar with Carla."

"She's not answering her phone. Guess she's still mad at me."

"Uh...Jonathan, while I have you on the phone." Rhiannon had not planned to talk to him tonight, but there was no time like the present. "I don't mean to pry, but Maggie May seemed upset tonight."

"It's because of the prenup and storm damage to the venue."

"She mentioned the damage but is there an issue with the prenup?" Rhiannon pretended not to know about it.

"Yeah."

Rhiannon heard Jonathan take a deep breath.

"Listen. I plan to be married to her forever, but this will be my third wedding, and it leaves me with nothing. I made a mistake that I am trying to resolve now. Plus, I love her."

Rhiannon felt Jonathan's sincerity. "Is there something that I can help you with?"

"No. I need to handle the situation myself."

"Then tell her how you feel and what you'd like in the prenup. You two need to work it out. The wedding is in two weeks for goodness' sake."

Fifteen minutes later, Rhiannon submerged herself into a soaking tub to take her mind off everything. Her brown Lab Luke and white Husky Lena rested on the black and white diamond patterned tile floor. Her son Jack, a paramedic, worked a late shift, and would be home later. Her daughter Diane lived with her boyfriend. She'd also named both after a rock song. For the first time in her life, the house was eerily quiet. The phone buzzed on the bathroom stand, taking her out of her thoughts. "Maggie May, what's up?"

"Thanks for telling Jonathan to negotiate the prenup in his favor."

"I just wanted to help."

"You made it worse."

Rhiannon sat up in the tub. "I'm sorry."

"I don't know if I should kill you or him first."

Oh brother.

After the phone went silent, Rhiannon stepped out of the tub and into bed, upset that she had allowed herself to get involved with her best friend's wedding tribulations. But right now, she needed rest and would worry about it tomorrow.

THE NEXT MORNING RHIANNON grabbed her ringing phone off the nightstand. "Hello." Her voice, coarse.

"Did I wake you, Mom?" Diane asked.

Rhiannon viewed her phone. Nine o'clock. "Uh…I can't believe I slept this late."

"Are you okay?"

"It's been a hard week at work plus planning the wedding is exhausting. I needed the sleep I guess. What's up?"

Luke and Lena stepped out of their dog beds and nudged Rhiannon to let them outside.

"I have exciting news," Diane said.

Rhiannon slipped out of bed and let the dogs out while holding the phone to her ear.

"I'm engaged!"

Just a week ago, Diane's boyfriend had asked Rhiannon for her daughter's hand in marriage. "Congratulations. When did it happen?"

"Nick asked me last night at dinner. Got on one knee and everything."

"I'm happy for you both. Do you have a date or location?"

"No. But I plan to ask Maggie May about her experience at the OBX Wedding Chapel."

She hoped that Maggie May and Jonathan could work out their differences. "That's a perfect location with an ocean view, minus the storm damage." She explained the repair situation to Diane.

"I agree. But I wanted to tell you first. Tell Jack I'll call him later. I must go. See you at the wedding."

At least there's some good wedding news. Rhiannon showered, dressed, and checked in on Jack asleep in his room. A few minutes later, she maneuvered through tourist traffic and crossed the Washington Baum Bridge into Manteo, a coastal community on Roanoke Island about fifteen miles from her cottage. Rhiannon eased into a parking spot in the historic downtown area to get a haircut at the Manteo Salon.

"So…what are we doing today?" Lisa Thompson, the shop owner, and stylist, stood behind the black metal chair.

"Trim the length and frame the curls around my face."

"The usual?"

Rhiannon smiled.

After receiving a massaging shampoo and a conditioner treatment,

Rhiannon sat in the chair while Lisa cut her hair. The two women chatted about tourist traffic and Maggie May's wedding.

"That's terrible about the storm damage." Lisa straightened Rhiannon's hair.

"They're working on the repairs."

"Well, I hope they get it ready in time. My staff and I are looking forward to styling the bride's and bridesmaids' hair that morning."

Rhiannon hoped to still be in the wedding since Maggie May hung up on her last night.

Lisa removed the bibbed apron off Rhiannon and held up a mirror for her to view the cut.

"Thank you." Rhiannon brushed a few loose strands of hair off her pants.

"My pleasure. Oh, by the way. Is everything okay with Jonathan and Maggie May?"

"Yeah, why?"

"When I cut Carla's hair yesterday, she mentioned that Jonathan wouldn't sign the prenup. Said he's using Maggie May for her money."

Oh, my goodness.

After leaving the salon, Rhiannon finished errands, dodging in and out of traffic. She did chores around the house with no word from Maggie May. *It's not like her to give me the cold shoulder for more than a few hours.* She wanted to tell her about Carla's discussion with Lisa but decided against it. So, she ended the weekend with ongoing wedding tasks and kept busy at work the following week to take her mind off the drama.

WHILE WALKING TO HER car on Friday after work, her phone rang. "Hey, Maggie May."

"We need to talk."

"Okay."

"Not on the phone. Where are you?"

Rhiannon opened her car door. "Just leaving work."

"Do you have plans now?"

"No. Is everything okay with the wedding?"

"That's what I need to talk to you about."

"All right."

"Let's meet at Mama Kwan's."

Nervous to see Maggie May, Rhiannon headed to the restaurant in Kill Devil Hills. Home of the Wright Brother's National Memorial. Fifteen minutes later she grabbed a spot in the parking lot.

Maggie May sat at a table near the bar.

Rhiannon eased into the chair opposite her friend, bracing herself to be uninvited from the wedding.

"Thanks for coming," Maggie May said.

Rhiannon didn't know what to expect.

"Something to drink?" A server approached the table and placed menus on it.

"Sweet tea." Rhiannon decided not to drink any alcohol to keep a level head.

"Same." Maggie May crossed her arms on the table. "So, Jonathan and I had a long talk about the prenup and came to an agreement."

"Oh?"

"Thanks to you, we discussed what we each want from the marriage. I'll talk to my parents soon and give them a prenup update."

"I'm glad it's working out," Rhiannon said.

The server placed tea glasses on the table and the women ordered dinner.

"I'm sorry for blaming you, but there's something else," Maggie May said.

Rhiannon dipped a lemon into her tea and took a sip. "What's that?"

"Jonathan has cold feet."

"What do you mean?"

"He's distant and distracted."

"But when I spoke to him last, he'd made positive changes to his life. He loves you."

"I hope so."

Rhiannon didn't mention what Lisa had told her since she didn't want to add fuel to the fire. She changed the subject. "How are the venue repairs?"

"I stopped by there today and some of the water damage is visible on the floor and back wall in the wedding room. There is damage to the boards on the back deck, so the cocktail hour will be held in the banquet room. The venue said it's the best they can do under the circumstances. They did offer a discount."

"I'm sorry. Everything will work out."

After finishing their food and saying goodnight, Rhiannon headed home. For the past two months her life revolved around the wedding. She would be glad when it was over and could get her life back on track. She pulled into the driveway and entered her house.

"Long time no see, Mom," Jack said. "How was dinner?"

"I'm still in the wedding." Rhiannon had talked to her son earlier about the situation.

"That's good news."

As she set her purse on the kitchen table, Luke and Lena ran toward her wagging their tails. She rubbed her forehead, exhausted from the drama.

"The wedding is stressing you out."

"It's an emotional roller coaster. I hadn't planned to be the unofficial wedding planner."

"I know. But there's only a week to go. Then you can celebrate Diane's engagement."

Three knocks on the front door took Rhiannon out of her conversation with Jack. The dogs barked as she opened it.

"Dexter?"

"Did you forget about me coming over?" Dexter Street, Rhiannon's handsome but rugged next-door neighbor, stood on her doorstep with his German Shepherd Duke.

"Uh...no," she lied. "Come in. Jack and I were just talking."

The two men nodded as the dogs sniffed each other.

"I'm heading out." Jack kissed his mom on the cheek.

"Don't leave on my account," Dexter said.

"I have a date. Catch y'all later."

Rhiannon closed the door behind Jack. She sensed that he didn't like her friendship with Dexter. But it had been two years since she'd divorced her cheating husband, and she needed to move on with her life.

"Did I catch you at a bad time?" Dexter asked.

"No. I just got home from having dinner with Maggie May."

"I'm looking forward to attending the wedding with you. I picked up my new suit today."

"Great." She paused. "Uh...I should freshen up. Would you like something to drink?"

"A beer sounds good."

After getting Dexter settled, Rhiannon grabbed a shower and changed her clothes. She poured herself a glass of rosé and joined him and the dogs on the back deck. "It's nice to chill out," she said.

"Especially with you." Dexter lifted his beer.

Rhiannon had met Dexter when he bought the house next door earlier this year. They became fast friends barbequing and hanging out together. Tense, Rhiannon rubbed her shoulder.

"I know you've been stressed about the wedding." He sat his beer on the table. "Here. Let me help." Dexter pulled his chair closer to Rhiannon and rubbed her shoulders. After a few minutes he stopped. "Better?"

"Much." She gazed into his eyes.

Dexter rubbed her arm, then lifted her chin and kissed her lips.

Rhiannon's heart began beating like mad.

"I would love to be more than friends."

Rhiannon smiled.

THE FOLLOWING WEEK, Rhiannon finished last-minute wedding tasks. The wedding would be over soon, and she could get to know Dexter better, spend more time with Jack, and focus on Diane's engagement.

On Friday, she headed to the wedding chapel for the rehearsal dinner. Dressed in a blue sheath, she entered the chapel and wedding room. Maggie May and the bridal party stood at the altar talking. Jonathan and the groomsmen stood to the right of them next to the officiant.

"You made it," Maggie May said.

Rhiannon hugged her best friend. "The room looks great," she whispered.

"The stains are camouflaged with room dividers," Maggie May said.

A few minutes later the rehearsal began. Maggie May walked down the aisle escorted by her father. Jonathan moved closer and the couple said their vows.

The wedding party shouted in excitement then headed to the banquet room for dinner, steps away. Once inside, they were greeted with shimmering candles in gold vases, giving the room a romantic ambience. Gold plated dinnerware and orchid flower centerpieces adorned round tables with gold chairs dressed in sheared organza sashes to complete the magical setting.

"Wow," the party said in unison.

The group sat at the tables while the wait staff served beverages followed by salad, oysters on the half shell, crab cakes, chicken, and a vegan pasta.

After the meal, Maggie May cut a special cake for the guests with her grandmother's wedding knife and server set. At eight o'clock, the group called it a night to get some much-needed rest before the big day.

THE NEXT AFTERNOON, the bride and bridesmaids gathered at one o'clock in the dressing room at the venue for Lisa and her staff to style their hair. This gave them time to do finishing touches before the four o'clock wedding.

As Rhiannon slipped into her soft, purple maid of honor's dress, a braid in her updo came loose. She searched for Lisa since the other stylists were busy but could not find her. A few minutes later a stylist finished a bridesmaid and fixed Rhiannon's braid. Moments later, Maggie May appeared in her wedding gown and veil. Everyone oohed and aahed over the bride.

When the guests arrived at the venue, the wedding party moved into position for the ceremony.

From the altar, Rhiannon gazed out over her family with thoughts of being married again. She smiled at Dexter dressed in a stylish gray suit. He sat next to Jack and Diane. Rhiannon looked forward to spending more time with them after the wedding.

Maggie May joined Jonathan at the altar and the officiant spoke of their love and commitment to each other. The bride read a poem, and the groom expressed true love to his bride. The couple exchanged rings and the officiant pronounced them husband and wife.

After the ceremony, guests enjoyed cocktails in the banquet room as the wedding party finished taking photos on the beach. The officiant, bride, and groom then walked to the wedding room to sign the marriage license.

Rhiannon sipped a long-awaited glass of wine with Dexter and her family as the officiant approached her about the missing marriage license.

Rhiannon's eyes widened.

"Come with me," he said.

Rhiannon followed him into the wedding room.

"Where is it?"

"I left in on the teal cabinet."

A man with the nametag Michael approached them. "Can I help you with something?"

The officiant explained the situation.

Michael checked under and behind the cabinet. "I'll ask the staff if anyone has seen it. Be right back."

Rhiannon rubbed her forehead. This was all she needed.

A few minutes later Michael returned. "No one's seen it."

"We can request a copy since they have sixty days to sign it," the officiant said.

"Would you like me to check the cameras to see what happened to it?" Michael asked.

"Yes. We'll go with you," the officiant said.

The three walked down a hallway and into an office at the back of the chapel.

Michael sat at the desk and motioned for them to sit in the two chairs opposite him. "What time did you place the envelope on the cabinet?"

"One o'clock," Rhiannon said.

Michael made several keystrokes on the keyboard. He ran his finger up and down the monitor screen. "Ah..." he said.

The officiant jumped out of his chair and walked around the desk.

Rhiannon viewed the screen from her chair.

"Do you know this person?" Michael asked.

"That's Lisa, the hair stylist," Rhiannon said.

Before she could think about what she saw on the camera feed, a scream echoed from the back deck.

Michael, the officiant, and Rhiannon ran to the deck.

Guests gathered in a circle in the sand dunes below.

Rhiannon rushed down the steps to the beach, careful not to step on the damaged boards and warning sign.

"Oh no." A woman covered her mouth.

Jonathan lay face down in the sand with Maggie May's grandmother's knife in his back.

"Excuse me. I'm a doctor." A distinguished man made his way through the crowd. He knelt and checked Jonathan's pulse. He shook his head.

"He's dead," a guest said.

Rhiannon glanced at Maggie May standing over Jonathan's body.

An hour later, the medical examiner placed the body in an unmarked van. As Rhiannon stood on the deck consoling Maggie May, a man in a navy suit approached them.

"I'm Detective Jake Haven," he said.

Maggie May wiped her tear-filled eyes with a tissue.

"My condolences, Ms. May. And you are?" the detective asked, gesturing to Rhiannon.

"Rhiannon Cassidy. The maid of honor."

The detective pulled a notebook from his pocket and opened it. "Ah...yes. Can you tell me what happened?"

Rhiannon explained the situation.

"Ms. May. I realize this is a challenging time, but what did you witness?"

Maggie May sniffed. "We just finished taking pictures on the beach when the officiant asked us to sign the marriage license inside the venue. But when he could not find the license, Jonathan stepped away to retrieve a lighter that he'd dropped on the beach."

"Did he find the lighter?" the detective asked.

"I don't know. He never came back." Maggie May started crying.

◊ If Buddy's killer is not human, poison was used. ◊

From the corner of her eye, Rhiannon spotted Lisa carrying supplies to her car in the parking lot. On a hunch, she walked down the steps and to her car. "You're packing up?"

"Uh...yeah." She opened her trunk.

"That's awful about Jonathan."

"What about him?" She placed the items in the trunk.

Rhiannon searched her eyes. "He was stabbed to death on the beach."

"What?"

"Do you know how it happened?"

"Why should I?"

"Because you took the marriage license from the cabinet earlier."

Lisa closed her trunk. "I took it, so what? I did Maggie May a favor. Especially since he dumped me when he met her. Call it childish if you like. But I didn't kill him."

Before responding, a speeding car approached Rhiannon, tossing her into the air like a rag doll. Seconds later, she landed on the pavement. The car crashed into a lamppost, and Carla exited the driver's seat. She ran to the deck, slipping through the damaged boards and falling into the sand. Detective Haven and Dexter trailed behind her in full pursuit.

Jack, Diane, and Maggie May headed toward Rhiannon.

"Mom, are you okay?" Jack examined her and called an ambulance.

TWO WEEKS LATER, RHIANNON and Diane met Maggie May for lunch at Mama Kwan's.

Rhiannon eased into a booth, careful not to cause more injury to her broken leg. She leaned her crutches against the booth.

"How are you doing?" Maggie May asked Rhiannon.

"Better each day, thanks to Jack's quick response."

"How are you Maggie May?" Diane asked.

"Still confused about Jonathan and Carla."

A waiter approached the table and the women ordered wine and salads.

"For what it's worth, Jonathan tried to tell me he was in trouble," Rhiannon said.

"When?" Maggie May asked.

"The night I talked to him about the prenup. I asked if I could help but he said he would handle it himself."

"Of course, we now know that he regretted getting involved with Carla. And when he tried to break it off she blackmailed him," Maggie May said.

Some protective friend.

The waiter placed wine glasses on the table. "Your food will be out soon."

"I'm glad Carla's in jail and will pay for killing him," Rhiannon said.

"She almost killed you too when trying to get away after the detective confronted her with the video that Michael had of her killing Jonathan," Diane added.

"Uh...there's something else," Maggie May said.

Rhiannon eyed her best friend.

"First, the detective found Jonathan's lighter and returned it to me."

"That's great," Diane said.

"And...?" Rhiannon asked.

"We never signed the prenup."

"Why?"

"In the end, we both agreed we didn't need it."

"Do your parents know?"

"No. And they never will."

The women grabbed their glasses and took a sip. They sat in silence at the revelation.

"Well...I have news," Diane said.

"What's that?" Rhiannon asked.

"Nick and I picked next June for our wedding."

"Did you decide on a location?" Maggie May asked.

"Uh...the OBX Wedding Chapel."

Rhiannon glanced at her daughter. "Are you sure about that?"

"Yes. Will you help me plan the wedding?" Diane asked.

Rhiannon hesitated before responding since Maggie May's wedding was exhausting. But in the end, she wanted nothing more than to heal from the accident and help her daughter plan the wedding. "Yes." She clinked glasses with the women.

FOR MORE INFORMATION about the author, please visit Teresa Inge's website: http://www.teresainge.com/

Icing on the Cake
Sally Milliken

A pair of feet appeared in front of Carrie as she tightened her skate laces. She didn't recognize the boots but the battered black hockey bag and stick that came with them were familiar. Her friend Ashley had arrived.

"Hey, nice boots."

"Like 'em?" Ashley turned the chunky leather boot to the side, showing the Sorel logo. "Pete gave them to me yesterday. He heard me saying how cold my feet were during the last tournament."

"That was very sweet of him."

"Wasn't it, though?" Ashley asked, flashing a wide smile. "You should have seen how I thanked him."

Carrie snickered and shook her head. "Ah, young love." As her friend and teammate laughed, Carrie patted the wooden bench next to her. "And the pièce de résistance? Come on, show it to me."

Sitting, Ashley held out her left hand. Carrie snagged her wrist and pulled it closer, examining the sparkling diamond resting comfortably on her left ring finger.

"We picked it out together." Ashley gently touched the jewel with her fingertips. "I don't usually like wearing rings, but this one—" Her eyes glittered as much as the ring itself. "It's perfect."

Carrie squeezed her hand. "The photos on Instagram of him proposing looked pretty perfect, too. Maggie looked as happy as you. You both deserve it."

"Mmmm. Thanks. He asked her first. Talk about sweet. And smart.

117

He knew the way to my heart is through that girl. She's as excited as I am to plan the wedding. She's already collecting ideas for my dress, her dress, the music, everything." Ashley began digging around in her bag. "And you know only too well that teenagers don't get excited about much. How did I get so lucky to find a new guy at this stage in my life?" She paused her search to look at Carrie. "I didn't know a relationship could be like this, especially after what happened with—you know." Her voice cracked. "And at my age."

"Fifty's not so old."

Scoffing, she said, "Says who? My legs and lungs say otherwise. Never mind the wrinkles and gray hair."

"Can't argue he doesn't know what he's getting." Carrie chuckled, then added, "We're still able to skate, aren't we? And we're here. Now let's go show the young ponytails we older players may not skate as fast but we have wisdom on our side."

Ashley nudged Carrie with her elbow. "We're going to get smoked, aren't we?" she teased.

Carrie returned the friendly gesture. "Yes, but we'll have fun in the process. And it's far more exciting than crunching numbers all day."

"Too true. Too true." Ashley attached her shin guard over her leggings before sliding on knitted uniform socks—black with five white stripes, one for each of them—as Carrie pulled shoulder pads over her head and added elbow pads.

The North Country Pond Hockey Classic was a favorite for Carrie because it brought together her former college teammates from different corners of the country. With their busy lives filled with jobs and families, she and Ashley, as well as Jennifer, Gretchen, and Katherine, didn't get to spend as much time together as they liked. Each team consisted of eight skaters—fewer than the more common number for indoor rink tournaments—and they filled the remaining three with skaters from Carrie's home team. Carrie was hopeful that the Ice Witches would make it beyond their first four games and into the playoffs for the first time.

Ashley pulled on her padded hockey pants. "A year is too long. Is everyone else here already?"

"Yes, I picked Gretchen and Jennifer up from the airport." Carrie waited until her head popped through her team jersey before adding,

"Katherine texted that she left her condo and so she should be here any minute."

The Ice Witches' team jersey—a black shirt with the profile of a hockey equipment-wearing witch flying across the front—was her favorite part of their uniform. Instead of a broomstick, the witch flew astride a hockey stick. Carrie had come up with the idea based on her daughter's favorite book as a child, *The Flying Hockey Stick*.

Carrie tapped Ashley on the shin guard with the blade of her stick. "Come on, move it, our game is in thirty." Pulling on her helmet, Carrie added, "Remember, we have to shovel the ice before we can begin."

"Right behind you. I want to send Pete a quick text to tell him I arrived."

Rolling her eyes, Carrie's mouth twitched. "As I said, young love." With her stick, gloves, and water bottle, she followed the rubber mat out of the warming hut, which was really a large white wedding tent pitched at the edge of the lake. How appropriate, she mused, thinking of Ashley's engagement. Seeing her friend's excitement about her upcoming marriage made her heart sing.

The shouts of players from multiple games reached her as she exited into the cold air. A storm was due later that weekend, but there was no sign of it yet. She blinked to let her eyes adjust to the blinding sunlight reflecting off the lake's snowy surface. Two neat rows of ten rinks made a total of twenty on the surface of Lake Wintergreen. Each of the rinks was already bustling with skaters and a few hardy fans. Taking a deep breath, she made her way to rink six, their assigned number for their first game. She was ready to kick some butt.

AND LOSE THEY DID, by ten points. Although, at this stage in their lives, any time they left the ice without an injury was considered a win by Carrie.

The five former teammates played together again as if no time had passed. Despite the loss, Ashley's playfulness was contagious and they joked and laughed throughout the game. She and her daughter had been through a lot. It had been far too long since Carrie had seen her so happy.

With their second game scheduled for two hours later, they had time to kill. Carrie removed her gear and sweaty clothes and bundled into her warmest down jacket. She pulled on one of the black knit hats she'd had made and given to each member of the team, a fun memento of the weekend. Topped with a furry black pompom, the hats had the phrase '#IceWitches' embroidered in white thread along one edge. It was the perfect accessory to her outfit as she joined the team around a fire pit and drank a hot chocolate while they waited for their next game.

LUGGING THEIR HOCKEY gear, Carrie and Gretchen chatted as they crossed the parking lot on their way back to the warming hut to dress for game two.

"What's the weather supposed to do?" Carrie asked. "Sure doesn't seem like we're still getting a storm this weekend."

"No, it doesn't," Gretchen said as she shook her head. "But, I just checked, and we are. And, it's due sooner than we anticipated." She worked at NOAA and was their source for the weather as well as the latest in science news.

"Will we still be able to—" Hearing voices raised in anger, Carrie paused mid-question to listen.

"Seriously?" the irate woman argued. "No. No more. I will not let you ruin my life. You've done that for far too long. And now our daughter's life too—"

It wasn't until they rounded a large pickup truck that Carrie saw that the heated words were coming from Ashley. She and her ex-husband Bob were facing each other like two dogs with their hackles up. Ashley's hockey bag was at her feet, and Carrie could see her body shaking and feel her friend's anger even from ten feet away. Carrie had hoped that chapter was over in Ashley's life.

"Uh oh, Bob the Bum," said Gretchen and looked at Carrie with her eyebrows high. "He's like the bad penny that keeps showing up. This can't be good." It had been a long and painful process for Ashley to admit that her marriage had failed. The Ice Witches heard it all: how he'd gone from a mediocre husband and father to a disastrous and self-destructive one. He seemed to relish dragging Ashley down with him.

"I'll make you pay, one way or the other," he growled, his fists clenched.

When Bob stepped aggressively toward Ashley, Carrie and Gretchen quickly moved in between them, and Bob backed off.

Ashley had never openly admitted that her husband had hit her but she'd arrived at the tournament three years before with evidence of a black eye. Carrie read between the lines and watched as the situation went from bad to worse as they untangled their marriage. Bob had fought the divorce at every turn, making up more excuses than a hockey team has injuries, and the Ice Witches supported Ashley every moment. Two years before, they celebrated together after she signed her divorce papers. A year later she met Pete, and they were all thrilled for her.

Carrie stepped closer. "You okay, Ash?"

Ashley did not take her eyes off her ex-husband. When she finally turned toward Carrie, she said, "Bob was just leaving."

"Okaaay—Don't be long. We need to be on the ice in forty." Carrie turned to leave but changed her mind. "Why don't I take your stick? You have your hands full." Carrie reached for Ashley's stick, but Ashley refused to release it. When Carrie tugged harder, Ashley let go so suddenly that Carrie fell back. "You sure you're okay, Ashley?"

Ashley blinked, shook her head, and lifted a corner of her mouth in a rueful smile. "Go on ahead, really." Waving a hand, she added, "I'm fine."

Without comment, Carrie and Gretchen continued toward the hut. Carrie could not hear Bob's muffled words—his voice was too low—but Ashley's angry response was crystal clear. "No. No more money. I'm done."

Gretchen glanced at Carrie. Gretchen looked as conflicted as Carrie felt.

"Do you think I should text Pete?" she asked.

"Maybe." Gretchen exhaled. "That sounded bad. What would he do with the information?"

"Good question." Carrie followed Gretchen into the hut. "I'm not sure, but he'll definitely want to know that Bob's harassing her."

"She's told us in the past that she needs to deal with it, with him, in her own way. Whatever she decides, we should support her."

"We will. Up to a point." In her mind, the Ice Witches were not just a team, they were family. As close as sisters. Carrie would do whatever it took to protect her family. They all would.

CARRIE WAS TYING HER skates when Ashley dropped her hockey bag and collapsed onto the bench next to her.

Ashley exhaled deeply. "Hey."

"Everything all right?"

"Ya, thanks. Nearly lost my cool." Ashley dropped her face in her hands. "I'm at the end of my rope. I don't know what to do."

"He still asking you for money?"

"Worse—he blew through most of Maggie's college fund."

"Oh, Ash." Carrie didn't know what else to say.

"How could he have done that?" Ashley smoothed her hair back from her face. "That's our daughter's future." She clutched her belly as if she were about to be sick. "He had the audacity to ask for more money? I mean, my shop is doing well, but not that well. I'm finally able to save a little. He said that I owe him for some of Maggie's expenses. Or was it her clothes? I can't remember, I was so angry I blocked out his words."

Gretchen said, "I think you need to call your lawyer."

"Already have." Ashley cradled her head in her hands. "With the divorce, I thought I'd be free of him. But now—"

Carrie waited, hoping her friend would tell them more. "But what?" she prompted.

"His behavior is becoming more and more erratic and paranoid. He even told me he thinks someone's following him. Watching him."

"Why would he think that?" asked Gretchen.

"He didn't say." Ashley rubbed her eyes. "Likely he borrowed money from some unscrupulous character again."

Carrie huffed. "He's put you and Maggie at risk before."

"Whatever happens," said Gretchen, "he owns his actions. You are not responsible for him."

"He won't take responsibility for anything." Ashley massaged her neck. Carrie had never seen her look so defeated, even in the middle of the divorce. "But he's Maggie's father—"

"Then he should act like it." Gretchen tugged the laces on her skate. "It may take a while, but—" she paused and shrugged. "I firmly believe what comes around goes around."

Carrie hugged her friend. "We'll do anything to help, you know that, right?"

"I appreciate that." Ashley's mouth wobbled. "Thanks for having my back. I don't know what I'd do without the Ice Witches. My ice sisters and the thought of a new life with Maggie and Pete are keeping me going."

Carrie prepared to put on her helmet. "Why's Bob here anyway?"

Ashley sighed. "He's here for the weekend. Said he needed to get out of town and mumbled something about ice fishing. I'm sure he conned someone out of a free condo. He must have found out I was skating this weekend from Maggie and thought it would be a good chance to confront me without her around."

"What are you going to do?" asked Gretchen.

Ashley opened her bag. "I don't think I can get married until this is settled. It wouldn't be fair to Pete."

"Ashley, no," said Carrie. "You've come so far—on your own and together. He'll be devastated. Don't do anything just yet. Just see what happens. See what your lawyer says. And talk to Pete. Maybe he can help."

Carrie pulled her game jersey over her shoulder pads but she stopped when Ashley placed a hand on her arm.

"Carrie, don't tell him that Bob's here, please. I don't want him dragged into my mess. Or do anything he might regret. Or worry about me."

"He should worry. He loves you."

"I know. I'll tell him." When Carrie lifted a brow, she added quickly, "I will, I promise."

"Has Bob—has he, you know, gotten physical again?" Gretchen asked.

"No." Ashley shook her head. "But I make sure I'm never alone with him, just in case."

Carrie noticed Ashley's feet: she was wearing an old pair of sneakers. "Wait, weren't you wearing your new boots?" When Ashley did not respond and refused to look her in the eyes, she asked, "Ash—Did Bob take them?"

Nodding slowly, Ashley's face fell. "I just wanted to get rid of him. Knowing Bob, he'd talk his way into here and 'borrow' them during our game anyway. This way, I saved him, and me, the trouble." Ashley exhaled and looked at her feet. "Ugh, I wish we weren't the same size. It was great for when we were married, but now—" She shrugged, then added, "Oh, and that's not the worst of it. He knows about my engagement."

"What'd he say?"

"I think he sees my remarriage as a new source of income for himself. Everything is always about him. And what he gets out of it."

"Unbelievable. At least you're much stronger now. You should be proud of that. You just can't go backward. Don't let him take advantage of your big heart. Don't let him walk all over you."

"With my own boots, especially. Darn. I loved those boots, especially because they were from Pete." Standing, Ashley gathered her gear. "Come on. Let's play hockey. I have some aggression I need to work out."

"Good idea. Imagine his face as the puck," offered Carrie.

Ashley barked a laugh. "Nice."

THE SECOND GAME OF the day was a loss also, but the score did not dampen their enthusiasm for a hot meal and a cold drink. With Katherine driving, Carrie and Gretchen stopped to shop at an outdoor store before joining the others at the Muffled Moose Pub for burgers and fries. As they crowded around a large wooden table, the waiter took one look at their red and tired faces and brought five glasses and two pitchers of water.

As they waited for their food, Carrie fiddled with the paper placemat on the table in front of her and searched her purse for a pen to play tic-tac-toe with Gretchen. Apparently, the previous diners had already used it for scrap paper, and she crossed out the words "If Buddy's killer's first name starts with the letter T, poison was not used" on the back, before drawing the required four lines.

After they inhaled warm brownie sundaes, Carrie revealed their purchase from the outdoor store, handing Ashley a large shopping bag. "We got you an engagement gift. Sorry, it's not wrapped."

"Wow, that wasn't necessary." Opening the heavy box from inside the bag, Ashley's eyes lit up. Lifting the new Sorel boots, she clutched them to her. "You got the same ones." She swallowed and looked each of them in the eyes. "Thanks, Witches. Bob can go jump in a lake, for all I care."

Pleased at Ashley's response, Carrie glanced at Gretchen and Katherine and grinned. Success.

"And by the way," Ashley said as she pulled on her new boots, "we'll be mailing the invitations to the wedding soon. We picked the second Saturday in June. It'll be a small ceremony and reception, but, after supporting me through these past years, Peter and I can't wait to celebrate with you all. Oh, and Jennifer, I'm hoping you can give us some technology advice, we want to put on some kind of multimedia show."

"I'm available for any help you need," said Jennifer and she bobbed her head as the conversation dissolved into several separate discussions of wedding details and planning.

"I'm so glad you've decided to go ahead," whispered Carrie, just loud enough for Ashley to hear. "What changed your mind?"

"I talked to Pete. He said he has a plan." Ashley beamed with a broad smile. "And no doubt, we're stronger together."

Carrie squeezed her hand. "We all are."

"Congratulations," interrupted Katherine.

Jennifer lifted her cup. "To Ash and Pete."

"To Ash and Pete," they all repeated.

"And to Maggie," added Carrie.

"Thanks, everyone." Ashley's smile wobbled, and she swallowed to control her emotions. "Your friendship means everything."

Carrie noticed that there wasn't a dry eye around the table.

After their meal, the friends caravaned in their cars to Katherine's condo on Pine Mountain where they were eager to soak their sore muscles in the outdoor hot tub under the stars. The clouds preceding the incoming storm still had not arrived. But despite the clear sky, Carrie could feel a chill down to her bones when she went to bed, and she shivered as she slipped between the ice-cold sheets. Bob's threats toward her friend swirled in her thoughts, making it hard to sleep. She was worried that the worst was yet to come.

THE NEXT MORNING, THEY returned to Lake Wintergreen. The quick bowl of oatmeal Carrie had wolfed down for breakfast felt like a lump in her belly. She'd slept badly and needed two full cups of coffee to feel fully awake.

After another loss, this time by only two goals, the teammates all tromped back to the warming hut together with Jennifer leaning heavily between Katherine and Gretchen.

"It's nothing," she said. "I tweaked my knee when I fell during that last play, that's all. I'll be fine."

Carrie scoffed. "Jennifer, you can't even walk."

"I'll take her to the hospital," interrupted Ashley. "I don't mind, really." She removed her game jersey. "And then I won't be here if Bob shows up again. I saw him unloading supplies last night. If we go now, we'll be back in plenty of time for the afternoon game."

WAITING FOR THEIR LAST game—as well as for Ashley and Jennifer to return—Carrie joined the rest of the team as they huddled in their thickest jackets on an assorted collection of tree stumps and Adirondack chairs circling one of the fire pits.

Carrie texted Ashley and then blew on the hot chocolate in her cup as she waited for a response. She took a sip and almost burned her tongue. With no reply, she then tried Jennifer.

"They must still be at the hospital," Carrie said as she pocketed her phone and quickly replaced her mitten.

"I know you hated to deceive her, but you guessed right that Ashley would offer to take Jennifer," Katherine said.

Carrie nodded. "Her kindness is her superpower, no doubt."

The expected storm was brewing: Carrie pulled down her hat to better cover her ears and pulled up her collar to protect her cheeks as the clouds gathered in the sky and the temperature plummeted. Katherine and Gretchen pulled their chairs closer to the roaring fire for warmth.

"Despite our losses, I'm glad the tournament is running this year," said Katherine, wrapped in a fleece blanket that she'd remembered to bring from her ski condo while Carrie wished she had thought to bring one, too.

"Darn global warming. It hasn't even been cold enough to freeze a pond in New Hampshire," said Gretchen as she gnawed on a granola bar. Carrie wondered how she wasn't breaking her teeth on the frozen snack.

"At moments like this, though, I could use a little global warming," Katherine said as she shivered, now covered by blanket so fully that Carrie could only see the tip of her nose. "And it's hard to sell houses in this kind of weather. My business suffers."

"Do I really need to explain to you again how climate change works?" Gretchen grumbled.

"I'm just glad Artie is back to ice fishing all weekend. He seems perfectly content to sit around freezing his butt off and drinking beer with his buddies," said Carrie. Rubbing her mittened hands together, she stomped her feet.

Carrie was distracted when Gretchen and Katherine cheered. Ashley and Jennifer had returned.

Ashley fist-bumped Carrie and then dropped herself into the adjacent Adirondack chair.

"What's the verdict?" asked Gretchen.

"It's feeling better already but I'm out, for the afternoon anyway," said Jennifer. "The doctor recommended scheduling an appointment with an orthopedist for a follow-up."

"Glad it doesn't sound serious," said Gretchen.

"Me too," said Carrie.

"I'm hungry—" Removing supplies from a grocery sack, Ashley held up a bag of marshmallows. "Look what we picked up on the way back from the hospital. S'more anyone?"

THEIR FOURTH GAME ALSO ended in a loss. They walked as a group back to the warming hut, far more slowly than their pace before the game. Another year without going to the playoffs. Oh well, there's always next year, thought Carrie. They were winners in other ways.

"At least we have a much cooler name," grumbled Katherine. "Who would name their team the Ice Kittens?"

"A bunch of twenty-somethings," answered Carrie. "And they weren't 'Kittens'; they were 'Panthers.'"

"Ha," Ashley cackled. "Hate to break it to you but I think they were in their forties."

Katherine scoffed. "Still babies, as far as I'm concerned."

"I think I strained my back," groaned Gretchen. "Another hot tub for me tonight."

They had nearly reached the warming hut when Carrie heard sirens. Two police cars rushed through the parking lot and out onto the ice—their sirens blaring and lights flashing—toward a spot on the edge of the lake about 100 yards away. They halted and watched as an ambulance followed them at great speed.

"I wonder what's up?" Ashley asked as the blue lights flashed in the gloom of the late afternoon. The storm was imminent and thick clouds hung low and heavy in the sky. The snow looked ready to drop at any moment. "I think I saw a fishing hut in that area," Ashley shared. "Perhaps an ice fisherman with a problem or something? Can't think what else it might be."

"Perhaps," Carrie said. They watched for another minute and when the emergency vehicles didn't return, she led the team into the hut as it began to snow.

Carrie shoved her hockey gear into her bag for the final time that weekend. Last to go was her flying witch jersey and she laid it carefully across the top of the bag. After a thorough washing, her uniform would be ready for their next tournament. She was already looking forward to it. Even better, they'd be together again in just a few short months for a June wedding. They'd made sure of it.

Gear in hand, Carrie, Gretchen, and Ashley crossed the parking lot on the way to their cars, stopping to watch the ambulance slowly creep back across the ice, then pick up speed through the lot, and exit onto the main road. Its lights were flashing but they heard no siren and the driver didn't appear to be in a hurry.

Ashley's gaze followed their route. "I guess it was a false alarm."

Carrie grunted. "I guess."

"JENNIFER, YOUR KNEE seems much better," said Ashley as they enjoyed a long and relaxing soaking in the hot tub. Carrie's side was hurting from laughing so hard as they relived their favorite moments of the weekend.

"Sure does. Feels almost like new. The warm water did the trick."

"Apparently. Now, let's eat."

Swaying to the music playing on Katherine's phone—they'd agreed on a song with a heavy bass beat—Carrie loaded sour cream and cheddar cheese on her bowl of veggie chili. Adding a slice of cornbread, she was just about to sit down with the others when a pounding knock on the front door interrupted them.

Katherine jumped up from the table, nearly knocking over her glass of red wine. "It's probably the owners of the condo next door. Maybe the music is too loud? They told me that they weren't coming this weekend but I guess they changed their minds with the fresh snow." She turned down the music, but only a fraction, on her way to the door.

Carrie watched as Katherine returned to the table thirty seconds later and whispered into Ashley's ear. Ashley's eyes widened, her head snapped up, and she hurried from the room, leaving Katherine to follow.

Jennifer was opening a second bottle of wine when Ashley returned several minutes later, her eyes red, her face pale. Katherine flipped off the music, which immediately quieted the table.

Carrie looked from one to the other. "You look like you've seen a ghost. What is it? What's happened?"

Ashley dropped heavily into her chair and placed her head in her hands. "It's Bob."

Carrie slapped the table. "What did that despicable leech do now?"

Ashley flinched and lifted her head to look at her. "He's dead."

Dropping her spoon, Carrie stared at her and then noticed Gretchen and Jennifer exchange looks.

Jennifer recovered first. "What? How?"

"Remember the ambulance we saw earlier today at Lake Wintergreen?" When they all nodded, she sputtered, "Well, that was—that was for him."

"I don't understand." Carrie wrapped her hands around Ashley's clenched fists, leaned closer and asked gently, "What happened?"

"I don't know," said Ashley. "The officers said he fell through the ice and drowned."

"Didn't you see him yesterday?" Jennifer glanced at Carrie and Gretchen who nodded.

"I guess that's why they want to question me. Apparently, they find it too much of a coincidence that we're in the area at the same time, the same weekend."

"Does that mean they think he was...murdered?" asked Gretchen, the words appearing slowly and hanging in the air, as heavy as the storm clouds outside.

Ashley twisted her hands together. "They didn't say. They must have found something to raise their suspicions."

"They didn't say anything?" asked Jennifer.

"Like what?"

"Like, were there witnesses?" asked Katherine. "Or, evidence that someone else was with him, such as, I don't know, more than one set of prints in the snow, for example?"

"So—" Ashley swallowed. "Do they think I was with him?" She looked at her teammates around the table. "They don't think I have anything to do with his death, do they? That I did it?"

"You couldn't have." Carrie grabbed her hands. "It doesn't matter what they think. You were with us all afternoon yesterday and all night, either at Katherine's condo, the hospital, or playing hockey." She waved a hand. "We're all witnesses."

"Well, the officers asked me to come to the station Monday morning, to answer some questions." She looked around at the women at the table. "They must think I was involved or why ask me? I mean, I can't say I haven't thought of—of—" she sputtered. "He's despicable. Or, rather, he was. But—I've—I've moved on." She roughly rubbed the tears gathering in her eyes with the back of her hand. "I can't believe it. The police think I had something to do with his death. What am I going to do? Just when I've dug myself out of the hole we were in. And what about Maggie?" Shaking her head, Ashley moaned. "I've spent so much on lawyers already. There's not much left. He gambled most of it away. Pete will never want to marry me now—"

"Of course, he will." Carrie patted her shoulder. "This won't change his mind one iota."

"It'll be okay." Katherine hugged her, adding, "We'll figure it out. The Ice Witches are here for you, whatever you need."

Katherine turned the music back on after switching to a slow tune but the arrival of the officers and their news had deflated the festive mood and the meal was finished in near silence. Deeply concerned, Carrie watched Ashley out of the corner of her eye. She noticed that she wasn't the only one.

After cleaning the kitchen, Carrie nudged Ashley. "Come on. Let's head to bed. We could all use the sleep."

After a hug from each of them, Ashley left the room.

As Carrie started to follow, Katherine snagged her arm, whispering, "Meet us back in the hot tub at eleven." After Carrie dipped her chin in acknowledgment, she added, "We need to go over the next phase of the plan."

To pass the time, Carrie searched the local news and social media apps for stories about Bob. Finding none, she opened a book on her Kindle but gave up after reading the same paragraph ten times. Finally, the time came and a few minutes before eleven, she quietly rose and closed the bedroom door without waking Ashley. Opening the slider door off the kitchen, she shuffled quickly across the deck, following fresh footprints in the snow. Two inches had already fallen and still the flakes fell. The others were already there and she slipped into the steaming tub with them.

"Ashley's asleep. She was exhausted," Carrie reported, as her body adjusted to the temperature. Her tense shoulders loosened as she relaxed into the warm water.

"Did she say anything?" asked Gretchen.

"Not much. Mostly she was in shock and worried about Maggie. She's concerned about what the police wanted. And, she feels guilty that she's relieved that he's dead."

"Well, we know what we need to do." Katherine looked around at each of them through the steam. "We need to be prepared to prove that she had no hand in what happened. Just in case."

"We saw the ambulance around three PM," Carrie remembered as she moved to allow the jet to pulse on her leg. "The last time I saw him was right before our second game yesterday when they were arguing."

"Ashley went to the hospital with Jennifer as we planned," Gretchen said. "She'll be on camera there."

"Yes." Jennifer nodded. "And I'll add that to a Google Sheet with an hour-by-hour summary of where she's been over the past 24 hours."

Carrie pressed her back against a jet and let it massage her sore muscles. "I've collected as many receipts as possible," she said.

"Good. Save everything—from food to gas to the coffee shop, parking from the hospital." Katherine brushed a loose strand of hair from her face. "Those will help confirm her whereabouts."

"Will do." Carrie's hair was starting to curl in the steam coming from the tub.

"Excellent. How about an update, Jennifer?"

"We were lucky Bob never changed his Apple ID and password. Gretchen and Carrie were gone long before he returned. Made it back here just before three AM. The signal stopped around five thirty, that must have been when the phone got wet."

"And there is no way the police can tell we've been tracking him for months?" Katherine asked. "No communication on his phone can be traced to us? That I arranged the ice fishing trip and the free lodging?"

Jennifer shook her head. "All clear. I used public wifi to cover our tracks. And we still have the recording of Bob taking the contract out on her as proof of his intentions. But I don't think we'll need to use it."

"Excellent. Carrie?" Katherine asked. They all turned to her.

"As easy as pie." Carrie's lips twitched. "They'll find only one set of Sorel tracks—" Her grin widened. "Well, one person going back and forth to their car for supplies several times. They won't find any evidence otherwise."

"We moved his tent and equipment only ten feet or so." Gretchen's eyelashes were dappled with snowflakes. "Just close enough to that underwater spring, and—" She lifted a shoulder.

Carrie nodded. "My husband's experience made all the difference. Good thing I listen when he talks about his ice fishing escapades."

"How'd you think of the idea?" asked Katherine.

"Once we knew for sure that the storm would be later than we expected, I knew we had to find another way to cover our tracks. So to speak. It popped into my head as soon as we learned that he'd all but stolen her boots," explained Gretchen. "I knew it could work when we were able to find several more pairs of the same model."

Carrie nodded her head. "We didn't come this far to not go through with it. Combined with what I'd learned about his plans of collecting Ashley's life insurance policy through Maggie—"

"It was becoming more and more dangerous for her," Katherine finished.

They all murmured their agreement.

"Are we going to tell Ashley?" asked Jennifer.

"No. No way." Katherine frowned. "This wedding gift is our secret. If he couldn't save himself, that's not our fault."

"He wasn't following recommended ice fishing protocols," agreed Carrie.

Following the others, Carrie leaned back against the side of the tub and closed her eyes, savoring the magic embrace of warm water and sisterhood.

Several quiet moments passed before Katherine reached behind her. "This should be chilled by now." Picking up a glass and brushing off the dusting of snow, she gave it to Carrie who passed it on to Gretchen until everyone in the circle had a glass.

A bottle of champagne followed. Carrie poured.

Carrie lifted her glass to tap the others already waiting in the center of the circle. "To Ashley and Pete. To a June wedding. And to second chances."

"And to the Ice Witches," added Katherine.

The sound of their glasses touching was muffled by the bubbling water and the wind stirring the tree branches above.

"To the Ice Witches," they each said in unison, their words mingling with the steam as it evaporated into the darkness.

FOR MORE INFORMATION about the author, please visit Sally Milliken's website: http://www.sallymillikenauthor.com/

Love and Death in Madison, Georgia
Rebecca Olmstead

I love my Mama Bea. She's bandaged every scrape and dried every tear since the day I was born. I almost feel guilty that my love for Mama Bea goes so much deeper than my love for Mother.

Almost.

Not that Mother is a bad person. Charlotte Olivia Davenport is a pillar of the community. Ask anyone in Madison, Georgia. Why, if there is a committee to be found, Mother will be on it, usually sitting at the head of the table. And if there isn't a committee, Mother will make one. In Madison, if your name doesn't mean cotton or tobacco, it doesn't mean much of anything.

Davenport means cotton, and has for a long, long time.

Mama Bea pulls the brush through my straight, blonde hair, like she's done every night for the last twenty years. I love the way the lamp on my dressing table makes her skin glow.

Mama Bea's real name is Begonia. She says her mama named her after her favorite flower. But she didn't like that name, so she goes by Bea. I was just a child when she told me this, and I said to her, "Why, Begonia is the perfect name for you, Mama Bea. Begonias like the shade, and have thick strong stems and leaves, and they're beautiful and colorful, just like you."

She laughed as big as life and drew me into one of her bear hugs that always made me feel safe and loved.

"My name's just awful," I said. "*Violet.*"

"Now, don't you go talkin' bad about violets, child. They're such pretty, delicate things, and they smell so sweet. They don't go actin' all proud and haughty, no sir! They're shy little flowers, happy to sit quietly and soak up the warm sunshine."

I looked up at her. "Like me?"

"Yes, baby. Just like you." She kissed my forehead. She was right, I was delicate. The doctor said I had a weak heart when I was born. I was always paler than the other girls. Always tired and cold. I was the only child in school who carried a medicine bottle. Little nitroglycerin pills to put under my tongue in case I overdid it on the playground. Little chance of that. No one wants to play with a sickly child.

When I was seven, I asked Mother if I could stop going to school. It was such a lonely place. Especially, watching all the other girls playing together. Mother's answer came swift and sharp. "Friends are overrated, Violet. You are a *Davenport*. That is all that matters."

That same day, Mama Bea baked me cookies. "Don't you worry none about those other girls. They don't know what they're missin'. Besides, you got somethin' none of them have."

"A bad heart?"

She laughed and dunked a warm snickerdoodle in her cold glass of milk. "No, silly. Don't you know? You got Mama Bea!" Her smile was so big and bright, and I giggled. I wanted that moment to last forever. Because it was true.

There isn't anything I wouldn't do for my Mama Bea. And there isn't anything she wouldn't do for me. I know because of what happened that day. I was just three, and I played in the yard, while Mama Bea shelled sweet peas on the veranda. She appeared beside me, stomping on the ground like a crazy woman and screaming, "You git back where you belong, devil!"

In shock, I stood still as a post. She gathered me up in her arms and held me tight as she turned back to the porch. A big old copperhead lay dead in the grass, near where I'd been playing. She rocked me in the white porch swing and stroked my hair. "Don't you worry, baby, Mama Bea ain't gonna let nothin' hurt you. Not now, not ever."

I was confused more than scared. I didn't know the devil lived in the creek next to the house. But I loved being in Mama Bea's arms and didn't say a thing.

"YOU LOOK MIGHTY MELANCHOLY for a young lady on the eve of her weddin'." The soothing melody of Mama Bea's voice brings me back from the past.

A heavy sigh escapes me. "Will you be comin' with me, Mama Bea? After the weddin'?"

Her dark eyes shine in the mirror. "Try an' stop me." She plaits my hair and ties it with a pink bow to finish. "Now, you climb into bed. You got a big day tomorra."

I do as she says, and she pulls the covers up to my chin. "Mama Bea?"

"What is it, child?"

"How did you know you loved Charlie?"

She chuckles. "Oh, I don't know that I'd call it *love*. I just knew when he come around, I'd get all fluttery in my stomach. And, when he kissed me, I liked ta float right up out of my shoes."

I sigh again. "Bobby Lee never made me fluttery. And, when he kisses me, I sure don't feel like I'm floatin'. I don't feel like anything at all."

Mama Bea sweeps her warm hand over my hair. "Oh, child, is that what's botherin' ya?"

I nod. "Mother seems more excited about this marriage than I do. I don't ever remember her askin' if I wanted to marry Bobby Lee. She just decided it would be. Like I was one of her committees."

"Honey, your mama—"

"Don't call her that."

She purses her mouth. "Your mother just wants you to have a good match, that's all. She doin' what she thinks is right for you. The Abernathys are an old tobacco family."

"I know, I know." Growing warmer under the covers, I pull my arms out. "And *rich*."

"And rich."

"But it's 1957, for Heaven's sake! Surely a girl should be able to decide what boy she wants to spend the rest of her life with!"

For the first time in my life, I see pity in Mama Bea's eyes as she looks down at me. "Baby, I think I done sheltered you a little too much."

"What do you mean?"

She takes my hand in hers, stroking the back of it gently. "I mean this, honey."

"My hand?"

She shakes her head. "No, child. I mean your skin." She must see the confusion in my face. "Most folks think dark-skinned folk like me aren't free like you white folk, and in some ways we aren't. But, when it comes to choosin' who we love and marry, we got all the freedom in the world." She grins. "Long as we stick to our own, that is. But you, with your soft, pale skin and your forefathers and all...well, you're expected ta marry *well*. Don't matter if ya love him or not, so long as you keep up the wealth and respectability of the family name."

I think about Mother and Daddy and realize for the first time why they are so unhappy. "That's just stupid." I could never use that kind of language with Mother, but Mother isn't here. "What good is money and respectability, if you don't have love?"

Mama Bea shakes her head, then smiles. "I don't know, child. I ain't never had no money." She rises from my bed. "Enough talkin', now. You're gettin' married tomorra, and you need your beauty sleep."

"But..."

"No buts." She pulls the duvet back over my shoulders. "You stop your frettin'. It's not good for your heart. Doctor McGill said so. Mama Bea gonna be right there with you. And the good Lord has a way of makin' everything work out. You'll see."

"I love ya, Mama Bea."

She bends over and kisses my forehead, like she's done as long as I can remember. "I love you, too, child."

◊ If Buddy's son committed the murder, poison was used. ◊

IN THE MORNING, DESPITE my lack of sleep, I can't help but smile when Mama Bea walks into my room carrying my breakfast tray. "What's all this?" I ask. "I'm not sick."

I'm usually expected to breakfast with Mother and Father in the dining room at seven o'clock sharp. I look at the clock on my bedside table. It's nine. "Oh, my goodness! Is that the time?"

"It shore is. And this is your special day. I talked your mama into lettin' you sleep in a little and breakfast in bed."

"*Mother.*"

She sets the tray over my lap and gives me one of her looks: *don't be a pill, young lady.* "Now, you git somethin' in ya, child. You have a long day ahead."

I look down at the steaming bowl of grits, just the way I like them, with a thick pat of butter melting on top and maple syrup swimming around the edges. My stomach lurches. Even the smell of the bacon on the side nauseates me.

"Don't you make me feed you like I did when you was a baby." She sees my tears well and sits down beside me. "Oh, child..."

Mother sweeps into my room in a tailored blue brushed silk dress, complete with pearls and heels. I swipe my tears away, and Mama Bea rises from my bedside.

"Well, my goodness, Violet. I understand it's your weddin' day, but you're actin' like you're royalty, or somethin'. Why, you aren't even outta bed." She fusses over my wedding dress on a dressmaker's form next to a full-length mirror. It's really Mother's "full lace gown with a princess neckline." It's been taken in and shortened to fit me. She arranges pieces of my trousseau, nodding her approval. Then she looks at me. "You haven't even touched your breakfast." She turns on Mama Bea. "Bea, I gave in to your whims, lettin' Violet sleep in and have breakfast in bed, but enough is enough. You get that breakfast down her and get her into the tub. Why, it's nearly noon." She is of course going by "Charlotte Davenport time," where every minute past nine in the morning is "nearly noon."

"It's not Mama Bea's fault, Mother. I'm not hungry."

Mother cringes at the use of my term of endearment. She's always hated that. Her eyes narrow, though the rest of her face remains wrinkle-free. "Young lady, we are expectin' some very important people today. I will not have you embarrass your father and me by faintin' dead away at the altar. Eat." She turns to Mama Bea one last time. "Make it happen." She sails out of the room.

I share the same look with Mama Bea that we'd shared a million times. Most of the time we don't have to say a word, that look is all we need.

"Try to drink some tea, honey. It'll help your appetite. I'll go draw your bath. Your Highness." We both laugh.

Mama Bea has been making me herbal tea as long as I can remember. She says the herbs are special, to make my heart stronger and calm my nerves. As a child, it took three spoons of honey for me to get it down. But now it's a comforting brew she makes every morning and at bedtime. I've come to see it as an extension of her love for me.

Having managed to eat some of the grits, I sink into a warm bath. Mama Bea pours warm water over my soapy hair, and I hear the voice of my best friend, Marcy. "Violet! We have arrived!"

The chorus of giggles must be from my bridesmaids.

"Oh, Lord," Mama Bea moans, and I know what's coming next. "I never did like that girl. Why in the world your mother ever asked her to be your maid of honor, I'll never know."

"She's my best friend, Mama Bea. Who else would she ask?" Marcy is actually my only friend. I don't even know my other bridesmaids. According to Mother, they're cousins of some sort. I don't have a problem with Mother planning my wedding down to the smallest detail. It's more her wedding than mine. I don't even know where I'm going for my honeymoon, but that's Bobby Lee's doing. No one is to know until the reception.

"Just what made that girl your best friend? The fact that she invites herself over here every chance she gets?"

"Shhh. They'll hear you."

"That's fine by me. The only thing that girl ever did for you was want everything you had. In fact, I better get out there and make sure things don't start disappearin'. You'll be walkin' down that aisle in your petticoat if she has her way."

She is barely out the door when I hear Marcy address her. "There you are, Bea! Fetch us a pitcher of sweet tea. I swear this Georgia heat is just murder!"

I cringe as I towel off. I have asked Marcy not to speak to Mama Bea like that. But it never seems to make a difference.

Marcy had once said I was far too familiar with *the help*. That got my blood up. "What would you know about help, Marcy? You never had any."

I felt bad after I said it, but it was true. Marcy wasn't from one of the old families. In fact, Mama Bea had confided in me that Marcy's mama had been a housekeeper, until she was impregnated by her employer. She didn't have to work now, as long as she kept her mouth shut.

But Marcy didn't even blush at my remark. "Oh, I will," she said. "Don't you worry about that."

I slip into a summer dress, wrap my hair in a towel, take a deep breath. My hand is on the doorknob when Marcy's voice stops me. Actually, it's just two words. "Honeymoon" and "Hawaii." I guess it isn't such a big secret after all.

I COULD HAVE KISSED Mother when she came to collect my tittering bridesmaids. One moment of peace before Daddy came to deliver me to my loveless future.

As Daddy escorts me down the spiral staircase, the air is heavily scented with roses and magnolias, and my mood takes a turn for the better. Mother has done a beautiful job decorating. Or directing the decorating, anyway. Blush roses and white, waxy magnolias entwined with baby's breath and fern fronds drip from every surface. I can see how it might be some girls' idea of the perfect wedding, but to be honest, it all makes me feel small...and a little lost. I'll do my best not to spoil it.

I look over my shoulder, and Mama Bea smiles down on me from the top of the stairs. She gives me a nod, and I take in a deep breath.

"You doin' all right, sweetheart?" Daddy's thick, bushy eyebrows worry above blue eyes that are very pretty when they aren't bloodshot. The familiar odor of his special bourbon and cigars wash over me with his breath.

"Yes, Daddy."

"Good. Your mother would be horrified if you were to faint in front of all her *friends*." He grins down at me, and I smile.

As we near the French doors leading out to the back garden, I go over my checklist once more, even though Mother has gone over it with me no less than seven times before I left my room. Something old: Great Gran's lace kerchief. Something new: a white garter of satin and lace, which mortified me when Marcy presented it to me in front of my giggling wedding party. Even worse when I learned what Bobby Lee would do with it at the reception. Something borrowed: Mother's string of pearls from her debutante ball. Something blue: a ribbon Mama Bea had tied my hair up with when I was a child. I tied it around my wrist when Mother wasn't looking, so Mama Bea would be close to me.

Lastly, Mother had given me a shiny copper penny to put in my shoe. "For good luck," she said. I'm pretty sure she meant good luck that I would get through the day without embarrassing her.

Daddy ushers me out into the garden. It blooms like I'd always imagined Eden did before the fall. Precisely placed urns overflow with blush roses, white gardenias, and greenery, and the flowerbeds just inside the neatly trimmed boxwood hedge that Mother likes to say, "embrace the perfectly greened and cut grass" burst with blooms in shades of pink and white. The "Wedding March" begins to play, and the guests rise. I feel the first lightness in my head, and my grip tightens on Daddy's arm.

"Steady on, Vi. It'll all be over before you know it."

I take another deep breath, and we start down the white cloth aisle that has been scattered with rose petals by some cousin's child. Halfway to the flower-draped archway at the end, I dare look up, and there he is—Bobby Lee.

Even from a distance, I can see him sway like a willow in a soft breeze. I feel my knees give under me, and Daddy's strong grip around my waist buoys me up. I find my legs and we carry on.

Do not faint! Do not faint!

I don't have to look at Mother to know she is white as a sheet and twisting her hankie in her lap.

Daddy gives me a little push forward when we get to the altar, before handing me off. Bobby Lee grins down at me and cocks an eyebrow over an eye every bit as blue, and as bloodshot, as Daddy's. Blinking through a haze of Daddy's cigars and bourbon, I feel the undigested grits roll in my stomach. Marcy's voice echoes in my mind, "Bobby Lee's a dream. Why, you're the luckiest girl in three counties, Violet."

I wonder if it's too late to move to another county.

When the minister tells us to repeat after him, I'm concentrating so hard on not losing my grits all over the groom and embarrassing Mother, it takes me three times to get it right.

By some miracle, I survive the ceremony, the congratulatory hugging and kissing, and the catered dinner al fresco. Bobby Lee revels in the attention, so I don't have to worry about making conversation with him. He's had an early start at the liquor with Daddy, so by the time we cut the cake, it's all he can do to stand. We do the marriage toast with Grandmother's crystal champagne flutes, one etched with *Mr.* and the other with *Mrs.*

Bobby Lee snatches one off the table, downs the contents, and tosses the flute back over his shoulder, to a resounding cheer from his entourage. The look on Mother's face should be accompanied by smoke curling from her ears.

My strength is waning when Bobby Lee grabs my hand and drags me onto the dance floor for our first dance. I'm sure it would have made a pretty sight with all the twinkling lights wrapped in tulle hanging from the ceiling of the giant reception tent, but I'm dead on my feet, and Bobby Lee's no longer work. My anxiety about what will happen after the party grows with each drink Bobby Lee takes.

Oh, Lord, please let him pass out before...

My new husband sways heavily in my arms to no other rhythm than his own. He stops, as his tan features take on a greenish hue. His face contorts into something quite the opposite of revelry, and he doubles over.

"My dress!" Mother hollers in a most unladylike fashion, before swooping in and pulling me away.

Bobby Lee's knees buckle, and he keels over right on the dance floor. Amused laughter spreads through the tent, and Doctor McGill steps forward to bend over the incapacitated groom. A moment later, the laughter stops.

Doctor McGill rises on unsteady feet. "He's dead."

At first, the words don't register. I'm busy thanking the good Lord for answering my prayer. But a screaming female voice brings me back.

From somewhere in the crowd, my best friend and maid of honor breaks though the circle that formed around Bobby Lee. "No!"

She throws herself down by Bobby Lee and shakes his shoulders violently. "No!" she screams again. "Do somethin'!" she yells at Doctor McGill, but he just shakes his head. She presses her lips to Bobby Lee's. I think she's trying to breathe life back into him, but she doesn't come up for more air. When she finally sits up, there's more screaming. "You killed him! You killed Bobby Lee!"

I search the faces all around me, trying to make sense of it all. Everyone stares back. Marcy is pointing at *me*. Everything begins to move around me, and I feel the strength abandon my legs. "I'm sorry, Mother," I manage to say as I go down.

I WAKE THE NEXT DAY to the warm Georgia sun filling my west-facing bedroom windows with soft golden light. Dr. McGill has my wrist in his large, warm hand, which is never a good sign. Trying to sit up, I call for Mama Bea, but Doctor McGill presses me back down to my pillows.

"Now, you just lie still, Miss Violet, and try to relax."

Mama Bea floats to my bedside like an angel. "I'm right here, honey."

"I had a terrible nightmare, Mama Bea. Bobby Lee was dead—why is Doctor McGill here?"

Mama Bea looks down at me, her eyes filled with concern. "The good doctor is here because that was no dream, baby." She sits on the edge of the bed and takes my free hand in her own. "Bobby Lee is sho 'nough dead."

I blink at her. "But...how? Why? Was he ill?"

Doctor McGill clears his throat and looks about to speak when a loud knock at the door draws all our attention. The door flies open, and Sheriff Baines strides in. I usually only see him sitting at a café table cracking jokes, drinking coffee, and reducing Millie's supply of fresh peach pie. He doesn't look like he's here for pie. He looks as if he's attempting to suck his sizable belly up into his chest. His thumbs are hooked in the belt loops of his already straining waistband, his face is set in a stern scowl, and the top of his scalp, revealed by his receding gray hairline, is red from the climb up the stairs.

Mama Bea stands and plants her hands on her hips. Thank goodness Doctor McGill sees she's about to launch into the sheriff, and jumps in.

"Sheriff," the doctor says, "it is customary to wait for an invitation before enterin' a lady's boudoir."

The sheriff's face reddens even more. "If you don't mind, Doctor, I am investigatin' a suspicious death, here."

"As a matter of fact, I do mind, Sheriff. There is no excuse for abandonin' the rules of comportment!"

Seeing as how the two men are members of the same Masonic Temple and regular checkers partners at Miller's Mercantile, this exchange is rather humorous.

"Miss Violet," the sheriff ignores the doctor, "why do you think Miss Marcy would accuse you of killin' Bobby Lee?"

My wedding night. I struggle to bring up memories. Isolated images flash in my mind, but all I can remember is exhaustion. Just thinking about it makes my eyelids heavy. I shake my head. "I have no idea."

"Mm-hm." The sheriff scribbles something in a brand-new pocket notebook. "How did you *feel* about Bobby Lee?"

"Feel? He's a nice boy. He comes from a good family. I'm so lucky to have him." When the sheriff's brows furrow I realize I sound like a recording of Mother—and Marcy.

"Don't you mean, *was,* Miss Violet?"

"I just can't believe he's gone."

The sheriff taps his pencil on his notebook. "You didn't quite answer the question, Miss Violet. How did you feel about Bobby Lee?"

"Why, I liked him just fine."

He studies my face a while before scribbling again. "Miss Violet, how long have you known Bobby Lee was carryin' on with Miss Marcy?"

I giggle at this. "Bobby Lee and Marcy? Is this some kind of joke, Sheriff? Marcy's my best friend. Bobby Lee would never..." I glance at Mama Bea and the doctor. No one else is laughing. In fact, everyone else in the room averts their gazes, wearing expressions of pity and shame that bring bile up into my throat.

There's a sharp pain in my chest. "No. You just go on over to Marcy's. She'll tell you. She'll put an end to all this...this...*nasty* gossip." Even though Mother had given me strict instructions to never make such a gesture in the company of gentlemen, I press both hands to my chest, in an attempt to ease the discomfort.

"Miss Violet." Doctor McGill is back at my side, pulling one of my arms free to check my pulse, but that doesn't stop Sheriff Baines's mouth.

"I'm afraid I can't do that, Miss Violet," the sheriff says. "Miss Marcy died early this mornin'."

WHEN I WAKE AN HOUR later, Mama Bea sits at my side, patting my hand. My other hand is in Doctor McGill's care again as he rechecks my pulse. He presses a warmed stethoscope to my chest and listens intently. Then he stands. "How ya feelin', Miss Violet?"

"I'm feelin' better. Thank you, Doctor."

"I apologize for that monkey's...I apologize for Sheriff Baines. I sure hope his sleuthin' skills are better than his people skills." He turns to put his stethoscope in his bag, and I catch his arm.

"Doctor?"

I ask the question that has to be asked. "Were Bobby Lee and Marcy— murdered?"

He gives my hand a squeeze and looks down at me with fatherly concern. It comes naturally to him, I suppose. He's been my doctor since he brought me into this world and laid me in Mama Bea's arms. "I can't say for certain, Miss Violet. I won't know for sure until I do the autopsies. You don't worry yourself about it now, ya hear?" He draws a small notepad from his bag. "I'm writing you a prescription, Miss Violet." He writes something on the pad and tears off the top page. He looks to Mama Bea. "You keep those nitro tablets close ta hand, Begonia. And I'd appreciate it if you'd sleep in here with Miss Violet, tonight. I'll stop by your place on my way home and let your family know."

Mama Bea nods. "Yes, sir. Thank you, sir."

Dr. McGill hands me the paper and excuses himself. I think about the big cooler in the cellar of his house, and I don't feel like laughing anymore. Bobby Lee and Marcy are in that cooler, like Romeo and Juliet, entwined in death forever. I turn to Mama Bea, who's gathering up the remains of the sweet tea and sandwiches she had made for the doctor. "Is it true, what the sheriff said about Bobby Lee and Marcy?"

She keeps her back to me. "I wouldn't be surprised. I never did like that girl. Always wantin' what you had." She lifts the tray and heads for the door.

"Seems like everyone knew but me. Did you know?"

She stops and looks back at me. "I had my suspicions."

"What made you suspect?"

She sets the tray back down. "Looks they shared, mostly. Lingerin' touches. That's one of the benefits of bein' dark-skinned. You blend right into the shadows. Folks forget you're there."

"Why didn't you tell me? Don't you love me?"

She comes to my bed and sits heavily on the edge. "Ah, honey. That's just why I *didn't* tell you. Men be men, and snakes be snakes. And sometimes you cain't hardly tell 'em apart. I knowed you didn't care for that boy. And I knowed you'd be marryin' him just the same. Your ma—your mother—always gets her way. Now, you don't know nothin' 'bout the facts of life; you just a child. But Mama Bea know. And I knowed that if that boy had someone else ta play with, he wouldn't be forcin' himself on you all the time. That part of life can be wonderful when you in love. But, when you with someone you don't love..." She shakes her head. "You just got ta trust me on this, baby girl."

She is right. I didn't care for Bobby Lee. Not that way. And Mother never talked to me about what happens between a man and his wife. Marcy tried once, but I just couldn't stand to listen, so I made her stop. She laughed at me in a way that made me feel small.

Mama Bea rises and takes up her tray again. "Now, I'm gonna make you somethin' to eat, and you gonna eat it. I promised the doc, and I ain't never broke a promise in my life."

DEPUTIES COME AND GO the next few days, asking questions and collecting garbage, of all things. A week later Sheriff Baines pays us another call. A week isn't long but feels like a lifetime when the whole town thinks I'm a cold-blooded killer. I just want the truth, so I can leave my house without people staring and whispering. Mother and Daddy and I take our seats around the drawing room. We look around as if it's the first time we've been here.

The sheriff straightens his shoulders in a very important manner and flips a page in his notebook. "I'm glad ta see you feelin' better, Miss Violet. I'm sorry to disrupt all ya'll's evenin', but we got the tests back from the autopsy. Looks like Bobby died of nicotine poisoning. Miss Marcy, too." He stares at me as he says it. I stare right back.

"Nicotine?" Daddy's voice is thick with disbelief. "How? Were they allergic?"

"No, sir." The sheriff shakes his head and flexes his back. "Bobby Lee had an extremely large quantity of nicotine in his system. Miss Marcy had enough to cause her death eventually, but not enough to kill her instantly."

I watch Daddy's face, remembering the smell of cigar smoke on Bobby Lee that night. Daddy's cigars. Bobby Lee had even lit one up after dinner. It was in his hand when he dropped on the dance floor. I clasp my hands to keep them from shaking as the sheriff continues.

"I understand Bobby Lee was smokin' cigars that fateful night, Mr. Davenport."

"As was I," Daddy shoots back, "and a lot of other men. It was a celebration afta' all." I can tell he's getting riled when his drawl thickens.

"How did you feel about Bobby Lee Abernathy, sir?"

Daddy's eyes narrow. "Just what are you insinuatin', Sheriff?"

"Don't get all het up," the sheriff urges, holding a nervous hand up. "I'm just doin' my job. I have ta follow the book on a murder investigation. This is routine, I assure you. Now, if you'd be so kind as to answer, Mr. Davenport."

Daddy draws in a deep controlled breath, like he does when Mother gets under his skin. "I liked him just fine. Known his family for years. I was happy to have him for a son-in-law."

Sheriff Baines scribbles in his notebook. He doesn't look up when he asks Mother the same question.

Mother's back straightens ever so much. Her chin rises slightly. "Well, I just *loved* Bobby Lee. He was the perfect gentleman." She smooths the skirt of her black silk dress over one knee, pressed tightly against its twin. I don't have to look to know her ankles are crossed beneath her chair. The perfect Southern lady. She only colors slightly when the sheriff asks his next question.

"Do you maintain that opinion knowin' Bobby Lee was havin' an affair with Miss Marcy?"

Mother shoots Daddy a look that would make most men burst into flame. "Men will be men."

My face heats, and I concentrate on controlling my breathing. Did everyone in Madison know about Marcy and Bobby Lee? Everyone but me? I force myself to breathe through the growing queasiness in my stomach.

"Mr. and Mrs. Davenport, were you aware that Bobby Lee's family is broke?"

Mother's eyes narrow and she begins to speak, but Daddy cuts her off with a cough. "That's just wicked gossip, Sheriff. You should know better than to go spreadin' it around."

The sheriff shakes his head. "No, sir. Not gossip. Fact. Verified by our own auditor. Seems Mr. Abernathy's got himself a pretty bad gamblin' habit. Owes his own company a fair bit of change. Not ta mention all the people he's been borrowin' from. Looks like this here marriage was his last hope of holdin' on to his family's legacy. Didn't they build one of the biggest plantations in the county?"

"Yes." Daddy nods. "I knew he had a little trouble, but nothin' like what you're suggesting."

I can feel the heat radiating from Mother across the room.

The sheriff rolls up on the toes of his worn black shoes. "And you *still* didn't mind Bobby Lee marryin' your daughter?"

Avoiding Mother's death stare, Daddy says, "I told you. He was a good boy. I don't see the reason for punishin' the son for the sins of his father."

"Mm-hm." The sheriff scribbles, then turns to Mother. "And you, Mrs. Davenport?"

Mother struggles to keep her composure. "I had no idea, Sheriff."

The sheriff writes more notes, then flips his notebook shut. "I won't take up any more of your evenin', folks. We're still waiting on some tests. Some of the things we retrieved from the reception, ya know, in order ta ascertain just *how* the nicotine was administered. Of course, all the dishes were washed before we found out about Miss Marcy. I congratulate you on the fastidiousness of your staff." He makes eye contact with each of us in turn. "But we do have some food samples. I am confident something will surface in due time. Until then, I thank you for your cooperation." He starts toward the door but turns back. "Mr. Davenport. I was curious. You seem to be good friends with Mr. Abernathy, who grows most of the tobacco in Madison. Yet, I understand that you have an exclusive contract with Mr. Everson, to purchase his crops, is that right?"

Daddy, who has risen to show the sheriff to the door, pales slightly. "Yes, that's right. Everson's land produces a...sweeter tobacco. I prefer it."

The sheriff nods. "I see. And Everson. That would be Miss Marcy's daddy, wouldn't it?"

Daddy's Adam's apple bobs in his throat. "Yes. That's right."

Sheriff Baines nods again and looks at Daddy for the longest time. "Well, goodnight, folks. I'll be in touch."

No sooner is he gone than Mother orders me to bed, despite the early hour. I'm old enough to marry off, but not old enough to choose my own bedtime. What she doesn't know, but I've known since I was a child, is that the ventilation shaft of the drawing room connects to the one in my bedroom.

I get up there just in time for the fireworks. As usual, Mother lights the fuse, which has been smoldering for some time.

"Why didn't you tell me? Why in Heaven's name would you let our daughter marry a man who has *nothin'*?" When Daddy doesn't respond, Mother says in a hushed tone, "*Oh, my lord*. He knows, doesn't he? *How?*"

"Marcy told Bobby Lee."

"*Marcy?* She wasn't supposed to know. I thought that was part of the agreement."

"Well, obviously, her mother didn't keep our agreement, Charlotte. Abernathy threatened to tell the whole sordid story if I didn't agree to the marriage. What was I supposed to do?"

150

"And do you think he's goin' to keep it quiet now? Now that you've killed his *son*?"

"What? *No!* How could you even think such a thing? I didn't kill Bobby Lee. And I certainly wouldn't kill my own *daughter*!"

I shrink back from the register as if it's a snake. I didn't hear Mama Bea enter, but she gathers me up off the floor and gets me to my bed before I have a chance to faint. "You just breathe, honey. Nice and slow." She pats my hand. "In and out. That's right. In and out."

It all feels like a dream. I'd had the sensation of sleepwalking since my wedding day. But now...

As the room settles from a dizzying spin to a gentle rocking, I find my voice. "Is it true, Mama Bea? Is Marcy my sister?"

"*Half*-sister, baby. Just *half*."

"Do you think she knew all this time?"

Mama Bea sighs. "Looks like."

I look into her eyes. "And you? Did you know?"

"Oh, I heard rumors. But it ain't no business of mine what folks get up to. You the only business I'm interested in, baby girl."

"Does this mean Daddy's a snake?"

"I reckon your daddy's as flawed as the next man."

My thoughts drift back to Daddy's cigars. "Mama Bea? Do you think Daddy killed Bobby Lee?"

"Like I said, child. Ain't none of my business."

"But the sheriff says they both died of nicotine poisoning. And Bobby Lee was smoking Daddy's cigars that night. And the sheriff said Mr. Abernathy—"

"I heard what Sheriff Baines said, all right. Why, this whole county was built on tobacco and cotton. Can't go ten miles in any direction without seein' a tobacco stand. Stop frettin' your pretty little head, ya hear? Sheriff Baines will get to the bottom of this, and whatever it is, we'll get through, you and me. Together. Now, you just get yourself ready for bed. You've had enough excitement for one day. I wouldn't want to have to call Dr. McGill."

SLEEP ELUDES ME. I keep trying to picture Daddy putting extra nicotine in Bobby Lee's cigars. How would he even do that? Had he planned it ahead of time, or was it a last-minute idea? And what about Marcy? I can't see it.

When sleep finally comes, I dream of a big snake sliding through the grass. As it comes closer to me, it has Bobby Lee's face. I scream, and Mama Bea comes running. She stomps on Bobby Lee's head and yells, "You git back where you come from, devil!" And then he's dead. I feel Mama Bea's arms around me, and I hear her gentle voice in my ear. "Don't you worry none, baby. Mama Bea ain't gonna let nothin' hurt you. Not now, not ever."

I wake with a start.

Mama Bea stands at my bedside with a breakfast tray. "My goodness," she says. "That must have been some dream." She waits for me to sit up, then places the tray over my lap. "Wanna talk about it?"

"I...I can't remember it now."

"Probably for the best. What do ya say we find you a pretty dress to put on and go out for some fresh air? Everything looks better in the mornin' light."

How I wish I could believe her.

THE WHOLE HOUSE HOLDS its breath when Sheriff Baines stops by three nights later. We take up our usual places in the drawing room, Mother in her blue jacquard with the full skirt, Daddy in his burgundy smoking jacket. He reaches for a cigar in his breast pocket, but Mother's razor-sharp gaze makes him think better of it. She doesn't like that "putrid smell" lingering in her furniture.

"Would you care for some coffee, Sheriff?" Mother asks in a tone that matches the black velvet lapel on Daddy's jacket.

"No thank you, ma'am." He pulls out his notebook, licks a thumb, and flips through the pages.

"How about somethin' a little stronger?" Daddy moves to the liquor cabinet and pours himself a double bourbon.

"As temptin' as that is, Mr. Davenport, I'm on duty."

Daddy takes his drink back to a comfortable reading chair and takes a seat. "Seems pretty soon to have gotten the lab results back from our...refuse."

Sheriff Baines looks up from his notes. "Not at all. Knowin' that we were lookin' for nicotine, I ran the samples over to the lab myself. Didn't take long at all."

Daddy's face takes on that roguish, devil-may-care look it always does under the influence of bourbon, and one corner of his mouth rises in a grin. "And did you find any nicotine in my cigar?"

Mother shoots him a contemptuous look.

Sheriff Baines takes Daddy's joke in stride. "Yes, we did, Mr. Davenport. But not enough to kill a man. Not outright, that is." My body sags with relief, and I don't care if Mother notices.

The sheriff continues. "We did, however find a considerable amount on some pieces of a broken champagne glass."

Mother shifts in her wingback chair. I'm not sure if her consternation is from the memory of Bobby Lee throwing Great Grandmother's champagne flute to the ground, or the fact that the sheriff called her precious crystal a *glass*. Surely, Mother wouldn't kill Bobby Lee. She adored him.

But it isn't Mother the sheriff turns his attention on. "Miss Violet, I understand there was some kind of toast between you and Bobby Lee at the reception." He dips his head sheepishly. "I didn't see it, unfortunately. I was...socializin' at the time."

He's right about that. I could smell the sociality all over him that night. Smelled an awful lot like whiskey.

"It's been brought to my attention that you did not actually partake in that celebratory drink. Is that correct?"

Daddy rises to his feet. "Now, you wait one doggone minute, Baines! That's my daughter you're talkin' to."

The sheriff raises a palm. "Just calm down, Mr. Davenport. I have ta follow every line of inquiry."

"Sit down, William," Mother commands. Daddy obeys. Then Mother turns a cool gaze on the sheriff. "Our daughter is no more capable of killin' someone than I am. Why, if it weren't for Begonia, she couldn't even get out of bed in the mornin.'"

I want to say, *I'm sitting right here, Mother. And if it weren't for Mama Bea, I wouldn't want to!* Instead, I squeeze my hands in my lap and stare at my shoes.

"This Begonia," the sheriff continues to look at me, "she that servant woman you're always with?"

A knot forms in my chest, but I look up at him without blinking. "She is my nurse."

"And how long have you known her?"

"She has been with me my entire life."

Sheriff Baines nods and scribbles something in his notebook. "I understand these *servants* can become very loyal to their...*employers*, over time. Would you say this..." He glances at his notes. "...*Begonia* is loyal to you, Miss Violet?"

Mama Bea ain't gonna let nothin' hurt you. Not now, not ever. My hands begin to tremble in my lap, and I push my shoulders back just like Mother taught me and take a breath. I look Sheriff Baines steadily in the eye. "I would say, Sheriff Baines, that Mama Bea is a good, Christian woman with no guile in her. And the world would be a much better place with more people like her in it."

Daddy gazes at me, wide-eyed. Despite Mother's cool gaze, her chin rises ever so slightly.

The sheriff clears his throat and flips more pages in his notebook. He turns to Mother. "Mrs. Davenport. We were only able to retrieve the partial remains of one of those champagne glasses. I believe it's one of a set of two, am I correct?"

"Yes. The other has been washed and put away. I can retrieve it if you like."

"I would appreciate that, ma'am."

To my surprise, instead of calling Sissy the kitchen maid, Mother rises from her chair with the grace of Queen Elizabeth and floats out of the room, returning moments later to place a champagne flute in the sheriff's hand. "I don't see how this can help you."

The sheriff raises the flute to the light. "Looks like someone did a very thorough job." He stops, his bushy eyebrows bunching.

"What is it, Sheriff?" Daddy joins the sheriff in the center of the room.

"Why, this glass says, Mister." He looks at Daddy, then they both turn to me.

Daddy says, "Bobby Lee drank from the wrong glass."

Everyone stares at me in silence, and I realize they are waiting for me to speak.

"Bobby Lee was drinking a lot that night. I don't think he was paying much attention. He just grabbed a glass and downed it. Then he yanked me out on the dance floor before I could take a drink. I was thankful, to tell the truth. I don't care much for alcohol."

Daddy and the sheriff exchange puzzled looks again. "But that would mean..." Daddy stops.

Sheriff Baines finishes his thought. "It wasn't Bobby Lee they meant to kill."

It takes a moment for the words to sink in. "Who would want to kill me?"

MAMA BEA DRAWS THE brush through my hair, and I feel more at peace than I ever have. It didn't take long for Sheriff Baines to solve his first murder case—if you could call it that. When he searched Bobby Lee's room, he only found one ticket to Kauai. He found the other ticket tucked away in Marcy's diary, where she was good enough to describe in detail their plan to poison me with nicotine. Since I already had a heart condition, my heart giving out wouldn't raise suspicion. After an acceptable grieving period, Bobby Lee would meet Marcy in Kauai to "comfort one another"—with my trust fund. But Bobby Lee drank from my glass, and as it turned out, Marcy wasn't trying to breathe life into Bobby Lee, she was *kissing* him.

Mama Bea says that's what she gets for wanting what someone else has.

I gaze at Mama Bea in the mirror as she finishes braiding my hair. "I'm sorry."

She looks surprised. "For what, child?"

"I thought *you* killed Bobby Lee. Because of what you told me when you killed that copperhead so long ago."

Mama Bea threw back her head and laughed, her hands shaking my shoulders. "Oh, baby girl. Don't you know? The good Lord's been dealin' with snakes for a long, long time. And He got a lot bigger shoes than Mama Bea."

I climb into bed and pull the covers up over me. "I love ya, Mama Bea."

She leans over me and kisses my forehead. "I know ya do, child. And I love you."

FOR MORE INFORMATION about the author, please visit Rebecca Olmstead's website: https://www.rebeccaolmstead.com/

Second Chances Are...Murder: A Vermont Radio Mystery

Nikki Knight

If you're getting married at 103, all anybody should say is *mazeltov*. Everybody at Grandpa Seymour's wedding could agree on that. And also that we didn't need a murder ruining the party.

Everything else? Well...

Let's just say we're not the usual family. For starters, Grandpa Seymour Metz is the grandfather of my ex-husband, and his 92-year-old bride Patsy is my priest pal Maeve's great-aunt. And did I mention that my new fella, the governor of our great state, performed the ceremony?

Oh, and that was all before the moose walked in.

Buckle in, friends, you'll need to keep up.

Here's the short course: my husband and I split after he survived cancer and wanted different (mostly blonde and bodacious) things, right about the same time the big New York City radio station where I worked dropped music for all-sports. I took our daughter, my broken heart and my severance up north and bought WSV, the tiny radio station in Simpson where I'd worked after college.

David, my ex, moved in with his parents and grandfather across the river in Charlestown. And so my new life began. Soon enough, I ran into my old crush, who happened to be governor again. Somewhere in there, Maeve and I decided to fix up Grandpa and Aunt Patsy.

Everyone gets along much better than you might think, because we're all where we belong, and we know what matters most: family.

And how better to celebrate family than the wedding of our two beloved elders?

They had a glorious day for it, with the late-September foliage and clear blue skies we get in Vermont, a perfect backdrop for the classic Victorian charm of the Telescope Inn.

It didn't get off to a great start, though, when the Inn tried to kill the bride and one of the maids, namely me. The new owner, a would-be wedding influencer, was clearly hoping for a big social media splash with this very special event. But probably not that kind of splash.

"Signature Cocktails!" Lucy Brabant announced brightly, waving to a tray as my tween daughter Ryan and I walked into the big Victorian foyer, trailing tulle and glitter, and bearing gifts. The celebrations were starting in very traditional fashion: the ladies dressing the bride and the gents watching the Sox in the Inn library.

"Kiwi Strawberry Fizz!" Lucy proclaimed.

For a second, I just looked at the tray.

I had to say something. I knew Great-Aunt Patsy was allergic. She'd turned down a beautiful fruit compote in a grapefruit shell at a family brunch a couple months ago, and Grandpa Seymour ended up with three of them, because I'm allergic too.

And Lucy Brabant should have known, because that brunch was on the patio right here, and she talked us up, charming Grandpa Seymour and Aunt Patsy into choosing the place for their wedding.

I figured homicide wasn't the plan...just the pretty contrast of pink and green.

Lucy, the granddaughter of the longtime former owners, seemed to be all about the visual. She was wearing a little black shift dress that would not have been out of place in Midtown, with a bright blue blazer, a perfect blonde blowout, and more makeup than even stylish Vermont women use in a year.

"Um, Lucy," I asked, "can we find a different cocktail?"

"Why?" Her voice was higher and more brittle than usual, which was an achievement.

"The bride's allergic to kiwi...and so are some members of the wedding party. Including me."

"Oh." A pout that might have been cute on a six-year-old but was more than annoying on an alleged adult food service professional. "Well, I don't know what else..."

"Bellinis?" I suggested. We'd had them at the bachelorette party, and everyone loved them.

"I guess." She sighed. "Are you sure about the kiwi thing?"

"Unless you want to kill us."

She thought about it.

I didn't imagine it. The wretch actually took a second.

But then a sunny smile. "Well, I suppose that will do. Don't tell anyone, okay?"

"It'll be our little secret."

"She's a piece of work, Ma," my daughter Ryan whispered to me as we headed upstairs.

"Not nice."

Ryan's light green eyes, sharper and savvier than any tween's had a right to be, held mine.

"But true," I admitted.

I picked up a Telescope Inn brochure as we headed for the bridal suite upstairs. The extravagant copy described the many amenities and services, with endorsements from some happy guests.

"If the fireplace poker was used, Buddy's killer was one of the groom's guests" was written on the back.

The shiny new brochure amused me; the Telescope had always been a family business, and known as THE place visiting relatives and the occasional (very occasional) dignitary stayed when in town.

I dropped the brochure in my tote bag and looked back at Lucy. She was marching off to the kitchen with the tray of signature cocktails, all puffed up with irritation. So puffy even the back of her bright blue blazer was tight.

Such an annoyance, to not have to kill a couple of your guests.

I shrugged. From the deepest and most honest depths of my soul: Whatever.

Kiwis, strawberries, and influencer innkeepers were the last thing that mattered right then. We had a bride to dress, and a wedding to celebrate.

The ceremony was everything a second-chance happy ending should be. When the sun began to set, and the breeze swished through the turning leaves, the party prepared to walk onto the patio behind the Inn, the principals and supporting cast all keyed up for the big moment.

Even Lucy Brabant was in the spirit, swapping the snug blue blazer for a pink boyfriend-style one with long sleeves. As we assembled in the hall, I complimented her on the choice of color, and the silver buttons, joking lightly about the long sleeves versus the short ones on the blue jacket, something I always notice because I'm six feet tall and sleeves are never long enough.

Then came showtime.

Out in the golden light, Grandpa Seymour was dapper in his tux, supported by his son Alan and grandson David, my ex. Great-Aunt Patsy glowed, rocking a cream silk and lace gown that recalled Princess Kate, only with less train and more sparkle. Maeve and I floated with a pack of maids in surprisingly attractive pink tulle, dresses somehow just right for even tall, dark-haired me—and my tiny adorable friend. We were led out by Ryan, enjoying her dream come true as a glitter-drenched flower girl.

Not that it was remotely conventional. We began with blessings from Maeve and the rabbi from David's college. Then Governor Will Ten Broeck took over for the legalities.

If anyone besides me noticed that our very handsome blond chief executive sent an adorable shy grin over to the maids as we assembled for the vows, well, that was just part of the fun. Everyone knew that Will and I were together after finding ourselves single and in the same state again, twenty years after we met for the first time. And everyone, even David, was happy for us. Or at least civil enough to keep their mouths shut.

Anyhow, this was Grandpa Seymour and Great-Aunt Patsy's day.

As they stood in front of Will, hand in hand, and promised to love, cherish, and stand by each other for life—a vow that was more than a little bittersweet, considering—there wasn't a dry eye in the house. As they exchanged rings, everyone just surrendered to the sheer joy and magic of the moment.

Finally, Will wrapped up the ceremony:

"So, by the power vested in me by the state of Vermont, it is my great pleasure to pronounce you married."

He beamed at the happy couple.

"This is the part where you kiss."

They did. We cheered.

"And this," Rabbi Sandi Carey said, walking up with a napkin-wrapped bundle, "is where you step on the glass."

She placed it on the patio tile. Grandpa wound up for a good stomp, as Patsy clasped her hands in delight.

BOOM!

"MAZEL TOV!"

And then the moose appeared.

No, that's not a reference to some obscure Vermont wedding custom. It was an actual moose, stalking onto the far end of the patio and gazing at all of us with wide-eyed curiosity.

"Heeeey! Charlemagne!" Grandpa crowed.

Well, the moose is a friend.

Sort of. He lives in the woods near my radio station transmitter, and sometimes we see him around. So he's used to us. And we, of course, just adore him.

Will put a careful hand on Grandpa's arm. "Watch out, Mr. Metz. Remember, it's moose mating season."

Aunt Patsy giggled. "Don't want to get between the big fella and his fun."

Charlemagne turned and loped away toward the woods.

For a moment, it seemed like nothing but a goofy, only-in-Vermont addition to the ceremony. And then, the server walking in with the champagne bucket dropped it, and screamed:

"Oh, good lord—it's blood!"

AT TRADITIONAL JEWISH weddings, the bride and groom are left alone for an hour after the ceremony, to give them a little private time to decompress (or whatever) after all the excitement of getting there. Since Grandpa and Aunt Patsy had planned to observe that tradition anyhow, it was easy enough to just bundle them off with champagne and a promise to let them know what happened.

On any other day, neither one of them would have let us get away with it.

Ryan and Great-Aunt Patsy's tween grandboys were easier: the other parents and I just handed over our phones, and the gaming began. This definitely qualified as a special exemption to the screen time rules.

Within minutes, a couple of state troopers were on the scene, and Major Crimes and the medical examiner were on the way. By then, we knew the blood was from a body a few hundred yards into the woods, a man who appeared to have been shot in the chest as he was approaching the Inn.

Yes, I looked.

I didn't plan on it, but once the old and young were safely settled, I joined most of the rest of the wedding party following the trail of bloody hoofprints into the woods.

The prints stopped at the slumped form of a guy in khakis and a green polo. At least it had been green, before.

Will was at the edge of the scene with his state trooper, Len Fortescue, all the security detail he required most of the time. Both moved protectively toward me.

"What happened?" I asked Len, who was technically the officer in charge of the scene until Major Crimes arrived.

"M.E. will confirm it, but it looks like he took two in the chest and bled out in the bushes. Probably a few hours ago. Nobody heard anything, right?"

"Not while I was here, for sure." I shrugged. "Even in Vermont, we'd notice a couple of gunshots."

"Not necessarily." Will nodded to the patio. "There's a lot of noise associated with setting up an event that big."

"And somebody could have dropped a tray or something to help camouflage the sound, if they were part of it," I agreed.

"Did you know him?" Fortescue asked me.

"I don't think so." I looked over again. The polo had lettering—originally sky blue. "But he's got some kind of connection to the place."

"Why?" Will asked.

"He's wearing a Telescope Inn shirt. Not the current ones." I pointed to the staff milling about behind us. "They switched to the black with white logos when Lucy Brabant took over."

"That's her name?" Fortescue asked. "The lady who's running it?"

"Yes. Granddaughter of the old owners—"

"Jeff! No!"

"NO!"

Two sets of running footsteps followed the cries of anguish.

Well, only the second was a real cry of anguish, almost a howl from a small blonde woman in a blue jacket and black slacks who ran to the victim, only to be caught by a sizeable state trooper. She struggled with him for a moment, finally going limp and just staring as the trooper held her arm.

I couldn't tell if he was holding her—or holding her up.

"What did you do?" A few steps behind came someone I recognized: Lucy Brabant.

"I didn't—" the small woman started, then broke off sobbing in the arms of the trooper.

Fortescue looked to Will with a shrug. "Sorry, Boss."

"You're in charge. And Ms. Jordan can defend me."

As Fortescue waded in, he pointed to the other trooper who was preserving the scene for Major Crimes. "Delorme, you just got promoted to protection detail."

Delorme, a tall woman with dark hair in a tight cop bun and bright brown eyes, gave him a quick smile, then strode over to Will.

While she and Will made acquaintances, I drifted over toward Fortescue.

"All right, Garfield, so what's going on here?" he asked the other trooper.

Garfield, which was a surprisingly appropriate name since he was short, round, and orange-haired, nodded to the women.

"That's my brother Jeff." Lucy's voice had an edge, but she didn't waver.

"My husband!" the blonde woman wailed. "Father of my poor little boys."

"Shut up, Alison!" Now, Lucy's voice cut like a lash. "You should have thought of them before you shot him."

163

"I didn't shoot him." Alison pulled away from Garfield and turned to Fortescue. "I don't know why she'd say that."

"Because you two had a huge fight last night and you threatened to kill him," Lucy said with an almost triumphant toss of her head.

"We always fight. It doesn't mean anything."

"Maybe it did this time, ma'am," Fortescue started.

Alison shook her head.

"And maybe it didn't," he continued.

"But this means something, Sergeant," Garfield said. "Look at her jacket, in the light."

Alison froze.

"Excuse me, ma'am," Fortescue said, leaning close to her. "I'm sorry, but that sure looks like gunpowder. Gunshot residue."

"See? I told you she did it!" Lucy pointed. She seemed more happy that Alison might be the killer than upset by the death.

"I didn't." Alison folded, sobbing.

"Well, ma'am," Fortescue said, "it certainly doesn't look good. You'll need to go with the fellas from Major Crimes and sort it all out."

And look who was just walking across the patio now.

An older white guy and a youngish Asian woman in the simple dark suits that marked them as State Police detectives.

I think, considering everything that led us to this day and this place, that we could be forgiven for being relieved at the fastest solution to a murder ever.

On any other day, my college journalism radar would have been buzzing. Sure, smart money is always on the spouse. But that doesn't mean that it's the only possibility. Or that you're supposed to accept the easy solution.

There was plenty of evidence pointing away from poor Alison. But I, and everyone else involved, just wanted to move past the horror.

I'm not proud of that.

Especially not considering how it all turned out.

After Major Crimes walked Alison out, Lucy tossed her hair like a cat shaking off an unwanted pat.

"Well, we can't let this unpleasantness ruin this magical day!"

Maeve shot me a glance. The same dubious expression that was currently clouding Will's face. Sure, the show must go on, but this woman's brother had just been found dead in a bloody heap not two hundred yards from the Telescope.

And at the hands of the mother of his children, yet.

I walked over to her, figuring that my street cred as the hard luck kid might give me a chance to convince her to take a little grace.

"Lucy," I said, "I'm sure the event will pretty much run on its own from here. You can go look after your brother's kids if you want to."

"Why would I want to do that? They're with a sitter anyhow."

"Oh, okay, well..." That shocked me into backing off. It was almost like she was glad he was gone.

Weird.

She held my gaze a moment too long, and I finally just shrugged.

"I'm sorry," I said. "Of course, everyone deals in their own way. I'm sorry for your loss."

Lucy's nod was gracious, but there was still something off in her affect. "We don't want to keep the happy couple waiting, now. Don't you need to introduce them and start the first dance?"

"Well, now that you mention it..." Of course, I was jocking the reception.

As Lucy swept off to the room where our happy couple had thankfully missed all of the bad stuff, I shrugged and walked over to the DJ booth. Like everything else in this newly renovated place, it was busy and a bit over-the-top. When I'd looked at the space a few days ago, I'd needed some extra time to figure out where everything was. It was fancier than my setup at the station.

This, at least, was fun.

I loaded my first few songs. "Chances Are" for the first dance, followed by some Sinatra and Percy Faith. Classic slow dance stuff to start our newlyweds...with some salsa and other up-tempo stuff to come.

At the ballroom door, Grandpa, his bride on his arm, shot me a big thumbs-up.

From their smiles, it was clear they, at least, had enjoyed their hour of privacy. None of my—or anyone else's—business how they enjoyed it.

I grinned back and picked up the mic.

"Ladies and gentlemen, it is my great, great pleasure to introduce, for the very first time, Mr. and Mrs. Seymour Metz."

The room erupted in cheers as they walked in. I hit the song.

"Now, let's give our happy couple the floor for their first dance, to their song."

A tap on my shoulder as I turned off the mic.

"Can I get a dance later, Jacqueline?" Will asked, using the French pronunciation of my name as an endearment, the way only he did, *Zhak-leen.*

"Last one, maybe." I smiled. "I'm on duty."

"Me too." His smile was shy, and a bit wistful. "I'll think of you while I'm working the room."

"Sounds like a plan."

He bent down for a quick and entirely appropriate kiss on the cheek, lacing fingers with mine for a moment.

"Have fun," I told him. "I know you like this stuff."

The wistful smile gave way to a little-boy grin. "Sure do."

I chuckled to myself as I watched him go. A natural pol, Will might have gone all the way if he had been blessed with as much steel as charisma. These days, a decade after an ugly crash and burn on the national stage, he was perfectly happy with the fact that he wasn't that guy...and so was I.

As Johnny Mathis' glorious voice faded, most of the guests filtered onto the floor. Grandpa and Aunt Patsy mixed it up with all the available and willing relatives. Will took duty spins with my former mother-in-law, and a local lawmaker who's a friend of the family, and then found himself salsa'ing with Aunt Patsy, fox-trotting with one of her pals, and next to Ryan during the constitutionally mandated "Electric Slide." My ex David and his parents were in the line behind them, and everyone was too busy having fun for it to be weird.

Exactly as it should be.

After that, though, everyone was in the mood for a slowdown. I put on "The Way You Look Tonight," and most of the couples returned to their partners, and the singletons to the open bar.

Best way to guarantee a happy wedding: an open bar.

166

Will wasn't interested in free drinks. He worked his way back to the DJ booth and pulled up a chair. All flushed and lit up from dancing, he was even cuter than usual. Okay, so I love the guy.

A waiter set the water I'd asked for beside me. It was dressed up with some nice little lemon and lime peels.

Will motioned to him. "Mind getting me one, too?"

"Sure thing, Gov."

The guy scuffled off.

"Nice job D-J, J-J," Grandpa said with a teasing grin as he and his wife came over.

"Doing my best." I grinned. "You two are definitely showing off the moves."

"Need to get you two on the floor together," Patsy said.

"Maybe later. I'm happy here."

"Company's good anyhow," Will added. "And I needed a break and some water."

"Should have had one of those funny cocktails."

"Well, they tried to kill us with the first ones," I said.

All three stared at me.

"Just kidding," I clarified quickly. Probably not the best joke right now. "There was kiwi in the original signature cocktail."

"So?" Aunt Patsy asked.

"Well, you're dangerously allergic too, right? Remember that brunch right after you two got engaged?"

"No. It's grapefruit I can't have, because of one of my medications." She shrugged. "I always kind of liked kiwi. Cute little things."

"Then..." I thought about it, picking up my new glass of water.

"Don't drink that, Jacqueline." Will's voice was suddenly gravelly.

As I pulled the glass away, I caught a scent, under the sharp citrus peels. Fruity. Tropical. I recognized it from the one time I'd eaten kiwi as a kid. I'd almost ended up in the hospital—my whole mouth swelled up. Nowadays, they'd probably call an ambulance and pump me full of atropine...but where I grew up, back in the day, if you didn't actively keel over, there was no reason to waste the cost of an ER visit.

"It is, isn't it?" he asked, taking the glass. "Fortescue!"

The state trooper, who'd seemed happy enough to return to his usual duties, had been watching the dancers and sipping club soda at arm's length. He was at Will's elbow before he finished the second syllable of his name. "What's wrong, Boss?"

"Somebody just tried to poison Ms. Jordan."

Grandpa Seymour shot me an approving glance at Will's respectful reference to me.

Fortescue took the glass from me.

"There's kiwi in it," I said. "I'm allergic."

"Anybody know that besides close family?" the trooper asked.

"You *are* going to play the chicken dance, aren't you?" Lucy asked, clattering over, puffed up with irritation and oblivious. "There are too many slow songs. You need to keep this party moving, you know."

As Fortescue pulled out his phone, I looked down at her incredibly noisy heels and noticed the pink piping on the vamp. Matching her pink blazer, which had sleeves that hit at exactly the right spot on the wrist bone, instead of the bracelet-length sleeves on the blue jacket she'd worn earlier today.

The same shade of blue as the one the much smaller Alison had been wearing.

Not just the same shade. The same jacket.

We'd all made a terrible mistake.

And more.

"It was you," I said. "And you thought I knew because I saw you in her blue blazer."

"You had to comment on the sleeves, didn't you?"

"I'm six feet tall." I couldn't stop the defensive note in my voice. "I always notice sleeve length."

"Sure you do."

"And you knew I'm allergic to kiwi because of the cocktail this morning."

"Meddling hag that you are," Lucy snapped.

"Hey!" Grandpa shot back. "You don't get to talk to J-J like that—especially in front of my wife."

"Seymour, the cops have got this." Patsy's voice, and the hand she placed on her husband's arm were soothing. Even if she looked just as mad at Lucy as he did.

A muscle flicked in Will's jaw. He was pretty mad too.

That was for later. Right now, we had bigger things to settle with this woman. "Did you really think you could kill your brother, frame his wife, and get away with it?" I asked.

"Why not? Everyone bought it. The spouse is always the best suspect."

"Unless maybe there's somebody else with a better motive." I looked around the ballroom. "Say this place?"

It was a guess, but a good one. Lucy's face flushed.

"I wasn't going to let Jeff's trashy wife and their grubby children ruin my chance at turning this Inn into the showpiece of Vermont," she snapped.

"Won't be your showpiece now," I said.

"It won't be theirs, either." Her prideful tone suggested there was a lot more going on here than event planning. "I still get his share."

"No," Will said, his tone cold slashing steel, "his family will get his share, and probably more. You can't profit from the proceeds of the crime."

"It's in the contract and—"

"Vermont," said its current governor, "has a Son of Sam law. No contract can override it."

"But—but—" sputtered Lucy.

"I signed it," Will said. "I know."

Lucy wilted. "It was for nothing."

"Absolutely nothing." I held her gaze.

Grandpa Seymour patted Fortescue's arm. "Any chance we can dispose of this trash and return to the party?"

"Already called my pals at Major Crimes. Again." He gave Grandpa a grim little smile. "Should have a couple more troopers in the lobby in five."

If it were possible for Lucy to look more miserable, she did.

It took less than one song for the troopers to arrive and one more for them to bag my glass and walk Lucy out. We'd all be hearing from Major Crimes in the morning...or maybe the afternoon, in the case of the newlyweds. Fortescue could—and would—get his pals to give them some room, anyway.

After that, we finally got back to wonderful.

For good.

I started "Chances Are."

Grandpa and Aunt Patsy quickly returned to the floor, swaying together, lost in love and joy. A happy ending after two lifetimes of love and loss, not to mention the horrible events of the day.

"Can the DJ step out for just a moment?" Will asked.

Last song of the evening. Why not?

Maybe we deserve a little happy ending too.

Will led me out to the floor, and pulled me in. "I love this stuff."

"Weddings?"

"Yeah. I think marrying people may be the most fun part of my job."

"Even knowing..." I started, thinking not just of our own marital disasters, but Grandpa and Great-Aunt Patsy, who'd overcome everything to take their chances on whatever forever they got.

"Even then." He pulled me closer, holding me the careful way he does, not like I'm fragile, but like I'm precious. It's pretty great.

"Even with moose and murder plots in the middle of the wedding?" I asked.

"Well, that was a little much."

We shared a laugh.

I rested my head on his shoulder.

"I'd like to step on a glass one of these days, Jacqueline."

"I think we can arrange that."

FOR MORE INFORMATION about the author, please visit Nikki Knight's website: https://kathleenmarplekalb.com/nikki-knight

Wedding Vows & Vipers
Shari Held

I was going to be late! I accelerated, hoping I wouldn't encounter any law enforcement, and pulled up at the Briarwood B&B in Charity close enough to six o'clock to qualify as being on time. I'd hoped to avoid heavy traffic when I'd left Indianapolis, but I had miscalculated. Since when had rush hour started before four?

I was looking forward to catching up with Dora in person and relaxing in a charming Victorian B&B for several days prior to her wedding. It was just what I needed after grading close to seventy-five English Lit term papers in which my college students slaughtered the English language in a myriad of creative ways.

Other than having to squeeze into a one-size-too-small, hot pink maid-of-honor dress, what could go wrong?

I hauled my bag from my lime green Beetle, and met Sarah, the Briarwood proprietor, at the door.

"You must be Casey Kelly," Sarah said, handing me the guestbook to sign. "The other members of the wedding party arrived two days ago. The groom's father and stepmother are on a Caribbean cruise and not expected to arrive until the day before the wedding."

"It was very generous of Mr. Mann to foot the bill for all of us."

Sarah's face lit up. "It certainly was. He reserved the entire B&B for a week. Dora will be so glad you're here. It's lovely when the bride and maid of honor have known one another since grade school. You don't see that often these days."

"To be honest, I haven't seen Dora in years. We gradually grew apart after her parents were killed in a car accident and she moved four states away to live with her aunt and uncle. But we recently became reacquainted on Facebook. She'd already invited me to her wedding, but when her sister's National Guard unit was called up for active duty, Dora asked me to fill in as maid of honor."

Sarah showed me to my room. "As soon as you're settled, come on down and join everyone in the parlor for drinks and hors d'oeuvres. I'll see you there." She left me alone to freshen up in a pleasant, pastel blue room featuring Victorian décor. I ran a comb through my hair, applied some lipstick, and started downstairs.

My Sketchers hadn't yet touched the bottom step of the staircase when I overheard two people engaged in a heated conversation. One of them was Dora.

"I wish you wouldn't leave me alone day and night. We should be having fun, sharing this time with friends and family. Making memories."

"I don't think you understand how much is at stake here. Ace-Cardinal Food Services is headquartered in Charity, and they're expanding—opening operations in Chicago, New York, and LA. If I land that account, I'll be the next VP of Sales for Mann & Associates, for sure. I'm sorry to leave you here alone, but your friend will be here soon, and I'm so close to convincing Ace's executive team to sign on the dotted line. This next meeting could be it. You know I'm only doing this for us."

"Not all for us, Tom. It's mainly for you. When are you going to stop trying to prove yourself? Go on then. Work on that precious account of yours. I'll cover for you one more time with the wedding party. But you'd better be here tomorrow at ten o'clock sharp for the bridal brunch, and for every bridal event from that point on, or you'll regret it. I don't care if Ace has signed the contract or not. You hear?"

"Maybe I should have stayed with Freya. At least *she* understood what my job means to me." Tom slammed the door as he left.

If Dora and Tom thought their conversation was private, they were mistaken. From my vantage point on the stairs, I could see the entrance to the parlor, where they had been standing, the dining room, where Sarah stood in the doorway, and the back door, where a blond guy with a scruffy beard couldn't help but get an earful. Their voices had been loud enough that those inside the parlor might have heard every word as well. This Happy Hour was going to be anything but happy.

I watched as Dora took a few deep breaths and strode into the parlor with a big smile plastered on her face. I tiptoed into the parlor behind her and liberated two flutes of champagne from a tray. Dora would need one. And what was a maid of honor for if not to cater to the needs of the bride? Especially when it appeared the groom was doing a less than stellar job of fulfilling his role.

When Dora saw me, her eyes lit up. She rushed over and hugged me as if I were the last friend she had on earth. This was the Dora I remembered. She pulled me into an alcove, and we sat on a red velvet settee, secluded from the others, to catch up.

"You don't know how happy I am to see you," Dora said. "Everyone else in the wedding party is from Tom's camp. Even my bridesmaid." She nodded toward a plump, plain girl, who looked all of fourteen, holding a plate stacked with appetizers. "That's Megan. Her mother recently married Tom's father. She insisted Megan be a bridesmaid when she found out I didn't have one." She shrugged. "At least Megan's nice."

"Aren't the others nice?"

Dora snatched one of the flutes from my hand and gulped the entire contents. "I don't really know them well. They're okay. Polite. Speak when spoken to. But they're more cliquish than the Rosebuds back in high school. Remember them? I keep getting Death Ray vibes from Freya, Tom's ex. I can't believe she's here, but she came as Larry's plus one. Larry's the best man." She shuddered. "I feel like I've landed in a nest of vipers. And Tom's never here. I'm beginning to wonder if I've made a big mistake." Her bottom lip quivered.

I took Dora's hand. "That's the wedding jitters talking. Everything will be fine. You've got me to lean on now."

I sized up those two as Dora gave me a hug. Freya, a busty redhead, looked like trouble, while Larry was thin with a pensive air about him and a receding hairline he kept touching as if to ensure himself it hadn't disappeared.

Dora collected herself and resumed her conversation in a hushed tone. "Larry works with Tom at Tom's father's company, Mann & Associates.

Freya used to work there, too. The blond guy is Scott, Tom's cousin. Scott also works for the company." She blushed. "I thought you two might hit it off. Wouldn't it be fun if we married cousins?"

I glanced at Scott as he talked on his iPhone, eyebrows scrunched together, fingers forcefully tapping on the chair top. I didn't want to disillusion Dora, but somehow, I thought Scott and I would have as much chance of becoming a couple as I would of winning the Miss Universe contest.

A few minutes later, Scott was off the phone and hunkered down talking with Freya and Larry. I walked over to introduce myself, but stopped short when I overheard their conversation. Scott was complaining about Tom having "an unfair home advantage." Larry told Scott not to worry about Tom—the competition was between the two of them, and Tom wouldn't even have qualified "without Daddy's help."

Freya was every bit as vindictive. "All that matters to Tom is pleasing his father and maintaining a squeaky-clean corporate image. I was good enough for a fling, but I fell short of his idea of the perfect corporate wife. Now he's got what he wants—Dora, the sickening sweet girl next door." She slammed her drink on the table so hard I feared the stem would break.

If these were Tom's friends, I'd hate to bump into his enemies. I hightailed it back to Dora's side.

"Let's see if we can loosen things up a bit," I said, replacing the Classical channel on Sirius XM with the '70s channel for some good old rock and roll. Fifteen minutes later Larry, Freya, and Scott were gone, making it very clear they wanted nothing to do with Dora, Megan, and me.

Dora tried to make excuses for their behavior. But I wasn't buying it. The undercurrent was dark. The tension crackling. I hadn't felt a vibe this sinister since I found a dead body in the restaurant I'd worked at one summer.

TEN O'CLOCK THE NEXT morning we assembled in the dining room for the bridal brunch. Everyone was present except Tom.

Sarah kept Dora distracted, asking questions and commenting on how lovely she looked. And she did. She was a picture perfect, glowing bride-to-be. I hoped Tom would arrive soon and keep her in good spirits.

No such luck. Ten minutes later, he was still missing. So was Dora's smile. I was about to ask Larry if he knew where Tom was, but Dora was one step ahead of me.

"Has anyone seen Tom?" Her voice rose with each syllable as she paced the room. They shook their heads and instinctively backed away.

I'd been chatting with Megan on the other side of the room. But as Dora's maid of honor, I needed to calm her down. Before I could, she brushed me aside and dashed out of the room, yelling, "Where is he? I swear I'm gonna kill him."

I was right behind her as she bolted up the stairs and flung Tom's door open without knocking. Her shriek reached a high note any soprano would be proud of. She backtracked into the hallway, then slid down a wall.

Leaving me staring down at Tom's bludgeoned body.

Blood pooled around his head. His skin was an unflattering purple-ish hue. Having encountered dead bodies before didn't make the experience any easier. Steering clear of his blood, I knelt to feel his pulse. Nothing. Tom was cold, stiff, and dead.

Who could have done this? And why?

I closed the door and joined Dora in the hall as the rest of the wedding party came rushing up the stairs to see what was wrong.

I'd worked with the Indianapolis Metropolitan Police Department on several cases—unofficially, of course. I knew the drill. "Someone call 911 and tell them we've discovered a dead body. No one can go inside. We need to keep the crime scene intact."

I caught Megan's eye. "Megan, let Sarah know what's happened and that we've called for help. The rest of us should gather in the dining room."

Scott helped Dora up and supported her down the stairs. Everyone else, including me, followed.

The white honeycomb paper wedding bells, hot pink crepe paper streamers, and picture of the happy couple on the mantel were cruel reminders of a wedding that would never be. The cloying scent of the showy pink peonies reminded me of a funeral.

Sarah appeared unflappable, as if she found dead bodies in her B&B

every day. Only the trembling of her hands betrayed her concern. "There's water, juice, and fresh coffee on the buffet," she said. "Help yourselves."

I poured a glass of water for Dora who was sitting in a chair, tears streaming down her face. One minute she looked angry. The next, stricken. I stood behind her and rubbed her shoulders. I hoped it helped.

I know it steadied my nerves as I prepared to confront this group. "Please, no talking. The sheriff should arrive soon. He'll want our unbiased impressions. Until then, keep your thoughts to yourself."

Scott challenged my authority. "Who put you in charge? You didn't even know Tom."

I countered, "How many police investigations have you helped solve?"

He opened and closed his mouth, poured a cup of coffee, and plunked into a chair next to Freya and Larry. His hand jerked as he ran his fingers through his hair.

Larry patted Freya's arm with an intensity that made me suspect it was his own nerves that needed soothing. Freya touched her fingers to her face and mouth with no regard for her perfectly applied makeup.

Scott had put his coffee aside and now was talking on his iPhone. He was probably contacting Tom's or his parents. I didn't envy him that job. I crossed over to the beverage table to pour some orange juice, when I overheard a snippet of his conversation and realized he was conducting a business transaction.

Not one of the three offered Dora their condolences. I shook my head. Dora was right. She had landed in a nest of vipers.

Sirens blasted through the quiet and two sheriff cars pulled up.

"That will be Sheriff Craig and Deputy Pyle," Sarah said as she scurried to the front door to let them in. They introduced themselves, then Sheriff Craig tromped upstairs to view the body. Deputy Pyle stayed with us, probably to ensure we wouldn't talk amongst ourselves.

The sheriff returned and lowered his bulky body into a chair. "Walt, go on up and record your initial impressions of the crime scene." Then he took a notepad and pen from his pocket and asked us each to identify ourselves and our relationship to the victim.

He also asked us when we'd last seen Tom alive. For all of us it was yesterday evening when he'd stormed out after his fight with Dora.

"I see. Now, what did each of you do the rest of the evening until this morning at ten?"

Everyone's movements the previous night were mundane. None of us had solid alibis. After Megan, Dora, and I had retired to our respective rooms, Dora had downed some anxiety pills with wine and was out cold. Megan had played a video game on her iPad, and I had revisited some of my favorites in a book on the Romantic poets.

Larry and Freya had gone into town for a pizza, then spent the night together in Larry's room.

Scott had gone into town looking for Tom. When he couldn't find him, he had a couple drinks, chatted up a few girls, came back around midnight, and went to bed.

Sarah had cleaned up, then left for her apartment above the garage around nine.

No one had heard Tom return. Unless he'd brought his murderer back to the B&B with him, someone in this room was most likely the killer.

The sheriff droned on. "Did Mr. Mann have any enemies?"

Dora, Freya, Larry, and Scott all shook their heads.

"Anyone ever threaten Mr. Mann?"

All eyes swerved to Dora.

Freya coughed, then said, "Well, Dora and Tom did have a nasty fight yesterday before he left, and she did threaten to kill Tom when he didn't show up for the breakfast this morning."

The sheriff turned his attention to Dora. "Is that so?"

Dora's skin blanched. "Technically I did say that, but it was...a misunderstanding. I didn't mean it. I was upset. You've heard of bridal jitters. Right?" She looked at the sheriff hopefully. Then bowed her head.

Sarah excused herself to check on the cinnamon rolls in the oven.

"Do you really have to do this now?" I asked the sheriff. "My friend found her fiancé's body minutes ago. She should be resting. Not answering your questions."

Before the sheriff could respond, Deputy Pyle burst into the room with what looked like a bloody fireplace poker, held aloft. At least he was wearing plastic gloves. "Sorry to interrupt, Sheriff, but you want me to put this in an evidence bag and take it to the station now or leave it until the coroner arrives?"

"Dang it, Walt. Didn't they teach you proper procedure for handling evidence at that community college where you received your so-called training? Leave the poker where you found it until it's photographed, documented, and bagged. You could have lost vital evidence by carrying it down here. Now, put it back."

"Sorry, sir," the deputy said, his face turning red as the filigreed poker handle. "This is my first homicide case. I got excited about finding the murder weapon." He turned to go back upstairs.

"Just a minute," Sheriff Craig said. "Where did you find it?"

"The room across the hall from the deceased," the deputy said. "Under the bed."

Dora gasped and her skin turned gray. "That's my room. There was no bloody poker under my bed. I swear."

The sheriff ignored her outburst. "Did you find anything else interesting in her room?"

"A prescription bottle for Xanax. I opened it and looked inside, but it's filled with Bayer aspirin."

The sheriff turned to Dora. "I thought you said you took anxiety medication with some wine and the combination knocked you out for the night?"

Dora twisted her engagement ring and swallowed hard. "I did."

"Then how do you explain the aspirin?"

"I can't."

"More importantly, how do you explain the bloody poker under your bed? The poker that I'm ninety-nine percent sure was the murder weapon."

Dora burst into tears. This situation had gone from bad to worse.

"Miss Green, I'm arresting you on suspicion of the murder of your fiancé, Mr. Thomas Mann." He turned toward his deputy. "Cuff Miss Green, read her her rights, take her to the station, and start processing her. I'll wait to see what the coroner has to say, then I'll come in and we'll interrogate her."

"Casey," Dora wailed as the deputy cuffed her. "Do something. Don't let them put me in jail. Find out who really did this."

"You know I'll do everything I can," I said, sounding more positive than

I was feeling.

The sheriff stood to go upstairs. "That doesn't mean the rest of you are free to go. We'll question Miss Green, examine the collected evidence, and autopsy the victim. Then, we'll likely bring all of you in separately for questioning. Nobody leaves town until I give the all clear. Understood?"

I hugged Megan as we watched the deputy walk Dora to his car. I had just reconnected with her. I wasn't going to let some trigger-happy, small-town sheriff put her in jail for murder when the killer was likely someone in this room who'd set Dora up to take the fall.

ONCE WE WERE ALLOWED to return to our rooms, I took a long, hot shower. I do my best thinking in the shower. Tom's body was cold and stiff when I'd found him. It takes at least eight hours for a body to exhibit rigor mortis in all its limbs. That meant time of death was between half-past six Thursday evening when he left the B&B to two o'clock this morning.

It's possible someone came back to the B&B with him, did the dirty deed, then left undetected—the B&B didn't have security cameras—but for now I was going to assume the killer was one of us.

But who?

Sarah, the proprietor? While she seemingly had no motive, what if Tom's business deal in Charity impacted her B&B in a negative way? It was a long shot. I'd put that thought on the backburner and concentrate on the three people closest to Tom—Scott, Larry, and Freya.

Someone knocked on my door. I opened it, and Megan came in and sat on the bed, rubbing her arms with her hands.

"What are you going to do?" she blurted out, a tear sliding down her cheek. "I didn't know Tom, but he is, er was, my stepbrother. And I don't think Dora did it, do you?"

"No, I don't. Are you okay? Is anyone coming to get you?"

"Mom and Tom's father will arrive as planned. They can't get here any faster. Besides, she said her hands are full helping Tom's father. She told me to stay out of everyone's hair."

Poor Megan. She was left to fend on her own while her mother tended to Tom's father. No doubt he needed consoling, but so did this young girl. Well, I'd do what I could to make the next few days more bearable for her.

I sat on the bed next to her. "How about if you and I get in everyone's hair? Shake things up. You want to help me figure out what really happened?"

Her eyes lit up and she pulled her body upright. "Sure. What can I do?"

"Well, for starters, tell me everything you know about Scott, Larry, and Freya. You've been around them for the past three days now, right?"

She perked up. "I can tell you something about Larry and Freya. They aren't a real couple. I overheard Larry talking on the phone to someone named Bernard. Have you ever heard of a woman named Bernard?" She rolled her eyes. "Larry was saying all kinds of mushy stuff, telling Bernard how much he loved him and how he'd come out of the closet soon, even if it meant he'd have to quit his job and give up the big bucks." She grabbed a pillow and made loud smooching sounds on it, then burst into giggles. Her antics elicited the first smile out of me since Dora was taken in for questioning.

"I certainly didn't expect that. Good job, Megan. That means Larry and Freya probably weren't together all night. There go their alibis. I wonder why Larry feels he has to keep his sexual orientation a secret at work? It's no longer the Dark Ages."

"It is at Mann & Associates. At the dinner table Tom's father rants and raves about how the world is 'going to the dogs.' He doesn't much like powerful women, people of color, LGBTQs, and anyone else that doesn't think or look like him. I don't know what Mom sees in him."

"So, Freya was Larry's cover. That makes sense. But I don't see that Larry had a motive for murder. You said you had something on Freya?"

A smug look spread over Megan's face. "Freya used to date Scott. Scott crushed on her big time. But Tom stole her away, told her he loved her, then dumped her a few months later. That's why she left Mann & Associates. She couldn't stand to see him once he started dating Dora."

That explained those laser-like looks Freya shot at Dora. Jealousy had long been a motive for murder. But wouldn't Freya have killed Dora instead of the man she had once loved? Or had her hurt turned into a desire for revenge? She certainly looked capable of murder. Framing Dora for Tom's murder would be a twofer. And how did Scott feel about Tom taking his girl?

"Anything else?"

"Not much. But I do know all three of the guys—Tom, Larry, and Scott—were competing for the VP position. Each one was assigned an account. Whoever landed theirs first would win."

That gave both Larry and Scott a motive. "You're simply amazing, Megan. That gives me several avenues to investigate."

"Thank you. I hear a lot, you know. No one pays attention to a fat, pimple-faced teen."

"Oh, Megan. No one else sees you like that. You're a lovely, intelligent young woman with a wicked sense of humor. Don't put yourself down." I gave her a hug. "You want to go into town for a late lunch? My treat."

"You bet! I'll meet you downstairs."

We found a quaint country restaurant in downtown Charity offering "all you can eat" meals, with breakfast served all day long. What can I say? When I'm upset, I eat. My cholesterol took a direct hit when I succumbed to that Hoosier staple, biscuits and sausage gravy served with hash browns, three strips of bacon, and two eggs over easy. Megan was in hog heaven as she dived into the fried shrimp and coleslaw. As the waitress delivered our order, our trio of suspects walked in. They were engrossed in conversation and didn't see us.

I couldn't hear what they were saying, but I studied their body language. Larry and Freya had given up any pretense of being a couple. If there had ever been a spark between Scott and Freya, it must have dissipated long ago—at least on Freya's side. I couldn't read Scott well enough to come to a meaningful conclusion.

I wondered what a search of their rooms might reveal.

WHEN WE ARRIVED BACK at the B&B, I was so busy contemplating a snooping mission before the others came back, I nearly stepped on an envelope someone had slipped under the door to my room. The sender cut to the chase: "Don't stick your nose in where it doesn't belong. Or else."

Being threatened doesn't exactly make my day, but at least it confirmed what I'd suspected. The killer was right here in Briarwood B&B. Not exactly a comforting thought, but a motivating one. Should I tell Sheriff Craig about the note? If this had happened in Indianapolis, I would have contacted my friend in the IMPD, but I didn't have much faith in this sheriff. He'd probably accuse me of writing the note to help Dora. I was on the alert. I'd take my chances.

I heard doors open and close. The treacherous trio were back. I'd missed my opportunity to snoop. Instead, I studied the note. It was hand-written in navy ink on cream-colored paper. It was the point on the bar used to cross each T that interested me. All three points ended on the left, suggesting the note's author was left-handed. I thought back to last evening. Freya held her wine glass in her left hand. Both men held theirs in their right hand.

It was time for a conversation with the woman scorned. I tapped on Freya's door. She looked surprised when she opened it and saw me. I waved the envelope in her face. She plastered an amused look on her face.

"I see you found my note."

She wasn't going to refute it was hers. What a cool customer. "I did. Want to explain what it's about?"

"Maybe I'm bored. Maybe I like watching people squirm. Tom sure did when I turned up here with Larry. Or maybe I wanted to see if you're as good as you think you are, little Miss Hotshot Detective." Her eyes glittered with venom.

I smacked my hand with the envelope. "This note sounds like it comes from someone who doesn't want the killer found. Is that because you're Tom's killer?"

"What? No!" She glanced at a painting on the wall, then back to me. "Tom treated me badly. So I wanted a little revenge. To see him sweat when I showed up. That's all."

"And you conned Larry into bringing you?"

She shrugged. "Larry owed me one. I called in the favor. That's all. Watching all the dramatic twists and turns is a bonus." Her smile could freeze water. "I'm not sorry your friend's the top suspect. She took someone who was once mine. I'd say she's getting her just rewards."

Freya opened the door wider and gestured for me to leave. "I'm done talking. I warned you. If I were you, I'd stop detecting before you find something you can't handle."

Back in my room I reflected on what Freya had said and how she'd said it—verbally and non-verbally. Was she guilty or not? I wasn't sure.

My analysis was going nowhere. I plopped on the bed and picked up the Briarwood B&B album on the bedside table. I hadn't paid much attention to the house itself, but as I read through the album's pages I was transported back to the Victorian era—when Charlotte Brontë, George Eliot, Charles Dickens, and Elizabeth Barrett Browning had penned their prose for prosperity. According to the album, the B&B had its share of authentic Victorian wrought iron, from the ornamental fence to the showy front door to the elegant stair railing. The original fireplaces featured marble surrounds with ornate carvings and decorative cast iron inserts. But what caught my attention was the fact that each fireplace had a distinctive set of fireplace tools.

The fireplace poker used to kill Tom could be a clue to his killer.

When everyone was out for dinner, I was going to examine the fireplace tools—in every room, if necessary. The poker that killed Tom most likely came from the set of fireplace tools in his room. But what if it hadn't? And what if it hadn't come from Dora's set either?

EVERYONE GATHERED IN the parlor for Happy Hour. I sipped on a glass of Oliver cabernet sauvignon while I played a game of backgammon with Megan. When the three suspects left, I begged off another game and was glad when Sarah took my place. I made a quick detour to the complimentary office space, grabbed several paper clips, and went to my room. I'd picked interior door locks out of necessity before. A paper clip technique worked for most. I hoped luck would smile on me again. I felt bad about not including Megan, but this could be dangerous. I'd rather risk her ire than her life.

I would search the guys' rooms for two things: their fireplace tool sets and their clothing and shoes. The sheriff and his deputy had supposedly checked, but by that time, they'd already nailed Dora as the suspect. Maybe I could uncover some telltale blood spatter on the killer's clothes.

I searched Larry's room first. Other than revealing a hidden stash of bite-sized Snickers and a penchant for Avenger comics, which he must have brought from home, I found nothing. His fireplace tool set was intact. Everything matched. His clothes were wrinkled, but I didn't detect any suspicious stains. I backed out of Larry's room and ran into Scott.

"You seem to be at the wrong room," he said. "Looking for anything in particular?"

Scott thought I was about to enter Larry's room instead of exiting. "Not at all. Larry's door was ajar, and I closed it for him. That's all." I turned to leave, but Scott blocked the way.

"I think you were about to poke your nose where it shouldn't be."

I noticed he was carrying a gym bag. He must have left the group, come back, gone to his room, and was on his way out again. I shook my head and used my most innocent look on him—the one I used on my dad when he asked if I were faking being sick during junior high. "Excuse me. I'm going to my room now." I moved past him and unlocked my door. Once I heard him leave, I used the paperclip trick on his door and let myself in.

No candy and comic books for Scott. His room was all business, with folders and papers scattered over the desk. I picked up a stray sheet of paper from the floor. It said "If Buddy's killer is a cousin of the bride, the murder weapon starts with the letter P" on the back. That meant nothing to me. But folders labeled with the name of two accounts did stand out—the Claybourne Media Group in Indianapolis and Ace-Cardinal Food Services in Charity. The first one must be the account Scott was assigned, but the Charity-based one was the one assigned to Tom. The one Tom had been working on so hard these last few days. Had Scott been going behind Tom's back, trying to show him up by landing this account as well?

An open, nearly empty Bayer bottle lay on its side on top of his bureau. I'd bet he switched them out with Dora's Xanax to discredit her. What a jerk.

Shoes. Scott had been wearing a nice pair of Cole Hann leather shoes last evening. I'd noticed because they were similar to those worn by a certain Indianapolis detective I know. I found the shoes under Scott's bed.

If I hadn't been searching for evidence, I never would have discovered the faint stains on his shoes I anticipated would be blood. Instead of placing them back under the bed, I put them in plain sight next to the bed where the sheriff might find them.

I fist-pumped, then checked Scott's clothes but found nothing suspect. Could his blood-spattered clothes have been in that gym bag?

Now for the fireplace tools. Scott's tool set was red with a filigreed ornamental design. The same design and color as the poker Deputy Pyle had bagged as evidence. It had been replaced with a green poker with a cross at the top. I'd be willing to bet Tom's fireplace tool set was green—and that it was missing a poker that was now in Scott's room.

This evidence was every bit as damaging as what Sheriff Craig had used to arrest Dora.

I closed Scott's door and hurried to my room to call Sheriff Craig. I informed him I had new information pertaining to the case and asked him to please come ASAP. No siren.

IT WAS ALMOST TIME for Happy Hour once again at Briarwood B&B. Everyone would soon gather in the parlor. I ran downstairs and waited.

Larry and Freya were the first to arrive. Larry left the room to help Sarah bring in the refreshments. Freya became intensely interested in the flower arrangement, actively ignoring me. Thank goodness Megan arrived soon after, giving me someone to talk with. Scott arrived next, looking smug.

That look slid off his face when Sheriff Craig walked through the parlor door.

"I understand you have some new evidence you wanted me to look at," he said to me. "This better be good. My oldest has a baseball game. I don't want to miss it."

Too bad. "Yes, sir. I'd like to bring a couple things to your attention. After I'm done, I think you'll reconsider holding Dora as a suspect in Tom Mann's murder."

Freya, Larry, and Scott looked nervous. Megan flashed me a look that told me she thought I should have shared my info with her.

The sheriff made a show of checking his watch. "Okay. This had better be good. And make it quick."

"Sarah, is it correct that every fireplace in Briarwood B&B has its own unique set of fireplace tools?"

Sarah looked confused. "Well, yes."

"And what color are the fireplace tools in Scott Mann's room?"

"Red. They're the prettiest set in the house. I found those in Williamsburg the summer before I opened the B&B and—"

I had to break in to get to the point. "I see. And what color are the fireplace tools in Tom Mann's room?"

"They're green with a large cross on the handle."

I was on a roll now. Maybe I should have been a lawyer instead of a professor of English Literature. "Sheriff Craig, was the poker Deputy Pyle found in Dora's room the murder weapon?"

"Yes, the coroner said it matched the blow to Mr. Mann's head and the fibers and materials on it were a match to Mr. Mann."

"What color was that poker?"

"It was red." The sheriff slapped his thigh. "I can't believe we didn't think of that."

I threw the sheriff a bone. "It's an easy thing to overlook if you aren't looking for it specifically."

"Poker shmoker," Scott said. "This means nothing. Those fireplace tools could have been mixed up days ago."

Sarah coughed. "But they weren't. I cleaned the rooms yesterday. I would have noticed."

Freya and Larry moved, almost as one, away from Scott.

"Sheriff, I think if you check Scott's room again, you might find other evidence," I said. "Plus, I saw him carrying a duffel bag out of his room earlier today. It might have held blood-spattered clothes."

Scott stood up with such force the elaborately carved chair he'd been sitting in toppled to the floor. "Well, you little...I knew you were trouble when I saw you sneaking around earlier. Sheriff, I demand you arrest her for breaking and entering. How else could she know about my fireplace tools?"

I rushed to speak before the sheriff could respond to Scott's question. "There's a picture of your room in the B&B album featuring the fireplace. I put two and two together from there." I hoped this was a good enough explanation for the sheriff. If he asked me point blank if I had broken into Scott's room, I could be in big trouble.

The sheriff motioned to Scott. "Let's mosey on up to your room, son, and take a look-see. The rest of you stay put."

I crossed my fingers the sheriff would find the shoes where I'd left them—and that the stains were, indeed, Tom's blood.

When Scott and the sheriff returned, Scott was in handcuffs, and the sheriff was carrying the shoes with him.

I spoke up. "Sheriff, does this mean you'll be releasing Dora?"

"Yes, follow me. You can drive her back to the B&B." His cheeks turned a shade of pink I hadn't seen on him before. "Thank you for your assistance, ma'am. We'll be checking for that duffel bag as well."

WITHIN A COUPLE HOURS, Dora and I were back at the B&B. Sheriff Craig called to say they'd found the duffel bag Scott had tossed in a dumpster near the B&B. He gave Larry and Freya the all clear to leave. They took off soon after.

The first thing Dora did was take a bath, then she came down and nibbled on a few goodies Sarah laid out for us. Megan, showing more maturity than most adults, disappeared into her room with two slices of chocolate cheesecake and a pint of Rocky Road, leaving Dora and me to talk.

Sarah opened a bottle of champagne for us. Instead of a wedding, we were celebrating Dora's release from jail.

"I want to sleep for a million years, then wake up to find this was all a nightmare," Dora said. "Wish I still had some Xanax, but this champagne will do." She took a sip. "Why did Scott do this? And why put the blame on me?" Her eyes filled with tears. "Thank you for staying here with me until Tom's parents arrive. What a horrible thing for the Mann family—they are grieving two young men."

That was so typical of Dora. Thinking about someone else's problems when her own were so earth-shattering. "It's tragic, and I'm so sorry you're going through this. As for Scott, I suspect he was tired of Tom getting everything he wanted—first, Freya and potentially the VP position. Scott saw an opportunity and took it. You were the easiest person to blame."

"He failed, though, thanks to you," Dora said.

I gave her a hug. "This only goes to show, it pays to read the B&B literature on your bedside table."

FOR MORE INFORMATION about the author, please visit Shari Held's website: http://www.shariheld.com/

The Bride Wore Death
Barbara Howard

The videographer, Alexander Lee, arrived at the sprawling Blue Ledges estate just as the sun was beginning to set. The soft glow of twilight enveloped the surroundings, casting a romantic hue over the grandeur of the property. He took a moment to appreciate the breathtaking beauty of the estate before unloading his equipment from the van.

He made his way to the designated area, a picturesque garden where the wedding reception would take place. As he set up his cameras and adjusted the tripods, Alexander felt a sense of anticipation. Capturing these precious moments on film was not only his profession, but his passion.

He positioned one camera at the edge of the garden, overlooking the ceremony area, ready to capture the exchange of vows and the bride's radiant entrance. Another camera was placed strategically near the dance floor, ensuring that every twirl and dip would be immortalized in film.

Alexander adjusted the lenses, ensuring that everything was in focus and the lighting was just right. He knew that these videos and photographs would become cherished memories for the couple and their families, a testament to their love and the beauty of their special day.

With his equipment set up, Alexander took a moment to soak in the atmosphere. The fragrant scent of flowers hung in the air, and he marveled at the meticulously manicured gardens that surrounded him. The estate exuded an air of timeless elegance, the perfect backdrop for a wedding celebration.

As the first guests began to arrive, Alexander started to move discreetly, capturing candid shots of the attendees mingling and enjoying the festivities. He took care to document the intricate details - the delicate floral arrangements, the ornate table settings, and the joyous expressions on the faces of the loved ones in attendance.

Throughout the evening, Alexander seamlessly moved around, skillfully capturing every significant moment - the cutting of the cake, the heartfelt speeches, and the emotional first dance. He expertly maneuvered his cameras, knowing that he had the power to preserve these fleeting moments for a lifetime of love. And murder.

MIA GRANT, THE FLORIST, stepped out of her van and gazed up at the sprawling mansion in front of her. She made her way inside and approached the table in the center of the room, where she began to carefully arrange the various bouquets and centerpieces that she had brought with her. She worked quickly and efficiently, the soft rustling of flowers the only sound in the otherwise silent room.

Mia had awakened early on the day of her sister-in-law's wedding. She arrived at the hall before dawn, the quiet of the early morning air punctuated only by the sound of her own footsteps as she unlocked the door.

The ballroom was a vast, open space with soaring ceilings and an abundance of natural light with a towering centerpiece for the main table. Tall, slender branches of cherry blossom and peach blossom trees created a dramatic, eye-catching effect.

In addition to the centerpiece, there were a variety of smaller arrangements to adorn the guest tables, using a mix of flowers in shades of white, cream, and blush pink. Roses, peonies, hydrangeas, and ranunculus created lush, full arrangements that exuded romance and elegance. To enhance the natural beauty of the mansion's gardens, a series of cascading floral installations hung from the ceiling, spilling over with blooms in shades of pink and white that would make the guests feel as though they were in a fairytale garden.

The room was empty, and Mia took a deep breath before setting to work. She moved quietly and efficiently, her fingers deftly arranging bouquets of roses, lilies, and peonies into vases and placing them carefully on tables around the room. She paused every so often to step back and admire her handiwork, a small smile playing at the corners of her mouth.

As she worked, the morning light slowly filtered into the hall, casting a soft glow over everything. Just as she finished placing the last of the centerpieces, the door opened and Candace walked in, her wedding dress trailing behind her. "Mia, it looks amazing!" she exclaimed, her eyes shining with excitement. "Thank you so much for all of your hard work." Candace rushed back down the grand hall to the residence.

As she put the finishing touches on another table setting, she heard the sound of footsteps approaching. She turned to see the groom, Daniel Delaney, walking towards her with a smile on his face.

"Hi, Mia," Daniel said, his eyes taking in the beautiful hall that she had transformed with her exquisite style. "Everything looks incredible."

"Thanks, Danny," Mia replied, her voice low and sultry. "I'm glad you like it."

Daniel shifted nervously, sensing a change in the atmosphere. He felt a sudden flush of heat as she walked towards him, her eyes fixed intently on his own.

"It's funny," Mia said, her voice dropping to a whisper. "I remember when we used to walk through the orchards together late at night back in college."

Daniel froze, his heart racing. He had always been attracted to Mia. Now, with her so close, he found it hard to resist her.

"It won't be long but for now—" Daniel stammered, trying to maintain his composure.

Mia chuckled, her voice like music in his ears. "Relax, Danny," she said, her eyes twinkling mischievously. "I'm just having a little fun with you. I know you're *almost* married now, and it's been a long time since college. Candace won you fair and square, I suppose."

"Give me a little time," Daniel whispered, almost pleading but she turned away from him.

"Anyway," Mia said, regaining her composure. "I'm glad you like the flowers."

Daniel's gaze softened, and he took a step closer to her. "Yes, I remember. We had some incredible moments, didn't we? It's strange to think how much has changed since then."

Mia nodded, her fingers delicately arranging a spray of roses. "Life has a way of taking unexpected turns."

Their eyes locked, and for a fleeting second, the weight of their shared history hung in the air between them. The energy crackled with unspoken words and emotions.

But just as quickly as it came, the moment passed. Daniel glanced down at his watch, a look of regret crossing his face.

"I should get going," he said, his voice tinged with disappointment. "Candace will be wondering where I am."

Mia nodded. "Of course. She's a lucky woman, Danny." She watched him leave the hall, her gaze lingering until the trace of his shadow had disappeared.

SHE REFOCUSED HER THOUGHTS and returned to her worktable, surrounded by an array of colorful blooms. She had set aside some of the prettiest flowers for her little girl, Lily, who stood beside her, eagerly watching as her mother arranged them into a lovely bouquet.

"Can I help, Mommy?" Lily asked, her big brown eyes shining with excitement.

"Of course, my love," Mia replied with a warm smile. "I have something special for you to make - a flower crown to wear at your aunt's wedding."

Lily's face lit up with joy as she clapped her hands. Mia guided her daughter's small fingers to select the right flowers and showed her how to carefully weave them together using thin wire. As they worked, Mia felt a sense of pride in her daughter's budding talent. Lily had a natural eye for color and design, and her flower crown was shaping up to be a work of art. But as they neared the end of their project, Mia noticed that one of the flowers was missing - a delicate white rose that she had set aside for the crown's centerpiece. She searched through her pile of blooms, but it was nowhere to be found.

"Lily, did you see a white rose anywhere?" Mia asked, her tone turning serious.

Her daughter shook her head, her eyes filling with concern. "No, Mommy. I didn't touch it, I promise."

Mia's mind raced as she realized the implications of the missing flower. The wedding was only a few hours away, and the flower crown was a crucial part of Lily's role as the flower girl. She took a deep breath and tried to calm her nerves. "It's okay, sweetie. Let's finish up the crown with the flowers we have, and I'll go and see if I can find another white rose somewhere else."

Lily beamed with pride as she watched her mother place the flower crown atop her head, the delicate blooms perfectly framing her face. "Mommy, I want to make something for Aunt Candace."

"Of course, sweetheart," Mia said, preoccupied with searching through her supplies for the perfect white rose. "But do not touch my flowers. Go into one of the gardens and pick something nice, but don't go too far."

"Okay," Lily said cheerfully and raced outside, bumping into Dr. Grace Wilson who was laboring with a set of pruners against a nearby shrub who patted the little girl on the cheek and sent her along.

The sun bathed the sprawling gardens in a golden hue, casting long shadows across the vibrant blooms. Lily's steps skipped lightly as she approached the groundskeeper, Liam Hawthorne. Dressed in weathered overalls and a worn hat, his hands calloused from years of toiling with the earth, he glanced up, his eyes twinkling with gentle warmth. "Ah, Miss Lily, a fine day for a garden adventure, don't you think?"

Lily nodded eagerly, her small hand clutching a wicker basket. "Mr. Liam, I want to make something special for my Aunt Candace. A necklace made of flowers. Will you help me find the most beautiful ones?"

A smile tugged at the corners of his lips. "A splendid idea, Miss Lily. You are free to embark on a treasure hunt, seeking the most exquisite blossoms this garden has to offer. Take whatever your heart desires." He smiled and waved her off toward the rows of colorful blooms.

AFTER THE CEREMONY, as the guests began to file into the reception hall, Lily spotted Candace standing alone in the corner of the room, looking pensive.

Without a second thought, she ran up to the bride and tugged on her dress. "Aunt Candace! I made you something!"

Candace looked down and smiled as Lily held up a delicate flower necklace, crafted from some of the same blooms that had adorned her crown. The petals were woven together with thin wire, forming a delicate and intricate design that shimmered in the light. Her eyes widened in surprise as she accepted the necklace, her fingers tracing the smooth petals, then draped it around her neck. "Oh my goodness, Lily. This is beautiful." Her niece smiled and skipped away to join the other children at a nearby table.

Mia re-entered the hall after stowing away her supplies and noticed Daniel wearing a scowl and knew immediately that something was amiss. She approached him while Candace was talking with Ava Johnson, the executive housekeeper.

"Mia, I need to talk to you," Daniel said, his voice low and urgent. "I'm having a problem with Liam and Ava. I wanted to fire them, but Candace won't let me. She said it wouldn't be fair to let them go right before the wedding. So, I've waited but now—" He looked over his shoulder. "I need to take control around here."

"I understand your frustration, Danny," Mia said, placing a gentle hand on his shoulder. "But perhaps it would be best to wait until after *everything* is over. Let this be a joyous occasion for Candace, and we don't want any unnecessary drama."

Daniel nodded, relieved to have someone to confide in. He trusted Mia implicitly, knowing that she had a way of calming his nerves and offering sound advice.

"You're right," he said, a hint of a smile creeping onto his face. "I'll wait a little longer. I just needed to get it off my chest."

"I'm here for you, Danny," Mia said, her voice soft and reassuring. "Whatever you need, just let me know."

As the weight of the situation settled on Mia's shoulders, she understood the delicate dance Daniel was forced to perform. Balancing the desire for perfection with the need to preserve harmony and peace during the wedding day was a challenging tightrope to walk.

Mia continued, "But perhaps there's an alternative solution. Would it be possible to express your concerns to the estate's trustees, allowing them to address the issues discreetly without disrupting the relationship between the siblings?"

"That's a thought." Daniel perked up. "Your husband and my wife have enough acrimony between them after their father left Stephen out of the will. How are things with you two?"

"You know Stephen." Mia rolled her eyes. "He's like a toddler most days. Trying to keep up with each mess he makes is exhausting. The plan for controlling his gambling is working out perfectly. Thank you for that."

"You're welcome," Daniel said with a little smile. "Anything for you."

THE GRAND HALL EXUDED an air of anticipation, the soft glow of candlelight flickering against the walls adorned with delicate floral arrangements. Amidst the elegant setting, the bride, Candace, stood in her resplendent gown, her hands trembling with nerves. Her heart raced, and a flurry of anxious thoughts swirled within her mind. It was her wedding day, a day filled with joy and celebration, yet her inner turmoil threatened to overshadow the momentous occasion.

As the final touch-ups were applied to her hair and makeup for the final photoshoot, her eyes darted around the room, seeking solace amidst the chaos. Her gaze fell upon a small tray of mints, strategically placed nearby. A wistful sigh escaped her lips, for she had recently quit smoking, and the habit of putting things in her mouth to soothe the cravings still lingered.

Her fingers twitched, yearning for the comfort of a cigarette. The familiar ritual of lighting up and inhaling the smoke had been a source of solace during moments of stress and anxiety. She still had nightmares from seeing the crash photos of her parents' private jet over Honduras and the months of their suffering. But on this momentous day, she had resolved to quit reaching for good, for the sake of her health and to start her new life smoke-free.

Candace glanced around, her eyes catching the gaze once again of her best friend and employee, Ava, who stood nearby, her expression filled with concern.

Ava, attuned to her struggle, approached with gentle steps. "Miss Candace, are you okay?"

Candace's trembling hand reached for the mint tray, her fingertips hovering hesitantly above the collection of colorful candies. Her voice quivered as she confessed, "I'm so nervous, Ava. I've been craving a cigarette, and I don't know how to cope with these jitters."

Ava's eyes softened with empathy as she took Candace's hands into her own. "I understand. It's natural to feel anxious on your wedding day. But remember why you quit smoking in the first place, for your health and the future you want to build with your new husband."

Ava gently squeezed her hands, offering words of encouragement. "You're strong, Miss Candace. You've made it this far. Let's find a healthier way to soothe those cravings, something that won't compromise your progress."

Candace nodded, tears glistening in her eyes as she relinquished her grasp on the mints. "You're right, Ava. I don't want to give in. I want to embrace this new chapter of my life with Daniel without the chains of nicotine addiction."

Ava wrapped an arm around Candace's trembling shoulders, guiding her towards the ornate balcony overlooking the picturesque garden. Together, they took a deep breath, allowing the soothing breeze to wash over them.

Candace closed her eyes, picturing Daniel's loving smile for her at the end of the aisle during the wedding ceremony. Reliving the moment when she said, "I do." She inhaled the fresh, fragrant air. She turned to Ava, gratitude shining through her teary eyes. "Thank you, Ava. I couldn't have done this without you."

Ava embraced her, holding her tight. "You're stronger than you realize, Miss Candace. Today marks a new beginning, not just in your marriage but in your journey towards a healthier, happier life." She hugged her again, then returned to her duties overseeing the caterers and uniformed wait staff.

Candace walked inside and took a detour into her late father's study. She studied his portrait of Roman Grant above the fireplace and wondered what he would have thought of her new husband. She was nothing like her father but hoped to live up to the responsibility that he placed on her shoulders as the only heir to his fortune. Suddenly, she spotted a small object on the ground at the edge of the mantel. It was a small, silver cigarette case. Her eyes widened with temptation. Without thinking, she leaned over and picked it up, running her fingers over the smooth surface.

Before she knew it, she had opened the case, revealing two slim cigarettes nestled inside. Her heart raced with excitement. She knew she shouldn't smoke, especially not on her wedding day, but the craving was too strong to ignore. She slipped one of the cigarettes out of the case and put it to her lips, lighting it with the candle on the mantel.

The familiar taste of smoke filled her mouth, and she felt a sense of relief wash over her. She took a deep drag, inhaling the smoke deeply. But her moment of peace was short-lived. Just as she was about to take another puff, she heard a loud gasp.

She turned to see Daniel standing in the doorway, his face contorted with anger. "Candace, how dare you lie to me. You told me that you gave up smoking," Daniel said, his voice dripping with disgust. "What else are you keeping from me?"

Candace froze, her face turning red with embarrassment. "Nothing, I swear." She tossed the cigarette into the fireplace and chased after Daniel, who had stormed out of the room. As she rushed back toward the residence, her brother Stephen cornered her at the end of the hall.

"Isn't it a beautiful day for my wedding?" Candace beamed. "Everything has been perfect. The weather. The food. The music."

"Really?" Stephen huffed. "I can't believe how much money you're wasting on this monstrosity."

"Stephen, why are you so—"

"You are responsible for Blue Ledges. *Every-thing*. Do you have any idea of how much money it takes to manage an estate of this size? The maintenance of the facilities, the grounds, the staff, the taxes. Not to mention the social commitments. The handouts this community *expects* from the Grant Foundation for all of their pet projects. We're at the top of the donors list for every fundraiser across Varset County." He shook his head in disgust. "Good grief, Candace. Snap out of this fairytale idea of life."

"Stephen, this is not the time or the day to get into this."

"Oh, it's exactly the time, little sister. Our parents would have never approved of you throwing such a lavish, garish wedding and throwing open the gates of Blue Ledges for the kind of people on your guest list. They must be rolling over in their graves. To put you in charge of our family's finances, the Grant legacy, was the biggest mistake of their lives."

"Stephen, please." Candace took a deep breath. "Just stop."

"Fine, we'll talk about this later."

"Okay, great. Thank you." She pressed past him. "I have to go and find Daniel. We got married today, remember?"

Candace found her husband in the main hall mingling with the guests. She wrapped her arm in his and looked into his eyes. "Come on, my love. This is the most important day of our lives." Daniel's countenance softened. He took her hand and led her onto the dance floor.

The wedding reception was in full swing, the ballroom a sea of laughter, music, and dancing. Candace looked radiant, her smile bright and infectious as she twirled around the dance floor with her new husband.

But as the night wore on, something seemed off. Her smile faltered, and she stumbled on the dance floor, her hand flying to her chest as she gasped for air. Daniel caught her just in time, but her face had turned pale, her eyes wide with fear.

The guests gathered around them, concern etched on their faces, as Candace collapsed to the floor, her breathing labored and shallow. The music ground to a halt, the joyous celebration suddenly transformed into a scene of chaos and confusion.

Officer Ryan had just arrived at the wedding reception to bolster the security on the estate grounds when he heard a commotion coming from the dance floor. He pushed his way through the crowd of guests, his eyes scanning the room for any sign of trouble.

Suddenly, he spotted the bride lying on the floor. Her husband was beside her, his face twisted with fear and grief. He quickly knelt beside Candace, his fingers searching for a pulse. But it was too late. Her body had gone still, her eyes staring blankly up at the ceiling.

The guests gathered around them, their faces a mask of horror and disbelief. As the paramedics arrived on the scene, Officer Ryan worked to calm the crowd, his heart heavy with sympathy for the grieving husband, who was inconsolable, his body shaking with sobs.

"I need everyone to step into the adjacent courtyard but do not leave the grounds until we release you," he shouted to the crowd. "I'll need a statement from each of you. So be prepared. This is going to be a long night."

DETECTIVE JAMES ANDERSON stepped into the opulent foyer of the grand estate, his eyes scanning the surroundings as he awaited the arrival of the security manager, Robert Matthews. The air hung heavy with an unspoken sorrow, the lingering presence of a tragic event that had unfolded just days ago. As footsteps approached, he turned to see a middle-aged man with a grave expression making his way towards him.

"Mr. Matthews, I presume?" Anderson extended a hand in greeting, his voice laced with a professional tone.

"Yes, Detective Anderson. I'm the security manager," Robert replied, his voice drenched with sadness.

"I understand this is a difficult time for everyone involved. My condolences for the loss of Mrs. Candace Delaney. Officer Ryan shared details regarding the terrible incident. I've been assigned to investigate the circumstances surrounding her death."

Robert's eyes flickered with a mix of apprehension and a desire for justice. "Anything I can do to assist, Detective. I want to find out what happened."

"Thank you, Mr. Matthews. I'd like to review the security footage from the day of the incident. I believe it may hold crucial information that can aid our investigation," he explained, his voice steady as he conveyed his intentions.

Robert nodded, his gaze resolute. "Of course, Detective. I can give you access to the security room. Please follow me."

They proceeded through the corridors. As they reached the security room, a bank of monitors flickered with images capturing moments from within the estate. Anderson took a seat before the central console, his eyes scanning the multitude of screens.

"Can you bring up the footage from the wedding day, starting from the early morning?" James requested, his voice focused.

Robert operated the controls, skillfully navigating the system until the desired timeline appeared before them. The screens split into multiple views, capturing different angles of the estate's grounds and interior spaces.

The detective leaned forward, studying the events leading up to the tragic incident. He meticulously observed the comings and goings of staff, guests, and the victim herself, searching for any peculiarities, anomalies, or signs of foul play. Every frame was scrutinized, every minute detail noted, as the detective sought the truth hidden within the shadows of the video feeds.

Hours slipped away as Anderson meticulously examined the footage, pausing, rewinding, and jotting down observations. The room was filled with a tense silence, broken only by the soft hum of the surveillance system and occasional exchanges between the two men.

The detective's eyes were glued to the screen, searching for any clues that might reveal what had happened. The footage showed the bride getting ready in her private chambers, surrounded by her bridesmaids. Everything seemed normal, until—

Anderson leaned forward, his gaze sharpening. "Can you zoom in on that?"

The security manager complied, and the detective could now make out a woman's figure approaching the bride.

"Pause that," he exclaimed. "Is there audio?"

"Yes," Robert said and ran the playback with sound.

The bride was sitting gracefully next to a small table on the balcony of the master suite.

"Candace," Emily, the maid of honor, began, her voice laced with concern. "I have to say something, and I hope you'll listen."

"What is it, Emily? You know you can speak freely."

"I can't help but wonder if this marriage is truly right for you. I mean, he's from a modest background, and you come from a wealthy family. It just seems like such a vast divide."

"I understand your concern, Emily. But you have to believe me when I say that I have never felt more loved and accepted than I do with him. Daniel sees me for who I am, not for the money or the status."

"But Candace, the wealth you bring to the table—it's substantial. Can you truly be sure that Daniel isn't swayed by it?"

"Emily, I've known Daniel for years. We met long before he even knew the extent of my family's fortune. He fell in love with me, not my bank account. If anything, my wealth has been a challenge for him, one that he's embraced wholeheartedly."

"I suppose it's just hard for me to grasp, Candace. But if you truly believe in this love, then I'll stand by you."

"Thank you, Emily. Your support means the world to me. Daniel and I have faced doubts and obstacles, but together, we've grown stronger. I'm entering this marriage with open eyes and an open heart."

James jotted down some notes, then motioned for Robert to continue showing more video of the master suite balcony.

"Zoom in on that, please." He studied the screen, rewinding and replaying the footage until he was sure of what he had seen. "This woman, do you know who she is?"

The security manager nodded. "Yes, I believe so. She's a member of the staff. I can give you a list of employees and guests who were on the grounds on the day of the wedding, if you need it."

"Yes and the contact information for the videographer." The detective frowned, his mind racing with possibilities. "What have you got from the rear of the hall?"

"There's an outside camera near the rear door."

"Play it."

Outside of the ballroom, the brother of the bride, Stephen, and his wife, Mia, were having a heated argument. Stephen was pacing back and forth, his face flushed with anger, while Mia stood with her arms crossed, her expression cold and unforgiving.

> "You promised me you would stop gambling," Mia said. "But here we are, on your sister's wedding day, and you're still knee-deep in debt even after your sister pays me for all of the arrangements and decorating. Do you know how hard I had to work today while knowing that we won't break even? How could you do this to us?"

> Stephen shot her a withering glare. "It's not like I want to be in debt," he snapped. "Things have been tight lately, and I thought I could win big and get us out of this mess."

> Mia scoffed. "And how's that working out for you?"

> They both froze, then ran out of the frame.

The detective turned to Robert as the video ended. "What happened?"

"That's when they found Miss Candace, I mean Mrs. Delaney," Robert said. "She was—"

Detective Anderson stood up and put away his notebook. "I need you to make a copy of this segment of footage for me as soon as possible." He thanked the security manager and assured him that he could find his own way out of the house. The solo walk through the courtyard would help clear his thoughts. There were several key individuals that he needed to question, and one was sitting in plain sight.

The detective set his gaze on the grief-stricken groom, who sat slumped in an adirondack chair. The air was heavy with a mix of sorrow and suspicion as the detective took the seat opposite him.

"Mr. Delaney, I understand this is an incredibly difficult time for you," Detective Anderson said, his voice steady yet empathetic. "But I need to ask you a few questions regarding the tragic incident that occurred at your wedding reception. Can you please provide me with your contact information so that we can arrange a time to meet?"

Daniel nodded, his eyes filled with sadness and confusion. He reached into his pocket and retrieved a business card, handing it to the detective. As he did, a second business card slipped from his grasp and fluttered to the ground. Detective Anderson swiftly bent down, retrieving the fallen card. His eyes briefly scanned the information on the back, and a flicker of surprise crossed his face. "If the knife is the murder weapon, Buddy's killer's last name is the same as his own." He maintained his composure, however, as he handed the second business card back to Daniel.

"Thank you, Mr. Delaney," the detective said, his voice masking the curiosity within. "I appreciate your cooperation."

Daniel offered a weak smile, his hands trembling slightly. "Of course, Detective. Anything to help find out what happened to Candace."

Anderson returned the smile, his mind swirling with questions, but he would tread cautiously. He had learned long ago that jumping to conclusions too quickly could lead to grave mistakes. The mysterious second business card, although seemingly innocuous, added another layer of intrigue to the investigation.

BACK AT THE VARSET County Police Department, the detective leaned back in his chair, his gaze fixed on the evidence board adorned with photographs, newspaper clippings, and strings connecting various suspects. The investigation into the mysterious events surrounding the wedding had taken an unexpected turn. As he studied the board, a series of financial documents caught his eye. The figures hinted at a secret business venture, one that involved the groom, Daniel, and a familiar face. The wedding florist, Mia. Intrigued, he delved deeper into their backgrounds, searching for any link that could explain their connection beyond the wedding. Hours of tireless investigation led him to a hidden online exchange, a private chatroom where they communicated covertly. He accessed the chat logs, his heart pounding with anticipation as he scrolled through the messages and read the cryptic conversations between them. They spoke in code, using aliases and carefully chosen phrases to conceal their true intentions. The truth unfolded before him, the groom and the florist had crafted their plan.

"I can't wait for our new venture," Mia's message read. "Our dreams are finally coming true, and we can leave Varset behind us."

Detective Anderson's mind raced, connecting the dots with newfound clarity. Daniel and Mia had orchestrated the marriage as a mere façade, while secretly plotting to meet abroad and establish their own international import/export business, leaving the unsuspecting bride in the dust. He reached for a photograph, a picture of Candace, radiant in her bridal gown. Her joyous celebration had been nothing more than a smokescreen for the groom's ulterior motives, and the florist had been his willing accomplice. All along Delaney had been planning their escape, a new life together without his bride.

The emails detailed a business venture, a secret enterprise that they had established behind her back. It was to be their ticket to freedom, to a life of wealth and prosperity. They had made arrangements to meet in a foreign country with some unscrupulous suppliers less than a month after the wedding. Passports and airline tickets were already secured. With this newfound knowledge, Detective Anderson had another layer to add to the intricate tapestry of the case.

He picked up the phone, ready to summon Daniel and Mia for questioning. It was time to confront them with the evidence and force them to answer for their actions. His gaze fell upon a photograph, a snapshot of the groom, Daniel, and the wedding florist, Mia, engaged in a seemingly innocent conversation during the reception. However, he had learned that their connection ran much deeper than a professional relationship.

With the evidence before him, Detective Anderson knew he had stumbled upon a motive, a motive fueled by greed, betrayal, and a desire to leave their spouses and rekindle their relationship. Infidelity, yes. But murder?

He put the phone back down and spent several more hours meticulously reviewing the video recordings from Alexander Lee, searching for any clues that could shed light on the tragic events of that fateful evening. As the footage played out before him, a particular moment caught his attention, causing him to lean forward, his focus honing in on the nervous bride.

On the screen, Candace appeared visibly tense, her fingers fidgeting as she glanced around anxiously. Detective Anderson observed her subtle movements, noting the telltale signs of a deep-seated nervousness. Her gaze shifted to her necklace.

Curiosity piqued, he watched intently as Candace reached for the necklace, delicately twirling it between her fingers. Her actions betrayed a familiar habit, one driven by anxiety and longing. The detective's brow furrowed as he contemplated the significance of her action. Could it be a mere nervous tic, a habitual gesture in times of stress? Or was there something more to it? He rewound the footage, replaying the moment several times, his mind searching for answers.

Finally, he saw something that caught his attention. It was the bride, looking nervous and fidgety. She glanced around the room before taking her necklace and twirling it between her fingers. Then, she put it in her mouth, pressing it against her lips. He rewound the footage and watched it again. He noticed that the bride seemed to be struggling to breathe, her chest heaving as she tried to inhale.

Then, she collapsed to the floor.

The detective leaned forward in his seat, his heart racing. He knew that he had found a crucial piece of evidence. He quickly made a note of the timestamp of the incident and called the lab to ask them to analyze the necklace for any trace of poison.

As he hung up the phone, he couldn't help but wonder who could have wanted the bride dead, and why they would choose such a sinister way to do it.

DETECTIVE ANDERSON stood in the cluttered office of Dr. Grace Wilson, the renowned botanist known for her expertise in toxicology, who also served as the Community Beautification League Captain for Varset

County which included Blue Ledges. She had been on the grounds on the day of the wedding. However, not as an invited guest. The room was filled with an assortment of plant specimens, books, and scientific equipment, creating an atmosphere of knowledge and intrigue. The detective needed her assistance in solving a puzzling case, and he knew Dr. Wilson's expertise would shed light on a critical piece of evidence.

"Dr. Wilson," Detective Anderson began, his voice laced with a sense of urgency. "I have a crucial question for you regarding a necklace worn by the victim at the time of her death."

Dr. Wilson adjusted her glasses and looked up from her desk, her eyes gleaming with curiosity. "Please, Detective, ask me whatever you need to know. But I must say, I'm no expert on jewelry. If you need a gemologist, I have a colleague that I can refer you to."

The detective reached into his pocket, retrieving a small plastic bag. Carefully, he placed it on Dr. Wilson's desk, revealing a cluster of red seed pods resting inside.

"These seed pods were found on the victim's necklace," he explained, his gaze fixed on Dr. Wilson's face. "I need to know if they contain any poisonous properties, specifically if they can cause harm to a person."

Dr. Wilson donned a pair of gloves, her hands expertly examining the seed pods. Her gaze was focused and analytical, her mind already analyzing the possible outcomes.

After a few moments of intense scrutiny, Dr. Wilson looked up at him, her voice measured and authoritative. "Detective, these seed pods belong to the Abrus Precatorius plant, commonly known as the Rosary Pea. They are indeed poisonous."

Detective Anderson leaned forward, his interest piqued. "Can you clarify, Dr. Wilson? How dangerous are these seed pods?"

Dr. Wilson adjusted her glasses, her tone informative yet cautious. "The Rosary Pea contains a toxic substance known as abrin, which can cause severe harm if ingested. However, the concentration of abrin in these particular seed pods appears to be relatively low. It would likely cause discomfort, but not enough to result in death."

A sense of relief washed over him, knowing that the seed pods were not lethal. However, the realization of foul play still lingered.

"Dr. Wilson," Anderson pressed further, his gaze unwavering, "is it possible to extract abrin from these seed pods and administer it in a concentrated form?"

Dr. Wilson nodded, her expression somber. "Yes, Detective. Abrin can be extracted and purified to create a highly potent toxin. In concentrated amounts, it becomes a lethal weapon."

The seed pods were not directly responsible for the victim's death, but they hinted at a calculated attempt to cause harm, the detective surmised.

"Thank you, Dr. Wilson," Detective Anderson said, his gratitude evident. "Your expertise has shed light on a crucial aspect of this case. It seems someone may have intended to cause harm but stopped short of taking a life."

Dr. Wilson offered a solemn nod, fully aware of the weight of her revelation.

"Detective, please let me know if there's anything else I can do to assist in your investigation. Finding the truth is of utmost importance."

As Detective Anderson left the botanist's office, his mind buzzed with newfound clarity. The seed pods, once enigmatic, now held a vital clue. He was one step closer to unraveling the web of deception that shrouded the victim's death, determined to bring justice to those responsible.

THE SOMBER ATMOSPHERE of the study hung heavy as the three individuals anxiously awaited the reading of the late bride's will. Daniel, the bereaved husband, sat with clenched fists, his eyes red-rimmed with grief. Beside him, his brother-in-law, Stephen, offered a supportive presence, though his brow furrowed with concern at the presence of Detective James Anderson. Across the table seated under the portrait of Roman Grant, the lawyer, Jonathan Collins, cleared his throat and began.

"Ladies and gentlemen, we are gathered here today to execute the last will and testament of the late Mrs. Candace Grant Delaney." Mr. Collins's voice resonated with a touch of formality, emphasizing the gravity of the occasion. He opened the portfolio and revealed the document before him, adjusting his glasses to read the contents.

"To my beloved husband, Daniel Delaney, I leave my heartfelt love and cherished memories, but regretfully, I have not left any financial bequest."

A mixture of surprise and confusion flickered across Daniel's face, his gaze searching for answers in the lawyer's eyes. "But how is that possible? Candace and I shared everything. She wouldn't have excluded me from her will."

Mr. Collins raised a hand, his tone measured and compassionate. "Please, allow me to continue. Mrs. Delaney had her reasons, and they are outlined in the will."

The lawyer's voice resumed, now carrying a weight that seemed to increase with each passing word. "To my dear brother Stephen Grant and his wife, Mia, I also must inform you that no financial bequest has been allocated to either of you."

Stephen's jaw dropped; his astonishment mirrored by Mia. "But Candace was my sister. My *only* sibling. I am the rightful heir of the estate. This is madness. Why would she exclude us like this?"

Mr. Collins's gaze met Daniel's brimming with empathy. "Mrs. Delaney's intentions are further revealed in the subsequent clause. She has chosen to bestow her entire estate, including her financial assets and the ownership of this grand estate, to the one person who has remained by her side, faithfully caring for her and attending to her needs. She has left everything to the executive housekeeper, Ms. Ava Johnson."

A gasp escaped Mia's lips, her hand instinctively reaching for her husband's arm. "Ava? But she's the *maid*. Why would she receive everything?" Stephen's brows furrowed, his disbelief mirrored in his wife's eyes. "This cannot be true!"

Mr. Collins continued, his voice laden with the weight of the truth. "Mrs. Delaney believed that Ms. Johnson exhibited unwavering loyalty and devotion, tending to the needs of her parents during their final days after the plane crash in Honduras. Mrs. Delaney recognized the invaluable service Ms. Johnson provided, and thus, she rewarded her with her entire estate."

Stephen's hands clenched into fists, his voice trembling with a mix of anger and grief. "How could Candace do this? We are her family! We deserve to inherit what is rightfully ours!"

Mr. Collins raised a hand, his tone firm yet compassionate. "I understand your pain and disappointment, Mr. Grant. However, it is within Mrs. Delaney's legal rights to distribute her estate as she saw fit. Her wishes were expressed clearly in this will, and it is my duty as her attorney to execute them accordingly."

Mia's voice quivered as she confronted the reality before her. "What about us? What will become of our future?"

Silence enveloped the room, broken only by the muffled sounds of disbelief. Daniel struggled to find his voice, his emotions conflicting within him. "This changes everything," he murmured under his breath. "Blue Ledges belongs to *her*?" He stared at Ava with confusion and growing contempt.

Mr. Collins sighed, his gaze softening with empathy. "It appears that Mrs. Delaney held a deep trust and appreciation for Ms. Johnson's unwavering dedication and loyalty. The will expresses Mrs. Delaney's attitude for her years of service and the integral role she played in the upkeep and management of the estate."

As the weight of the revelation settled, Daniel, Stephen, and Mia exchanged glances, grappling with a mix of emotions that ranged from bewilderment to resentment. The implications of Candace's decision, veiled in mystery, hung heavy in the room, demanding answers yet offering none.

Mr. Collins folded the will, his voice gentle but firm. "While this decision may be unexpected and undoubtedly raises questions, it is my duty to execute Mrs. Delaney's wishes as stated in her will. I am here to provide legal guidance and assistance to all parties involved."

The room fell into a heavy silence once more, each person left to grapple with their thoughts and feelings. Ava Johnson sat silent, avoiding the glare of the others, staring at the floor, her eyes welling over with tears.

Detective Anderson stood and opened the office door. "At this time, I would like three more important people to join us. I have concluded my investigation and need them to be present. This portion of the meeting is being recorded. Please enter the room when I call your name."

Dr. Grace Wilson

Mr. Liam Hawthorne
Mr. Robert Matthews

The three filed into the room and took their seats along the wall.

"Dr. Wilson, I visited you at your office and you explained that the necklace worn by Mrs. Delaney during her wedding reception contained red seed pods that belong to the Abrus Precatorius, or Rosary Pea. Isn't that correct?"

"Yes, that is correct."

"And the seed pods are considered poisonous. Correct?"

"Yes."

"Wait, are you saying that my daughter poisoned Candace?" Mia blurted out. "She's a *child*. That's ridiculous."

"Although Mrs. Delaney brushed the seed pods to her mouth, it would be necessary to create a concentrated dosage of the key ingredient abrin before it became lethal."

"Yes, that's true."

"I noticed when you examined the seed pods, you wore gloves."

"Yes, of course. I always take precautions when handling a plant species that—"

"Dr. Wilson. Did you ever warn other members of the household about the dangers of this plant?"

"Yes, of course."

"Who were they?"

"Liam, the groundskeeper, of course. Miss Candace and Mr. Stephen."

"Anyone else?"

"Yes, Ava, the executive housekeeper."

Detective Anderson turned to face all three of them, taking the time to study their faces.

"Is that true? Were you both warned not to handle the plant pods?"

"Yes, I suggested destroying it but—" Liam said, voice breaking as the realization hit that there might have been something he could have done to prevent the bride's death. "It's an invasive species. Almost impossible to get rid of it all no matter how much you try."

"Ms. Johnson, were you aware of this plant and its properties?"

"It's possible. I mean, I suppose so. If Dr. Wilson says she told me, then I guess she did."

"Are you saying that you don't recall the conversation?"

"Yes, that's it. I don't recall."

"Ms. Johnson surveillance video footage before the reception shows you going to the work table used for staging and preparation of florist materials that belonged to Ms. Mia Grant and her florist shop."

"Maybe so. I was in a lot of places that day. There was so much to do and I had to keep on top of it all."

"You took several white roses."

"Umm, possibly. What has that got to do with—"

"And you intertwined them into a corsage that fit upon the wrist."

Ava became agitated.

"Come on, Detective," Daniel interrupted, his impatience with the questioning rising to a boiling point. "We have more important things to concern ourselves with at this point. Do you really think we care about my wife's bridal flowers now?"

"We discovered a pair of gloves on the dressing table in Mrs. Delaney's suite with the residue of abrin." The detective circled the room. "But they were not gardening gloves like those that Dr. Wilson wears. They are the style for polishing furniture." He stopped next to Ava Johnson. "For housekeeping."

"What happened to my wife?" Daniel's words slipped out of his mouth like steam from a kettle.

"The pin pricks along Mrs. Delaney's wrist served as the entry point for the poison, in concentrated form." He turned to Dr. Wilson. "A lethal level."

Dr. Wilson dropped her head and whispered, "What?"

"Ms. Johnson, the evidence is clear. You entered the master suite carrying the corsage wearing the gloves. And exited without the corsage and barehanded. Shortly thereafter, Mrs. Delaney appeared leaving the suite wearing the corsage on her wrist on her way to the wedding reception downstairs."

Daniel inhaled and released a deep sigh, trying to control his rage. The others sat still, their faces covered in shock and disbelief.

"It's time to reveal the truth," Detective Anderson said, his voice sharp and demanding. "I've uncovered a disturbing connection between you and Mrs. Delaney. A connection that goes beyond your role as a housekeeper."

Ava's gaze faltered for a fraction of a second before regaining its composure. Her voice was laced with a calculated calmness as she responded, "Detective, I have faithfully served Miss Candace for years. I am as shocked and devastated by her death as anyone else."

Detective Anderson leaned forward, his eyes burning with intensity. "But the truth cannot be hidden forever. The evidence has led me to an incredible discovery. You are not just Mrs. Delaney's loyal housekeeper; you are her long-lost sister."

"What?" Stephen said. "Is this some kind of joke?"

Ava's expression wavered, her eyes darting momentarily before she regained her composure.

"I don't know what you're talking about, Detective. I have no family. Miss Candace and I were merely employer and employee."

Detective Anderson took a step closer, his voice steady yet laden with accusation.

"Oh, but the evidence suggests otherwise. All point to the undeniable fact that you are Roman Grant's daughter, half-sister to Stephen Grant and Candace Grant Delaney."

Ava's mask cracked, fear and anger surfacing in her eyes. "Yes, fine, it's true. I am," she exclaimed, her voice trembling with a mix of despair and bitterness. "He brought me here from Honduras to live as a servant, not as a daughter. But Candace, she had everything, Detective. The wealth, the attention. I had nothing."

Detective Anderson's gaze remained fixed on Ava's, his voice filled with determination. "And so, in your desperation, you devised a plan to kill her and inherit her fortune."

Ava's lips curled into a chilling smile, her true intentions laid bare. "She had it all."

"You see, Ms. Johnson," Detective Anderson continued, intense resolve in his eyes, "we discovered a hidden letter. A letter Mrs. Delaney had written to her *sister*, unbeknownst to anyone else. She had confided in you, revealing her fears and doubts, seeking solace in the only family she felt that she could trust. But instead of offering comfort, you saw an opportunity."

Ava's voice quivered as she whispered, "It was never about the money. It was about what Candace had that I didn't. The life she had, the love she found. I couldn't bear it any longer."

Officer Ryan walked into the room and approached Ava with a set of handcuffs.

"Those won't be necessary," Detective Anderson said, as they watched Ava stand up, straighten the creases in her Blue Ledges uniform and step out of the room with the officer.

THE SPRAWLING ESTATE stood in eerie silence, its grandeur contrasting with the weight of the secrets that lay hidden within its walls. Ava, the housekeeper who had faithfully served the late bride, Candace, found herself in an unexpected and sinister position, a holding cell in Varset County. She had inherited everything, but her true identity and sinister motives remained concealed until that day in Roman Grant's study. Stephen Grant would retain ownership of the family legacy in name only, while his wife, Mia, made haste to escape media scrutiny bound for an unknown foreign location with the money he believed she used to place his bets, but were in actuality invested in the import/export business along with the husband of his deceased sister. Detective Anderson made one last walk through the courtyard and waved to Liam Hawthorne who fastidiously trimmed the fine fescue grass around the legs of the For Sale sign in front of Blue Ledges.

FOR MORE INFORMATION about the author, please visit Barbara Howard's website: http://www.authorbarbarahoward.com/

Chill: A Naomi Sinclair Short Story
Ashley-Ruth M. Bernier

I'm *that* bridesmaid.

Not the Maid of Honor, who needs the mental strength and physical endurance to manage bouquets and bustles. Not the style savior, who can reverse hairstyle malfunctions and blot out any stain from white silk. Nah. I'm the fixer. The problem-solver. My job is to keep a smile on the bride's face no matter what, whether it's an ex showing up at the ceremony or a cousin going for round 7 at the bar. Or a no-show bridesmaid, four days before the wedding. We're forty-five minutes into a Bridesmaids Day that includes drinks in plush lounge chairs and a catamaran waiting for us just past the buoys in the sparkling aquamarine waves of St. Thomas' most beautiful beach, and still—there's a bridal meltdown looming, right there in the words falling from Rina Douglas's mouth and the flash flood building in her eyes.

"The photographer charges by the hour, and he can't start until *she's* here," Ri tells me at the charcuterie table set up on the sand between our lounge chairs. She's not wailing, not yet—but I hear the beginnings of it building in her voice. "How the pictures gon' look with an empty lounge chair and an unclaimed swag bag? With only four of us instead of five? My pictures need to be *symmetrical* and *perfect,* and they won't look right without her. Naomi, I jus'—I can't have lopsided pictures!"

I fill Ri's glass of passionfruit mimosa a little higher than I'd originally intended. "Hey. Eboni's probably jus' running late, okay? Just—breathe, Ri. You don't want tear tracks in your photos."

"Late? No, gyul. Not at all. I saw Eboni drive through the beach gates half an hour ago," Rina says. "She's up at her ice cream hut instead of here with us. She promised she wouldn't work today. She *promised,* but..." There's a gulp of the mimosa, and I raise the pitcher, ready to top her off again. "I know she wants to make me look bad. Entitled. Like a spoiled Bridezilla, while she's down there scraping pennies together."

"Or maybe it's not about you at all, love," I try.

"You're right," Rina realizes. "Mussbe she tryin' to make *herself* look *good.* Like, better than everyone else. With her 'unshakable work ethic', or whatever."

I'm about to respond to that, but then I remember—bridal happiness, no matter what. "Right. Sure. Of course." I reach for her free hand. "Ri. Look, I know weddings are stressful and all, but this day is supposed to be for you to relax and enjoy. Maybe if you took a moment to—"

"Can you talk to her for me, Nay?" She's gripping the glass stem with the same force she's using on my fingers. "I'd do it myself, but conversations with her always end with at least one of us crying—and like you said, my makeup's already done. Please, can you tell her to close up shop and get her behind down here?"

"With those exact words?"

At least this gets a grin. "See? You get it. Talking to people is your whole job."

"I interview chefs, Rina."

"That's talking to them, right? This is why it has to be you," she says. I begin to say something about her spending the bulk of her days talking, too—persuading people to buy million-dollar villas, no less—but she barrels right over my words. "And I hate to ask you to do this when you're not working, when you back *home* for a few days to unwind."

"Rina, I'm back home for a few days...for you. To be the best bridesmaid I can be. To help you be the best bride you can be. If talking to your sister is something I can do so that you enjoy today a bit more..."

"Oh, Nay. Thank you. It is. I can always count on you," she says, blinking back the flood and widening the grin. She sets her glass next to the charcuterie board and hugs me. I've just convinced myself she's settled down when she speaks again. "I see my photographer checkin' he watch, though," she murmurs into my hair. "Think you could try talkin' to her, like, right now?"

This is how I find myself trudging down Magens Bay, feeling every grain of the soft white sand under my fresh pedicure and the mid-morning sun on my lower back just below the tips of my sisterlocs; to talk to Eboni Douglas. Eboni is Rina's sister—half, not full—and her role in the bridal party can be neatly summed up as "The Token". Big win for Mama Douglas, who gets to look sacrosanct for including her husband's older daughter on Rina's big day. Not so much of a win for Rina...or for Eboni. The love between the two of them is hard to see clearly through the layer of ice that also exists in that space. Lots of Eboni freezing Rina out. Lots of Rina pretending she never wanted to be let in in the first place. It's been like this their entire lives, even on days like today—when basking in all the warmth of sisterhood, in the midst of an abundance of sunshine; should be the only thing on our agenda.

I find Ebbi struggling with the blue shutters of her Cool Vybez ice cream hut, which is sandwiched between a wing bar and an overpriced swimwear store at the pagoda near the beach entrance. Rina's told me all about it—how Eboni took over the homemade ice cream business after her mother died a little over a year ago; how she'd changed the name and the business model from a pop-up canopy on the side of the beach road to a tiny haven promising the ultimate cool bayside treat. She looks up and sees me, and I meet her exasperated sigh with the most disarming smile I can manage. My TV audience buys it all the time. Not the case with Ebbi.

"I knew she'd send somebody," she mutters. "Figured it would be you."

"Oh—no, I volunteered, Ebbi. I've been meaning to come for some of your ice cream my last few visits home," I tell her. "Hey, there are nights I lie awake thinking about your mother's soursop or guava ice cream. Geez, and the mango. You still makin' that, right? Nobody could make mango ice cream like she could."

"Gelato Dreams could," a skinny guy says as he walks past us into the wing bar's kitchen. Everything about him is out of place—the cadence of his words sounds like something straight out of the southern U.S., and his jheri curl looks like something straight out of my daddy's high school yearbook. The man wipes his hands on his dirty apron and shoots Eboni a glare over a sunburned shoulder. She sighs and continues to tug on the shutters, but I can't let his tone slide by unchecked.

"Incorrect...oh, and *entirely* unsolicited," I snap back after him. Eboni shakes her head at me desperately, so I leave it at that. "What's his problem, Ebbi? Iss one thing to interrupt a conversation he wasn't even a part of, but to interrupt it with something rude is even—"

"Garland's always rude. That's why I don't talk to him. Man can't get over me dipping into his profits. His grill used to make a good bit from gourmet ice cream sales before I opened," she mumbles. "He can't move that Gelato Dreams and Haagen-Dazs like he used to. And it ain' cheap."

"He's mad he's losing money to a better, locally made, more authentic product?"

"Mad he losin' money. That's what it's always about, right?" Eboni finally gets her shutters hooked up, and then stops to face me fully. "So...enough now, Naomi. I know she sent you with a message. You have something you need to say? Go ahead. Say it."

I pause for a moment to get my words right. It's long enough for me to see the redness in Ebbi's eyes and the bags right under them; the tension in her jawline and shoulders. I begin to wonder when she last slept. Or sat. Or unclenched. "She just wants you there, Eboni. She planned this whole day for us and wants to share it with you. Rina's—"

"Those definitely ain' the words she sen' you with. That's TV Naomi right there," Eboni cuts me off with a dry laugh. "Rina planned this whole day...for *her*...on a day with seven ships in town, when this beach will be packed with tourists and I could make three, four times what I normally do. She never cared about my—"

"Morning, Eboni," a lady interrupts. She's jangling a lanyard full of keys as she walks past us to the swimwear store. There's a sullen looking teenager behind her, messy twists and acne; with a backpack the size of a dromedary hump weighing down her shoulders. On a Saturday. "I was looking for you yesterday afternoon. You clocked out early?"

There's something like a sigh from Ebbi. "Yeah. Sorry, Simone. I forgot you wanted to talk," she says. "I had...an errand to run."

"Well. You picked a nice, slow afternoon to run it," the lady says. "Not like today, though. Seven ships! Beach gon' be full, so our registers should be too, right?" She nods pointedly. "Maybe I'll get close to affordin' my electric bill this month."

Eboni responds with a grimace. "Yeah, your bill last month was something, for sure. Again. But it's like I keep telling you, it really can't be because of my coolers. We don't share breakers, and *my* bill hasn't been—I mean, did you ever call the office to ask if there might be any mistakes with your meter, or with your..."

Ebbi trails off. Simone isn't really listening anymore; she's looking over at me. "Hey—you ain' deh girl from EAT TV? With the restaurant show?"

"That's her," Eboni mumbles as I do the whole smile-and-introduction thing.

"Well, well! Naomi Sinclair, here in our li'l corner of the beach. You back home for a few days? Wait, you back on St. Thomas to feature Eboni's shop on *A Word from the Kitchen*?" The woman's brown eyes go as wide and bright as her smile.

"Naomi's home for...an entirely different reason," Eboni says. "Not to work. She's got the kind of job where she can afford to take a week off and still be fine."

There are words that come to mind—quick, hot, defensive ones, right there on my lips—but then I catch a glimpse of that catamaran waiting for us out in the water. I remember I'm supposed to be putting out a fire, not drenching it with more fuel. "If you say so, Ebbi," I say instead. "Also, my producers pick the restaurants I visit and the chefs I interview. I can make suggestions, but..."

"Suggest Eboni, no? Then get some shots of my Bikini Hut in the background." Simone chuckles. She's only half-joking. "Eh-eh—maybe you could even interview my daughter, too, you know? She's never been shy in front a camera. Tell her, Monet. Tell Ms. Sinclair what an industrious businesswoman Ms. Douglas is."

"Um. She really works *all* the time," the girl with the backpack mumbles after a not-so-subtle nudge from her mother.

There's actually a laugh from Eboni. Not much body or warmth to it, but it's there. "Thanks, Monet. Every time I see you, you're working hard, too."

"College scholarships don't jus' hand themselves out," Simone says, pulling open the door to her store. "An' on that note, Monet, you'd better get back to work on your essay. Eboni, get ready for that cruise ship traffic, gyul. First taxi vans should be here soon."

Eboni sighs and checks her watch. "Thanks, Simone."

I wait until the two of them have disappeared into their store before I speak. "Maybe I'm mistaken, Ebbi, but it doesn't sound like drinks on the catamaran deck fit into your plans for today."

"You're not mistaken. I already took off yesterday afternoon to get fitted for my bridesmaid dress, and that in itself was a big ol' sacrifice. Maybe if you—maybe if my *sister*—would actually listen, allyou would understan' that this is the way it is for people who live in the real world. One of you in front of a camera on cable TV, and the other staging and selling homes for millionaires, and suddenly allyou forget about the rest of us who don't get to live that kin' of life. Who didn't get their dream job handed to them. Who have to hustle and grind every day to pay bills." She opens the door to a small hallway between her nook and the grill kitchen, where I can hear Garland cursing quietly about something.

"Yeah, but this is Rina," I try. Eboni's a fast walker, and I can barely keep up with her as she moves down the narrow space. "She's not even thinking about money and businesses. All she wants is a beautiful day in the sun with the girls she loves best before she gets married. Drinks on the deck and cheers in the breeze. Can't you put the hustle aside for a day and just chill with her?"

"When Daddy left to marry her mother, my mother had to work even harder," Eboni mutters, pulling out a key of her own and opening a small door in the hallway that leads to the back of her shop. "Running herself ragged teaching during the week, and then doing the ice cream thing on the weekends and summers. Making the ice cream late into the night. Selling it late into the day. She worked right up to the day she had her stroke. She wanted *this* so badly, a li'l place of her own; and she never got a chance to have it. But I did. I got it. And I won't let it fail. So no, Naomi, I can't put the hustle aside for a day. Especially not for someone who never understood how her very presence made it all necessary. Go tell my sister I hope today is everything she wanted it to be, but I need to—"

She stops. Curses loudly. "What the...what is *this*?"

I begin to ask if she's okay, but swallow the rest of my question when

I see why Eboni's yelling. Her two freezers sit at the front of the hut, silent and still. Which they shouldn't be. They should be humming away as electricity powers through them, keeping that heavenly ice cream perfectly chilled. But the thick freezer cord lies in the middle of the floor like a lifeless snake. It's been unplugged from the wall.

Eboni's frozen, staring at the unplugged cord. I grab her arm gently. "Ebbi, your ice cream," I say. Those are the words she needs. Her eyes go wide and she bolts over to the freezer. I follow, bending over to take a look behind the unit while Eboni pulls the sliding glass doors open to check her product. That's when I notice the cord's also been cut. It's been sliced straight through, severed neatly into a short piece still connected to the freezer unit and the other long, winding piece that ends with the plug; the piece visible to us when we walked in.

"Oh, man—it's not just unplugged. Someone cut the cord," I tell her.

I'm not sure she even hears me. "It's all ruined," she wails.

"Yes, but Ebbi? Your *cord*—"

"My ice cream's soft. Good for another couple hours, maybe, but it won't last the whole day. It's been sitting like this...I'm guessing since last night?" Eboni sounds dazed and hurt all at the same time. "How am I going to...? I can't sell...how...how am I going to do this?"

Ebbi's mind hasn't arrived here yet, in the space beyond *how*, where *who* and *why* need answers. I'm about to yank her over to my line of thought, but a voice interrupts me.

"Um, hello?"

Ebbi's still rummaging around in the freezers, so I'm the one who answers the petite redheaded lady in the back doorway. "Can I help you with something?"

There's an embarrassed smile. The lady's not dressed for the beach at all—long khakis, sensible flats, and an orange polo with the Gelato Dreams logo stitched right above her heart. "Sorry to disturb you," she says in smooth tones that remind me of stateside friends from the midwest. "I'm looking for Garland McHale?"

"I can help you find him," I tell the lady. Eboni's behind me, muttering to herself and sniffling back tears. "Ebbi, I'll be right back, okay? Hey—in the meantime, does Simone have a fridge in her shop that can house at least some of this?" Eboni grunts, but she heads out when the other lady and I do, stalking in the other direction toward Simone's store.

"Everything okay back there?" the Gelato Dreams lady asks as I lead her down the hallway. The narrow space connects the back entrances of all three businesses. Monet's backpack and several thick textbooks are strewn across a desk in a corner nook, along with a battery-powered lantern and an old manual pencil sharpener.

"Just...um...a warmer welcome than we expected," I mutter. "Are you with the company? Gelato Dreams?"

"I absolutely am! Are you a fan of ice cream?" the lady answers me in her best seller's voice, instantly making me sorry I'd asked. "Gelato Dreams is synonymous with gourmet frozen goodness worldwide, but our footprint in this region is smaller than we'd like it to be. We're trying our best to change that. Are you a vendor or store owner?"

I smile faintly. "Neither. My only ice cream-related goal is stuffing my face with it on the deck of that boat out there."

"Oh, I wish," the lady responds, dropping the corporate voice for a moment. "We came down four months ago for our first trial meeting with Mr. McHale. All I wanted to do was jump in those waves. Today would've been ideal for that, no? But he insisted the re-eval had to be today, so work it is."

"I'm so sorry," I tell her. We walk through the door I'd seen Garland move through earlier, which leads to a large kitchen. Nothing's cooking—not yet—but Garland's got several huge unopened bags of chicken drummettes thawing on the counter, and the heavy scent of cooking oil hangs in the air. "Maybe you'll get to relax after your meeting?"

"Probably not," the woman says. "Garland seemed to think he'd be pretty busy today."

"Colleen!" The voice that calls out is Garland McHale's, just without the curt tones he'd used with me and Eboni earlier. He's changed into a clean apron and switched out the scowl on his face for a cool grin. "Thrilled you could make it today. Welcome *bock* to *di islan', mon.*" He delivers the last line in a miserable attempt at a Thomian accent, which sparks the beginning of a giggle from Colleen. The eye-roll and screw-face from me douses the rest of it.

"Glad to be here, Garland," she says instead, and then turns to me. "Um, thank you for helping me find him."

"It was her pleasure," Garland answers for me. There's a chilly wind behind his words. "Just watch your step on your way out, ma'am. I'm doing some rewiring—got things laid out on the floor behind you."

"I noticed," I say, glancing over at the enormous tangle of colorful wires in the exposed studs and then down at the piles of sheetrock and tool bags next to the hallway door. "Before I take that watched step, though, Mr. McHale—were you here yesterday afternoon? Did you see anyone inside Eboni's place after she left?"

"No, but it's not like I was looking." He pauses. "Wait. Now that I think about it, what's-her-name, Simone's kid? She went in there yesterday. She had her computer with her. Why? Did something happen?"

"Well, actually—"

"Know what? Tell me later. Colleen and I have lots to discuss before the beach gets full. We won't have time once that lunch rush hits." He looks over at Colleen and turns the warmth back on in his voice. "See that big catamaran out there past the buoys, Colleen? Wealthy clientele like that is always pleased to see we carry Gelato Dreams. I bet whoever's rented it will have lunch here, too."

"I wouldn't count on it," I mutter as I step over the cords and leave Garland's kitchen.

I find Eboni and Simone examining the vat of soursop ice cream in one of the coolers. The ice cream isn't soup, not yet, but it's certainly got the consistency of soft-serve more than the firm, smooth texture Eboni's mom's recipe has always delivered. They're both too busy to notice the way Monet's face turns the more they talk about *selling* and *loss* and *ruin*—like she's eaten a bellyful of spoiled ice cream and rotten fruit. The look gets even worse when I ask her to join me outside, to see if we can grab some ice from Garland's big machine to try to buy Eboni's ice cream a little more time. The kid's practically hugging herself as we make our way back down the hallway toward Garland's kitchen.

"You okay?" I ask over my shoulder.

"I'm good," she mumbles. I stop and raise my eyebrows at her—just a little—and that's all it takes for her to sigh and shake her head.

"Monet?" I ask again quietly, and the kid folds.

"Geez. Okay, Ms. Sinclair. Look, I...think this might be all my fault," she squeaks.

"What, this thing with Eboni's coolers?" I turn to face her, ready with reassurance—but then it kicks in, my journalistic training; and different words pop out instead. "Why would you think that?"

Kid looks terrified. "So yesterday, I needed to finish a practice AP Chemistry test. And where I sit in the hall out here...it's quiet, but—"

"...you don't have an outlet," I realize, glancing over at her lantern and twisty handheld pencil sharpener. "Was your computer battery running low?"

Monet nods. "Yeah. I usually go into my mother's store to plug in, but Mr. McHale was working with the wires in his place and he said the...um...the breaker in the wall he shares with my mom was shut off. He suggested I work in Ms. Douglas's spot."

"He suggested it?"

There's another nod. "I jus' needed to plug in to finish the test. It's timed, so I was rushing. I unplugged her cooler. I knew I wasn't going to leave it like that for a long time. Mr. McHale let me in and went back to cutting up his chicken, and I finished my test. But I'm almost positive I plugged the cord back in before I—"

"Hold up," I interrupt. "You said he was cutting up chicken?"

Her look of confusion is probably mirrored on my own face. "Um...yes? That's what he said those weird scissors were for. I...don't exactly remember plugging the cord back in, but I'm pretty sure..."

She's still talking, going on and on about her steps yesterday, but I've stopped listening. There's something unfreezing in my mind, a truth that's becoming more apparent as every detail adds a little more heat to thaw it out. "Monet," I interrupt. "Can you get your mom and Eboni? Meet me over there in Garland's kitchen."

The confusion on her face only grows. "For...the ice?"

"For the truth," I tell her. "Don't worry—none of this is your fault, okay? And if we're fast, we can do this before the tourists get here."

Garland and Colleen are setting up an enormous fabric feather flag advertisement with the Gelato Dreams logo on it when I walk into the kitchen a few moments later. I hear Monet, Eboni, and Simone coming down the hallway behind me, but my eyes are on Garland.

"Hey, Garland?" I call out. He turns away from Colleen and the smile drops from his face. "Do you have a sec? I need to talk to you."

"I'm actually in the middle of something, and I still have no idea who you are," he returns.

"You don't know? She's—" Simone begins from behind me, but I shoot a little smile her way, one that signals *I got this* more than the words themselves could. She pauses, and I turn back to Garland.

"I think Simone wants to tell you who I am when I'm working, about how my job is to interview exceptional chefs on TV. That's not who I am today, though. Today, I'm just trying my best to get Eboni to join me and her sister on the deck of that boat out there for our Bridesmaids Day. Her sister, the bride, can't start without her." I look over at Eboni. "She really can't, Ebbi."

"Your sister's getting married?" asks Simone.

Garland's voice is far less enthusiastic. "*You're* the ones renting that catamaran?"

"Yes, and yes," I say. I want to point out how this moment feels so far away from both of those things, but I point at the Gelato Dreams banner instead. "Pretty big flag you've got there."

"It is," Colleen says brightly, "but can I just say how much I absolutely *love* weddings? All the sweetness and all the beauty...look, I've even got the announcement for my niece's stepcousin Buddy Bill Corey's wedding right here in my purse. And—well. That's weird. Looks like it says "If Buddy's killer's first name starts with the letter R, the gun was not used" on the back. Never saw that before. But—goodness, you don't want to hear about all that, and I've gotten way off topic. Yes, the flag. I'm glad I brought it. Garland's expecting a lot of business today."

"I'm sure he is," I say. "Why don't you go and set it up out front, Colleen? I just need to talk to Mr. McHale for a second. He'll be out to help in a few. I promise."

She gives me an odd look, but ultimately she picks up the banner and heads out through the front door of the kitchen. Garland watches her go and then turns back to me, ready to say something as fiery, I imagine, as the look on his face. I cut him off before he even begins.

"So why *would* you, Garland? Why would you expect a lot of business—and invite your Gelato Dreams distribution rep to visit—today, when Eboni's ice cream has been outselling yours for months now? When the same thing is likely to happen on a larger scale with so many people on the beach?" I ask. "The answer is, you wouldn't—unless you didn't expect Eboni to be open."

"W-well, of course I didn't," Garland stammers. "Why would she be working? Her sister's getting married."

"Yeah, but you didn't know that. Not before I told you. Eboni's intensely private. She talks to Simone more than she talks to you, and Simone didn't even know until just now." I take a small step toward him. "Garland. Colleen told me she was here a few months ago. Trial visit. I'm betting that since then, with Eboni's shop open, you sold a lot less ice cream than you expected to, and you didn't want Gelato Dreams to know. That stuff has a shelf life of, like, three or four months. If you were the only one selling ice cream on a day like today, you'd not only move a lot of product close to its expiration date, but it would also make your business look really lucrative to a corporate sponsor."

"You're saying a bunch of words that sound like something, but mean nothing," Garland whips back at me.

"They make a lot of sense to me," Simone pipes up from the doorway. "I know how nice it is to have support from a company. I have several swimwear reps who visit, maybe give a little bonus to make sure their products are placed well or promoted. Gelato Dreams would be a big one for you." There's a little pause. "So—wait, Ms. Sinclair. You sayin' Garland did that thing to Eboni's freezer cord?"

"Your daughter was the only one in Eboni's place yesterday afternoon. Maybe you should ask her," Garland says.

"Monet was in there. Yes. And she unplugged the freezer—yes," I explain. Eboni's eyes—and Simone's, too—go wide, and she's just opened her mouth to say something when I continue. "But Monet didn't sever the cord. In fact, she didn't even know it had been cut—just unplugged. I believe you were lookin' to set her up for ruining Ebbi's ice cream, but that was all you, Garland. Monet told me something she remembered when you sent her to Eboni's shop for an outlet. She said you had 'chicken scissors.'"

There's a scornful sniff. "That's probably because I run a chicken place, sweetheart."

I can do scorn, too. "You run a chicken *wing* place, dahlin'. I've seen your kitchen. Those wings you buy come prepackaged, already cut up, ready for frying and saucing. You don't need to cut up a thing. Well, except for the freezer cords of your competition. So here's what I'm thinking," I say. "Eboni can call the police. One thing I know about our St. Thomas police, they'll be thorough. They'll investigate and stick around for a few hours. Maybe all day. They'll poke around and explore every inch of Ebbi's place. Yours, too. And nobody gets to sell anything while they're here. Or..."

"Or what?"

"Or maybe, Garland, you let your line cooks manage the wings and burgers today and you declare a change of plans. Take Colleen to lunch in town. Encourage her to spend the rest of the day relaxing—back here on the beach, maybe, like she was talking about earlier. And in the meantime, you go buy Eboni a new freezer."

"I say you go for option two, Garland," Simone says evenly.

Garland folds his arms across his chest. He's quiet—frozen—for a couple of moments. And then, in a voice chilly enough to give Eboni's ice cream a boost: "Exactly who...*are* you?"

"Like I said—today, I'm just a bridesmaid," I repeat. There are other voices coming from the hallway now. Voices I recognize. I sigh and suck my teeth. "A bridesmaid who's really failing at her duties right now, Garland. Look, if you think I'm rough, there's a disgruntled bride heading your way right now. And if she finds out you're the one keeping her back from her day sail, you'll wish you'd used those scissors to slit something else."

"I'll take Colleen to town," Garland mutters. "Lost my mind for a moment, Eboni. I'll replace that cooler, all right? No need to get anyone else involved." He sends a curt nod Eboni's way, and he's gone, headed out through the front door of the kitchen, before she can say anything in return.

"I...didn't see that coming," Eboni says quietly.

Simone's shocked, too. "Never in my mind did I see Garland McHale folding so quick. Scared of a young lady in a bikini an' sarong."

226

I look over my shoulder. Rina's getting closer. "What Garland's scared of, I think, is the police showing up and looking into his illegal wiring. Did you see that crazy hookup in his wall? I mean, I'm no electrician, but that many plugs in one exchange doesn't look safe. I'm, um, willing to bet he's trying to save on his electric bill by tapping into your power source, Simone. Which is why—"

Simone opens her mouth, and some words saltier than the ocean water beyond us jump out. "Is *that* what's been goin' on with my power bill?"

"I think so. You might want to call the police anyway. You know, while he's out," I say.

"Oh, you bes' believe I will," Simone says. She storms back through the door, right before Rina bursts into the kitchen, followed by the other two bridesmaids in their own bikinis and monogrammed sarongs. Ri's already mid-tantrum, hot words falling from her mouth like sparks.

"I sent you to bring Eboni back, not get lost yourself, Naomi! Deh two of allyou—" she begins, but I'm already walking toward her, doing my job; ending the crisis. I take Rina's arm and point her towards her sister.

"Ri, Eboni needed help with a problem. And we figured it all out, okay; but...I think she needs you too," I tell her.

Eboni's crying softly, and Rina's eyes go wide. When she speaks, there's a different kind of heat in her voice—one that's gentle enough to defrost more than strong enough to scald. "What happened, E? Hey, what's—"

"Jus' forget it, Rina. Let's j-just go out on the boat an' celebrate you, okay?" Eboni says between sniffles. "It's all...ruined. All my work. Naomi solved deh one problem, but the bigger problem...all that melting ice cream...I can't do anything about that. I suppose I deserve it, right? Always working, always putting *this* first. I chased it too hard. I wanted it too much."

"Ebbi, no. Ay, I don't know what happened, but you don't deserve this feeling. No way," Rina murmurs.

"I wanted to do this for Mommy. Show the world what a gift she had. I wanted everyone to see this place thrive. Today was supposed to be all about that." Eboni wipes her eyes and cheeks. "Forget it, though. It's your day. I'll close up, and then we'll go take your pictures and get on the boat."

"Take pictures? When you feelin' like this? How could I ever—"

"Rina, wait," I cut her off. "Look, we need to get started on our epic day, and Eboni needs to sell something like three hundred ice cream cones in the next forty-five minutes. Am I right? Okay. I...think I know how we can get it all done in a way that makes everyone happy."

Ri makes a face. "How is it you always know exactly what to do?"

"I'm *that* bridesmaid," I remind her. "Go call your photographer over here, Rina. He'll get some cool shots, for sure."

This is why most of the pictures of Rina's Bridesmaids Day aren't staged photos of us posing on the sand in matching towels or toasting bellinis. Instead, he's got the five of us in matching Cool Vybez aprons, handing out cones of sugar apple, guava, mango, and soursop ice cream to surprised tourists across the beach. I've bought the first eighty cones, and Rina, Chelsea, and K'Niya have followed suit and covered the rest. By the time we empty the last tub, 317 tourists have gotten free ice cream and the beach is buzzing with visitors discovering the cool, cozy delight of our native fruits. With our four checks—and the plenty of tips from satisfied customers—locked away in Eboni's cash box, we help Eboni close up shop right before the lunch rush. By early afternoon, we're all on the deck of the catamaran.

The sun's high in the sky and the heat index is soaring, but warmth has a funny way of making things evaporate. Like all the tension in Eboni's face and shoulders. Like all that iciness between her and Rina. In the shade of a canopy on the catamaran's deck, we feel the breeze on our faces and the cool ocean spray on our toes as we laugh and chat and *chill*. And when we finally do toast Rina, when we bump our glasses of frozen daiquiris together and cheer, there's nothing but the echo of our voices in the tradewinds ahead. Drinks on the deck. Cheers in the breeze. Nothing on our agendas but all the warmth of sisterhood and standing behind one of our own as she prepares to take her next big step.

FOR MORE INFORMATION about the author, please visit Ashley-Ruth M. Bernier's website: http://ashleyruthbernier.com/

A Bit of a Do
KD Sherrinford

Ok, let's start from the beginning.

You see, I remember precisely where I was when I received the invitation to my cousin Rachel's wedding. I was alone at breakfast, in the kitchen of my cottage, in the sedate village of Woodplumpton, a stone's throw from the Great River Stour.

I glanced out the window as torrential rain poured down when I heard the gate swing open and saw Tom, our village postman, walk past. He grimaced, pulling his hat down firmly over his head, before closing the gate behind him.

Recognising the Oxfordshire postmark and my aunt Matilda's distinctive handwriting, I took a breath and opened the envelope. It was out of character for Matilda to write to me. I received the odd chaste telephone call complaining I rarely came to see her, but I had good reason.

The invitation also enclosed a letter, although it was more of a summons, to the wedding of my cousin Rachel Fiona Barnaby and her fiancé Stephen Alastair King, a high-flying barrister from Knightsbridge. The marriage would occur at St. Mary's church in the village of Cottam on Saturday the 27th of May. A reception would follow at my aunt and uncle's country pile, The Grange.

Matilda was expecting me on Thursday for a family dinner. The thought of meeting up with my family again filled me with dread.

My aunt and cousin, Richard, were pretentious social climbers considering themselves a cut above everyone else. Richard took after Matilda: condescending and pompous, while Rachel differed from them, self-aware, kind and tolerant. We had always been close. Rachel shared the same blue eyes and infectious sense of humour as her father, my uncle Robert, whom I adored. A proud Yorkshireman, Robert hailed from Harrogate where he honed his craft in the family business and became a renowned vintner.

When I was twelve my mom Susan tragically died of cancer. I had led an unconventional lifestyle up until that point. Susan home-schooled me and encouraged my intellectual curiosity. Despite my numerous questions my mom never revealed my father's identity. Instead, she told me they loved each other but couldn't be together, and that's all she would say on the matter, apart from the fact they shared a mutual appreciation for the works of Thomas Moore. Aunt Matilda (my mom's sister) and Uncle Robert took me in and raised me as their own. Matilda enrolled me in the local grammar school, I found the transition challenging interacting with other children and adhering to my aunt's strict rules and regulations. Those feelings of vulnerability and insecurity were a sharp contrast to my idyllic life with Mom.

Then when Robert and Matilda decided to send me to a girls' boarding school, I finally came into my own. I excelled at boarding school and won a scholarship to Cambridge, graduating with a first in English Literature. After graduation, I found work as a part-time journalist for *The Levington Post* which gave me time to concentrate on my first love, writing. There is magic in bringing your characters to life on the page, I always found it intoxicating.

Two years later, Penguin published my first two books as part of The Hilary Mallory detective series. Although the books sold relatively well, I wasn't rich by any stretch of the imagination. But I had a few loyal fans and my royalties and salary from *The Post* were enough for me to get by, pay my rent, and continue writing.

After covering some intriguing cases, my editor Andrew Hoyle encouraged me to apply for The Police Now Graduation scheme—a two-year course for the training and development of future detectives. My A-Level in Law stood me in good stead at the interview and I was subsequently accepted into the two-year programme. After eighteen months of working under Detective Inspector Peter Blythe's eagle eye, it was quite an experience. Blythe was a hard taskmaster and expected a lot from his rookie detectives. I didn't want to disappoint him; I was determined to graduate.

So, with a sigh of resignation and some trepidation I wrote back to my aunt accepting the invitation.

I ARRIVED AT THE GRANGE just after 3pm on Thursday.

It was a pleasant journey in the afternoon sun. I marvelled at the natural beauty of the green

Cotswold hillsides, epitomising the best of the quintessential English countryside and the gorgeous honey-coloured stone villages as the car rolled into the picturesque village of Cottam.

Cottam was gentrified with baristas, vegan cafes, and its pièce de résistance, a Michelin-star restaurant, The Bowers. I took a sharp right at The Dew Drop Inn, which took me onto a long winding country lane, continuing to the end before finally reaching my destination.

Pulling into the large gravel driveway, I gazed at the splendour of the double-fronted manor house and its colourful well-established garden. The cottages in the village seemed minuscule in comparison. To the side were the stables and outbuildings overlooking a twenty-acre stretch of the meadow where I played as a child.

As I removed my case from the boot of my car, my uncle's gun dog Rufus, a beautiful Golden retriever, ran over to greet me, barking and wagging his tail. I bent down to stroke his head. I heard a whistle, looked around and saw my uncle, Robert, walking towards me from the direction of the stables. He smiled broadly, dashing over to embrace me. He was dressed in tweeds, plus-fours, and a flat cap covering his be-speckled grey hair.

"So, our very own Jessica Fletcher decided to come to our bit of a do after all," he joked in his broad Yorkshire accent.

"Yes, of course." I laughed. "I wouldn't miss Rachel's wedding for the world, and it's hardly a bit of a do. Aunt Matilda would have a fit if she heard you describe the most prominent society wedding this side of The

Cotswolds as such."

Robert chuckled. "You got that right, lass. *Country Life* will take photographs on the big day!" Robert picked up my case, and we strolled to the house together.

"Who's here for dinner?" I quizzed. "Will the rector, John Jemson, be coming?"

John was the vicar of Saint Mary's church and one of my favourite human beings, he had shown nothing but kindness towards me since being a child. As an active church member, my aunt held John in high esteem. A staunch church committee member, Matilda was there every Sunday, helping gauge the congregation's spiritual health in robust participation. When Mom was alive, we helped with the flower arranging.

"John, James and my PA Lesley will join us for dinner." Robert smiled at my startled expression. "You must remember me telling you that James qualified as a doctor? He shares a practice in the village with Joe Calvert."

I stared at my uncle; I vaguely remember him mentioning something. James was my ex, the son of my uncle's business partner, Simon Ashe. We spent an unforgettable summer together in 2016, backpacking in Paris, strolling around the banks of the Seine and the Arc De Triomphe, captivated by the lovers walking hand in hand, endorsing Paris as the city of love.

I was stunned when James proposed at the top of The Eiffel Tower on the last day of our trip. I had a massive crush on him; he was modest and thoughtful. But I gently turned him down, explaining we were both too young to contemplate marriage. James took my rejection badly; he became sullen and withdrawn. When we returned home, he shunned my request that we wait until I finished uni and stormed off angrily. My calls and emails remained unanswered; he blocked me on social media. After all this time, I still had a frisson of regret about how our relationship ended. I missed his engaging sense of humour and infectious smile. Tall, darkly handsome, with mesmerising blue eyes, James was my first love. I have dated a few guys since but never found anyone who compared.

Robert escorted me to the drawing room for afternoon tea. He explained we were alone in the house, except for the servants and his PA, Lesley, working in the study. A corporate lawyer and partner at SH legal in Cheltenham, Richard was expected home shortly while Matilda and Rachel had gone into town for some last-minute shopping.

Robert glanced at his watch. "I was expecting them back before now. You know what Rachel's like when she hits the shops." He chuckled.

We were waited on by Caroline, a pretty, slim-built girl with auburn hair and freckles. Before leaving the room, she poured the tea, serving us from delicate silver trays holding cucumber sandwiches and freshly baked scones with homemade raspberry jam and Cornish clotted cream.

Robert took a sip from his cup, gazing at me fondly. "Your mother would have been thrilled that your dreams are eventually taking flight. Oh, that reminds me, I was having a clear-out the other day. I found this." He opened the top drawer of his bureau and handed me a book. I scanned the title, *The Poems of Sir Thomas Moore.*

I nodded, smiling at the mention of Mom. Robert continued, "I meant to return it and then she died. You take it, lass; it's what Susan would have wanted."

I felt tears welling in my eyes. "Thank you, I will cherish it forever."

After tea, I headed to my old bedroom in the west wing. Walking through the large hallway, I heard raised voices coming from the direction of the dining room. The door was slightly ajar, so I peered through the crack to find my cousin Richard and Caroline in a heated altercation.

Richard's hands were on her shoulders, his face like thunder. "Threaten my family, and I'll finish you. You'll not get another penny, you scheming minx."

Caroline pushed him away with a ferocity that made me gasp. "Lay your hands on me again and I'll report you to your parents. I'm not afraid of you, Mr big shot lawyer. If you want to keep your dirty little secret, you'd better start treating me respectfully." Caroline laughed mockingly, approaching the door.

I slipped into the morning room until I heard the entrance to the dining room slam shut. After a few minutes, I listened to another set of footsteps descending the hallway. I made my way upstairs, wondering what on earth was happening. I contemplated confronting Richard but then realised I was the last person he would discuss his personal life with.

As for Caroline, she appeared more than capable of looking after herself; nevertheless, I wondered what juicy gossip she had about my cousin. Was Richard seeing someone my aunt disapproved of? I wouldn't put it past Richard. He had always been a lady's man.

As the heir to The Grange and my uncle's fortune, that frustrated Matilda; her dearest wish was for Richard to marry well, and start a family, to carry on the family tradition. But, unfortunately, so far, he had shown little interest in walking down the aisle.

One glance around my old bedroom brought my childhood memories flooding back. The comfortable double divan bed with a multi-coloured bedspread was as I left it. My poster of Justin Bieber still hung on the wall next to the window, which looked out onto the car park and open fields. I stared out the window in quiet self-reflection as Matilda's Bentley drew into the car park. I watched as she got out of the car, wrinkling her nose, undoubtedly at the sight of my battered old Citroen parked nearby.

My thoughts were interrupted by the sound of my cell ringing. Recognising Rachel's number flashing on the screen of my iPhone, I answered. I smiled upon hearing her dulcet tones. "Hi, Liv; where are you?"

"I'm here at The Grange, but where are you, Rachel? I thought you were out with Matilda. She arrived home alone."

"Yes, I know; mother dropped me off at The Randolph to meet Stephen. She refused our lunch invitation; she didn't want to be late for an appointment with her accountant. However, the strangest thing happened when we got to the hotel lobby. I noticed my mother's accountant Jonathan Keenan walking into the restaurant with his wife, Josie." She sighed. "Mother must have got her dates wrong; she will be furious when she realises her mistake." Rachel paused. "Did Dad explain that James is joining us for dinner?"

"Yes, he did, although I have mixed feelings about seeing him again."

"Would have, should have, could have." Rachel laughed. "It will be fine, you'll see. I had lunch with James recently, and your name cropped up during the conversation. He said he was gutted when you split. He dated a few other girls but said none held a candle to you."

I rolled my eyes. "Oh, so no pressure there, then."

"I'm sure James will be on his best behaviour."

"Ok," I conceded. "You're right. I'm looking forward to seeing you, although surprised you're getting married so soon. You and Stephen haven't known each other that long."

"You know I'm a hopeless romantic." Rachel sighed. "I can't wait to marry Stephen. I love you, Liv."

"Yes, I know; I love you too."

I sat on the bed reading through Mom's book, reminiscing about the poems she recited to me as a child. Finally, my fingers stopped at a page. "The Meeting of the Waters" had always been Mom's favourite. I noticed a short inscription at the end, *until we meet again*. I furrowed my brow, trying to read the initials which were smudged. I often wondered if Robert was my biological father. He and my mom were extremely close, but then I dismissed the absurd notion; I knew Robert would never be unfaithful to Matilda.

I must have dozed off because it was 7 o'clock when I awoke. I showered and changed into a black silk evening dress. I gazed into the mirror, applying Clarins Ombre satin eye shadows to the baby blue eyes I inherited from Mom, then mascara and lipstick, tying my auburn hair into an elaborate up-do with a velvet band before spraying a liberal amount of Chanel no. 5 to my wrists and neck.

Slipping on my stilettos, I went downstairs into the kitchen to be greeted with the familiar sight of my aunt's housekeeper and cook, Cassie, stirring a large pot of soup on the Aga.

Cassie beamed when she saw me. "My, Miss Olivia. Well, you are a sight for sore eyes, that's for sure." She laughed, gazing at me with her astute green eyes.

"How are you?" I asked, hugging her reassuring corpulent frame. We chatted for a while, catching up on old times. Before I left, I promised to get coffee with Cassie in the morning.

I entered the drawing room with some trepidation to find the guests enjoying pre-dinner drinks. The rector smiled warmly, acknowledging my presence from the opposite side of the room before continuing his conversation with Lesley, a tall slim lady with ash-blonde hair. My eyes scoured the room; there was no sign of James, perhaps the thought of seeing me again was too much. I hoped not.

Matilda acknowledged my presence with a curt nod. She was

impeccably dressed in a Ponte midnight blue evening gown, her silver hair swept off her face in an elaborate chignon. "Ah, Olivia, at last, there you are. We'd almost given up on you," she said as I moved forward and kissed her rouged cheeks. Matilda addressed the room. "May I introduce my niece, Olivia Williams, an aspiring author and a trainee detective." She frowned. "Must you insist on risking your life and continuing with that ghastly job?"

"I suppose I could sit around all day drinking wine, but I don't think my inspector would be too impressed." I heard my cousin Richard snigger as he sipped from his glass.

I diverted my eyes away from Richard and Matilda on hearing Rachel's distinct laugh, and in a moment, her arms were around me hugging me. As elegant as ever, my beautiful cousin was dressed in a Stella McCartney red silk evening dress, enhancing her lovely figure. Her thick long blonde hair cascaded over her delicate shoulders. Rachel introduced me to her fiancé Stephen, a tall, red-haired young man with piercing grey eyes and an engaging manner.

"How are you, Liv?" quipped my cousin Richard. "Have you arrested any villains or written any best sellers lately?" he mocked. I blushed as curious eyes stared at me from within the room.

"Not yet," I replied, forcing a smile. "I'm still training to be a detective. I don't write for money, it's a vocation."

Look at him now, a respectable lawyer, as if butter wouldn't melt. However, admittedly Richard looked rather handsome in his tuxedo, tall and slim with deep-set blue eyes. His usual light brown floppy hair, now cut short, gave him an air of distinction.

My aunt glared at me, staring at me over her glasses. "I think it's time we went in for dinner."

◊ If the gun was used, Buddy's killer was one of the groom's guests. ◊

We retired to the dining room. The table was laid exquisitely with white linen and matching serviettes. I sat between Robert and an empty chair. After a few moments, I gasped in surprise as my ex James entered the room. "So sorry I'm late, my last patient overran his appointment." He laughed as my aunt briefly introduced him to the other guests. His smile immediately vanished when he discovered he was seated beside me.

Matilda smiled at James, waving her hand dismissively. "It's not a problem, young man, at least you are here now. That's all that matters." I stared at her in bewilderment, and shook my head, a stark contrast to my tepid reception.

Robert filled up the wine glasses while I made small talk with James. "You look well, Liv," he said stiffly, barely glancing at me.

"Thank you, so do you," I replied and meant every word. James was dressed in a black three-piece evening suit and a white shirt with a black bow tie. I could smell the faint aroma of his cologne, Creed Aventus, which I always found alluring.

"I heard you graduated from med school and now share a practice in the village?" I asked, attempting to converse politely.

"Yes, that's right. I took a sabbatical in Africa after graduating from Barts. So here I am now, a respectable practitioner." He looked at me curiously. "I read your books. You're incredibly talented, but then I guess the life of an author and an aspiring detective is far more glamorous than one of domestic drudgery."

I glared at James, speechless at the impudence. I could sense the voyeuristic interest in the room—the sly glances in each tilted head. "We no longer live in the dark ages, there's no reason a woman cannot have it all," I expounded. I could feel my cheeks burning. Sitting there next to James, who could hardly bear to look at me, was the loneliest feeling in the world.

I glanced up as Rector John Jemson spoke softly from across the table, breaking off his conversation with Lesley, his brow creased in concern. "You are right to value your independence, Olivia. Finding the right work is like discovering your soul in the world. I greatly admire strong-minded women such as Susan, your late mother, who survived and thrived in what is still classed today as a male-dominated world. It never ceases to amaze me the number of women prepared to turn a blind eye to their partner's decrepitude. In my opinion, that's no basis for a successful relationship."

I smiled at John, grateful for his intervention. He was an attractive-looking man, over six foot tall with silver hair swept off his face and kind expressive brown eyes that gazed at me with a hint of humour.

I sat in quiet contemplation, trying to remember where I had heard that quote before when my thoughts were interrupted by James. "I'm sorry that was rude of me, shall we start again? Perhaps we can talk later in private?"

My uncle squeezed my hand under the table. "Keep smiling, lass," he whispered. "The night will soon be over, you'll see."

Well, he was wrong about that. As Caroline served the coffee, I overheard her whisper to Cassie that she felt unwell. Stephen rose from his seat, gesturing for Caroline to sit down. He poured coffee into his cup, which Caroline sipped from slowly. Finally, she smiled at Stephen, explaining she felt much better and standing to resume her duties. A few minutes later, we were disturbed by a sudden commotion. As Caroline stumbled the tray she was carrying crashed to the floor.

"Are you drunk?" my aunt reprimanded, staring at Caroline disgustingly.

Caroline turned to face Matilda, shaking her head. "No, mam. It was the coffee, it was too sweet," she said before collapsing.

There was a collective gasp as James rose from his chair, ordering everyone to stand aside to give Caroline room to breathe. He quickly checked her pulse and temperature, explaining both were high. Finally, he instructed Robert to call for an ambulance. James reached into his pocket and pulled out his car keys, throwing them at me.

"Liv, please get my medical bag, it's in the boot of the black Mondeo." James turned his attention to Matilda. "There's no easy way to say this, Mrs Barnaby, but this girl isn't drunk. She's been poisoned and from the looks of it by ethylene."

THE AMBULANCE ARRIVED fifteen minutes later to take Caroline to the North Cotswolds hospital; she was barely conscious. We watched James inject Caroline with Fomepizole from the tiny vial which he removed from his medical bag. Cassie offered to accompany Caroline to the hospital.

"I'm sorry," I said. "But we must all stay here."

"Why?" said Cassie, staring at me, eyes wide. "So, you are saying that someone deliberately planted the poison?"

"We can't rule out the possibility. But, if James's diagnosis proves correct this could be the scene of an attempted murder and I'm afraid everyone will be under suspicion."

I glanced over to Matilda. "I'm sorry, but I need to call this in. I suggest we all return to the dining room until the inspector arrives."

"Is this entirely necessary?" asked Matilda.

"It's standard procedure in a case like this."

Cassie nodded. "Aye, right then, I will clear the table and organise some tea. I will be in the kitchen if needed."

I called Peter Blythe on my cell; he answered after three rings. "I'm sorry to disturb you, sir, but there's been an incident at The Grange; my aunt's maid Caroline O'Connor is on her way to Cotswold North, suspected of ethylene poisoning."

Blythe sighed. "Right, Williams. I shall send a constable to the hospital, Sergeant Dixon, and I will be with you within the hour."

When I entered the dining room Matilda was deathly pale, no doubt traumatised by the poisoning and realisation Cottam was no longer the picture-perfect, chocolate box, idyllic village she was used to.

"I have no wish to appear insensitive," said Matilda. "But I don't want a circus this close to the wedding, the house crawling with police."

I smiled at her sympathetically. "It's alright; it will only be me, Inspector Blythe and his sergeant. We have to find out what happened." Matilda smiled weakly as Robert put his arm around his wife's shoulders, pouring a liberal dash of brandy into her coffee.

I turned my attention to James. "I hope for everyone's sake there's a reasonable explanation and that this was an accident."

He furrowed his brow. "It's possible, although the stumbling and slurring symptoms displayed earlier are classic signs of ethylene intoxication."

I SLIPPED INTO THE kitchen with the offending pot of coffee, which I locked in the pantry for safe keeping. Noticing the integral door to the garage was open, I slipped out to the triple garage to find immaculately filled shelves containing an assortment of oil, sponges and windscreen wipes, liquid dripping onto the floor.

Wrinkling my nose, I recognised the pungent sweet fruity odour. I then made several phone calls; finally, entering Caroline's bedroom, I searched through the wardrobe and drawers, finding nothing unusual until I picked up her handbag from the bed, revealing a leather purse holding several notes, loose change, and debit cards. Then tucked inside the wallet, I pulled out a bank statement and stared in disbelief at the transaction dated two weeks earlier and, on the back, the highlighted words "If Buddy's killer is his mother, she used poison".

It was nine o'clock when Sergeant Dixon and Inspector Blythe arrived. I quickly filled them in on the events that had occurred. Blythe was a tall, built, imposing figure with a receding hairline, his face sombre as he waved his badge and introduced himself and Sergeant Dixon, a well-built man with wavy black hair. Everyone sat around the dining table as Blythe took a sip from his cup, addressing the room.

"You will all remain here with Sergeant Dixon. Williams and I will interview everyone separately in the drawing room, starting with Doctor Ashe."

Blythe smiled grimly. "It would appear that your diagnosis was correct, Doctor. When Miss O'Connor arrived in the ER the hospital said she was sliding into renal failure and would likely require dialysis. My brother's a surgeon so I know that ethylene is a solvent often used in medical research and, therefore, easily accessed by medical practitioners." He looked at James questioningly.

"That's true." James shrugged. "But then ethylene is much more available than people think, due to its shallow freezing temperatures, it is better known as the primary compound in many commercial colourants and formulas, such as—"

"Antifreeze?" Blythe interrupted.

"Exactly."

"Williams found spilt antifreeze on the garage floor. Unfortunately, the bottle appears to be missing."

"I hope you are not suggesting I was responsible, Inspector. I swore an oath to save lives, not end them," said James. Blythe smiled sardonically.

"You would be amazed how many doctors turned into murderers. Shipman and Crippin, for example. I understand you arrived late for dinner, giving you ample time to sneak into the garage and remove the antifreeze."

James laughed. "If I intended to murder someone, Inspector, I could think of more subtle ways. But, in any case, ask Cassie if you don't believe me. She let me in and escorted me to the dining room."

I looked at James. "I called Stella, your receptionist. She confirmed she locked up at 7:45. Ten minutes after you left the building, corroborating your story."

"That will be all for now, Doctor," said Blythe, appearing satisfied. "But I'm afraid everyone is a person of interest until we get to the bottom of this unfortunate incident; we may need to question you again later."

James nodded, staring at me, nonplussed, as he left the room.

A few minutes later, the inspector and I sat across from Cassie. She confirmed escorting James to the dining room. "Did you get on with Caroline O'Connor?" asked Blythe.

"Yes, she was a nice enough girl, that poor lass." Cassie blinked tears from her eyes.

"Did you notice anything strange about her behaviour?"

"No, nothing, Inspector."

"Was Caroline seeing anyone, a boyfriend, anyone special?" I quizzed.

Cassie shook her head. "No, Caroline kept herself to herself. She rarely discussed her personal life."

"What about family?" I asked.

"There are no relatives except for a distant cousin in Weymouth."

After Cassie left the room, the inspector went for a cigarette break. I wished I'd joined him, Richard was in next, and I wasn't looking forward to that conversation. Blythe eventually re-entered the room and I stared at my cousin in stunned disbelief as he protested his innocence to the inspector until, finally, I interrupted the conversation.

"I heard you and Caroline having a heated altercation in the drawing room."

Richard stared at me incredulously. "You must be insane if you think our one trivial disagreement had anything to do with that wretched girl's predicament."

"I saw you, Richard, and the argument did not sound trivial; on the contrary, you had your arms around Caroline's shoulders, speaking to her threateningly."

"Do you often lose your temper like that?" asked Blythe.

"Only when provoked, Inspector." Richard ran his fingers through his hair, a look of exasperation on his face. "I'm no saint, Liv, but you've got it all wrong."

"Was it a lovers' tiff, perhaps?" quizzed Blythe, leaning forward in his chair, staring at Richard keenly.

Richard shook his head. "Good grief, on the contrary, we enjoyed a healthy mutual dislike."

"Then what was the argument about?" quizzed Blythe.

"Caroline O'Connor was blackmailing me."

"So that's why you deposited £5,000 into her account earlier this month. What exactly did she have over you?" I quizzed.

"Caroline knew things I have kept from my parents." Richard swallowed hard before meeting my gaze. "The only crime I have committed is falling in love."

"With whom?"

"Cassandra."

"Cassandra Turnbull, the daughter of your parents' best friends, but isn't she married?"

"Yes, she is, but there is an added complication."

"What complication?"

"Cassandra's expecting my child, if my mother finds out, she will disown me, and I will lose everything. But then, after Caroline attempted to blackmail me again, I decided to come clean." He sighed. "I intended to tell Mother later this evening, and then this dreadful poisoning business occurred. I know how this sounds, but I did not poison that woman."

"Then who do you think did?" asked Blythe.

Richard smiled wearily. "I have no idea, Inspector."

Blythe stepped out of the room to take a phone call while I accompanied Richard back into the dining room. I listened spellbound as he told his parents he was about to become a father. Matilda looked as though she was about to faint.

"But why keep it a secret? We're living in the twenty-first century," said Robert.

"That old aphorism." Matilda scoffed, exasperated. "As though it justifies everything. So, your father and I are to be grandparents, and you didn't even think to tell us? Are we really that unapproachable?"

"Mother, I know your expectations of me are high, I'm sorry to be such a disappointment, but my lover, the mother of my unborn child, is Cassandra Turnbull."

"You impregnated a married woman, the daughter of our close friend Johnathan," Matilda spluttered, falling back in her seat horrified. "What on earth will they think of us at the golf club?"

"Cassandra is a great girl," I said, suddenly feeling the need to defend Richard. "We were at uni together, she's compassionate and kind with a first-class mind. Richard would be lucky to have her."

Richard nodded, smiling gratefully; witnessing his unexpected devotion to Cassandra and his unborn child was endearing. Richard diverted his gaze to Matilda, who shook her head in disbelief.

"Cassandra and I intend to marry as soon as her divorce from Julian comes through. So, if you and Dad decide to disown me, that's fine."

"Don't look at me that way," said Matilda.

"Why not?"

"Because I never could refuse you anything. You are my son, and I love you." She paused for a moment.

"Alright," Matilda conceded. "We are all distraught; we shall talk later once the inspector's resolved this dreadful business."

"Might I remind you that we are still conducting an attempted murder investigation?" interrupted Blythe as he entered the room. "If Miss O'Connor dies, then this will become a suspected murder enquiry." The inspector's narrative quietened the room. Sergeant Dixon gestured for Lesley to join us in the drawing room.

Before I left, I noticed Rachel rise from her chair to embrace Richard. "Well bro, you've managed to upstage my big day, that's for sure."

"I don't think I can deal with any more drama; goodness knows what the villagers will make of this," Matilda wailed.

John placed his hand on her shoulder. "They will think like everyone else, Mrs Barnaby, how fortunate your children are to have found love and how blessed you and your husband will be as grandparents."

Lesley sat across from Blythe and me, sipping from a glass of water; she looked pale and drawn, her ash-blonde hair tied up in a knot, and her brown eyes staring at us from behind gold-rimmed spectacles.

"Can you confirm your whereabouts today?" asked Blythe.

"I have been here since 9am, Inspector, catching up on paperwork. Mr Barnaby and the servants can vouch for me."

"And where is your office?"

"At the far end of the house, next to the orangery."

"Did you see or hear anything suspicious?"

"No, not at all."

"Do you normally have dinner with your employers?"

"No, I don't live in. I rented a cottage in the village; Mr Barnaby kindly invited me. You see, today is the anniversary of my sister's death. She died in London under tragic circumstances last year. So, I moved here shortly after and started work for Mr Barnaby."

"What was your sister's name?" I asked.

"Her name was Helen Bruini. She was only 24 when she passed away. An intern at a legal practice in London. She was a bright girl with a promising career ahead of her."

"We are sorry for your loss," said the inspector, smiling at Lesley sympathetically.

We were interrupted by my cell ringing, I glanced at the screen. "Sorry, sir, I need to take this." I left the room to speak to Jonathan Keenan, who confirmed what I already knew.

Matilda entered the room; taking a seat, she stared at us defiantly. Blythe returned her gaze with a flicker of amusement.

"What about you, Mrs Barnaby? You told your family you had an accountant's appointment this afternoon, but we checked with Mr Keenan, and you cancelled that appointment yesterday."

Matilda raised her eyebrow. "Ah, so you thought I bought antifreeze instead, then popped back to bump off my maid; why on earth would I do that," she sneered.

"I don't know, you tell me, Mrs Barnaby. Perhaps you discovered Miss O'Connor was blackmailing your precious son and wanted to silence her."

"Ridiculous."

"Then please enlighten me, tell us where you were this afternoon?"

Matilda hesitated. "I was at the hospital visiting the oncology suite, I have stage two breast cancer."

I gasped in astonishment.

"But why didn't you tell anyone? You have a family to support you; you don't have to face this alone." I fought back the tears.

"I know, I'm sorry. I didn't want to put a damper on the big day."

"What did the doctors say?"

"They said it's treatable, the cancer is in the lymph node, but I will need an operation soon."

"How soon?"

"After the wedding, but please don't say anything to the others; I promise to tell them after the honeymoon." I stared at Matilda in stunned silence. Sensing her vulnerability I squeezed her hand, she squeezed mine back.

I FOUND MAKING EYE contact difficult when Robert entered the drawing room so soon after Matilda's shocking revelation. He confirmed Lesley Bruini was at The Grange all day working in her office. The last time Robert saw Caroline was in the drawing room, where we took afternoon tea. When we quizzed Robert about the antifreeze, he explained the bottle had been unopened when he last visited the garage two days earlier.

Our next interviewee was Reverend Jemson. He smiled reassuringly before taking a seat. "This is a dreadful business, Inspector. Rest assured I will do anything I can to help." John confirmed he was in the church all afternoon, officiating two funerals. He showed us his work diary. John said he arrived at The Grange at 7:30, where he enjoyed pre-dinner drinks, striking up several conversations with Lesley, Robert and Matilda, who'd confirmed his story.

Rachel was in next; she shrugged, staring at me perplexedly. She confirmed she spent the morning shopping in town with Matilda before meeting Stephen at The Randolph. The Sergeant had already checked, and the concierge confirmed Rachel and Stephen only left their suite at

7:30pm, ordering coffee from room service at 5:30pm, verified by the bellboy, who received a tip for his trouble.

Blythe stared at me curiously as Rachel exited the room. "Well, Williams, we only have one more witness to interview. So, what have you deduced so far?"

"On the face of it, it would appear that Richard had the means and motive, but then if he was about to confess why would he put himself at risk? It makes no sense."

"Although we only have his word for that," said Blythe.

"That's true," I agreed. "Then we have Lesley Bruini. She was here all day and had the time and opportunity, but what was her motive? I remember that incident she mentioned with her sister; my colleague David Dunnett wrote an article for the paper I was working on."

"Could you find the article?" asked Blythe.

"I can do better than that, sir." I glanced at my cell. "I still have David's number."

Blythe consulted with his sergeant while I phoned David.

"Hi Liv, I was about to go to bed. You know how tough life is for us old hacks?" He laughed.

After I explained the reason for my call, David immediately emailed the article. I showed it to Blythe and Sergeant Dixon when they re-entered the room.

"I understand if you want to sit this out," said Blythe, his face a mask of concern.

I shook my head. "No, sir, it's fine."

Blythe gestured to the sergeant. "In that case, Dixon, send in our next person of interest, Stephen King."

"Is this a joke?" asked Stephen, leaning back in his chair, staring at Blythe with a thunderous gaze. "This is my first visit to The Grange, Inspector. I had never met any of the staff before. Why would you suspect me?"

"Do you remember Helen Bruini?" I quizzed.

Stephen looked at me in amazement. "Yes, of course, she was my co-worker. It's tragic what happened. But what on earth has this got to do with anything?"

"Could you talk us through what happened that night?"

"I already gave a statement to the London Metropolitan Police."

"We understand that," said Blythe. "But please humour us, the information may be relevant to the case."

"Right." Stephen sighed. "We went out to dinner in Soho, Helen, me and Simon Henderson, the clerk working with us on the Santi case. After receiving a guilty verdict on the indictment, we decided to celebrate. After the meal, Helen and I wanted to go home, but Simon insisted we go to a nightclub. Helen's sister was on the way to pick her up. So, Simon and I walked ahead to get the drinks. Helen arrived soon after. To be honest, Simon was pretty wasted by then. So, when he and Helen disappeared for a while, I had an idea what they were doing. When they came back, they were both high on Charlie."

He shook his head. "I have never taken drugs, Officer, only the occasional drink and social cigarette. But there was no filter with Simon. So, I told them I was going home I called a cab, but Helen collapsed onto the floor before I had a chance to leave. Simon panicked. He told me to call for an ambulance and then ran out of the club, he said he couldn't risk the police discovering him with drugs. So, I called for an ambulance and stayed with Helen until the paramedics arrived. She might have recovered if it had just been the cocaine; we could not know that someone spiked Helen's drink with Rohypnol. She died on the way to the hospital."

"Yes, we're aware," said Blythe, staring at Simon grimly. "The Metropolitan police reported that the perpetrator Ian Ambrose was later arrested and charged with involuntary manslaughter. He is currently serving time in Pentonville. We understand that your colleague Simon later killed himself with an overdose, although the coroner recorded an open verdict. Why do you think he did that?" asked Blythe.

"Oh, he was heartbroken; Simon adored Helen. He was nuts about her."

"I take it she never returned those feelings; she had another lover, perhaps," said Blythe.

Stephen laughed. "No, Inspector, Helen did have a lover, but it wasn't Simon or me, you see, Helen was gay. As for Simon, he couldn't cope with the fact that he was indirectly responsible for the death of the only woman he ever loved, even if it was unreciprocated. So, Simon took his own life, and I lost two close friends within days of each other." He sighed. "So, it's been a challenging year, and then I met Rachel. But I don't see what this has to do with the suspected poisoning of Barnaby's maid."

"Oh, believe me, it has everything to do with it, but perhaps not in the way you might think," I said.

Stephen looked at me perplexed. "May I go outside for a cigarette?" he asked. Blythe nodded; Sergeant Dixon escorted Stephen into the garden while Blythe recalled Lesley.

She sat on the chesterfield with an aloof expression, all pretence of amiability removed from her face.

"It's been a long day, Inspector; I'd like to go home now."

Blythe nodded. "As would everyone else, Miss Bruini. We have a few more questions. The night your sister died, we understand you picked her up from The Blue Dolphin."

"That's right, but then Helen insisted I drop her off at The Black Cat nightclub. I pleaded with her to come home, but she insisted on going. So, I drove her there. A work colleague waited outside, smoking a cigarette." She sighed. "He escorted Helen into the club. That was the last time I saw my sister alive."

I stared at her hard. "The person responsible for spiking your sister's drink is in prison, and Simon Henderson paid with his life. But it was the third man you also held accountable, and you recognised him when he arrived earlier this evening. The barrister and your sister's work colleague from Pump Court Temple, Stephen King?"

Lesley started to cry. "I was shocked when I saw him, the arrogant young man who stood outside that nightclub twelve months ago and led Helen to her death."

"But you've got it all wrong," I said. "Stephen had nothing to do with your sister's death. He wasn't responsible for the cocaine or spiking her drink. On the contrary, Stephen tried to help Helen. He was the one who stayed and gave her CPR."

Lesley dabbed her eyes with a tissue. "I'm so sorry about the girl, Caroline. How is she?"

"Thanks to Doctor Ashe's timely intervention, Miss O'Connor is now conscious and expected to recover. So, I'm curious, how did you administer the poison?" asked Blythe.

"I was responsible for the place settings and ensured I sat next to Stephen King at dinner, when Caroline complained of feeling unwell and drew the room's attention, I poured a dash of antifreeze I found in the garage into King's coffee cup. But I was mortified when Caroline drank from the cup and the rest, you know." Lesley's voice trailed off, her eyes on the floor.

Blythe sighed. "Lesley Bruini I am arresting you for the attempted manslaughter of Caroline O'Connor." He read Lesley her rights as Dixon deftly handcuffed her.

"What will happen to me now?" she sobbed.

"Once you arrive at the Station you will be formally charged and questioned further. You will be advised of your rights and offered legal representation. Be thankful you are not looking at a more severe charge."

Sergeant Dixon quietly led Lesley out through the patio doors.

Blythe spoke to me softly. "You did well today, Liv. Go and enjoy the wedding; family is everything. I intend to return to mine after I've written this up at the station."

I stared at Blythe in surprise; it was the first time he had ever called me by my first name. "I will sir, thank you, and goodnight."

I entered the dining room to find everyone chatting among themselves. They were staggered when I filled them in on Lesley's subsequent arrest. Matilda smiled. "Thank you, Olivia. I hope the police realise how lucky they are to have you."

"I want to apologise for my behaviour in the past," said Richard. "I promise to do better. Susan once told me that when you become a parent, you look at the world differently when you see life through the eyes of a child; she was right."

After the inspector left everyone retired to bed, leaving John, James and me in the dining room. James went to the kitchen to uncork another bottle of wine.

I stared at John with curiosity. "That quote you said at dinner, I have been wracking my brain to try and remember where I heard it before, and then it came to me."

"Ah, that." He laughed. "Why it's from Thomas Moore?"

"Yes, I remember now; he was my mom's favourite."

John looked at me in astonishment. "You worked it out then?"

"Yes, but why did you never say anything?"

"Because Susan asked me not to. You see, I was married, albeit unhappily, and my wife refused to divorce me; then she had the accident and was confined to a wheelchair. I couldn't leave her then. So, after Yvonne passed away last year, I wanted to come forward, but I was afraid to approach you after all this time."

"It's alright, I understand. We have much to discuss."

"Yes, and by the looks of it, not just with me." He chuckled as James entered the room.

"No, thank you," said John refusing James's top-up offer. "I must go, I have a wedding to officiate."

I stood up and hugged John. "Goodnight, I'll see you on Saturday."

"I look forward to seeing you both," said John, beaming as he shook James by the hand before quietly leaving the room.

James sipped from his glass, staring at me pensively. "I need to apologise, Liv, for how I handled things when we split. I was an idiot. And then later, when I decided to try and make amends, Richard told me that you had found someone else."

"And you believed him?" I scoffed.

"I told you I was an idiot."

"While we're in the confession box, you don't have the monopoly on idiocy. I didn't realise how much I cared for you until it was too late."

Gazing into my eyes, James put his arms around me, and the years rolled away as though it was only yesterday as he gently kissed me, my heart beating wildly.

"Do you want the same again?" asked James, gesturing to the bottle of Merlot on the table.

I met his gaze, smiling demurely. "Oh, yes, I want the same again, but first I must ask my father for his blessing."

"Your father?" he quizzed, raising an eyebrow.

"Yes, I finally discovered his identity," I said, laughing at James's perplexed expression.

"But, how?"

"Why, it's all thanks to my mother, of course, and a little help from Thomas Moore."

FOR MORE INFORMATION about the author, please visit KD Sherrinford's website: http://www.kdsherrinford.co.uk/

Goes Around
Stephen D. Rogers

M iss Havisham tapped Estelle on the shoulder.

Estelle unclenched her teeth. "Now what? Boss."

"Why do today's bride and groom have to get married?"

"As you're well aware, since you own SatisFaction and booked this very reception, I'm desperately trying to assemble these fruit cups before the wedding guests arrive. Your interruptions? Not helping."

Miss Havisham merely repeated the question.

"Fine. I don't know. Why do they have to get married?"

"Because they cantaloupe."

Estelle turned to face her boss. "That's your worst one yet."

"I should have quit when I was ahead?"

"You should have been in another room doing something... administrative, instead of bothering me."

"I'm telling jokes to keep up your spirits. The guests are going to be here shortly, and look at how many containers you still need to fill."

"You could actually, I don't know: wash fruit, dry fruit, cut fruit, place fruit in the still empty containers."

Miss Havisham laughed. "You're such a delight, Estelle. Such a wit!"

"I wasn't joking. In ten minutes, a mob of hungry people is going to start storming through our front door."

"If I did the work, there would be nobody to supervise."

Estelle resumed making fruit cups. "Is that what you call what you're doing?"

"Supervising, and keeping up your spirits."

"Why did you even agree to fruit cups? What's wrong with the usual candy-covered almonds? So simple."

"The entire wedding is fruit-themed."

"Yes, I know that. Your idea. A bad idea, I might add."

"Posh. You can get candy-covered almonds anywhere. Here at SatisFaction Betrothals, we strive to create an experience worthy of your special day."

"Are you sure you weren't simply getting back at me for some small slight?"

"'Revenge' is such a harsh word."

"And fruit smoothies? Do you have any idea what it's going to be like making over a hundred individual fruit smoothies?"

"Just wait until you see my profit margin this quarter."

"That's all and well for you, but is any of that extra income destined for your most valuable employee?"

"You do keep me in stitches, Estelle."

"Hmm."

"Besides, you're my only employee, which already makes you my highest paid employee. Where's my motivation to pay you even more?"

"Maybe because I'm also your lowest paid employee."

"Is it any wonder, you chatting away when we're in such a tight spot? There's a mob preparing to storm through our front door!"

"You don't say."

"Someone did, but I wouldn't want to name names."

"How thoughtful of you."

"Let it never be said I don't protect my underlings."

Estelle shook her head. "One of these days, there's going to be a reckoning."

"There's a reckoning every week I calculate payroll. All that money I give you, and when was the last time I received a thank-you gift from a member of my adoring staff?"

"You have adoring staff?"

"Adoring me would at least explain what they do with all their time." Miss Havisham motioned at the worktable. "Storming mob. Empty containers."

Estelle straightened. "Hark. Is that a doorbell I hear?"

"We don't have a doorbell."

"Maybe the mob installed one." Estelle shooed away her boss. "You better go check."

MISS HAVISHAM FROWNED at the time.

While it was not uncommon for the wedding party to be late for the reception—the staged photographs and all—it was extremely rare for the guests, having survived the ceremony, not to be in a rush to celebrate with food and drink.

So where was everybody? Had they heard about the fruit smoothies, decided they needed stronger fortification, and stopped at a bar?

Miss Havisham stepped outside to see a limousine enter the circular drive.

Finally, somebody who couldn't wait to decide between a Strawberry Matrimony and a Will You Berry Me?

As soon as the lone vehicle stopped, the doors were flung open and the sobbing bride and gesticulating groom jumped out, she beating him up the stairs, past Miss Havisham, and through the front door.

The driver climbed out of the car, met Miss Havisham's questioning gaze, and shrugged. "Love."

Miss Havisham followed the happy couple inside.

THE BRIDE AND GROOM slumped at one of the round tables, her head in her hands, his fingers covering his eyes.

Miss Havisham asked brightly, "The ceremony?"

The bride thrust out an arm, a hand, a ring finger unadorned except for the diamond engagement.

"What happened?"

The groom shuddered. "I asked the best man for the ring."

"Yes?"

"I opened the box, and discovered a banana chip."

"Keeping to the fruit theme. But where was the ring?"

"That's what I'd like to know."

The bride groaned. "What we'd all like to know! We somehow staggered through the rest of the ceremony, and the two of us came here to recover while the guests and the rest of the wedding party search the church."

"Congratulations to you both. And my condolences. Remember, just in case nobody locates the ring, it's only a symbol."

"So's a bad omen."

Miss Havisham clapped twice to change the energy. "Pip, pip. I can't have you two all mopey during the reception, ruining everything for everybody."

"I'd almost rather call it off."

"Nonsense. All those people came out to watch you get married and then celebrate here afterwards." She paused, thinking the thing through. "Tell me, was there a ring bearer?"

"They weren't the real rings. We thought we were playing it safe, having her carry a pillow with replicas."

"My niece is a bit of a klutz."

"But she was so adorable."

"The best man and maid of honor were given the boxes this morning at the wedding breakfast."

"That narrows down the timeline of the theft."

The groom straightened. "Theft? Are you suggesting someone stole the ring?"

"Not just stole it, but replaced it with a banana chip. That's not what happens if someone opens the box and the ring rolls away. That's intentional." Miss Havisham lowered her voice for dramatic effect. "It's a message."

The bride sighed. "I wanted today to be perfect."

"It will be once I solve this mystery. Buck up, you two. Everybody should be here shortly, and they're coming to celebrate."

MISS HAVISHAM STOOD behind the bar with Estelle, each responsible for three blenders.

Estelle frowned. "Looking out into the crowd, I see blue tuxedos and suits, and I see red blouses and dresses."

"Yes, blueberries and strawberries. The brilliant fruit theme you mentioned earlier." Miss Havisham noted a slip someone had left on the bar. "If Buddy's killer is the bride's college friend, poison is not the murder weapon" was written on the back.

"Then why am I in yellow? I don't look good in yellow."

"You're the banana. Or pineapple, if you prefer. Even if you're a bit of a lemon."

Estelle examined what her boss was wearing. "And what are you, a blackberry?"

"I'm management."

"That's convenient."

"For me it is. You still look like a banana. You're not missing any chips, are you?"

"I should hope not. Why, would it give you an excuse to dock my pay?"

"You know, that's the best idea you've had all day."

"Thank you. I think."

"A little less chatting." Miss Havisham nodded towards the people coming towards the bar. "Customers."

Customers who would be talking amongst themselves about what happened during the ceremony, feeling free to gossip while waiting for their smoothie since Miss Havisham was merely the person pulping the fruits they chose.

The noise of the blenders complicated the eavesdropping, but Miss Havisham was careful to be inefficient, taking longer than necessary to rinse and pre-cut the items to be mushed so that she could listen longer without interruption. In fact, she was moving so slowly that Estelle kept glancing over, probably trying to decide whether her boss had just handed her a reason to ask for a raise.

The next time Miss Havisham caught Estelle's eye, she mouthed: "No."

Miss Havisham smiled at the person waiting next in line. "Which smoothie would you like me to make for you?"

"I guess I'll settle for a Watermelon Wedding."

"Would you like mint?"

"Yes, please."

She turned to the man standing next to her. "Can you believe I can't even get a decent glass of bourbon here? It's no wonder the ceremony was such a mess."

"I wouldn't be surprised if the whole thing was faked."

She nodded. "Cut ring expenses in half. Cheap out on the alcohol. It's definitely them."

Miss Havisham handed her a Watermelon Wedding before meeting his gaze. "Sir?"

He shuddered. "I don't think so."

She looked past the couple. "Next."

The young woman shouldered her way through. "Can I have a double expresso mocha cappuccino?"

"I'm afraid we just have fruit smoothies."

"So put a strawberry on top."

"We're not set up to make coffee drinks. But I'm more than happy to make you a Strawberry Matrimony."

"Fine." She pulled out her phone and started scrolling.

As Miss Havisham slowly prepared the fruit, she took advantage of the fact that her customer wasn't fully present. "Bride's side or the groom's?"

"Neither, really." She didn't bother looking up while she answered. "My brother's an usher."

"How'd you score an invitation?"

"More like, why couldn't I get out of doing my brother a favor?"

"What's that?"

"He works with the groom, but he's shy, doesn't know anybody here. If I come, that's at least one friendly face."

"Plus the groom."

"I think he has other things on his mind today."

"What did you think about the ring fiasco?"

"I can't believe people still put themselves through all this."

"You don't believe in marriage?"

She finally looked up from her phone. "What does anything that happened today have to do with two people falling in love?"

Miss Havisham handed over the smoothie. "It's about making private feelings public in a way that allows others to witness and take part."

"Whatever."

Once the customer flounced away, Miss Havisham turned her attention to the next couple in line. "What'll you have?"

The guy elbowed the woman standing next to him. "Two extra-large dramas, straight up. No, I'm just kidding. Two of the blueberry smoothies."

He boasted to the woman, "I promised you today was going to be entertaining."

"You were right, no doubt about it. As soon you told me that Sharon was going to be there, I said to myself I had to attend, but I never imagined everybody in fancy clothes crawling around on the floor of the church."

"The bride and groom couldn't very well tell the best man his wife wasn't welcome just because she was once involved with him."

"Actually, Sharon was a bit of a letdown. I half expected her to take a swing at the bride."

"Probably too busy searching for the missing ring."

They traded an evil laugh.

Miss Havisham quickly finished their smoothies so as to move their nastiness along.

She washed her hands before turning to the next in line. "Yes?"

"You don't happen to have anything hot, do you? My wife still hasn't shaken the chill from the place where we all went to breakfast."

"I could make her a tea."

"That would be great, thank you. It was so cold at that restaurant, I put my jacket over my wife's shoulders, and she still couldn't get warm."

"I'll be back in a minute."

After letting Estelle know she was going to the kitchen, Miss Havisham put on a kettle, reviewing all she'd overheard. Mix in all she'd learned about human nature from working in food service, and everything that happened made sense except for one small detail.

Once she returned to the reception, she would have to ask the thief about the banana chip.

MISS HAVISHAM STOPPED in front of Sharon and waited for the woman to acknowledge her presence. "Yes?"

"Why the banana chip?"

Sharon laughed nervously. "What?"

"At breakfast this morning, your husband was given a wedding ring to hold, and he placed the box in his jacket pocket for safekeeping. You caught a chill in the restaurant, and the man you don't deserve slipped his jacket over your shoulders. Maybe you stole the ring there and then, or maybe you went to the bathroom to perform the deed. After all, you once dated the groom. Why should somebody else enjoy her wedding day with him?"

She licked her lips. "It wasn't quite like that."

"What I don't understand: why the banana chip?"

"I always keep some in my purse in case I get hungry."

Miss Havisham held out her hand. "The ring."

Sharon reluctantly retrieved the stolen item, and Miss Havisham marched over to the bride and groom. "Enjoying the reception?"

"Yes, thank you."

"They say that what comes around goes around, and I think this goes around the bride's finger." Miss Havisham handed the ring to the startled groom.

"Where did you find it?"

"We at SatisFaction Betrothals are here to serve."

After wishing the couple a happy life, Miss Havisham hurried back to behind the bar before Estelle filed a grievance.

FOR MORE INFORMATION about the author, please visit Stephen D. Rogers's website: http://www.StephenDRogers.com/

Jilted
Elaine Togneri

I stare down Grace Lutheran Church's center aisle with what I'm sure is a big, goofy grin, waiting for the love of my life to arrive. My fiancée Valerie searched for weeks to find the perfect wedding dress, and today is the great unveiling. Stress killed her appetite, so she opted for a smaller size. But I've been eating nonstop since we ordered my tux. My shirt collar pinches. I slip a finger between it and my neck trying to stretch it without dislocating my white bowtie, hoping no one is watching or videoing. The flower girl, my five-year-old niece, scatters rose petals as she takes slow, well-practiced steps. She reaches the altar. We are waiting for Wagner's "Bridal Chorus" to sound and announce the bride. All my family and friends are standing and facing the back of the church.

Val's only living relative, her gray-haired Uncle Jack, sits at the piano. He looks at me and raises his bushy eyebrows. He's playing another chorus of the flower girl's song. The bride has missed her cue. I stare at Reverend North, who's only been shaving ten years longer than me. He shifts from foot to foot and clears his throat, more keyed up than I am. People standing in the pews look forward as if somehow, they may have missed the bride's entrance. Hushed voices whisper.

I stare at the empty doorway. I don't know how long I wait. My heart crashes against my chest and threatens to break through. I strain to breathe. Where is Valerie? My family and friends look at each other, unsure what to do. I stride down the aisle. Murmuring, sorrowful voices follow. I dash toward the bride's chamber and throw open the door.

Empty. I race toward the main church entrance followed by the minister. Her bridal bouquet of red roses lies abandoned on the grass, wilting in the hot Florida sun. She's gone. So is the limo scheduled to drive us to the reception. Her uncle hurries past me to his car and doesn't respond when I ask where he's going. I trudge back to the church, push past everyone without a word, and return to the bride's room.

Valerie's engagement ring sits on a folded piece of paper in the center of the vanity. I pocket the ring and unfold the note. The paper is battered, the creases worn in. How long did she carry this around waiting for the right time? Our relationship moved fast, maybe too fast? The note reads:

This is really difficult. We're just not right for each other. I'm so sorry. I don't know what else to say. Wishing you the best with someone who truly loves you. Val.

My brother taps on the doorframe, holding my wailing niece in his arms. Tears stream down her face. "Hey, Shawn. What's going on? Can I help?"

I shrug. "Guess we're not lucky in love." My brother is divorced. His daughter, the only good thing to come from his marriage. I nod toward my niece. "You'd better take her home. Don't worry about me."

The minister has shooed everyone else out of the church. He appears at my side, his face frozen in the serious expression he has evidently practiced for consoling jilted grooms. "Cold feet," he announces. "Some people can't take the pressure. Better off eloping."

"Then how do you explain this?" I hand him the note as I call Valerie on my cell. It goes straight to voicemail.

"I had a bad feeling after the rehearsal dinner," he says, frowning. He returns the paper.

I remember us drinking too much and laughing our way through the practice run. "What do you mean?" I ask.

"She was troubled," he says. "She didn't have that love light shining in her eyes."

"Why didn't you say something?" I ask. Valerie and I made love three times that night. She seemed happy enough though we hadn't spent time looking into each other's eyes.

"I'm here for you, Son." He pats my back. "Whatever I can do to help."

Lines plagiarized from a sappy Hallmark movie; the kind Valerie turned on when she couldn't stand watching the Buccaneers lose another game. How out of touch this minister is. Has he ever managed a situation like this before? I need to ditch him. "I've got to cancel the reception, our hotel room, our honeymoon. Change my whole life." I stare at my shoes. I have to return them and the tux too. I stick my hand in my pocket. Empty. Valerie has our keys in the satin money bag she was going to use for a purse. I look at Reverend North. His black suit. The white stole, with Alpha and Omega embroidered in gold lettering that drapes his shoulders. His face still fake. I'm sure to regret this, but there's no one else around. "I need a ride home."

"Of course." His lips turn up slightly. "Glad to be of service." He slips the stole off his shoulders and onto a hanger. We walk to his car, a tan van with over a hundred thousand miles, a broken passenger handle and a sticky dash. I lean back in the passenger seat, wondering if Valerie will be there waiting. She's not answering my calls.

I give the minister credit for letting me stew on the way there, only asking for directions, not stupid questions about my feelings. Fifteen minutes later, we arrive at the apartment I share with Valerie. I try to lose him, but he says he fears I'll need him if she's here. He trails me to the door. I don't have the key, but it swings open when I try the handle.

◊ If Buddy's killer once dated the bride, the gun is the murder weapon. ◊

Papers lie scattered on the floor. My big screen TV is gone, the Blu-ray player, even the cable box. I catch myself before cursing as I remember the reverend and forget him again as I dash into the bedroom. Also missing, my laptop, and all things Valerie, her clothing, makeup, hair dryer. So much for avoiding bad luck by sleeping at my brother's last night. I'm sliding open drawers to see if she left anything behind when I hear the minister's calm voice.

"I need to report a robbery," he says into his cell.

Cops are the last thing I need. I turn and consider ripping the phone out of his hand, assault on a man of the cloth, or police climbing all over my life, two unthinkable choices. "You need to leave," I say instead.

He shakes his head and gives my address to dispatch. He whispers to me, "She cleaned you out good. But remember, Son, it's blessed to forgive."

"No way Valerie would..." But who else? I believed she loved me, not that she'd ditch me at the altar at the last minute. I don't want the cops involved. I'm not sure about forgiveness, but I won't press charges.

HOURS LATER AFTER FIVE shots of coconut vodka, the only liquor left in the apartment, I toss and turn. Around four a.m., sleep overtakes me. After I wake up, I'm actually grateful to Reverend North. I barely had to say two words to the cops. He handled them, cancelled travel arrangements, and returned my tux and shoes on his way back home. So, when the phone rings and I hear his voice, I'm not annoyed.

"I found something," he says. "You need to see this." He sounds breathless.

"What is it?"

"Just come to the church," he says and hangs up.

My car is a dented and scraped former rental that I bought at one of those credit union car sales days. I'm grateful Valerie hated it so much she left it behind. It's low on gas, but I estimate I have enough and barrel down the road to the church. The foyer door is locked. I bang on it and pace as I wait for the reverend to answer.

He draws the door open slowly and scans the roadway before he lets me in.

"What do you have?" I ask.

"Our security video captured something. I don't want to jump to conclusions."

That didn't stop him yesterday. Still, I want to grasp at any chance my relationship with Valerie wasn't a sham. "Show me."

He leads me to an office crowded with bookcases, jammed full of Bibles and hymnals. He sits in front of a rundown desktop monitor squeezed in between piles of papers on an ancient metal desk and works the mouse. A video plays, showing a man, slightly younger than me, at the church's side door. If I can believe the time and date stamp, he's there twenty minutes before our ceremony. I bend close to the display for a better look. The hair on the top of the guy's head is long and streaked red. It hangs over black stubble on the sides. Matching shadow covers his chin and cheeks. The rest of his face is a dark shade of pale. A sweatshirt and jeans don't hide his powerful muscular frame. Not dressed to attend the wedding.

"Who is it?" I ask.

"You don't know?" Reverend North turns to face me, his forehead furrowed.

"No. Should I? What's he got to do with Valerie?"

North leans his forehead on his hand and shakes his head. "She should have told you. It's not my place."

I snap upright. "Don't give me crap, man. Why did you bring me down here?"

"Watch your language please."

"Don't play games with me, Father." I say that instead of the words I want to use. "Show me the rest of the video. Does Valerie leave with him?"

"That's all I've got. The camera on the main entrance is broken. We don't have the funds to replace it. He must have gone out that way. I've checked everything else."

I step forward and stare down at him. "I think I'm owed an explanation."

He sighs and puffs out a breath. "You're not the first groom Valerie left at the altar." He nods at the screen. "Meet Fabio. Her ex-fiancé."

My jaw clenches and I speak through my teeth. "How long ago?"

"Six months."

"Did you counsel her, Father?" I taunt him again with the title. "Didn't you think it was too soon to jump into another relationship?"

"I thought you knew."

Evidently there's a lot I don't know about Valerie. "Maybe—"

"Maybe they got back together," he says. "We never know God's plan."

Not what I was going to say. "Only one way to find out. Where does Fabio live?"

"Bad idea, Son."

I finally figure out he uses that word when he's trying to exert authority.

His phone plays "Amazing Grace" and he snatches it up to escape. "What? Yes, I understand. Right away. Can you give me any more information? Of course." When he finally hangs up, he turns back to me.

"There's a dead body the police need me to identify at Moby's Funeral Home."

I close my eyes for a few seconds and brace myself. "Valerie?"

"A male. I must go." He stands and walks toward the exit.

I follow along. "Please give me Fabio's address. I just want to talk to Valerie."

He stops and locks the door behind us. "If you come with me now, I'll take you there afterwards."

I frown. I don't want to waste time. "How long will you be tied up?"

"However long it takes. I will not be a party to violence. I'm not sure you have control of your feelings," he says, walking to his van and not looking at me.

"You don't trust me."

He pierces me with a glance. "I place my trust entirely in God, not man." He sits in the driver's seat.

I have no play without his information. I climb into the passenger side.

THIRTY MINUTES LATER, while I'm waiting in the van for the reverend, I call Valerie again. No answer. I check her accounts. No activity since yesterday, our wedding day. In the morning, she posted a message.

Dear Mom, Please look down from heaven and bless Shawn and me on this special day. I love you and miss you. Val

Reverend North is totally wrong. No cold feet, no reuniting with a former lover. Why would she post this and then abandon me? Only answer, she couldn't have left of her own free will. But what about her note? To understand I need to find Valerie. I peer out the windshield toward the redbrick funeral home. The minister's still inside.

What's taking so long? I stretch my fingers and take a long breath. Time's a wasting. I jump out of the van and head for the double door.

A man dressed in a suit and tie is in the foyer. He offers to help me.

"I'm looking for Reverend North," I say.

"Are you a friend?" the man asks.

I lie. "Yes."

"Please come with me." I follow him to an office where North is seated in a large brown leather chair. The acrid smell of vomit fills the room, and another man holds a small plastic garbage can next to the reverend.

"What happened?" I ask.

Reverend North greets me with a wan smile before upchucking bile.

Whoa, not good.

The guy holding the bucket says, "Some dudes can't take looking at dead people."

The reverend shakes his head. "It's Valerie's uncle and his head is smashed in." He gags, but this time nothing comes out.

"I was hoping for Fabio," I say. Could this have anything to do with her disappearance? "Are you going to be okay, Father?"

He nods but doesn't look up.

"We've got to get going," I say. "Maybe some fresh air." I hope because I don't have time to play nurse. I head toward him and help him up. "Let's go."

Once he's standing, his brain seems to activate. "I need to talk to the police."

"Not now," I insist, holding him by the elbow and aiming toward the exit. I worry the guy in reception won't let us leave, but he opens the door and holds it until we're both through. I march the reverend to his car and plop him in the passenger seat. "You're in no shape to drive, and I'm afraid Fabio kidnapped Valerie. Maybe Uncle Jack got in the way."

Reverend North wipes his mouth with a crumpled-up napkin from the glove compartment. "It's the complex off Ratner Road."

I pull out onto the highway into the fast lane and sink the accelerator. The fifteen-minute drive takes me seven. Weeds plan to reclaim the apartment complex's parking lot, but I just run them over until I find a spot by Building One.

"Upstairs, two-oh-one," North says.

I leave him to fend for himself, bound up the steps, and follow the concrete walkway. I'm banging on the door before he catches up.

The door finally opens, and I see a woman with long brown hair, highlighted with blonde streaks. For a minute, I think it's Valerie, but then I notice wrinkles around her eyes and jowls weighing down her cheeks. She's also heavier and shorter. "Can I help you?" she asks.

The reverend jumps in. "We're looking for Fabio."

"He used to live here, but he got married and moved."

"When?" North asks while I ask, "Where?"

Her face turns from one of us to the other and the reverend wins. "Six, seven months ago, I think. I'm here six months."

"Do you know where he moved?" I ask again.

"Super told me the guy was so great. He bought a brand-new house. A surprise gift for his bride. How cool is that?"

"Where?" Reverend North asks.

"That's all I know, guys."

"Thanks," I say.

On the way back to the van, Reverend North says, "Not much help."

"You know what I do, right?" I ask.

"You work in a bank."

"I write mortgages. If I can find the sale, I'll get the address." I open the van and get back into the driver's seat. No need to discuss my sideline of private high interest loans for those who don't qualify for bank mortgages.

"No guarantee he went through with it." The minister slides in.

"I need a computer." I shift into drive.

"We've got a brand-new one at the church."

"Not that I saw. Besides, I thought you didn't have funds." I pull out into traffic.

"The deacons insist on the top of the line."

I look at him, the question on my face.

"For collecting tithes."

THE CHURCH TREASURER'S computer is a superfast laptop with the latest toys, but all I need is Fabio's last name to plug into county websites. Within minutes I find the deed, lot, and plat listed in local property records. There's no mortgage. I use the information I've gathered to find a street address. I remember the Rivercress development. I processed mortgages for a few clients. It's in the middle of the county, one of the endless series of developments in our bedroom community.

"You never mentioned Fabio was rich," I say to Reverend North.

"Not to my knowledge. I shouldn't say this, but not based on the engagement ring."

"Paid for the house in cash," I announce.

"Where did he get the money?"

"Are you coming?" I ask, jogging toward the door. I've got to get to Valerie. Even though the minister is no help since he's been wrong about everything, he might come in handy.

He hurries behind me to his van and we're off. He clips on the seatbelt.

I don't make excuses for how I drive, and he braces one hand on the dash when we zoom around turns.

THE HOUSE SITS ON A narrow lot between two others. The front has a stacked stone façade and a fancy door with a glass insert. I park strategically blocking the green pickup truck in the driveway. "You go and ring the bell," I instruct. "I'll be out of sight over here." I head for the side of the house. Once I'm in position, I hear the peal of the doorbell.

There's a window, but I can't see through the blinds. I admit to myself I'm using the reverend for entrance to the home. We're not friends or comrades. He came of his own accord. If he gets hurt, it's on him. When the front door unlocks, I zoom around the corner and launch myself at the opening. I knock down North and the person who answered the door: Valerie.

"Sorry," I say and help her to her feet. I leave the minister to struggle up on his own.

"You can't be here," she says, moving her pupils to the side as if willing me to look there. She's dressed not in her bridal gown but in a casual sundress that ends mid-thigh.

"What's going on?" a voice calls down the hall. It's Fabio, wearing only gym shorts. His bare chest and stomach sport tanned, well-defined muscles. He clenches one fist and his knuckles crack. "Father, what are you doing here?" he asks.

I don't let go of Valerie's hand. It is warm and smooth and presses mine. "Don't you mean what am I doing here?"

"Don't," Valerie says, pulling away.

Fabio yells, "Get in the kitchen."

Valerie doesn't move. "I'm here with you. You don't need to hurt anyone else."

"I haven't hurt anyone," Fabio declares.

She rubs her neck and I notice small purple blotches that could be bruises. I breathe deeply to restrain the urge to smack him. A plastic strap is wrapped around her wrist. It looks like a fitness band.

"Shawn, you and Reverend North can't be here," she says.

"Exactly right," Fabio says, looking down the street.

A white van approaches from the south, moving slowly. Emblazoned on the sides is Miller's Electric, Inc.

"We've got a short in the garage," Fabio says. "Our insurance won't cover you if anything happens. You need to go."

Two burly guys exit the work van. Neither one has a clipboard or tool belt. They open the van's back door and just stand there. I look at Valerie.

Her eyes appear moist and her voice rises with each word. "I'm sorry, Shawn. Just go. Go now."

"Tell him you love me," Fabio says. "That should wake him up."

"I, I don't love you, Shawn. I love Fabio." She raises her eyebrows and looks only at Fabio. "You don't have to do this," she tells him.

"Oh, but I do."

Reverend North's eyes open wide. "I think we need to pray on this."

Fabio shoves him back against the door. "Why are you in the middle of this, Father? It's not good for your health." Fabio holds him off balance.

The men start walking toward the house.

I want to intervene. Guess the rev is getting to me. While Fabio is occupied with him, I pull out my phone and quickly search. No such electric company.

Fabio releases North as the men step onto the porch. "Service call. What's with the crowd?" the taller one says.

"Just leaving," the reverend replies.

"Wrong again," I say.

"Listen, buddy," the talker says. "Time to move on."

I grab Valerie's hand and whisper, "Run." I dash away, dragging her behind.

"Stop!" the talker shouts. "Go get her," he tells Fabio. "The boss won't be happy about this."

I yank the rev's van side door and slide it open. I shove Valerie inside, shut the door and sidestep just as Fabio attempts to tackle me. "Lock the door," I yell. This isn't a fair fight. Fabio outweighs me. I sit behind a desk, and he works out daily. I dredge up memories of youthful karate training. But since he came at me with full force, his head hit the side of the van when I moved out of the way. He fell to the ground without me even touching him. I kick him a couple of times to make sure he stays down. I only stop when the tall guy is on me, twisting my arm until I'm afraid it will break. I chop his throat in just the right spot with my other hand and he loses his grip.

"Stop," a voice calls.

I look back to see the other burly guy pressing a handgun to the side of Reverend North's head. I can't let that stop me. We could all end up dead. I chop at the tall guy's throat a couple more times.

He chokes and clutches his neck.

"I said stop or I'll shoot," the guy holding the gun yells.

"Go ahead," I say. "He does God's work, going straight to heaven. Can't say the same for you."

"Are you a priest?" the guy asks the reverend, pulling the gun slightly away.

North's neck is bent, his eyes closed in prayer, but he nods.

"Sorry, Father." He holsters his weapon. He marches over to Fabio who lies on the ground, blood dripping from his mouth, looking dazed. "Your debt is still due. We want cash this time. We'll be in touch."

I hear the reverend on the phone, doing his favorite thing, calling the police.

I open the van door and hug Valerie to my chest. "Are you okay?"

"I've got a lot to tell you," she says. "I'm so sorry I wasn't honest with you. I'm not supposed to tell anyone I'm in witness protection. I testified against the Manhattan mob. There's a price on my head." She pulls back and tears pool in her eyes.

"I don't care, Valerie." I try to pull her close again, but she resists.

"Wait. Let me finish. The feds relocated me here ten months ago. I made a big mistake and trusted this guy." She points at Fabio. "We broke up, but he blames me for the money he owes the local gangs. He robbed our apartment and kidnapped me. He told them I was worth big bucks to the Manhattan mob." She shudders. "The gang was going to trade me to them for the cash."

"That explains a lot. Except Uncle Jack."

"He's not really my uncle, a bodyguard assigned by WITSEC. He checked the bridal room and thought I'd be okay with so many people around."

"He's dead."

She looks to the heavens and blinks. "Fabio found him checking out the garage and hit him over the head. He got the local crew to drop the body in a dumpster. If you know, I guess the police found him there." She pulls at the band on her arm. "I've got to get this off. It's a tracker."

I grab the plastic and stretch it until it slides over her hand. "What about that note you left me?"

She drops the band on the ground. "I wrote that to Fabio six months ago. I guess he saved it. He must have figured he could reuse it on you. You're the one I want to be with, Shawn. I love you."

"I love you too." I kiss her.

"Let's get out of here," I say, tapping my phone to order a ride service.

"What about Reverend North?"

"Hey, Father," I call, "you came here on a visitation and Fabio went berserk."

He considers this for a minute. "All true. See you in church Sunday?" he asks.

We both nod and walk to the corner to wait for the car. It arrives and thankfully, we're on our way before a police cruiser passes and turns toward Fabio's.

"I want to tell you everything," Valerie says as we cuddle in the ride's back seat.

I silence her with a kiss. That's enough sharing for a while. As for my loan shark secrets, they can wait until after we marry. I want to make sure she can't testify against me.

FOR MORE INFORMATION about the author, please visit Elaine Togneri's website: http://www.elainetogneri.com/

Sabotage and a Murder Mystery

Lynn Hesse

I fold the bank statements and stick them underneath the spice caddy on our dinette table. Half of Sissy's wedding expenses are charged to my credit card and half to my husband's. The birds are pecking at the wet feeder outside our bay window. A bee lights on a daffodil. The Georgia morning shower has vanished, leaving spring sunshine, blooming flowers, and pollen streams on my neighbor's work truck parked across the street.

My husband, Jim, traces the curve of his coffee cup handle with his thumb. "Where are they going on their honeymoon?"

"Not sure. Sissy wanted to go on a three-day mystery cruise but they can't afford it."

"I bet Ray hates murder mysteries. He dodged a bullet." Jim pats my hand and puts on his Atlanta Braves ball cap. "I should be going. Traffic. Don't want the floor manager to regret giving me the overtime."

"Maybe interactive mystery dinner theatre tickets will suffice. See you tonight, hon." I hear the door slam as I stack the dishes in the dishwasher, turn off the lights, and grab my "teacher-of-the-year" tote.

THE COFFEE WITH MADELINE:

His mother disliked me from the start.

The line is long at the coffee shop, and I can't think of anything else to say.

Madeline arches her back, pushes her store-bought breasts out, and sticks a photo of Susan in my face. "This beauty was Ray's fiancée before you came along. She sings in the Better Hope Baptist choir *and* acts. Look at that skin. Flawless." She shakes her highlighted feathered hairdo and narrows her gaze, scanning my freckles.

I order a croissant and cappuccino and scratch at the bug bites on my chin and neck. At least she can't see the red bumps on my backside, but her son didn't object to them last night.

Madeline sits on the shady side of the table and ogles my croissant. "So, Susan, I'm sorry. It's Sissy. You're lucky you do yard work for a living and don't need to count calories."

"I own a landscaping business. As I've mentioned before, I'm a master gardener and have ten employees." I scoot and angle my chair away from the sun. I don't bother to explain that during a recent landscaping job, my field manager asked me to drop by for a consult on the customer's Japanese maple tree. I stepped into a mound of Georgia's red ants. Those suckers climbed like Olympic runners up my boots and jeans and into my panties. I'm a bit unlucky.

THE PHONE CALL AND AFTER:

I'm trying not to hyperventilate. "Hi, Mom. Sissy here. We need to talk."

"I'm not mad, sweetheart, disappointed, sure. I thought we, mother and daughter, would pick out your dress next week. Why would Ray's mom—"

"We met for a coffee in downtown Mobile. She asked me if I'd seen any dresses I liked and didn't I know Mobile was famous for its designer gowns. When we leave the coffee shop, she doesn't tell me where we are going. Before I can object, I'm being fitted in a wedding dress by this old guy who has been The Jester for the Mystic Society balls for a million years and runs the Mardi Gras Museum."

In the background, Dad says, "How much?" I realize I'm on speakerphone.

"Tell Dad I'll pay for the dress." My guilt meter runs into the red zone.

"No, you won't," Mom says. I can visualize her scowling at Dad in their living room over three-hundred miles away.

"We can drive from Atlanta and save the plane fare," Dad says. "The boss won't be happy. Probably lose a day's pay, but dads want to see their little girls happy."

AT THE GROOM'S MOTHER'S HOUSE, A SNAG IN AND SNAG OUT:

Madeline puts the finishing touches on a quiche and slides it into the oven. "The good news is the caterer. Susan's new boyfriend, Tray, can make a groom's cake by Saturday, but Darlene—the sister who practically raised me—can't make the bridal shower Thursday night. I told her you wouldn't object if we changed it to Friday afternoon."

"Actually, I do. My parents are taking vacation days from work and arriving early on Thursday for the shower. On Friday, the rehearsal starts at five at the church, and then the rehearsal dinner's that night."

Two hours later Ray hugs me in his mom's territory, her kitchen. The dishwasher is humming, and Madeline and her husband are on the veranda watching the sunset. "Don't worry, babe. It will all work out. Mom is only trying to make everyone happy. How about we go to bed?" Ray tickles my neck with his trimmed beard.

The next morning I'm feeling optimistic until Madeline drops her bomb on the way out of the house. "I got the most fabulous deal from Joc, a florist in Daphne. For a hundred dollars more, he'll put flowers on the ends of the pews."

"My family has a budget, and we can't afford extra flowers."

"I'm sure they won't mind. Of course, it's your wedding and you only get married once, or so we hope."

THREE DAYS BEFORE THE WEDDING:

"I'll talk to Mom. I promise." Ray kisses me, and the doorbell rings.

"That will be my dad and Gerry. We're off for the tux fitting. Smile. That's my girl."

"Why is your brother going? Isn't my brother your best man?" I'm aware I'm standing at the bottom of the stairs and my curly hair is loose and bushy. Glamorous, Sissy.

Somebody taps on the door. Bob, Ray's dad, doesn't bother to wait and steps into the foyer of his used-to-be house, now the home his ex-wife shares with her current husband.

I pull my mid-thigh robe closed over one of Ray's tee shirts. "Hello, Bob," I say forcing a smile. "Ray will be with you soon. Give us a minute."

Ray's father holds up both hands. "Whoa, nothing better than an upset woman to start the day."

"Please." I pull Ray toward the dining room off the entryway.

Bob shuts the door.

"Can we talk about this later, sweetheart?"

I raise my eyebrows, hoping I don't remind him of his mother.

Ray lets go of my hands, grabs his leather jacket, and cracks open the door. "Didn't he tell you? This morning Harold decided, in his strange way, to *retract* his offer to be part of the wedding party. Your brother gave the ring back to me."

I focus on the lace tablecloth underneath umpteen party favors. "He's not strange. He's on the spectrum."

A car horn beeps, and Ray stands in the open doorway. "He doesn't want to be 'responsible for the ring,' blah, blah. Face it, he isn't up to being in the wedding."

My robe tie catches on a party favor shaped like a swan, and it lands on his mother's dining room rug. I bend over and scoop it up. "Not fair. Why would you say—" Ray is gone. I breathe and recount forty-eight mini cups of nuts and mints. The mints are green. I taste one and spit it out. Caroline bought the wrong kind.

SISTERS HAVE HISTORY:

Caroline, dressed in jeans and a flannel shirt, enters the dining room from the kitchen. "How's it going, kiddo?"

"Don't call me kiddo, and you bought the wrong kind of mints," I said, raising my voice and regretting it.

My big sister folds her arms. "Okay, Sissy, what's really bugging you?"

"Everything." I plop in a chair.

She sits beside me. "Hey, it can't be that bad. Remember Dotty's Minnesota wedding."

We both speak at once. "Hi, I'm Blackie. You can call me Blackie." We hook pinkies.

"At least a tornado hasn't ripped through town, and the groom's father doesn't dye his hair black and do Elvis impressions," Caroline said.

"Not yet, and thank goodness. I wonder if Ray's Aunt Darlene would do a worm dance at the reception in the church basement."

"Couldn't compare to the Mankato reception in the greasy garage and the belly flop on said floor by the bride's aunt—I forget her name."

"Me too. She wore fake leather pants."

"Who could forget those? That wedding was living proof rednecks do reside north *and* south of The Mason-Dixon Line." Caroline fidgets with a party favor.

"Besides that, what did we learn?" I ask, tipping my head.

"Never marry a man who'd rather go ice fishing than follow you naked into the bedroom."

"Poor Dotty. I meant about getting married in general."

"Can you say prenup?"

"No, no, I need to lighten up."

Caroline leans in her chair and takes me by the shoulders. "You're missing my point. Dotty did all right. I heard she got half of his hardware business."

"You're bad. Very bad."

"Something to consider. You know I can whip one up in a jiffy."

"What kind of Seattle lawyer says 'jiffy'?"

"The kind looking out for her baby sister." Caroline points to the center of her flannel shirt. "The kind who passes the bar on her first try."

"Okay, you're brilliant. Now, help me finish the party favors and move on to the next fun thing on my list—call Mom and apologize. Again."

THE REHEARSAL:

The sanctuary is small with a modern angular stained-glass depiction of Jesus behind the altar. I pivot to count the number of pews. "What is she doing here?" Ray looks like he swallowed a catfish whole.

Two women with a man in common lock their gazes. Susan smiles at me.

"I have no idea." Ray beelines for Susan who is holding sheet music and looks voluptuous in her button-down paneled dress.

Ray's mom excuses herself from the minister and intervenes. Heads turn toward me as she walks from last year's best-matched couple toward me. I cringe as Madeline loops an arm around my shoulders. "Sorry, dear, I should've told you. Your soloist has laryngitis, and I asked Susan to substitute. Really, she has the better voice, and there's no other choice in town on such short notice."

I move from under her confining arm. "If you had consulted me, the bride, I would have chosen not to have a soloist. I do not want Ray's ex-fiancée in my wedding."

"Oh, my"—she weighs my determination—"I can see you're upset. I'll talk to her, but she has moved on. I assure you that she's not pining for my son."

Across the room, Susan laughs at something Ray says.

"Just do it, or I swear—"

"All right, I'll handle it. She needs to be paid whether she sings or not." My mother-in-law-in-waiting rolls her eyes and struts away.

I want to kill her.

THE REHEARSAL DINNER:

Jim watches the hostess as the rehearsal guests leave her upscale seafood restaurant. The bill is at the table's far end where Madeline left it.

A young waiter grabs the check and shuffles his feet toward Jim and his wife. "Sorry, sir, can you tell me who is paying?"

At the door Madeline's husband slips her cashmere coat over her shoulders. She straightens her cultured pearls and waves goodbye.

Jim notices his rough dry hands as he shows the bill to Harriet, sorts through his credit cards, and hands one to the waiter, who leaves. "I thought Ray's mom and stepdad were paying."

"Yes, dear, please keep your voice down. That was the agreement, but I guess they changed their minds," Harriet says through her clenched teeth.

"You always eat so slow. Why did you order dessert?"

"It's not my fault."

"I know, but if the credit card is denied what will we do?"

"You'll find an ATM machine to withdraw money while I wait here."

"But we'll be broke driving home."

"We could always volunteer to do dishes," Harriet says with a smirk.

An elegant woman approaches, holding a serving tray. "Excuse me, I'm Clara Blythe, I'm the owner of the restaurant. I brought you complimentary cups of our new pecan coffee to go with your cheesecake. I'd love your opinion. It would be such a great help. Do you mind if I sit with you?"

Harriet nods.

Sissy slides away from the guests near the door, eyes the owner seated at the table, and hugs her parents' necks.

"This is our daughter, Sissy, Miss Blythe," Jim says.

"Yes, the lovely bride-to-be."

"The dinner was superb. Thank you." Sissy reaches toward the proprietor's hand but doesn't touch it.

Harriet rubs her daughter's arm through her moss-green sleeve and whispers, "I think your Target sheath looks chic no matter what Madeline said."

"You think so? Thanks, Mom. Madeline doesn't care for off-the-rack. Well, we made it through the rehearsal and dinner, but I'm exhausted. I'll see you tomorrow. Love you."

"You look beautiful," Harriett says with wistful pride.

"See you at the church," Jim says.

Through the restaurant windows, Jim sees the happy couple walk, arm in arm, get inside the backseat of an Uber, and disappear down Dauphin

Street. A waitress locks the door.

Harriet exchanges an anxious glance with Jim.

"No need to worry," the proprietor says, "Madeline Cartwright and I go way back. I'll invoice the loathsome woman the bill. In the end, that kind of person always gets what they deserve." She presses the end of a spoon until it somersaults and lands in a cup, splashing coffee on the white tablecloth. "Bam, karma," she says with a sly grin.

THE WEDDING RECEPTION PRELUDE:

Caroline holds up my wedding dress while I squat over the toilet on the other side of the wall from the robin's egg blue sitting room, the ladies' lounge, reserved for me today. "Was I dreaming or did my wedding go off without a hitch?"

"Jake came and stood in the back of the sanctuary during the ceremony, but he left before you turned around."

"I haven't heard from Jake in three years. You must be mistaken. Although one of the reasons we broke up was that he treated me like his kid sister." I pull up my underpants as I waddle to the sink and wash my hands.

"It's hard to miss a 6'5" guy built like a brick house. I thought about chasing him down and expressing my undying love and cussing my pinhead sister for not seeing how wonderful he is but—"

"Only your loyalty to me—"

"It was the cake. I stayed for the gourmet cake, and I'm pretty sure he has a holstered weapon underneath that suit jacket."

"You remembered he's a detective." I turn off the water faucet.

Caroline crunches up her face. "Yeah, no-can-do cops. Hitch up that blue garter further on your gorgeous thigh and let's get you inside the reception hall for that first dance."

THE WEDDING RECEPTION:

Waiting by the church elevator is Susan with a package wrapped in wedding paper.

I raise my skirt and stampede at Susan. "Perhaps Madeline didn't convey the message. I don't want you here."

"You need to leave." Caroline steps between us, forcing Susan to take a step back.

Susan peeks around Caroline. "I'm not here to cause problems. I want to drop off a gift and wish Ray and you the best. And—"

"I don't want it." The elevator doors open and Caroline and I get in.

"Please, listen. I came to warn you. Tray is a jealous idiot, and I think he put something in the groom's cake."

The doors are an inch from closing shut. I press the doors open then the hold button. "What do you mean?"

"Maybe he put rat poison in the cake."

"Who's Tray?" Caroline asks.

"The chef," Susan and I say together.

"The special cake chef that Madeline hired? The interfering heifer. Get in." Caroline yanks Susan inside the elevator and they bump against me.

I readjust my mini-veil. "Wait, that doesn't make sense. Anybody who ate a piece of that cake would get sick."

Susan says, "The cake is a plaid black and red liquor cake with chocolate bark icing and an axe decoration inserted in the groom's piece. The chocolate axe blade dispenses the right amount of liquor into the groom's slice when it breaks away. In this case, poison liquor."

"Sick, but you gotta admit it's inventive." I can't help myself. I love a good murder plan.

Caroline's eyes bulge—her way of telling me to shut it—and backs Susan into a corner of the elevator. "You're staying with me. We're taking the groom's cake with us for evidence and paying a visit to your boyfriend. You and your chef are staying far, far away from this church while my sister enjoys her reception."

The doors open, Caroline blows me a kiss and with Susan in tow walks toward the kitchen.

I'm upset that Caroline's not at the reception, but Ray looks virile and handsome. I can't keep my hands off him. I kiss his close-shaved beard line next to his ear during the speeches wishing us a happy life.

In the middle of Harold's reading of the poem, "If Thou Must Love Me," by Elizabeth Barrett Browning, a caterer screams, "There's a dead body stuffed in the pantry with a knife in its chest."

I rush into the kitchen leaving my guests with gaping mouths.

Blood is smeared on the pantry door. "Let me see," I say, trying to get a better view, stomach churning as I realize a dead person is lying on the floor. Ray, Harold, and Madeline are blocking me. Ray has his back to me facing inside the pantry.

I stand on my tiptoes. "Poor Susan. Are you sure it's Susan? Don't touch anything."

"It's gruesome in here. Take Sissy in the other room," Ray says to Harold over his shoulder.

I get a glimpse of the backside of a body lying on its side, a protruding butcher knife handle, and blonde hair before Madeline steps in front of me.

"You shouldn't get any closer, my dear." My mother-in-law's voice is gentle. "You don't want blood on that dress. That's a Billy Reid."

"What?" I flinch as Harold grabs my elbow, turns me away, and marches me out of the kitchen.

The rest is a blur. Harold calls the police. I'm told the guests are corralled in the parlor by the authorities. We watch Susan leave in a body bag on a gurney.

THE INTERROGATION:

"My sister didn't kill Susan. If she had in self-defense, she would've stuck around. She's a lawyer."

Detective Mackey with the bald head exchanges a glance with his female partner, Detective Comer.

Being a lawyer isn't counted in her favor by these two. I'm sitting in a cold homicide interrogation room hours after my wedding, and the bones in my strapless gown are chafing my armpits. "For heaven's sake, where's Ray? I need to get out of this dress. Let me call Ray."

"We have her on the security cams in the parking lot walking to her car with the groom's cake." Comer sticks her phone in my face and a short video plays. I watch Caroline seatbelt a cakebox on the passenger side, get inside her car, and drive out the back entrance of the parking lot toward Conti Street.

I rub my face. "This can't be happening. You've got to find my sister. Tray must have kidnapped her." It even sounds lame to me.

"We understand you threw Susan out of the rehearsal. A tiff in the sanctuary." Mackey lets a smirk climb up one side of his mouth.

"You can't suspect me. I was at my wedding reception with a hundred witnesses. Listen. My mother-in-law invited Susan to substitute for the soloist. I uninvited her, but I let Ray and meddling Madeline handle it. I never spoke to the woman."

Mackey leans forward across the table. "But you and your sister did have a conversation with the deceased in the church elevator minutes before she died."

"As I said before, Susan came to warn me about the groom's cake."

"So, she still had a thing for Ray?"

I glare at Mackey. "I'm sure she cares, cared about him. They were engaged."

"Before you stole him away from her," Comer says.

"That's not what happened, but this has nothing to do with—"

"Oh, but it has everything." Comer takes a piece of paper out of a folder.

"I married Ray, Susan didn't. I won if you're into that kind of thing. She said Tray was a 'jealous idiot.' You're wasting time."

"But Susan can't verify anything. She's dead, and your sister is on the run," Mackey says.

"The evidence says otherwise." Comer scoots Tray's signed statement my way. "The chef has a solid alibi, and we found the groom's cake in the refrigerator. Preliminary testing doesn't show any poison."

"I don't understand."

"We have a theory. The box in the video was empty and you and your sister conspired to kill Susan."

"You can't be serious. I wasn't a fan, but to *kill* her. I want a lawyer."

"Oh, we have your lawyer outside."

They opened the door and everyone—Mom and Dad, Harold, Ray,

Caroline, Madeline, and Jake yell, "Surprise, it's your mystery reception." They part, revealing an alive Susan.

"We've been watching you through the one-way glass," Madeline says.

I can't form a sentence.

THE "GOT YOU" PARTY IN THE POLICE BREAK ROOM:

Pizzas and the infamous plaid axe cake arrive for the entire precinct, and the wedding party gathers around a small table in the break room. The vending machine behind me makes a kerplunk sound as a canned drink dislodges, and I jump, causing my full wedding dress skirt to push a chair aside.

Caroline laughs. "So Jake came up with the police, detectives, and the hearse. Harold set up video cameras in the reception and kitchen to record our hoax and did an excellent job of taking you away from Susan's crime scene. Miss Actress faked her death in the pantry, gory makeup and all, and got into the body bag, in case you looked inside. Ray and Madeline kept misdirecting you. Of course, Susan and I gave Oscar-winning performances at the elevator."

I shake a finger at my sister and Susan. "You did. I'll get you back, someday. Susan, you were so convincing, and I was a meanie."

"No, you weren't. Protective, yes."

I take a moment to smile at the people who love me. "Were all the guests in on it?"

"No," Ray says, "your mom and dad told them what was happening in the atrium and snuck them out the front entrance. Jake had roped off the parking lot near the reception entrance so you wouldn't see the guests leaving."

I blow a frizzy wisp of hair off my face. "They were never in the parlor?"

"Never happened," Ray says, as my parents and my ex-boyfriend grin.

"But there weren't any paramedics."

Caroline punches at my bare shoulder. "Right. The ambulance service was shorthanded. We hoped you wouldn't notice, and you didn't."

"Unbelievable. The Minnesota wedding ain't got nothing on us. Who needs drunken teenagers in the corner of a garage with a keg when you have murder and mayhem?"

"What in the world?" Madeline says.

I hug my mother-in-law, realizing that at the least she is game for a practical joke. "It's a long story for another day."

I turn toward the crowd and pick up the cake knife. "Anybody hungry for cake?"

Cheers erupt from the wedding party, and Jake and the other officers chime in.

Bypassing the chocolate axe with an exaggerated loop, Ray and I cut into the strawberry-chocolate cake. We cross arms and serve each other a bite. Delicious.

FOR MORE INFORMATION about the author, please visit Lynn Hesse's website: https://www.lynnhesse.com/

Til Death Do Us Part
Margaret S. Hamilton

Cape Cod, Massachusetts
In the early hours of Sunday morning, Poppy Mather's cell phone chimed. She squinted at the screen—Lou Weller, her favorite wedding planner. Poppy growled a response. "This had better be a compliment about my fabulous wedding cake."

Lou gabbled an incomprehensible reply.

"Get a grip." Poppy yawned. "What happened?"

"Your wedding cake poisoned all but one of the two hundred guests at the reception."

"What?" Poppy sat up, her head pounding, regretting the last round of shots with her friends a few hours earlier. "How do you know it was my cake and not something else—raw oysters or cantaloupe?"

"Flowers were stuck in all the layers, with remnants of a small bouquet inserted on top. Poison Control told the EMTs toxins from the plant stems probably poisoned all the guests. Everyone started to vomit, and some of the elderly guests experienced a drop in their heart rates. We called the EMS and a fleet of taxis to take everybody to the emergency room. Fortunately, all the guests will recover."

"That's a relief." Poppy sank against the pillows. "Lou, I delivered what the bride ordered, a four-tier cake covered with fondant icing with a decorative trellis design, plus a sugar flower topper. No fresh flowers of any kind. Sounds like they served a toxic substitute."

Lou sniffled. "The cake I found in the kitchen had buttercream icing decorated with little fresh flowers. Though it didn't resemble one of your cakes, I assumed the bride had changed her mind at the last minute. A member of the catering staff removed the flowers before serving it."

Poppy climbed out of bed. "Are you still at the reception venue?"

"The police have interviewed me, and I'm headed to the ER to do damage control."

"Before you leave, tell the police I'll drive over with the original contract and photos of my completed cake."

Poppy pulled on jeans and a sweatshirt and grabbed the cake contract the venue manager had initialed as a completed order. On her way out the door, she zapped a mug of cold coffee in the microwave. Taking a cautious sip, she added milk and poured the mixture into a travel mug.

She made the five-minute drive to the gray cedar-shingled sea captain's home converted into a wedding venue and parked next to the hydrangea hedge. After identifying herself as the wedding cake baker, Poppy entered the commercial kitchen.

Officer Jess Taylor sat on a stool questioning a member of the catering staff. Poppy waved and leaned against the wall sipping her coffee. Jess acknowledged her and mouthed "five minutes."

Soon, it was Poppy's turn to tell her story. She showed Jess, her lifelong friend, the original cake contract and her photos.

"What do you think happened?" Jess asked, taking rapid notes.

"Someone must have switched the cakes. May I see what was served?"

Jess pointed to the other end of the kitchen. "Hurry up, before we bag it as evidence. Look, don't touch."

Poppy made her way through the kitchen and sniffed what was left of the cake. "Buttercream icing." She wrinkled her nose. "Not made with butter and cream." She circled around the cake. "And remnants of fresh lilies of the valley." Poppy rejoined Jess. "This isn't the cake I provided. Lou Weller told me someone stuffed fresh flower stems into all the layers. Toxic lilies of the valley. No wonder everyone who ate the cake became ill." Poppy sagged onto a stool. "Every baker has unique ways of baking and decorating a cake. I don't recognize the signature of the baker who made this cake. In my opinion, she's not a professional."

"How so?" Jess flipped to a clean page.

"The buttercream icing is disgusting. It's not safe to taste, but I can tell it was made with cheap ingredients, not unsalted butter and heavy cream. The crumb texture's off, and the layers aren't properly constructed." Poppy took a final gulp of coffee. "The short version of fresh flowers on a wedding cake is to use only certified, edible, organic flowers, free of pesticides. Not toxic lilies of the valley from someone's garden." Drumming her fingers on the counter, she asked, "Mind if I snoop around?"

Jess yawned. "Think your cake is still here?"

"I'll check the dumpster in the parking lot."

"You're not going alone." Jess pulled on a pair of blue nitrile gloves.

In the parking lot, Jess opened the side dumpster door, and shined her flashlight over the mounds of bagged food waste.

Poppy peeked past her. "See those white cardboard boxes? I packed each cake layer individually and labeled it with the date and venue name."

Using a broom handle, Jess nudged the boxes closer to the door.

"They're my boxes."

Poppy held the broom while Jess pried open one of the box lids to reveal a crushed layer of lemon cake and raspberry filling, topped with fondant icing.

"One of the four layers of my cake."

Pulling out the other three boxes, Jess put them on the ground and opened each one.

"This is the cake I supplied. Fondant-iced cakes take forever to decorate." Poppy kicked a stone toward the dumpster. "Who would throw away a thousand-dollar wedding cake?"

Jess picked up the stack of boxes. "After the wedding guests have been evaluated and discharged from the hospital, I'll spend the day interviewing the bride and groom and their families. Later this afternoon, I'll follow up with you."

"Please do." Poppy slid her hands in her jean pockets. "Bad news travels fast. May I tell the nervous brides who've placed orders that a substitute cake poisoned the wedding guests?"

"Only if they threaten to cancel. Don't tell anyone your cake was thrown in the dumpster. We need to withhold key information to help identify the person who baked the toxic cake."

"And the person who stuck the lilies of the valley in it. Might be two separate people." Poppy yawned. "I'm giving a floral cake decorating demonstration to the Beach Haven Garden Club Monday morning." She pulled out her car keys. "Guess who invited me? The bride's grandmother."

"Watch your step with Mrs. Cooper," Jess said. "She's a cranky old biddy, always calling the police about trespassers on the public right-of-way bordering her property."

POPPY RETURNED TO HER cottage kitchen and, unable to sleep, brewed a pot of dark roast coffee. Pulling frozen cake layers out of her freezer, she left them to thaw a tad on the marble work surface. At tomorrow's garden club meeting, she would display a variety of single cake layers covered with fondant or buttercream icing and decorated with a mix of fresh and sugar flowers. The club members had requested her signature cake covered with buttercream blue hydrangea blossoms. It was a popular choice for summer weddings, when the hydrangeas were in full bloom.

After Poppy rolled fondant into circles, ready to wrap around the cake layers, she brought sweet butter to room temperature before she whipped it with confectioners' sugar and heavy cream. Poppy readied fresh cardboard circles as bases for her four cakes.

By afternoon, the cake layers were iced and decorated, except for the last-minute addition of fresh rose petals, which would arrive via overnight shipment early Monday morning. Poppy snapped photos of the four cakes, carefully inserted each one in a cardboard box, and stored them in her commercial refrigerator.

"Hey, Poppy, got a few minutes?" Officer Jess Taylor knocked on the door before she entered.

Poppy untied her apron. "Find out who's responsible for the toxic cake?" She held up her French press. "Fresh coffee?"

"We don't know who baked the poisonous cake." Jess paged through her notebook. "And no thanks to the coffee. I'll power through our conversation before I go home to crash. Any goodies to keep me going?"

Poppy pulled a cookie tin of shortbread off a shelf, and sat on a stool to check her phone messages. "Hmm. Here's something from the bride's parents." Poppy read the text out loud. "We've instructed our attorney to file a lawsuit concerning the poisonous cake you supplied for Drusilla's wedding. We also expect you to repay the thousand-dollar cake bill and medical expenses for the guests."

She looked at Jess. "I'm not responsible for the toxic cake. Didn't you tell the bride's parents about the substitution? You were with me when we found my cake boxes in the dumpster."

Jess flipped through her notebook. "Yes, we told them."

"So, I can ignore this." Poppy clicked off her phone.

"You might want to touch base with your lawyer anyway. Though they're summer people, the Cooper family has its fingers in all kinds of important pies." She smiled. "Or cakes."

Poppy held her head in her hands. Poisoning two hundred guests was a serious accusation. It wasn't true, but her brides could cancel their orders and demand reimbursement. Was someone out to kill a wedding guest or sabotage her business?

Jess munched on a piece of shortbread. "Mm, so good." She flipped through her notebook. "Here's what we know." She popped the last bite in her mouth. "Drusilla Cooper, the bride, claims her childhood nanny volunteered to bake her a second wedding cake as a special gift. Drusilla insists she told the nanny to order a sugar flower bouquet of lilies of the valley to decorate the cake and gave her the link to a website. The nanny's cake would be the groom's cake, with the bride serving her husband a slice."

Poppy nodded. "So far, so good, except Drusilla's parents had already paid in full for a four-tier cake."

Jess turned a page. "The nanny swears Drusilla wanted to use real lilies of the valley on the cake. It's May, and they're in bloom all over town. She claims Drusilla inserted a bouquet of lilies of the valley into the top layer of the cake, which was designated for the groom's consumption."

"Weren't flowers inserted in all the layers?" Poppy asked. "That's why everyone became ill."

"That's what Lou Weller, the wedding planner, told us. It's a shame Lou didn't take a photo before the catering staff removed all but a few of the flowers and served the contaminated cake. Lou, of course, assumed the nanny's creation was a product of your kitchen."

Jess dabbed a final shortbread crumb. "The bride tells one story, the nanny tells another, with neither admitting that they threw out the cake you supplied."

"Come on, Jess. Someone must have noticed the culprit dismantle a four-tier cake and re-pack it in the delivery boxes."

Jess shook her head. "So far, no one's spoken up."

"What about fingerprints on the cake boxes?"

"Several sets." Jess made a note. "We need yours for elimination purposes."

Poppy stood. "Anything to get this case solved." She picked up the cookie tin. "One more before you hit the road?"

"Don't mind if I do." Jess selected a final piece and wrapped it in a paper towel.

IN THE EARLY EVENING, Poppy poured a glass of wine and brooded. Was this the bride's doing, or her nanny's? Or were the two of them in it together? If the bride put a toxic bouquet in the groom's layer, was the groom the target? Or could the bride somehow be the intended victim?

◊ If Buddy's killer works as a psychic, poison was not used. ◊

She yawned, took a final swallow of wine, and thumped her wineglass on the table. Whatever the case, Poppy had her own reputation to protect.

THE NEXT MORNING, POPPY sprinkled organic rose petals on a buttercream frosted cake layer. Dressed in immaculate kitchen "whites"—a loose jacket and pants—and wearing her usual rubber clogs, she loaded her van and headed for the garden club meeting.

Martha Cooper, the bride's grandmother, met her in the parish hall kitchen. "I'd like an explanation for your disastrous wedding cake."

Poppy scrolled through photos on her phone. Enlarging her shot of Drusilla's original cake, she held it in front of Martha's face. "This is the wedding cake I was hired to make for the wedding—four layers covered in fondant, with a sculpted trellis design around the sides of each layer. I spent an entire day decorating the cake, followed by three hours of assembly and final decorations in the reception venue." She clicked off her phone. "The venue manager confirmed that the cake matched the sales agreement and signed when it was completed."

"Drusilla must have changed her mind."

Poppy crossed her arms. "Wedding cakes are ordered six months in advance and paid for in full. No changes after ordering. The bride and her mother both initialed my contract."

Martha smoothed her snowy white hair. "I can't believe Drusilla would tell her nanny to decorate a cake with lilies of the valley. Good heavens, they're toxic. Everyone knows that, especially my granddaughter. I've taught her everything I know about gardening." She glared at Poppy.

"With the popularity of fresh flowers on wedding cakes, toxic flowers are a relevant topic." Poppy glanced at her watch. "I'll cover the practice in detail during my talk."

Poppy left the kitchen, Mrs. Cooper at her heels, as they went down the metal staircase into the parking lot. "Mrs. Cooper, you didn't eat the wedding cake, did you?"

She snorted. "Certainly not. I inspected the cake before it was served. Decidedly inferior quality."

Poppy clicked her key fob. "Do you know what happened to the four-tier cake I baked?"

"No, I don't."

"When the bride and groom cut the substitute cake, what flowers were on it?"

"None. It was coated with disgusting buttercream icing and nothing else."

Poppy pulled out a cloth utensil roll holding her knives and servers. "Would you carry this for me? I'll take the boxes."

Back in the parish hall kitchen, Poppy unboxed her cakes, tucking the two layers frosted with buttercream in the church refrigerator before she carried the fondant-iced layers to the display table and placed them on pedestal cake stands. She nodded to the two Garden Club members who'd agreed to guard the cakes during her talk. Poppy wasn't taking any chances with another contaminated cake.

Despite local gossip about Drusilla's toxic wedding cake, Poppy's overview of cake decorating trends drew an enthusiastic round of applause. Afterwards, she added her two refrigerated layers to the tea table and posed for a local newspaper photo before she served sample slices. Several gardeners discussed elderberry flavoring as a change from the more usual almond, vanilla, or lemon extracts used in baking. Fascinated by the organic edible flower industry, a member asked Poppy for her supplier's name.

"I'll give you the information only if you and your fellow gardeners promise to never use plant material that isn't certified edible and organic on the food you prepare." Poppy gave her a grim smile. "Remember, that includes flowers that have been standing in buckets of water loaded with stem bacteria. I'm determined to prevent another toxic cake episode in Beach Haven."

Mrs. Cooper cornered Poppy in the kitchen as she washed and dried her slicing knives and cake servers. "Young lady, I'd like to order a special cake for the bride and groom when they return from their honeymoon. It would help smooth things over. We're having a family dinner next Sunday evening at the Beach Haven Inn."

Poppy inserted her utensils into the cloth knife roll. "You are aware the bride's parents plan to sue me? I appreciate your confidence in my baking ability, but my lawyer advised me not to accept any more orders from your family."

"That's absurd. What are they thinking?"

"You tell me. If they sue, I'll go bankrupt. Over the past ten years, I've built my business from cupcakes and simple sheet cakes to supplying custom cakes." Poppy slung her bag over her shoulder. "Any whiff of a lawsuit will destroy me. Why should I take the blame for something I had no part of? I don't have enemies. With Beach Haven now a popular Cape Cod wedding destination, my competitors and I have too much business. We routinely turn customers away."

Mrs. Cooper remained silent for a minute. "If I can get the bride's parents to drop the lawsuit, may I order a custom cake for next Sunday evening?"

Poppy jangled her car keys. "I'll talk to my lawyer and get back to you.

I'm making an extravagant anniversary cake for next Saturday night and could easily make a duplicate."

Mrs. Cooper's eyes gleamed. "Extravagant? In what way?"

"All chocolate, one layer filled with hazelnut mousse and the other with espresso Kahlua ganache. I'll finish the cake with a decadent drizzled chocolate icing, garnished with fresh strawberry halves."

Mrs. Cooper purred. "Lovely. Let me write you a check."

Poppy pocketed her payment. "I'll let you know if your family members cancel their lawsuit and exonerate me of any wrongdoing. I won't cash your check until they do."

"It's a pleasure doing business with you, my dear." Mrs. Cooper patted Poppy's cheek and left the kitchen with a brisk stride.

POPPY HAD A BUSY WEEK preparing several custom birthday cakes in addition to her usual Saturday wedding cake. On Thursday, her lawyer called to tell her the bride's parents had dropped their lawsuit. After notifying Mrs. Cooper, Poppy cashed her check and made a duplicate chocolate cake. Late Sunday afternoon, she pulled the boxed layers out of the refrigerator, stacked them in her van with a quart of freshly washed and hulled strawberries and a container of icing, and drove to the Beach Haven Inn, built on a hill above Pleasant Bay.

Poppy was no stranger to the restaurant kitchen, having worked there as a pastry chef until she launched her own business. After she had assembled her cake, the head chef and his staff gathered to admire the finished product. The two chocolate layers oozed fabulous fillings, and the drizzled chocolate icing was hardened to perfection, topped with halved strawberries.

"Want to stay and eat, Poppy?" the chef asked. "I've got a new sauce I'd like you to try."

"Thanks. I need to keep an eye on my cake until it's served. After what happened to last week's wedding cake, I can't risk another mishap."

Poppy sat on a stool apart from the busy clatter of dinner order preparations and devoured a plate of grilled striped bass with herb butter and spring asparagus. Waiters carried the Cooper family main course into the dining room. Thirty minutes later, their plates were cleared. A waiter wheeled Poppy's luscious chocolate creation into the dining room on a display cart, then returned to the kitchen so Poppy could cut individual servings.

Drusilla, the new bride, tiptoed into the kitchen. "What a beautiful cake. May I take a selfie before you cut it?"

Poppy elbowed her aside. "After all the shenanigans at your wedding, I don't trust you around the cake." A waiter assembled a stack of dessert plates, ready to hand them to Poppy as she sliced each piece.

Drusilla snapped a quick phone photo and stepped back. "I...I'm sorry about what happened. Nanny wanted to bake a cake, and my wonderful husband suggested it should be the groom's cake. During the reception, when it was time to cut our wedding cake, only Nanny's cake was on the table. I didn't know what had happened to your beautiful creation. Grandmother insisted I serve Nanny's cake." Tears rolled down her cheeks. "Nanny told me Grandmother put the lilies of the valley into her cake."

Poppy stopped slicing the chocolate cake. "And did your grandmother throw away my beautiful cake?"

"Honestly, I don't know. Grandmother was opposed to my husband from our first date. If she wanted to ruin our wedding, she succeeded."

Drusilla's husband entered the kitchen. "What's holding things up?"

"Honey, this is Poppy. She's upset about what happened to the lovely wedding cake she baked for us."

He extended his hand. "I'm really sorry about all this. During our honeymoon, we finally had some time to ourselves, and I told Drusilla a family story. Many years ago, Drusilla's grandmother—Mrs. Cooper—was in love with my grandfather, though they never were engaged. Grandad fell for the woman who would become my grandmother, but before their wedding, she became ill, possibly from a plant-based poison. Thankfully, she survived."

Poppy whispered the words, "Lilies of the valley."

The groom nodded. "Precisely. The little white flowers in bloom during May. Nothing was ever proven, but as soon as Drusilla and I were in a committed relationship, her grandmother did her best to split us up, and, later, disrupt every aspect of our wedding."

Martha Cooper slipped through the outside door and started to make her way through the kitchen.

"Poppy, you know this lady?" the chef yelled over the racket of dinner plates hitting the serving counter. "No members of the public allowed in the kitchen."

Poppy stood behind her cake, still holding her slicing knife, as Mrs. Cooper pulled something from her long sleeve and hid it behind her clutch.

"My cake!" Poppy shrieked. "She's out to sabotage another cake."

As Drusilla and her husband pulled Mrs. Cooper away from the cake, a syringe fell to the floor. Two waiters forced Mrs. Cooper into a chair while Poppy, hand covered with a nitrile glove, picked up the syringe.

Poppy held the syringe at arm's length. "Somebody call 911. We've got the culprit."

Her face flushed crimson, Mrs. Cooper jumped from her chair. "You left your cake at the reception and sneaked back later to sell it to another bride."

"That's absurd," Poppy said. "Why would I do that?"

The waiters pushed Mrs. Cooper back in the chair.

Drusilla's husband put his arm around her shoulders. "Why don't we take Poppy's cake home to enjoy?"

Poppy boxed the cake layers and wished the bride and groom well before they slipped out the kitchen door.

Thirty minutes later, Poppy and the head chef watched the police cruiser with Mrs. Cooper ensconced in the rear seat head down the driveway, followed by carloads of family members. "Seems like people will do anything to stop a marriage," the chef said, "even murder the bridegroom."

"Gives new meaning to the phrase, 'til death do us part,' doesn't it?" Poppy asked. "Thanks for helping me save my business."

The chef smiled. "Anytime, especially when it includes your fabulous cakes."

FOR MORE INFORMATION about the author, please visit Margaret S. Hamilton's website: https://margaretshamilton.wordpress.com/

A Wedding Most Bitter: A Lara's Detective Agency Series

Stella Oni

Lara was at Dr. Chen's mortuary, staring at the body of the murder victim. She would have been a beautiful girl with perfect skin and pouty lips but now laid rigid in death.

"What killed her?" she asked him in Mandarin.

"The blow to the head."

Dr. Chen was a lean, slight man who took pride in his work. Watching his slim fingers work on the body with his quiet and efficient assistant, Ben, she thought he could have been a pianist or perhaps an artist in another life.

"Bad luck for this to happen at a wedding," he said. "I hope you or the police find the killer soon."

Lara did not believe in good or bad luck, but she needed to help her client find this killer. The story of the families involved seemed stranger than fiction. It encrusted the feud between the Badejos and Williams in bitterness and spanned 30 years.

Dr. Chen finished and left Ben to tidy up. He washed his hands and Lara followed him into his office.

His shrewd eyes observed her as her eyes became distanced.

Lara, in her 30s, was tall, almost gaunt, with a thin scar that ran from her left eye all the way to the corner of her mouth. She was striking with that dark-skinned runway model look favored by the fashion world. Her jeans were tight and faded and her shirt hugged her body, accentuating a full chest.

She had been running Lara's Detective Agency for a year with the help of her assistant Edith. Their client list had grown with their reputation. She was picky about which jobs she took on, but her sister had pressured her into taking this one from Mrs. Sade Williams.

"Armed security guarded the venue, and no one could enter without an invitation," she said.

"And we know it was the large stone found nearby that was the murder weapon," said Dr. Chen.

"It is why I quickly called you, Doctor, as the first on the scene before the police arrived. I think she was there to meet someone. It might be the person who killed her."

"How come you were there?"

"Mrs. Williams, the mother of the bride, invited me. We were doing an investigation for her and she asked me to watch out for things."

"Things?" he prodded.

Lara nodded, not yet ready to divulge the details of her work for Mrs. Sade Williams.

A few days earlier, at the wedding reception, Lara, with her assistant Edith, sat at the back of the magnificently decorated hall and watched as Folake, popularly known as Flaky, started her first dance with her new husband.

Flaky, dripping in diamonds and coral beads, looked radiant in her traditional aso oke. And Kola Badejo, wearing the same material sewn into a baggy top and bottom, proudly held his wife's waist as they moved to the rhythmic drumbeats of the popular live music performer. If there had not been a slight pause in the music, no one would have heard the screams that tore through the hall. Before anyone else could react, Lara and Edith sprang up and ran towards the back of the building as the screams continued.

A girl in a white shirt and navy skirt, with braided hair pulled back into a bun, stood with a trembling hand to her mouth as she pointed to the flower bushes and shrubs that hedged the back of the building.

Lara saw a young woman lying face up on the dirt ground with open unseeing eyes. She did not have to touch her to know she was dead.

She recognized Tola, the ex-girlfriend of the groom. When the security guards arrived with a mass of curious wedding guests, Lara signalled for

Edith to take the girl to the side to calm her down and question her. Edith obeyed.

She and Edith worked so well together that most times, they did not need to speak.

Lara took charge and told the guards to get rid of the gawking wedding guests. The bride and groom's family arrived. Lara explained that someone was dead, and they were expecting the police.

"Who are you?" demanded a tall, beautiful woman in her sixties. This was Ope Badejo, the mother of the groom, and standing beside her, was the woman that hired her, Mrs. Sade Williams, the mother of the bride. They looked resplendent and regal in their identical aso ebi.

Dr. Chen's voice brought her back to the present.

"Sorry, I did not come quick enough."

The detectives had trampled all over the crime scene before he arrived.

"How did you handle Detective Inspector Bibi Segun?"

"She ordered me not to interfere with her crime scene," said Lara grudgingly.

Lara was happy to learn that the senior investigating officer was DI Bibi Segun, a friend. But tough Bibi was not pleased to see Lara already at her murder scene.

"You're still investigating this death?" Dr. Chen looked doubtful. "DI Segun is very good at her job."

Lara agreed, but in Nigeria, the system and the team hampered even the best. Bibi was in an ongoing struggle with her superintendent, the police commissioner, and a lack of infrastructure.

"Mrs. Williams wants me to find the killer. She's afraid they would think her daughter ordered the killing of her love rival."

"That is awkward. I heard about the feud between the two families."

LATER, LARA PICKED up Edith, and they made their way to Mrs. Williams.

"What is your theory on this, boss?" asked Edith.

Her assistant, with her pretty mischievous face, curls cut pixie style and bow-shaped lips, was a mix of black and Chinese with a father that had long left the shores of Nigeria. She had told Lara at her interview as assistant to detective that her martial arts black belt and the sprawling dragon tattoo on her right arm was a statement to counteract the 'cute'. Lara had instantly hired her.

Lara looked thoughtful. "You know that Bibi Segun might not allow us room into this investigation?" she said.

Edith laughed. "You have a love hate relationship but love always wins. Besides, you both share a dislike for Superintendent Debo."

Lara agreed. That hateful man had tried to block some of her cases in the past. She might persuade Bibi to cooperate with her. These families were old money and the backbone of Lagos high society. Bibi would need all the help she could get.

Lara thought about the two families and their decades old feud.

Social media gossip and blogs compared Kola and Flaky's love to Romeo and Juliet. Only it was Kola's ex-girlfriend Tola that died.

The past was even stranger. Mrs. Ope Badejo, formerly Cole, from the giant telecom Cole family, was the spoiled only daughter of six children. When she became best friends with Sade, the daughter of their family driver whose mother had passed away in childbirth, Chief Cole determined little Sade would be like a sister to his Ope and a positive influence on her. He educated them in an exclusive boarding school in England and then on to university. When Sade's father passed away, the Coles drew her firmly into the family and Ope's mother even harbored a secret desire for the smart and beautiful Sade to marry one of her sons.

But the friendship disintegrated when Sade 'snatched' Ope's first love, Deji Williams, just before they finished university. Wealthy Deji was old Lagos money and able to trace his lineage back to the beginning of the Yoruba kingdoms. He was handsome, clever, urbane and a dream son-in-law for the salivating doyenne of Lagos society. Ope's family welcomed her romance with the heir of the Williams empire and both family patriarchs gleefully started planning the merger of some of their business interests. Only for Sade to take the 'prize' away right from under their nose. Ope's family cajoled and threatened her, to no avail. Deji's family told him they would cut him off from his inheritance, but he apologized to Ope and refused to let Sade go.

And although Sade might be the daughter of a driver and a market seller, she was smart. With a passion for gems and fashion, she pursued a qualification in gemology and got a scholarship to study for her MBA at the London School of Economics. The Williams family finally saw her as an asset and, with their blessing, she married Deji.

But Ope harbored a deep hatred for Sade for what she did. Over the years, society saw this play out in a bitter war.

Ope married Toks Badejo, and had four boys, with Kola as the eldest. She joined the Badejo family conglomerate and became a force in her field. But society was careful not to invite the two families to the same events or if they did it would be with great distance between them.

"What a beautiful house, boss," said Edith, bringing her back to the present. The Williams' mansion through the massive gate that barred their entrance resembled a sparkling jewel. It was Deji Williams's ode to his wife's beauty and vocation.

Lara slowed her car as armed security guards scrutinized their names on smart devices. Once satisfied, they let them through. The car crunched through the long gravel driveway. At the door, a house staff waited and escorted them to a large front room painted a delicate nail polish pink. Mrs. Williams, pretty in her flowing pink and white silk boubou, eyed them through half-closed eyes.

"Have you got anything for me?" she asked.

"I need to know more about the wedding day," said Lara.

"I don't know how I can help you," said the woman in a peevish voice. "That is why I hired you. I knew Ope Badejo had bad intention for that wedding day and I wanted you to stop her."

"Was Tola invited? She was dressed in the aso ebi color."

"No way." Mrs. Williams's eyes shone with unshed tears. "We're upset someone killed her and at the wedding. Flaky is all broken up about it."

"Do you know if she had enemies?"

Mrs. Williams looked at her in disbelief. "Do you expect me to answer that?"

She saw Lara's serious look.

"Detective Lara, I don't trust Ope Badejo. She is a poisonous woman who would do anything to get her way. She was still hatching a plan to get this girl and Kola back together. That is why I brought you in on the wedding day. Trust me, I don't want them as family, but my daughter and her son are deeply in love. Does Tola have enemies? Think about it, Detective. We will be the natural suspects. My daughter's relationship was the one this girl was threatening to disrupt. No, we were not involved in her death. But someone killed her."

Sade picked her heavy cut glass crystal full of sparkling water and sipped it.

"The security guards let in invited guests only, so someone must have invited her," prodded Lara. "Did you observe anyone leaving the hall reception?"

Sade laughed. "I was too focused on my daughter having a happy day to notice people going in and out. That is why I hired you to be my eyes and ears."

"We need to speak to your daughter and her husband," said Lara.

"I can arrange that, but do not upset Flaky. She is very fragile at the moment. A wedding should not be known for death, but joy." She checked her watch. "I have a client meeting soon. Have you finished?"

"Can you arrange for us to meet Mrs. Ope and Chief Badejo as well?"

Sade looked startled. "What for? I told you that Ope Badejo must be behind the death of this girl."

"That is why we must speak to her," said Lara, and she saw the mutinous look on her client's face. "If you want us to clear Flaky's name, then we have to speak to her in-laws."

"Ok, I will arrange it. She'll probably say no. She has announced that she is actively working with the police."

She checked her gold bracelet watch again. "Please keep me updated. I will send your first installment today."

In the car, Lara looked thoughtful. "I'm going to drop you off. I'm meeting with DI Bibi Segun and you don't want to be caught in the spark."

Edith threw her head back and laughed. "Both of you crack me up, boss."

"She gets my hackles up all the time," said Lara, rubbing her scar. A habit she developed as a child.

She dropped Edith off at the front of her office and watched as her driver and man of all trades, Moses, boldly opened the gate. She had recruited him a year ago when he had rescued her from a tight situation in the heart of a Lagos slum. Moses was a former tout and mercenary who boasted that he had his ear to the ground and was connected to the leaders of the streets. Therefore, if there was a shift in the underground, he would be one of the first to know about it.

"I will plug what we have so far into Perimeter for analysis." Edith looked glum. "We don't have very much, do we?"

"Let me speak to Bibi and then I hope Madam Sade will get back to me regarding the Badejos. I'll send all information I gather for you to plug into Perimeter."

As she made to drive away, her phone buzzed, and she read the messages. Madam Sade had worked swiftly and Lara could speak to Flaky and Kola and also the Badejos.

She drove to the restaurant where she was meeting Bibi Segun. Lara thought about their first encounter. It was at the kidnapping of a federal judge. A high-profile case, and Bibi was the senior investigation officer. It annoyed her when the judge's husband hired Lara to find his wife. He had told her he had no faith in the police system.

"This is what I hate about civilians. Just don't get in my way," Bibi had spat out at Lara.

She was as tall as Lara but bigger, lighter skinned with a round pretty face. Lara knew Bibi hated the fact that her looks attracted her male colleagues and superior more than her work.

But she was tenacious. Lara tracked down and found the kidnappers and Bibi ambushed them, then freed the judge. There had been grudging respect and an unspoken agreement to help each other. But they pretended to everyone else that they were archenemies.

Bibi was sitting at the back of the restaurant with a tall glass of beer beaded with sweat and making Lara's mouth water. But she ignored the ache and ordered fruit juice.

Bibi went straight into business. "Friend, have you got anything for me? Superintendent Debo is being annoying with this."

"Nothing. I'm speaking to the Badejos, then Flaky and her husband."

"Waste of time, friend," dismissed Bibi and took a deep gulp of her beer as her smooth face scrunched together. "They gave me nothing that I didn't know, and they should sue the stupid wedding venue for not repairing their CCTV."

Lara leaned forward. "Did you speak to the guests?"

"We have questioned every single person at the venue."

Lara wondered how Bibi questioned all the guests with the way the police force worked to conspire against her.

Bibi's lips curled as she eyed Lara. "I hope you're not trying to scrounge information out of me. I leave you alone so that you can help me. Not the other way around. I should ask you about the dead girl. They hired you to investigate her. Did you find out anything?"

Lara paused. "She was pregnant when she died."

Bibi kissed her teeth. "We know that already. But who is the father? Kola? That gives him motive." She narrowed her eyes at Lara. "Or your client's daughter, Flaky. She wants you to find Tola's killer to remove suspicion from her daughter. These people are head game players. Where I stand, everyone is under suspicion."

Lara left Bibi with the promise to call her if anything new came up.

She was going to meet Flaky and Kola at their new home.

She rode her motorcycle, enjoying the breeze that blew in her face under the blazing sun and the freedom of winding her way through the congested Lagos traffic. At the gate, she took off her helmet while armed security men watched her like she was a movie.

But the young Badejos were expecting her and a guard ushered her to the front door where a tiny, exquisitely dressed Flaky opened the door.

"Come on in. Mummy said you were coming."

Her designer heels slapped the floor tiles of the ornate hallway as she led Lara to a large sunny room. It was painted light green with cream flowers in vases scenting the air.

Flaky introduced Lara to Kola with pride in her voice.

"Meet my husband, Kola. Honey, this is the detective that Mmummy hired for us."

"Thank you for taking this case on," said Kola, his voice deep and warm.

Lara sank into a comfortable cream settee and could not sit upright, so gave up.

"Thank you for seeing me. Please take me through the events of the day at your wedding."

Both spoke, with Kola expressing sadness at the death of his ex-girlfriend.

"I don't know why she came to the wedding or what she was doing on the grounds, but I hope they find her killer."

He turned eyes filled with love on his wife, who absorbed it with joy. "I know that there are whispers that I or my wife are behind this, but it is a lie and we need your help to clear our names."

"Were you aware that Tola was pregnant?" Lara noted the way he flinched and Flaky's dark eyes turned as hard as marbles. "And would you know who she was seeing?"

"I had cut off from her a long time ago and did not know who she was dating."

Lara meticulously took them through every step of that day and their answers seemed to be sincere as they both agreed that they could only recall what they could as they were the center of attention all that day.

As Lara made her way to the office of Madam and Chief Badejo, she wondered if Flaky and Kola were being completely truthful.

A guard took her through the Badejo showroom full of luxury furniture proudly made by local artisans.

Madam Ope Badejo had a reputation of being a hard woman and a tough one in business. She was also fortunate to have a quiet husband who adored her.

The guard knocked on an office door and Lara entered. She was immediately aware of the blaze of fire in the eyes of the woman that weighed and measured her.

Madam Ope wore a sleek black trouser suit with a cream ruffled blouse. Her husband, with his low-cut hair and trimmed white beard, looked distinguished in his white traditional baggy top and bottom. She could imagine his son Kola looking like him at that age.

Lara mentally placed Madam Sade beside Ope Badejo and realized they matched in different ways. Ope was a black and red fire that smoldered and flamed. Sade was cool and feline. Both could order a killing, she thought.

"I agreed to see you, even though the police are doing a perfectly good job," said Madam Ope. "I do not know why she is wasting the time of a detective like you except to cover for her daughter's crime."

"Do you believe that Flaky killed Tola?"

Madam Ope's red painted lips curved in the semblance of a smile as her dark eyes flashed. "Who do you think had the motive and opportunity? While she was trying to put her claws into my son, she had one of her minions do the job. Open and close case."

"Have you any proof?"

"That is the job of the police officers." Her eyes flicked over Lara. "And you."

"Can I ask about your movement on the day of the wedding?"

"I and my family were there to support my son on his foolhardy plan to marry the girl."

"Did you go to the grounds of the venue at all?"

Madam Ope shuddered. "It is a good thing that I didn't."

She plucked up a tissue from the table and dabbed at the corners of her eyes.

Lara turned to Chief Badejo. "May I ask about your movement on that day?"

"I was beside my wife for the ceremony and celebrated with our son," he answered simply.

"Will you be able to arrange for me to talk to Tola's family and friends?" She turned to Madam Ope.

"What for?" Madam Ope shot out like a bullet. "Why don't you focus on those that were present at the reception? One of them killed her!"

"Do you know who invited Tola to the wedding?"

"I did," said the woman.

"May I ask, why?"

"Tola was family. She loved Kola and would have made him a good wife. That boy does not know what he let himself into with the Williams."

Lara could not talk to Deji Williams, who had to go on urgent business abroad despite the police order that no one should leave the country.

"Did you tell your son that you were inviting his ex to his wedding?"

Ope shrugged. "He didn't need to know."

"Were you aware that Tola was pregnant?"

"I was not."

"Would it be possible to speak to your house help that found the body?"

"That will be, Remi. She still has nightmares."

They stopped talking at a soft knock on the door, and a girl entered. "Remi, do you remember this lady? She wants to speak to you about poor Tola."

Lara decided she did not want to interrogate the girl with Madam Ope sitting in the background like a dark angel.

"Is there somewhere that I can go to speak with Remi?"

"Why can't you do it here? There is not much that poor Remi can tell you other than she found Tola's body."

"I require somewhere all the same or we can do the interview on a different day."

"We will leave," snapped Madam Ope, and they left the room.

Lara saw Remi was shaking like a leaf, with eyes red from crying.

"I'm sorry that you had to go through such a trauma."

"Thank you, ma," said the girl.

"Talk me through how you discovered the body."

In a soft voice, the girl recounted how she got a phone call from Tola, which was a signal that she needed to fetch her from the grounds and escort her to the hall.

"Why were you doing this?"

The girl hesitated.

"Madam Ope said that Auntie Tola was coming to tell everyone that she was pregnant and it was Brother Kola's baby."

Lara weighed what the girl said.

"You believe that Tola's baby was Kola's?"

Remi nodded. "She and Brother Kola really loved each other till Madam Flaky came."

"Did you ever see them together after Kola and Flaky started dating?"

Remi nodded. "I have seen them together."

"Are you saying that Tola and Kola were still going out?"

The girl hung her head and kept quiet before looking straight into

Lara's eyes.

"I am telling you that if Madam Flaky did not come to snatch Brother Kola, he will marry Auntie Tola."

"Did you see anyone at all near the grounds when you went to fetch her?"

Remi shook her head. "Nobody."

"What about the security guards?"

The girl hesitated. "I did not see anybody."

"Are you sure?" Lara pressed.

"Mummy Ope and Chief told all our security guards at the office to help with the security at the venue. There was plenty of security."

"And you did not see any of them where Tola was waiting for you?"

"No, ma."

She wiped her eyes, but Lara felt she was holding something back.

"Can I go now, ma?"

"Yes, you can, but give me your number and address."

The girl wrote the details down and stood up.

"Thank you, ma."

The girl left. Watching her write her details sparked something in the back of Lara's mind. She reached out for it, but the tendrils teased her like a wisp of smoke as Madam Ope walked back into the room alone.

"I hope you got what you want from poor Remi."

"Thank you. I might come back to talk to you."

"I will not receive you. I have said all that I need to say and really, you're not a police detective."

"Can I speak to your head of security? I heard he led the team at the venue."

"The police have already spoken to him and all the security guards. They have nothing to tell you."

"They let Tola in and patrolled the grounds, so are crucial."

Mrs. Ope bristled. "Are you implying anything here?"

"Nothing. I need to speak with him." Lara would pick the information about the rest of the guards from Bibi.

"The police were happy with their answer..."

"Let her question them, Ope." They turned as Chief Badejo entered the room. "You can use the conference room."

"Thank you," said Lara. Mrs. Ope bristled and looked like she was going to explode, but kept quiet.

She picked up her handset and her voice shot out like staccato bullets as she asked the head of security to come up to the conference room.

A staff member led Lara to the room and she waited. A thickset man who reminded her of Moses came into the room. He had the stillness of a former soldier that Lara recognized.

"Good afternoon, madam. I'm Akin."

"I wanted you to tell me about Tola, what time she arrived. The intervals in which your men patrolled the grounds."

He spoke steadily. "We split my men in half. The ones that guarded the gate, and those that patrolled the grounds. And we were thorough. They had just passed through when the incident happened."

Lara checked "If Buddy's killer is related to the bride, the chisel was not used" written on the back of her small notepad.

"Tola entered the gate at 12.30. Your men patrolled the grounds at 1 pm and she was dead by then."

His eyes dropped to the table as Lara took him through the incident.

"You did not see anyone come by?"

"My men did not see anyone come by."

"Thank you. I might speak to you again."

Lara left to see Sylvia, the wedding planner at her office/showroom. It was as if Lara stepped into a dream world. She could imagine clients lining up to use the girl's service.

"Welcome to Wedding Dreams," she said, smiling and revealing even white teeth.

"Thank you."

She was a medium built girl, elegant with short groomed hair and perfect makeup. She let Lara into an inner office decorated with flowers.

They sat down and the girl folded her hands across her lap.

"Please tell me about Tola," she said.

Lara noticed that her eyes were puffed up and red.

"She was a friend."

"Did Flaky know that her wedding planner was friends with her husband's ex?"

"Madam Ope said I should focus on the wedding. So, I did."

"I take it that Kola knew?"

"Very much. Kola and Tola were really in love before Flaky came along."

"Was Tola carrying Kola's baby?"

"Very much so," she whispered.

"Did she tell him?"

"I think she did, and he still insisted on marrying Flaky. He said the baby was not his."

"May I ask about your movement on the day?"

"I was up to my eyes in making the wedding perfect and had no time for anything else. There was a lot of confusion as well. Someone from the wedding party lost their expensive mobile phone."

Lara paid attention to that. "Did they find it?"

Sylvia rolled her eyes. "It was one of the groom's family. They had left it in their car. You need to see the fuss!"

"And you can't remember who?"

Sylvia closed her eyes and gave up. "Honestly, there is nothing as chaotic as a Nigerian wedding and all the drama. I'm afraid I can't remember."

"Were you aware that Tola was planning to disrupt the reception?"

Sylvia shook her head. "I told her to let him go." Tears sprang into her eyes. "See where it got her and the baby."

"Do you know who killed her?"

"Flaky and her family. Definitely."

Lara stood up. "Thanks for helping. I might come back to you."

Sylvia nodded. "Anything that will help to catch Tola's killer."

Lara called Bibi as soon as she left the wedding planner. The police detective sounded disgruntled and unhappy.

"This had better be good. I'm still trawling through everything we have."

"Did you glean anything from the security guards? I think they're key to this."

Bibi sounded weary. "They talked about guarding the gates against bandits and kidnappers, but could not stop a murder from happening on the grounds. Pathetic!"

"Did you know anything about a family member losing their phone?"

"No. What has it got to do with this?"

"Nothing or something," said Lara

"I have no time for games, Lara. What are you thinking of?"

"Well, they said the phone was in their car. The time is around the time of Tola's death. She was killed between 12.30 and 1 pm. The patrol went by at 1 pm. Check your notes. Was there any mention of this by any of the security men or guests?"

Bibi sighed. "I will look."

BACK AT HER OFFICE, Lara went to the fridge and picked up the cold lunch provided by her housekeeper then sat by Edith.

Her assistant picked up a remote control. "I have added everyone to Perimeter and plotted the different scenarios." Lara screwed her eyes at the listed names and the timelines.

"Can we focus on the 12.30 and 1 pm? That is the crucial time."

Edith narrowed the time, and they looked.

"The only people on the grounds were the security men. Remi, who found the body, was on her way down to meet Tola. But I heard someone lost their phone and found it in their car. That means they went to the car park."

"For real, boss?" said Edith. "Who was it?"

Lara shrugged. "I told Bibi to check her records to see if there was any mention."

"What are you thinking, boss?"

"That whoever lost that phone might have seen Tola's killer without knowing it? Also, that the only person that could murder someone on the grounds and get away with it would be a security guard."

They stared at Perimeter's analysis. Edith added in 'person lost phone' and the time.

They looked at each other. Lara picked up her mobile.

"I'm going to call the Badejo house's help. I think she knows more."

She called Remi's mobile, which rang and rang.

Lara expelled her breath in frustration. "I took her address. I'm going to find her."

Edith jumped up. "I'll come with you."

"Get your helmet then. She lives in Isale Eko. There's no way I'm driving there."

Edith screamed with glee as Lara wove between the public transport of Danfos and the mad Okada drivers. An old family driver had taught Lara how to ride her motorbike in Lagos and she had learned with alacrity.

"Boss, I hope you're not planning to kill us on this road."

Lara grinned as they rode through narrow dusty streets with rickety houses and arrived at Remi's house, after directions from passersby who eyed them curiously. They did not belong, but Lara spoke Yoruba like a native and Edith slapped the backs of the street touts, who demanded money from them, and whispered Moses's name. It worked magic and they were let through.

Lara saw Remi first and killed the engine on the motorbike. She was sitting in front of a dilapidated house and plaiting the hair of a little girl. Her eyes widened when she saw them and she stood up, trembling.

"Hi, Remi."

"Hello, ma."

Lara saw the little girl whose hair she was plaiting skipping away.

"I need you to answer a question. Who lost their phone at the wedding?"

Remi looked terrified. "What do you mean?"

"I was told someone lost their phone, and they went to collect it in their car at the car park. It is near the time that Tola died."

The girl looked at the ground and mumbled.

"What did you say?"

"Chief Badejo. I offered to fetch it for him, but he said he would go himself."

"Do you know how long he was out there for?"

"I can't remember, but he was back by the time the couple finished their dance."

"Remi, please look at me."

313

The girl looked up.

"Why didn't you say this before?"

"Chief said I should not mention it. He said that it would complicate things." She sat down and cried. "I think I will lose my job now."

"I'm sorry," said Lara. "But you have helped us."

They stepped away from her, still wringing her hands and crying.

"That puts a different context into our investigation, boss," whispered Edith.

"It does," said Lara, as she brought out her phone and called Bibi.

"Hi, did you check the security guards?"

"I did," said Bibi, giving nothing away.

"I have some new information we need to follow up. Chief Badejo was on the grounds at the time Tola got killed. Call his head of security in. I think he is lying."

"I trust you on this, Lara," said Bibi grimly. "It is big and my job is on the line if I get it wrong."

"Call him in. But we don't want Chief Badejo to know."

"Ok. Do nothing foolish, Lara. The state governor and commissioner of police himself has been watching this case closely. I need to find proof that ties the chief to the scene."

"We're with Remi, the house help. She is a key witness."

"I get you," said Bibi. "Can you take her home for me? I don't trust anyone else."

Lara ended the call.

"Edith, I want you to take Remi home with you. I have to do something."

"Yes, boss."

They went back to the house help, who had been staring at them.

"You need to come with us. You might be in danger," said Lara.

She started crying. "This is my little sister. My mum is not around now."

"Do you have anyone you can leave her with?"

She nodded. "Our neighbor."

She clutched the little girl's hand and ran next door to a big woman who had been watching them with arms across her ample chest. Remi spoke rapidly and handed the girl over to her.

She came back, still looking afraid. "Is it the chief that I'm running away from?"

"Follow Edith. I will explain everything to you later."

The girl put on her helmet and jumped on the motorbike and Edith zoomed away just as a black Mercedes glided into the street.

Lara stared at the ground and strolled away. She would order an Uber on the main road. The car stopped and slowly reversed. She ignored it and continued walking.

"Miss Thompson." She stopped.

It was Chief Badejo. "I hope I can help you with your investigation?"

"Not at this moment. I'm surprised to see you here, though," said Lara.

"As I, you. My job is to protect my family. I think my wife is right. The Williams family is trying to use you as a weapon to destroy our family. I cannot allow that."

"I'm after the truth of Tola's death, Chief."

"Not at the cost of my family. Can I give you a ride by any chance?"

Lara eyed the darkened windows of the car. She did not know who else was in there with the chief. Probably his heavily armed security guards.

"I'm fine. I'll catch an Uber on the road."

She walked rapidly under the intense heat and waded through the curious residents who had gathered to watch the sleek car. At the main road, the touts did a salute military style and let her through. She was thankful to Moses for her freedom in the city.

She headed straight for Dr. Chen's mortuary. He was busy with Ben, said the receptionist. Lara waited for him in the lounge area as her phone rang.

"Where are you?" demanded Bibi. "I got the head of the security guards picked up. You were right, he was lying. Chief went to meet Tola. He's our main suspect. We have the guard and the house help as witnesses."

"But they didn't see him with Tola. I'll call you back," she said as Dr. Chen entered.

"Wait, wait...I need your help here."

"I'll call you back."

Lara ended the call and followed Dr. Chen to the office.

"I take it you have a breakthrough in the case?"

"We have some witnesses, but we need evidence."

"I might have something," he said.

He brought out the crime scene photos. Lara stared at them. She could see nothing. "What are you showing me?"

"I found a speck of foreign hair in the victim's hair. Had I not been looking closely, we would have missed it. I think the killer bent over her, perhaps to check if she was breathing and shed hair. Give me the DNA of your suspect and if it matches it, then you have your killer."

"Thank you, Doctor."

She called Bibi. "Arrest Chief, and get some DNA off him."

"Lara, I'm putting everything on the line for this."

"Nobody will believe the security guard and a house help without DNA. Dr. Chen found a hair on Tola. White hair."

A WEEK LATER, THEY were at the food and drinks parlor, favored by both. Bibi had her tall glass of beer and eyed Lara's Coke.

"One day you will tell me why you look at my glass with hunger and will not drink."

"Maybe."

Bibi took a deep sip.

"The boss and the higher-ups are all in hiding for the moment. Thanks to you." She grinned. "You leaked the arrest of Chief Badejo on social media, didn't you?"

"That's the only way we can get justice. But they might still cover it up."

"He had been carrying on with his son's ex-girlfriend under his wife's nose," said Bibi.

"Apparently, he was a known womanizer, but Tola threatened him when she found out she was pregnant. She was not coming to disrupt the reception but to speak to Chief. He used the cover of losing his phone to meet her near the bushes, and his chief security kept the guards away."

"I hear he has a ferocious temper," said Bibi, and Lara remembered the way Madam Ope meekly obeyed him when she asked to question their head of security.

"Do you think he will go to jail?"

Bibi shrugged. "How many wealthy people have you seen in our jails?"

"Mrs. Williams is grateful that she cleared her family's name. But she forgot that the Badejos are now Flaky's family," said Lara.

"Madam Ope has sworn not to forgive her for hiring a private investigator," laughed Bibi.

Their fish pepper soup arrived and smelled delicious.

"Thank you," she said to Lara, and picked up her spoon.

"You owe me," said Lara.

Bibi spluttered when the pepper hit the back of her throat. Her eyes watered as she croaked, "You wish!"

FOR MORE INFORMATION about the author, please visit Stella Oni's website: https://stellaonithewriter.com/

Better Late Than Murdered
Robert Petyo

"Do you remember when we first met?" Lisa looked down at the man seated beside her at the long table.

"Like it was yesterday," Conrad said as he surveyed the guests scattered before them.

Jake, seated at one of the small circular tables, noted that the groom-to-be seemed uncomfortable, tugging at his collar and twisting his shoulders.

Lisa continued, "Our college orientation. Quite a few years ago. Maybe a lot more than I'm willing to admit." She paused, waiting for a few chuckles from her audience. "But do you remember those three July days we spent on the campus?"

Conrad bobbed his head up and down but said nothing.

She reached over and stroked his forearm. "The very moment that we first spoke in the auditorium, that very second, I decided I wanted to marry you."

Gentle "oohs" and "aahs" wafted from the guests and family members seated around the small room. Lisa smiled as Conrad screeched his chair back to stand for a kiss.

Jake O'Malia did not consider himself an overly sentimental type. Years as a public defender had hardened him to the harsh realities of life. But something about the bride's words and the way the couple embraced tugged at his throat. Love was something he had long sought but never achieved.

"Then why the heck did it take you two so long to get hitched?" The garbled voice came from the back wall not far from where Jake sat.

Conrad peered toward the sound. "Gabby, you're drunk."

"Yeah. So are a lot of us, buddy. That's what this party's for, ain't it?" A woman beside him made shushing noises as she rapped the back of her palm against his arm.

Conrad started to move behind the other chairs at the head table as if to dash toward the man, but Lisa seized his arm and pulled him back into his seat. "No. No. He's right. It did take us a long time to find each other. But you know what they say. Better late than never. We waited years. Very many years. For a long time fate kept us apart. But now, finally, we are together. And that's what makes ours such a beautiful story."

Jake leaned toward the woman seated beside him at the small circular table. "You know that guy?" he asked softly, nodding his head in the direction of the drunken interloper who grumbled as he was scolded by his companion.

"Best man at Conrad's first two weddings," she said while watching the head table. "I think he's a little steamed he's not best man at this one."

"Why not?"

"Believe it or not, my cousin Conrad decided he's bad luck." She turned to Jake. "You do know they've been married before, right?"

He made patting motions for her to lower her voice, even though they were alone at their table and most people were focused on the head table, ignoring Gabby who was now being scolded by two men in sport coats with long floppy ties.

At the head table the bride-to-be clanged a fork against her wine glass to draw some silence. "It is a very beautiful story," she said. "For me it was love at first sight, but at first, Conrad didn't seem interested. And circumstances kept us apart. He was too busy with sports, and we didn't really see much of each other in college. And after school we returned to our separate homes in separate states." As she spoke, she stroked the thin necklace that hung to the top of her low cut blue dress. "I tried to keep in touch, but when Conrad found someone else, I stepped aside." She closed her eyes and bowed her head for a second.

Conrad reached for her hand but didn't quite get there.

"I, too, found someone," she continued. "So Conrad and I established separate lives, but I never stopped thinking of him. After my first marriage fell apart, I again tried contacting him." She pursed her lips as she gave him a scolding look. "But you never responded."

Conrad hunched his shoulders and pretended to pout as he turned away, which brought a few chuckles from the crowd.

"I tried a second marriage," she said. "It was a disaster like the first. And that scumbag took me for as much money as he could." She stopped and tapped her lips like she had just burped. "Sorry. Don't want to turn this into a vicious rant. But as I suffered through two marriages, I still knew Conrad was the only man for me. But he stayed unavailable. His first marriage failed, but then he found someone else. They were going to get married." She paused and squeezed her eyes shut for a moment. "But tragedy struck." Conrad placed his hand over hers on the table. "I'm sorry if I'm bringing up sad memories."

"No," he said. "I've accepted it. She'll always be a part of my life, but now, you are my wife."

"I never met Jill, but I know she must have been an incredible woman. This is my tribute to your fiancée," she said as she tapped the necklace again. "This was hers," she told the crowd. "A gift from Conrad." More "ooohs" from the audience. "She was wearing it the day—" She stopped and squeezed her eyes shut again. "He wanted me to have it."

"You are my true love," he said.

She bent to pick up her glass. She hesitated, and her throat bobbed. "It was a horrible accident, but I prefer to think of it as fate bringing us together. It took some time for it to happen, but here we are. Better late than never." She held her glass high in the air. "A toast to true love."

"True love," a few people shouted.

After a long drink, Lisa thumped her glass down. "Now, everybody, let's eat."

As people started clanging their silverware and chatting amongst themselves, Jake leaned toward the woman at his table. "I knew she was divorced, but I didn't know she was married twice."

"Well, they're both over sixty." She looked down and tapped her lips to stifle a burp. "Sorry. That's a little ageist, isn't it? You're what? Fifty-two? Fifty-three?"

He said nothing.

"I guess I shouldn't talk," she said. "I'm coming down on fifty myself and I'm still single." She sipped from her glass of wine. "I guess I never found the right guy. Not through lack of trying, though." She took a deep breath. "And I hope it's not too late to find someone." She leaned toward him and raised her eyebrows in a silent question.

But Jake cut off her self-analysis, trying to keep his voice pleasant. "Back to the wedding couple."

"Okay, yeah, they've both been through the wringer. Lisa was married twice. And Conrad one and a half." She munched on some lettuce from a salad dish that a waiter placed before her.

"One and a half? You mean that second marriage she mentioned? The one where the woman died?"

"Okay." She picked up her glass, studied it, and took a long sip. "You were still working in Jersey when all this happened," she said when she thumped it down.

Jake moved back to the city when he retired last year after twenty years in the public defender's office. He had no desire to stay in the legal profession. He had lived alone for years, saving his money and investing it wisely, and he figured that once he came back home, he would enjoy his early retirement, maybe find a nice quiet part-time job, if necessary. But he felt a little lost and lonely, since he no longer had family here, however, Rita, the younger sister of a high school friend of his, had quickly made him feel welcome and invited him to this little pre-wedding party being held for her cousin.

"What happened?" he asked.

"Cuz got divorced from a bimbo who just wanted to spend his money. She cheated on him and everything. Then, obviously not learning his lesson, he hooked up with another woman who enjoyed spending his money. That's the one Lisa was talking about. The one who died. They were together a few years before finally deciding to tie the knot." She dropped a sliced carrot to the table and studied it for a few seconds before shrugging and seeking another on her plate.

"What happened?" He tried to keep the impatience out of his voice.

"Okay. Well, before the wedding, his fiancée was murdered."

"That's not what Lisa said." Jake sucked in air, drying his lips as he watched her munch on a crouton. He didn't touch his own salad.

"Well, they officially ruled it an accident," she said. "But I know it was murder. She drowned in Porter's Lake."

"Why do you think it was murder?"

"Well, like I said, it was Cuz's second marriage. He has three adult kids from the first one, and all of them had their eyes on his money. I think one of her kids bumped her off before the new wife could really get her claws into his fortune."

He glanced at the head table where the couple worked at their salads, though the man still kept gazing toward the back of the room at Gabby, the drunk who had interrupted his bride-to-be's toast. Gabby's date hovered over him, still chastising him, while the others seated at the table pretended he wasn't there. Gabby seemed only interested in his glass of wine.

"You read too many Agatha Christie books," Jake said.

"You think so?" She smiled as a waiter removed her empty salad plate.

Jake nudged his own untouched plate away and, after a mocking stare, the waiter took it. When the plate was gone, he noted a small folded slip of paper on the table. "What's this?"

She finished her wine and watched him take the note. "Probably left over from the afternoon luncheon they had here. I've been here before. It's a classy place, but they don't have the best cleaning staff."

Jake read the note. On the back it said, "If Buddy's ex-wife is the killer, the knife was used." It made no sense to him and he tossed it aside, letting it waft to the floor.

She waved until another waiter approached and she handed him her glass. "More please." Looking at Jake, she said, "It was murder. If you knew Conrad's family you wouldn't be so quick to brush me off."

"I'm sure the police considered that possibility."

"Around here? You've been gone too long, my friend. The cops around here aren't too sharp." She licked her lips as another waiter approached with two plates dressed with steak, potatoes and mixed vegetables. "First of all, Jill went out at night on their rowboat, the one Conrad used to take her on trips across the lake in."

"So?"

"Jill was afraid of the water and would never go on that boat by herself."

"Did the police know that?"

"Sure they did." Rita sliced her steak in half. "But those morons didn't think it was a big deal. There's always a first time, they said. No big deal. She was sitting on the dock next to Conrad's boathouse and decided to go for a ride, they said. And, apparently, she was drunk."

"Oh."

"That's what the police said. There was a glass and two bottles down on the dock table."

"Did they find booze in her system?"

She held up her fork as she leaned back. "You definitely have been gone too long. This place is no CSI. The cops knew there was some liquor left in the glass and one bottle was empty. That was enough for them." She leaned toward him, pointing with her fork. "She was bombed and went out boating. End of story."

"Sounds plausible."

"Anyway, Alex confirmed that she went down to the dock alone."

"Alex?"

"He said it was a calm evening and she just wanted some alone time. Needed to think, she said. She didn't say she was going out on the boat, just that she wanted to sit and think. And maybe have a drink. One drink. That's what she said. There's a small wet bar down in the boathouse. Cuz's family likes their booze. But the thing is, not Jill. She wasn't much of a drinker. I could see her having one drink, but not getting loaded. Somebody must have pumped her with drinks to get her drunk and then knocked her in the water and let the boat loose."

"I think you're jumping to conclusions, but let's slow down. Who is this Alex you mentioned?"

"Conrad has three kids, Alex, and the twins Becky and Cheryl. Alex tried to follow his dad into the investment brokerage business that made Conrad big bucks, but he was a loser at it. Becky and Cheryl had other plans. Becky played tennis and hoped to turn professional. That didn't work out too well and now she still lives with her father. Cheryl looked for a rich husband." She sifted through her vegetables, looking for what she wanted.

"Did she find one?" Jake asked.

"Nope. Married a loser. Some guy who was big in that crypto garbage and ended up losing it all. She divorced him and started working in an art gallery. She gets by. I mean, at least she's got her own place. But let's face it. All three kids basically live off Conrad's money."

"How about Conrad's first wife?"

"Told you. She was a bimbo."

"Did she get any money in the divorce settlement?"

Rita turned away as she munched on a piece of meat, finally grabbing her napkin and wiping her lips. "This meat's too tough," she said with a slight cough.

Jake still hadn't touched his own meal. "The first wife?" he prompted.

"She didn't get anything. They had a prenup. Conrad's no fool. That's why he's got big bucks."

"But you say he lets his children take advantage of him."

"Okay, yeah. Kids. That's a different story." She shrugged her bony shoulders. "He'd do anything for his kids." She readjusted the strap of her beige dress. "You going to eat, or not?" She poked a fork at his plate.

Jake finally attacked his meal. "Let me just get this straight," he said after swallowing some potatoes. "You're convinced one of his kids drowned his potential second wife?"

"Yep."

"You have a favorite suspect?"

"I think it was one of the twins."

"Why do you say that?"

"I don't know." After another shrug, she had to again pull up the strap of her dress. "They're both kind of creepy." She sipped from her glass. "They're both thirty, yet they insist on dressing up identical, like they're still little kids."

"Creepy won't hold up in a court of law." Jake tried not to sound condescending, but the stern look on Rita's face told him she took offense. "Do you really think they killed her to protect their pending inheritance?"

"That's right. They didn't want her to spend any of Conrad's money. I think one of them joined her down on the dock, liquored her up, and put her on the boat."

"What about Alex? You said he was talking to her before she went down to the dock."

She rested both her palms on the table and gave him a long withering look. "Do you really think he would drown her, then admit to the police that he was there?"

"Maybe not."

"And a neighbor confirmed Jill was walking down to the dock after Alex left."

"Nosy neighbor?"

After a slow shrug of her shoulders, she adjusted her strap.

"Did the nosy neighbor see one of the twins go down with her?"

"No."

"See her get into the boat?"

"No. People can't really see the dock. It's kinda isolated. Just the wooden stairs leading down from the road are visible."

"Well, did the nosy neighbor see her taking liquor down with her?"

"No. But there's a liquor cabinet and fridge in the boathouse. In fact, one of the bottles of rum was empty."

"Did anybody see anybody else go down there?"

"No. But that doesn't mean no one else was there. The nosy neighbors don't keep watch twenty-four seven." Her lips twisted into a bit of a sneer which she quickly converted into a smile.

"I guess you're right," he acknowledged with a smile of his own.

"The boat was seen drifting out on the water. That's when somebody called the Lake police. Jill was found in the water a few feet offshore. The twins waited until dark, got her drunk, then knocked her in the water and let the boat loose. She couldn't swim."

"And how do you know all this? Was it in the paper?"

"Some of it." She sipped her wine and attacked her meal again, chomping on a piece of meat like she was punishing it.

"Rita?"

She swallowed the piece of meat and took another sip of wine. "I shouldn't tell you this, but my ex-boyfriend works as a dispatcher in the department. He was always telling me how he was trying to get the cops to do their jobs and look into things. He's the one who told me about the booze and other stuff. Told me to keep it quiet."

"Ex?" That was the only part of her speech that stayed with him.

She nodded.

"How long?"

That brought a brief smile. "I'm well over him if that's what you're concerned about." She reached across the table as if to grab his hand, then reconsidered and pulled back. "I'm definitely on the market for a new companion."

"Me, too," Jake said. Then he loudly cleared his throat. "Let's get back to being detectives. How about this new wife?" He pointed toward the main table where two waitresses were distributing desserts to the six people seated there.

Rita's fork clattered against her plate then fell off the table. She made no move to retrieve it.

Jake said, "If the twins killed his potential second wife to keep her away from Conrad's money, wouldn't they be after the new bride, too?"

Her eyes widened and she started to gag like a piece of steak was caught in her throat. She pointed, jabbing her finger toward the head table like she was banging a computer key.

Jake saw a tall woman in spiked heels with a sleek red dress that hampered her stride as she waddled in front of the bride-to-be. She set a tall cocktail glass on the table. "One for you, too, Dad," she said as she stepped to the right and placed one in front of Conrad.

"Thank you, Becky."

"No." Rita stood.

"A special mixture from Cheryl and I," the woman said. "Drink up."

Rita started toward the head table.

Conrad guzzled half his drink in one swig.

Lisa sipped hers. "Mmmm. I can taste the rum. That was Jill's favorite, wasn't it?" She looked down at Conrad who leaned away from her with wide eyes. As she took his hand he turned toward his daughter standing before them. He started to say something, but instead clamped his mouth shut in a meek grin.

Lisa looked at Becky and raised the glass. "You made this in tribute to her. How sweet."

"Stop," Rita said.

Another woman in a similar red dress cut in front of her. "Let them enjoy this," she said in a voice slightly deeper than the first woman's.

"Stop." Rita pushed her aside. When she reached the head table, she grabbed Lisa's drink.

"What are you doing?"

She sniffed the drink like she was a wine connoisseur and held it up to the light. She turned toward the woman who had blocked her way and held out the glass. "If this drink is okay, then you drink it."

"What?"

"It's fine," Conrad said, thumping his now empty glass on the table. "Don't be such a doofus, little lady."

"I'll drink it." Gabby stumbled to the floor in front of his table. On all fours, he crawled toward the head table like a rabid dog, but one of the men with long ties grabbed his ankles and yanked him back, holding his legs in the air like he was getting ready to plow the field.

Jake stood and approached Rita.

Becky, the first woman in red, took the glass from Rita and, again, approached the head table, holding out the glass toward Lisa.

"No." Rita grabbed for the glass. The woman turned slightly hoping to block her but Rita crashed into her elbow, knocking the glass from her hand. Its contents sloshed through the air as it crashed against the front edge of the head table. It tottered there for a second before dropping to the floor where it shattered.

"You goof!" Becky shoved Rita away and she stumbled back into Jake's arms.

"A waste of good liquor," Gabby wailed as he broke free from the man holding his legs and again crawled toward the head table.

"What was in that drink?" Rita demanded, still sagging against Jake.

"What? Some rum, chocolate whiskey, and a little soda."

"Nothing else?"

As Jake helped her straighten up, he whispered, "The groom drank it. No problems."

Gabby tapped his palms on the wet floor, then held up his hands and licked them. "Mmmm. Maybe a little too much rum."

Laughter showered the room.

Two men grabbed him this time, lifting him and carrying him back to the table.

Rita pointed at Conrad. "Are you okay?"

"I agree. A little too much rum." He paused for more laughter as he wiped his knuckles across his lips. "But very good. There's nothing wrong with the drink."

"That one was meant for you." She finally stood without Jake's help. "But I'm talking about the drink that was meant for Lisa." She pointed toward the shattered glass on the floor and looked at Cheryl. "What else did you put in it?"

"That's enough, little lady." Conrad had come around the head table and stood before his cousin, his voice taking the scolding tone of an angry parent. "You've had too much to drink. I won't let you ruin our party." He looked at Jake, his eyes twitching as he realized he had no idea who he was. "I suggest you take her home, sir. Please."

Jake took Rita's arm but she immediately shook free. "Sure. Send me home. I won't spoil your little party. The food was lousy anyway." She leaned to one side so she could see past Conrad to Lisa at the head table. "But please promise me you won't drink anything these twins bring you."

Lisa said nothing as she dropped into her seat.

"You don't want to end up like Jill."

Conrad slapped her. Hard.

Jake winced at the sound and Rita bent nearly in half at the waist, pressing her hand against her cheek. Jake moved in front of her, blocking her from Conrad, and bent to gently take her shoulders. "Let's go," he said as he straightened her. He helped her back to the table and grabbed her purse.

The laughter had snapped off at the sound of the slap. Jake felt the stares like boulders.

"I want another drink," Gabby said loud enough to draw some twitters.

Rita was sobbing. "They're trying to kill her," she said, but the words came out garbled and only Jake heard her.

He kept one arm locked in hers as they walked toward the exit. "You're overreacting," he said.

"No, I'm not." She tried to shake free.

They stepped into the small anteroom that served as a coat room. Jake looked for her jacket.

"Look." Rita pointed.

He turned and saw confusion at the main table. Lisa lay with her head on the table and a thin man was slapping at her wrist, trying to wake her. People were chattering as they pointed. Then, as Jake watched, Lisa popped her head up and flashed a broad smile.

Everyone started to laugh.

"Those bums," Rita mumbled as Jake helped her put on her jacket. "Trying to make fun of me."

"I tried to tell you," he said. "You were overreacting." He pulled on his own jacket.

"I think they were trying to poison her. And I think they'll try again." Her words trembled with tears as she tapped pleading fists on his chest. "You believe me, don't you?"

He twisted slightly, taking her hand and leading her outside. "I believe you when you say your cousin's last wife was murdered."

"What?" She pulled her hand free. "You do?"

"But it wasn't his children who killed her." He kept walking and she had to hurry to catch up. It wasn't until he reached his car in the parking lot when he said, "I think Lisa killed her."

"What?"

He held her door open and waited for her to get in. "You have the motive right. Money." He closed her door and hurried to the other side. "But not the kids. Lisa. She wanted to get her hands on his money and saw her opportunity slipping away when he got engaged to Jill."

"What? How could you know that?"

"She said it herself. She had eyes on him all the way back in college. She never forgot him. And she watched him hit the jackpot moneywise. When it finally looked like she had a chance to get him, Jill screwed up her plans. So she acted."

"I can't believe that."

"In the morning, we have to go talk to the police."

"We," she said with a weak smile as she took his arm. "I like the sound of that."

He pressed his hand over hers, feeling the warmth.

She asked, "But why are you so sure it was Lisa?"

"Lisa said she never met Jill. Then, how did she know what her favorite drink was? Because she was with her down on the dock as she was having her 'one' drink." He absorbed the smell of all the wine Rita had drunk as she pressed closer. "She asked what she was drinking so she could make her another one, or two. She emptied the bottle. You said Jill wasn't much of a drinker. She didn't have a favorite. That's why your cousin seemed confused when Lisa said that." Was it the wine making Rita overly friendly, or was she actually hugging him? He tried to keep his head clear. "They had a long chat before she knocked her into the water and set the rowboat adrift so people would think Jill went out rowing. Lisa killed her."

"My hero," she mumbled as she kissed him.

Charm City Wedding
Pamela Kyel

"We're gonna be like sisters, I tell ya. Sisters." It's true what they say, you can take the girl out of Jersey, but you can't take Jersey out of the girl. I mean the state, not the cow.

Leona Scola, Jersey girl through and through. From the tip of her teased hair to the scarlet toes crammed into sky-high stilettos. She was saccharine sweet tea—with excitement dripping off her like sweat on a Pimlico racehorse crossing the finish line.

Leona and I stood outside the sanctuary waiting for rehearsal to start. I knew I should have run when Antonio and his brother Giancarlo approached me a month ago, asking me to join the wedding party. I had never met her before I got roped into being a bridesmaid.

The mood around me was happy, but my heart just wasn't in it. The back of the Baptist church was like I remembered, from the merlot red carpet to the pale blue and ivory walls rising around me. The walls echoed with the sounds of a past I didn't want to remember.

This was the church of my childhood. Yes, I, Special Agent Laci Duvall, was baptized up there under the painting of the Jordan River. I was twelve—I think.

"Hiya, hon."

My hand flew to my mouth to cover the not-so-church-like word that threatened to come out.

"Hi, Rev," I said. "How are you?"

"I'm good. Never thought I'd willingly step foot into one of these places again, I tell you what." He eyed the crowd in the sanctuary like you would an exhibit at the zoo. Rev was a happily retired preacher who owned a car driving service—which is how I met him. He was performing the ceremony for Giancarlo as a favor to me.

"Have you been in here before?" I asked.

"This church? Nah—never seen it before. They're all the same to me, though. Seen one—seen 'em all. You been here before?" he asked.

"Oh, yes," I replied. "I grew up in this church. Any time the doors were open, we were here. Whether I wanted to or not."

"Now, that don' sound like a happy memory if you ask me," Rev said.

"Some were—some weren't."

"You gonna be okay while I get this show on the road?" Rev asked.

"For now, yes," I said.

Rev left and waded through the wedding party and their families. I stood on my toes looking for Antonio, but I didn't see him, so I pulled my phone out and shot him a text asking where he was. Detective Antonio Desio, Baltimore Police Department, and I were complicated. We recently got thrown into each other's orbit, along with feelings I never could quite shake. Twenty years ago, we were going to get married. We didn't.

While I waited to hear from him, I returned to the foyer to look around. The stairs to the balcony flanked the rear double-door exit from the building. The other side of the foyer held wooden steps which took you to the basement. I spent many a Friday night racing through this place with other youth at a lock-in.

There was a mirror above the lobby table, and I caught sight of myself. As a Special Agent for the Air Forces Office of Special Investigations, I was more comfortable in combat boots and OCPs than a flowery dress and heels. My roommates Sammie and Cassy spent the last month teaching me how to walk in four-inch heels. Luckily, I'm a fast learner and have a low center of gravity.

Just then, the wedding coordinator passed behind me in a blur. She was a Long Island iced tea of a woman named Pat, with hair rivaling Leona's height. Pat was in her sixties but dressed like she was in her twenties. She wore more leopard than an actual leopard, and none of it was the same pattern.

Even now, Pat teetered on a pair of sky-high leopard print heels which clashed with her pink leopard print dress. She occasionally placed her hand against her stomach and covered her mouth with a fist.

"Are we ready yet?" Pat pushed the button on her walkie-talkie and spoke to someone inside the church. The walkie-talkie squawked in reply, but I don't know what was said. Apparently, neither did Pat. "What?" she asked. She rubbed her temple and eyes with her right hand.

"Sisters, you say?" I kept one eye on Pat and one on Leona.

"Oh yes," Leona said. "We gonna double date and do lotsa couple's things with you and Anthony."

"You mean *Antonio*?" I asked.

"Ain' that what I said?" she asked.

I bit my tongue. I didn't want to get off on the wrong foot with Giancarlo's wife-to-be and Antonio's sister-in-law.

Pat's clapping hands alerted us that rehearsal was starting. I took my place in front of Leona, and Pat opened the door for me to enter the church. I stepped into a sea of faces. All of them stared at me, and I froze in place. I didn't do well with a lot of attention.

Cassy and Sammie, who were somewhere in the gathered mass of family watching the rehearsal, insisted it was best to rehearse in the shoes I would wear in the wedding. But instead of placing one foot in front of the other in the sedate manner we'd practiced at home, I jumped at the sound of the door closing behind me and tripped and fell onto the white paper running down the aisle.

The songbook I carried in place of flowers flew off in front of me and slid to a stop halfway down the aisle. I heard a snort from the crowd that I knew belonged to Cassy. Before I could right myself, someone stepped from behind me and reached for my elbow. I looked up at my rescuer. *Antonio.*

One glance at his face was all I needed to know—he was doing everything in his power not to laugh at me. Instead, his eyes danced, and his mouth twisted in the grin I loved so much.

He helped me up, and together we walked down the aisle. Walking beside Antonio felt surreal, and Mrs. Desio's face revealed her train of thought was at the same station as mine. In retaliation for Antonio calling off our wedding, I went and got married. Antonio recently helped me investigate and find who killed my ex-husband—but that's another story.

We reached the front, and I took my place opposite Antonio beside Rev. The wedding party was small, just me and my Charm City heartthrob. Giancarlo's eyes were glued to the back door while we waited for Leona to emerge.

We waited. And we waited. And after about five minutes of waiting, a scream erupted from the foyer. Antonio and I jumped into action, but halfway down the aisle, I stumbled in my heels and crashed to the floor. I waved Antonio on, took my shoes off, and ran the rest of the way with Giancarlo a step behind me. When we reached the back, Desio told Giancarlo to keep everyone out of the area.

"What's going o—" I asked.

Pat was spread eagle on the ground in a semblance of a toddler making a snow angel—blood dripping on the floor beside her head. Leona was on her knees waving a hand in front of Pat, her face as white as a sheet.

"She won' wake up," Leona said.

"WHAT HAPPENED?" I ASKED.

"Who is this?" Antonio took Leona's place beside Pat and analyzed Pat's temple. On the right side of her head was an open wound where a bullet grazed her head and left a trail.

I grabbed the trash can from under the lobby table. It usually began with my mouth watering, and this time was no exception. After I emptied my rehearsal dinner into the trash can, I checked her vitals, careful not to analyze where the blood was dripping from. Strong pulse. "Oh good, she's alive."

"We was outside when her phone went off, and I came in to give her privacy. I turned when the door opened, and she came inside hand to her head, and a funny look on her face, and the next thing I knew, she was like this." Leona windmilled her arms, and her rehearsal bouquet missed Antonio by inches.

"Why were you outside? Wasn't she supposed to tell you it was your turn to enter the church?" I asked.

"Yeah, but she said she needed a cigarette."

"What's going on?" Giancarlo joined us.

"NO," Leona screeched, and I covered my ears. "You ain' supposed to see me before we're married."

"I thought that was just the wedding day." Giancarlo's hands flew to cover his eyes just in case.

"Oh yeah." "It is." Leona and I spoke at the same time.

"Again. Who is she?" Antonio dialed dispatch for an ambulance.

"She's the wedding coordinator," I replied. "Her name is Pat."

"We ain' gonna be married tomorrow." Leona wailed into her flowers and used them to dry her tears. I grabbed a wad of tissues from the lobby table and pushed them into her hands. Giancarlo gathered her in his arms and patted her back. Leona was short, but the top of her hair reached Giancarlo's nose, and he started to sneeze. I grabbed another tissue and shoved it at him.

"Do you know who she was talking to?" Desio asked. He took a tissue from the box to pick up Pat's phone. He couldn't turn it on due to the password request, though.

"She didn' say. Just went outside."

Antonio and I looked at each other. Someone was calling her to get her outside so they could shoot her.

"Giancarlo, why don't you and Leona finish the rehearsal while Laci and I wait here until the ME arrives."

"Hey, hon." Rev came into the back room. "What's going on? What happened to her?"

"We don't know," I said.

"Her dress reminds me of one my aunt Pat has." He stepped beside me and looked at her spread eagle before us. "Hey, whatta you know? It is my aunt Pat."

"What a coincidence," I said, "since, according to Leona, her name is Pat. How are you so sure?"

"According to who?" Rev asked.

"Leona...the bride?"

"She had the cabbage ear when I was growing up. She's my mom's sister."

"Cabbage ear? You mean cauliflower ear?" I looked at the left side of Pat's head. "Has your mom seen her lately?"

"Yeah, that. She got it in a fight at her salon a long time ago. I'll call and ask my mom once I finish the rehearsal." He stepped back into the church to finish his job for the evening.

Desio took his phone out again and started taking pictures of Pat from every angle you could imagine. He also included the lint and whatnot on the carpet around her.

"Someone called her outside so they could shoot her." I spoke the moment Rev walked away.

"Yeah, it looks that way. The question is, who would want to kill a wedding coordinator? And why?"

WE STAYED WITH PAT until the paramedics arrived, then slipped into the back pew while the rehearsal finished. I noticed Rev took out his phone the minute Giancarlo and Leona walked down the aisle to the rear of the church and out the doors into the foyer. We had minimal success cleaning up the blood but ended up covering it and putting one of those wet floor signs over it.

Giancarlo and Leona met us in the foyer and had a million questions which we answered as best we could. Cassy and Sammie joined in, and I explained what happened while Antonio ushered his family out of the church, including Giancarlo and Leona.

"Now, what's he doin'?" Cassy looked past me to the sanctuary, where Rev paced back and forth in front of the wedding flowers.

"He mentioned calling his mom once the rehearsal was over and asking if it's his Aunt Pat," I said. Rev closed his phone before I finished explaining, and with a grim look, he joined us in the foyer. "Was that your mom?"

"Yeah, she can't reach Aunt Pat, and my cousin ain't answering. So, she's going to run over to her house and check, but she's pretty sure it's her. Said Aunt Pat's been more drama lately than she normally is, whatever that means."

"What do you know about your aunt you can tell us?" I asked. "Did she work other than being a wedding coordinator?"

"Oh yeah, she owns a salon down in the city," he said. "Down on Howard Street—coupla blocks from the Hippodrome. Been there about thirty years. She never got married—said her life was her work, but she had my cousin back in the '90s. He's a little younger than I am and don't work. Usually lives off his girlfriends. Always claims to have something cooking and will get his big break soon. Had a garage band back in the early 2000s—nothing ever came of it, though."

Antonio caught the end of the conversation with Rev and asked his own questions. Was she in the red? Did she get along with her employees? Stuff like that. He must have been satisfied with the answers because he didn't pursue anything else.

We parted ways with nothing left to do tonight but research. Antonio was staying with Giancarlo tonight, and I drove home with Cassy and Sammie. We would recon after the wedding tomorrow and look for Pat's house, assuming the search warrant came through.

While I didn't have a dog in this fight, as an agency, the Air Force Office of Special Operations was known to help out the local police, and this time was no exception. I mean, we helped each other nab my ex-husband's killer, after all.

Rev headed off to his mom's house and would let me know what he found out. If I didn't hear from him tonight, we would catch up tomorrow at the wedding.

THE WEDDING WENT OFF without a hitch, and I considered my maid-of-honor duties a thing of the past. We posed for pictures with the happy couple until my face hurt, but seeing the smile on Giancarlo's and Leona's faces was worth it. We left the church and went to the Desio Family Restaurant in Little Italy for the reception.

They were honeymooning in the Poconos. Leona showed me the website where they would sleep in a heart-shaped bed and bathe in a martini glass. Her enthusiasm bubbled up as much as the tub, and I laughed with her when she wondered aloud whether it was real champagne in there or not. She was a sweet girl, and she and Giancarlo were so obviously in love you couldn't help but wish them the best.

Antonio's phone went off right after the happy couple took to the dance floor for their first dance.

"Search warrant came through." He leaned over and spoke in my ear. I probably would have punched him if I hadn't been expecting it. I hated being snuck up on—it never ended well for the sneaker.

"How long do we need to hang out here before it's acceptable that we leave?" I asked.

He looked at me like I was crazy. "We leave now," he said.

"I'll wait while you tell your parents." I grinned big because I knew how this would end. Sure enough, he retraced his steps to me and sat down. His face set in an adorable frown.

"We have to wait until they cut the cake," he said. I looked at him and burst out laughing, which drew the attention of everybody.

"Fine. If I have to suffer, so do you." He snagged my wrist and hauled me onto the dance floor, where various couples joined Giancarlo and Leona.

"Oh no. No. No. No. No." I tried to put the brakes on, but my strength was no match for his. Next thing I knew, I was in his arms with a sea of people watching us. Most were his family, who knew and disapproved of me because of how things ended with our engagement twenty or so years ago.

I closed my eyes to the audience and held on for dear life instead. Antonio held my left hand with his right, and my other was on his shoulder. I leaned my forehead against the knot in his tie. It was the perfect height and the perfect pillow. After a few minutes, I felt him lean his chin against my forehead and relax.

We never went to prom—he'd worked instead, and I chose to spend prom night propped up on a stool in the kitchen of this same restaurant. We talked and laughed, and, oh yes when things got slow in the kitchen, we danced—one slow dance.

When the song ended, everyone exited the dance floor, and Antonio bypassed our seats and made a beeline for Giancarlo. I joined Cassy, Sammie, and Amaré, Cassy's old partner on the police force, while he went and presented his case to his brother and sister-in-law.

"Where he goin'?" Cassy asked.

"To see if Giancarlo can move up the cake cutting. They approved the search warrant, but his mom won't let him leave until they cut the cake."

Cassy threw back her head and laughed.

"That was my reaction, too," I said.

"Only thing is none of us brought a car," Cassy said.

"I'm using Giancarlo's car." Desio returned and picked up the conversation. "Laci and I will go to the salon if you and Amaré want to go to her townhouse in Dundalk."

"Me too," Sammie said. "But how are we going to get there?"

"Get where?" Rev joined our small party in the corner.

"Perfect," I said.

"Oh no. No. No. No. No." Cassy was waving her arms back and forth behind Rev's back.

"Rev, do you think you could help us out and drive Cassy, Amaré, and Sammie to your aunt's townhouse?" I asked. "We have a warrant for her house and the salon. We're splitting up duties."

"Sure, hon. I'd be glad to help out," he said.

"What'd Giancarlo say?" I asked.

"They're cutting the cake as we speak." Antonio pointed to the center of the dining room, where a table with a white cake stood.

"What kind is it?" I asked.

"Wedding cake," Antonio said.

My eyes rolled on their own, I swear. "What flavor is inside the wedding cake?"

"Oh. I don't know. Something red."

"Red velvet? Oooh, can I get one to go?" I asked.

"Me too." Sammie appeared at my elbow with an earnest look on her face.

Antonio looked at us like we were nuts.

"Don't judge," I said. "Red velvet is my favorite."

"Mine too," Sammie said. "Does it have cream cheese frosting?"

"It's white. That's all I know. You get to the parking lot, and I'll grab the extra cake from the kitchen."

"Oh yumm," I said. I snagged all my gear and followed the train to say goodbye to Giancarlo and Leona.

"Call me." Leona grabbed my hand in both hers and looked me in the eyes. "We're gonna be like sisters. Oh, but not yet. We don't get back from the Poconos for a week an' a half. So, after that. Call me. And let me know what happens with Ms. Pat, too."

THE SALON SPILLED ONTO the sidewalk between an abandoned storefront and a liquor store. The façade was painted bright aqua blue and sported a black and white striped awning. We were greeted with a wonderland of aqua, stripes, and leopard when we opened the door. The chairs were leopard, and the sinks were black and chrome. I assumed the pads on the floor were black and white stripes to match the awning outside.

"You take the reception area, and I'll go to the back room," Desio said.

I nodded and immediately got to work opening drawers, feeling around for hidden compartments, rifling through papers, then moving to the next one. Halfway through the third drawer, Desio called me to join him in the back.

The room was little more than a hallway sporting several black bookcases which reached the ceiling. Various needs of a modern salon filled the bookcases alongside a washer and dryer and lots of towels.

"Where are you?" I asked. When Desio stuck his head out a door about six feet in front of me, I went and joined him. Bathroom. "What's going on in here?"

He was on his hands and knees, rifling through the under-the-sink cabinet. He shoved a business-size manilla envelope at me, then another, and another. I set several on the sink and then opened the first one. Once Desio finished under the sink, he picked up an envelope and looked through it.

In my envelope, there were pictures of a blonde woman in her late twenties. She was doing everything from walking a small poodle, to grocery shopping, to standing outside another hair salon. Desio's held the same woman in different places. He whipped out his phone and looked up the salon's name from one of the pictures.

"This place is right around the corner on West Fayette Street. It can't hurt to stop and see if she's there."

"Yeah, she could work there," I said.

We were almost to the corner of Park Avenue when a nondescript salon appeared beside us. We would have missed it if we didn't know what it looked like. I tried the door and found it open.

The small petite blonde from the pictures greeted us.

"Oh honey, you came just in time. I can help you with your hair," she said.

Desio looked at me and eyed my hair while I tried to push it behind my ear. Unfortunately, my curly updo had become an up-don't with the day's activity.

"We're not here for her hair," Desio said.

"Oh, then what do you want?" she asked.

"Are you the owner of this salon?" I asked.

"Yeees. Why?"

"We foun—"

"Your salon was recommended to me by another salon. She said you knew what to do with curly hair." I was winging it here, but I didn't think telling her we found her picture around the corner in another salon would work.

Her face lit up when I finished. "I have time now to work my magic if you do."

"I'll give you a raincheck if that's okay. Pat said you were busy and—"

Her face seized up when I mentioned Pat's name. "Pat? Pat, who?"

"She has the salon around the corner." I pointed my finger in the general direction of the salon we had just left.

"Hunh," she said. "I don't know anyone by that name. I'll have to look her up. Maybe we can share stories. It's probably best you can't do it right now. I just remembered I have an appointment in fifteen minutes. You can take one of my cards and give me a call." She shoved a business card into my hand and ushered us to the door, which left us with no choice but to leave.

I gave Desio the side-eye when we stepped outside, and the clanging bell on her door stopped swaying.

"Interesting reaction, don't you think?" I asked.

"Yeah. We'll go to the park and sit and wait to see what she does next."

We crossed Park Avenue, went along the dog park to a bench, and sat down. Thankfully, it was a nice day since we didn't know how long we would be there. From here, we could remain out of sight while keeping an eye on the salon. According to the name on the card, her name was Nikki Parker.

"What'd you think of the wedding?" I asked.

"It was nice," Desio replied. "Thank you for standing in as a bridesmaid. I know it couldn't have been easy. Leona is...unique."

"But it's obvious Giancarlo is as over the moon with her as much as she is with him. She is very sweet, but even I could take her in a thumb war. Do your parents like her?"

"They want Giancarlo to be happy," he said.

"In other words, she's not good enough," I said. "Though I'm beginning to wonder if anyone would be good enough for their boys."

"You were," he said.

"At one time, yes. Not so much anymore."

"Lucky for you, we Desio boys get to choose our own women," he said. I snorted.

We lapsed into silence while traffic flowed around us. A few blocks over was the Hippodrome, and one block over from that was Edgar Allen Poe's grave. The Poe Toaster stopped their yearly salute in 2012, seventy years after they first appeared, and the mystery remained.

"I'm going to move the car to the parking garage next to her salon." Desio interrupted my historical thoughts. "I'll take West Fairmont so she doesn't see me. I should have thought of it earlier, but your curly hair distracted me."

I reached up and touched my hair again. I'd never been insecure about it, but I didn't know if Antonio liked it or not, and did I know why it mattered so much now after all these years? Not really.

I kept an eye on the salon door, and about fifteen minutes later, his police sedan pulled into the garage next to the salon.

"I'm going to stay with the car." Desio's text came across a couple of minutes later.

I couldn't play on my phone while in surveillance mode, so I came up with games to play about the cars going by. A tiny car honked as they passed me, and I looked over. Then out of the corner of my eye, I saw Nikki lock the salon's front door. She glanced in my direction, and I jerked my head to the right. When I turned back, she was at the entrance to the parking garage where Desio was parked.

"Incoming," I texted Desio. I quickly got up and followed her at a distance. When I reached the garage, she was exiting in a small yellow car. When Desio appeared in the next instant, I hopped inside. "At least she's easy to spot in the yellow car."

WITH FOUR CAR LENGTHS in front of us, we followed Nikki onto West Franklin, then Edmonson.

"Uh oh."

"What?" Desio asked.

"Ten to one. She's heading to the Purple Pelican."

"No way," he said.

"Look." I pointed out the front window, where Nikki turned into the gravel lot of the Purple Pelican. I snagged my phone and fired off a text to Cassy to meet us at the Pelican.

"Gotcha. We right around the corner and be there in five minutes," Cassy messaged back.

"How are they going to get there that fast from Mt. Vernon?" Desio asked.

"You obviously haven't ridden with Rev," I said. Sure enough, five minutes on the dot later, the battered hatchback pulled into the parking lot and headed right for us. At the last minute, Rev yanked his car into the spot next to us. I thought we were going to have to peel Amaré off the seat with a spatula, but he erupted from the car and went to the back, where he leaned over and threw up.

Cassy was hooting in the back seat, and Sammie giggled. Rev looked dazed and confused—which is odd because that's usually Sammie's MO.

"You okay back there, Amaré?" I asked. He waved his hand, and you could hear him gasping for breath.

"Come on," Desio said. "We've lost enough time already."

I trailed after him, with Cassy, Sammie, Rev, and Amaré bringing up the rear. I didn't know how we would find them in the club on a Saturday evening. Once inside, I scanned the place, looking for her.

The dancers were doing their thing on the stage beside the door leading to the dressing rooms. Nikki stood at the bar to my right and spoke to Adam, the bartender. I nudged Desio on my left and tilted my head in their direction. A second man, a giant, joined Nikki just then, and they took off for the dressing area.

"I'll take the girls and Rev and question Zucca," I said. "You and Amaré take those two."

He nodded, and I gathered my crew while he and Amaré fought the crowd to reach the back door. Zucca owned the Purple Pelican and stood tall in his five-foot-seven frame. We met when I investigated who killed my ex-husband this past summer. He was Italian down to his loafers. I accidentally called him Pumpkin the first time I met him, and I swear he hasn't forgotten it. I knew enough Italian to be dangerous, but this man *was* dangerous in every sense of the word. I knocked once on his door and let us in.

Zucca sat behind his desk, and Luca, his bodyguard, rose from the corner chair when we barged inside.

"Hey, now," Luca started.

"It's okay, Luca." Zucca waved him back into his chair before turning to us. "To what do I owe this pleasure?"

"Holy mole—" Rev spoke from behind me.

"What do you know about a petite hairdresser name Nikki Parker?" I asked.

"What makes you think I know anything about her?"

"Because we just seen her talkin' to Adam, the bartender, and leaving through the exit to the dressin' room with some big dude."

"That would be our newest bouncer, Chuck Nielson."

"Chuck 'The Wedge' Nielson?" Rev asked.

"Who gotta name like that? I'd like to know," Cassy said.

"Maybe his momma didn't like him very much," Sammie said.

Zucca wiped his hand down his face, and I admit it took a lot for me not to roll my eyes. I coughed to cover my laugh instead.

"'The Wedge' is a hitman," Rev said.

"Now, how you know that?" Cassy asked.

"My ol' church was a part of the neighborhood he grew up in—his momma used to brag about him. I thought he was long gone, though. When did he get back?" Rev asked.

"I know nothing of him leaving, but yes, he is a hitman."

"Nikki put a hit out on Pat." I spoke to myself, but Cassy heard me.

"Do what now?" she asked.

"What's his current location?" I asked.

After looking down his nose at me, Zucca removed a piece of paper from a stack on the corner of his desk and wrote down an address he apparently knew by heart. I snatched it from his hand and raced for the door. I glanced behind me to make sure everyone was with me, then turned and plowed into Desio outside the office.

"Quick—the bouncer is a hitman. I have his address."

Desio and Amaré about-faced, and we hot-footed it for the back door. Racing through the parking lot, Desio assigned duties as we went.

"Amaré, you and Cassy go straight to the hospital. They've gotten a head start on us, and we don't have any time to lose."

"Now, how we goin' to get there?"

"Rev, can you take them to the hospital on the way to drop Sammie off at her parents' house where the kiddos are? Keep track of how much we owe you, okay?"

"Aw, hon, you don't owe me nothing. This is the most excitement I've had since the last time."

"If you're sure," I said.

He nodded, and they all piled in the car. I noticed that Amaré beat Sammie to the back. How a six-foot-something man could fold himself into that back seat was beyond me. It just showed you how determined he was.

DESIO AND I BACKTRACKED down Edmonson until we hit the

Beacham Homes district of the West Baltimore Hoods. We found his house on Pennsylvania Avenue and made a U-turn at the corner of Pennsylvania and Gold. Parked around the corner—we could see the front door to a muffler shop alongside an alley. I took note of the time, 8:00 pm. Who knew how long we would have to wait until Chuck showed up. I didn't know where the day had gone. It seemed like just an hour ago we were leaving the wedding.

"What time did we leave the wedding?" I asked.

"I think after six. Why?"

"Just wondering where my day went, that's all," I said. "Do you suppose that muffler shop has snacks?"

"There's a taco place a couple blocks up. Do you want me to get something to eat?"

My stomach grumbled on cue, and Desio opened the door and got out. As a BPD cop, he knew these streets well, and one look at him would tell you not to mess with him.

I kept an eye on Chuck's place, but I couldn't resist the sight of Desio walking in the opposite direction. Lord, that man was fine.

Thirty-ish minutes later and Desio stepped into my line of sight again. About a block from the car, a homeless person stopped him. There was no threat, and Desio took something out of the bag, gave it to the guy, then continued to the car.

"You're so nice," I told him the second he sat down.

"Hunh?"

"You gave that man food," I said.

"Well, it's telling when he was hungry enough to take it."

"True, but you didn't have to offer."

We shared the remaining tacos and settled into silence while we waited. It didn't take long before I started nodding off, though. I tried my hardest to stay awake, but I slowly slid along the headrest until my head rested against the window. This was quite a day. The shaking of my shoulder woke me up, and with one glance at the dash, I saw we were going on midnight.

"Sorry about that," I said. I wiped my mouth and prayed I hadn't snored.

"Look." He nodded his chin at Chuck's house.

"He's there?" I asked.

"Yep." Desio reached for the door handle, and I did the same. We met at the front of the sedan and walked to the alley. One look down, and Chuck was nowhere in sight. Desio stepped in first, and I followed, watching our rear. When we reached the second door halfway down the alley, Desio knocked.

"Yeah?" Chuck answered the door in a dingy t-shirt and low-slung sweats. If he sneezed, we would see more than we cared to.

"Chuck Nielson?" Desio asked.

"Who wants to know?" Chuck asked.

Desio flashed his badge and stepped into the house. I remained at the door where I could see into the alley in case anyone else wanted to join the party.

"I ain' done nothin' wrong."

"Now, did we say you did?" Desio asked. "We have a few questions concerning the company you had tonight at the Purple Pelican."

"I ain' gotta say anything. I know my rights." Chuck crossed his arms on his chest and stared at Desio.

"You're right. You don't have to say anything. We can do all this down at the precinct. I have enough information to consider you a suspect in a murder attempt last night." Desio was good.

"I didn't shoot nobody," Chuck said.

"Who said they were shot?" Desio asked. With a glance at me, I knew my job was to call for more backup—someone who could take "The Wedge" here down to the station. I stepped outside and quickly placed the call.

"...it was that salon chick." I caught the tail end of the conversation when I came back inside.

"Pat?" I asked.

"Nah—it was the other one. Nikki."

"Nikki Parker hired you to kill Pat Brooks?" Desio was trying to get a confession.

"Was that her last name? I only know her as Pat. The salon owner Nikki used to work at," Chuck said.

"Nikki used to work for her?" I asked.

"Yeah, ain' that what I said?"

Before we could ask anything else, a patrolman came to the door, and Chuck took one look at him and went running for the stairs. Desio stuck out his foot and tripped him, and Chuck crashed into the small wooden table in the middle of the kitchen.

"You said yous wouldn't take me in," Chuck whined.

"That was before you confessed to shooting an innocent woman," Desio replied.

"Did I confess to that?"

"Yes," Desio and I said together.

WE LEFT THE PATROLMAN at his squad car with Chuck and headed for the sedan a block away. Our next call was the hospital. I messaged Cassy that we were on our way and to be expecting us. I told her we had Chuck.

We took Bel Air Road instead of traversing the tunnel. It was after midnight, so there wasn't a lot of traffic out, and we made it in a little less than a half hour. Funny how the roads were empty, but the parking lot wasn't. With not a lot of options for parking spots, we grabbed the closest one we could and still ended up a hundred yards from the front door.

Desio was in a hurry, but I struggled to keep up while running in heels. He stopped and waited for me twice before we reached the entrance to the hospital, where the information desk was happy to help once he flashed his badge. I checked my phone while he got directions, but I still hadn't heard from Cassy.

With room number in hand, we stepped past the information desk and pushed through the doors leading into the ER. Pat's door was firmly closed, and when I opened it, I couldn't believe my eyes. Cassy was sitting in the middle of the room, on the floor. While this wasn't so strange, the fact she was sitting on Nikki Parker is what drew all our attention.

"Is about time you two got here," Cassy said.

"Where's Amaré?" Desio asked.

"That fool went for coffee thirty minutes ago and still ain' come back."

Before she finished her sentence, the door opened behind us, and

Amaré stepped in, but he stopped short when he saw the room.

"Uh oh. What'd I miss?" Amaré asked.

Desio reached for Nikki, but in the time it took Cassy to stand up, and before he could grab her, Nikki was up and sprinting for the door. Desio tried the tripping trick again but missed her entirely and instead tripped Cassy, who was hot on Nikki's tail. Cassy tripped and fell into Amaré, and the tray of coffee went flying. Coffee flew in every direction, but mostly it landed on the floor, which Nikki slipped on, skidding across the linoleum, and crashing headfirst into the closed door. She didn't get up.

Desio grabbed the blanket off the unconscious Pat, laid it on the floor to sop up the coffee mess, and stepped over to check on Nikki.

"What's going on? Where am I?"

We turned as a unit to see a startled Pat struggling to sit up in the bed. I went over and pushed the button to get the bed in a chair position. On the heels of the leopard queen's awakening came Nikki's, who reared back on her knees in a failed attempt to leverage herself into a standing position. The only problem was she was cuffed and fell back on her chin. Desio reached down, picked her up, and placed her in the chair beside the bed, but still a good seven feet from reaching Pat.

"Now," Desio said. "Who wants to start?"

Neither woman spoke up. They eyed each other. Pat bit her bottom lip—trying not to say anything, I'd wager.

"I'll start," I said. "We spoke with Chuck Nielson before coming here. Does that name ring a bell, Nikki?" When she refused to answer, I went on. "He had some revealing things to say about you. How much did you pay him?"

"I don't believe you," Nikki said.

I reached out my hand, and Desio placed his notepad in it. I flipped to the page where he wrote down our convo with Chuck. I knew I could count on Desio to keep everything squared away. It's what made him such a fabulous detective.

"We asked Chuck, and I quote, 'Nikki Parker hired you to kill Pat Brooks?' To which Chuck replied, 'Was that her last name? I only know her as Pat, the salon owner where Nikki used to work.'"

"That's a lie." Nikki erupted out of her chair, and when Cassy stepped in front of her, she bounced off the front of Cassy like one of my dog Needles' balls off my tile floor. Nikki fell back into the chair with so much enthusiasm she would have fallen off the side if Cassy wasn't there to grab her.

"We have the testimony of the man you bought off," Desio said. "We don't need an admission of guilt from you. What I want to know is why?"

"She started it." Nikki angled her chin at Pat in the bed.

"I did not," Pat said. "She did."

"Will someone please tell me what this is all about?" I asked. "Because if you don't, the BPD will take you both off to jail."

"On what grounds?" Pat asked. "You don't have anything on me."

"Not right this second, we don't, but I guarantee that as we speak, Chuck is spilling his guts, and we'll find out any minute now what this is all about," I said.

"Fine," Nikki said. "She's been blackmailing me for the last six months."

My jaw fell open, and my eyes swung to the frail-looking Pat sitting in the bed. Her face was red, and her clenched fists sat on her lap.

"Over what?" I asked.

"On account of my previous profession," Nikki said. "I used to be a sex worker. I paid my way through beauty school that way, and soon as I graduated, I checked off the street and got a job with Ms. Pat. Everything was goin' great, even if the pay wasn't what I wanted. After two years of working my tail off for her, I decided to take a stab at goin' on my own. Bought the storefront I got now and set up shop.

"Pat didn't like I took my customers with me, who then went and brung people they knew. Next thing you know, I'm doin' better than she is. A year or so ago is when the blackmail started—threatened to tell my customers and to put it in the beauty school alumni e-newsletter, which she runs. I paid and paid, but it kept gettin' higher and higher. I was payin' her more than I paid in rent. I was through with being blackmailed, and Chuck offered to help. Yeah—funny how he left that part out, but I guess it's his word against mine. Anyways—that's it. That's the whole story."

"How did you find out about Nikki's previous job?" I asked Pat.

"My ex-fiancé, the dirty no-good rat, picked her up while she was on her corner, then bragged to me about it a couple years later when he saw her in my shop. I kicked him to the curb and began my plan. I knew she would eventually go out on her own, no matter how much I begged her st—"

"You never begged me for anything a day in your life," Nikki shouted. "If you'd only been civil and treated me fairly, I wouldn'a had a reason to leave."

"So, now we know," I said.

"What happens now?" Nikki asked.

"We'll have to arrest you both," Desio said. "One for blackmail and the other for hiring a hitman."

IT WAS NICE TO GET out of the bridesmaid dress I'd worn all day and sit outside with Cassy and Sammie in the humid night air. The cicadas were outdoing themselves tonight, and they almost drowned out the traffic on Philadelphia Road, which ran in front of my house. We finished at the hospital around one in the morning, but none of us were tired. We'd picked up Sammie from her parents' but left her twins, Ana and Ryan, sleeping for the night at their house.

"Well, I swanny, I didn't see that one coming." Cassy and I finished filling Sammie in on the story of Pat and Nikki. "What about that hitman?" Sammie asked.

"Well, he signed on to kill someone. So that means jail time," I said. "And you can bet the BPD is looking into unsolved cases he could have done."

The doorbell and knock on the door were out of the blue, but we all knew who it was.

"Well, I guess tha's all for us tonight," Cassy said.

"You guys don't have to leave, you know," I said.

"Uh-huh." Cassy snorted.

They went upstairs, and I went to answer the door and greet Antonio. He was still in his wedding attire when I let him inside.

"How come you didn't change?" I asked.

"I didn't have a chance to yet. I had to call and let Giancarlo and my family know what happened. You'll never guess what happened on the way to the station."

"Uh-oh, what?" I asked.

"I put them both in the back of the car, and they started going at it the second I shut the door. Before Amaré and I could pull them apart, Nikki delivered a swift kick to Pat's face, and with those shoes of hers, she broke her nose. Pat isn't one to suffer fools gladly and returned her kick with one of her own and knocked Nikki so hard her head hit the window, and I am now sporting a large spiderweb crack in my rear passenger door."

"Holy crap," I said. "Who knew those two had it in them."

"Yeah, no kidding. I didn't take Pat back to the hospital. I just put Amaré back there, holding a tissue to her nose. They took care of her at the station and bandaged her up before I left to take Amaré home."

"Oooh, he's going to get you for that one," I said.

"Yeah, well, if he'd stayed in the room like he was supposed to, then Nikki wouldn't have gotten in."

"But was that so bad?"

"Eh—Well, I just wanted to make sure you were recovering from the day. Giancarlo and Leona stopped in Hershey for the night, but I didn't wake them up when I called."

I snorted. "That's more than I wanted to know."

He turned and pulled the front door open. I grabbed it to hold it open, and he turned around and looked down at me.

"I've always loved your curly hair," he said. His voice was low and sent chills down my spine. "It reflects the passionate woman you don't let many others see. It's like a secret you save for those who really know you."

I stared after him with my mouth hanging open like a fish. Where on earth had that come from? When he waved from the sedan and pulled out of the lot, I still hadn't recovered from my surprise. I didn't know if it was the wedding festivities in the air or what, but suddenly mine and Desio's future looked brighter than it had in twenty years.

FOR MORE INFORMATION about the author, please visit Pamela Kyel's website: http://pamelakyel.com/

The Other Wedding Crasher
Karen McCullough

No one was checking invitations or credentials at the door, but just to be safe I waited for a small group of people to go by before I got out of the car and followed behind them. The chattering partygoers didn't notice me, but to anyone else I looked like a straggling member.

We went into the clubhouse, through the reception area, and up a few steps to an enormous room, comprised of three sections separated by widely spaced wood columns. None of the wedding party had arrived yet. Still posing for pictures, I imagined. That gave me time to scope things out—check angles and exposed areas. No one questioned me as I moved around the enormous room, studying the placement of windows, doors, and banquet tables. I wasn't sure if that indifference reflected the lack of interest from the minimum wage staff or was a testament to the power of a three-hundred-dollar dress and killer high heels. I just hoped those killer heels didn't slay my feet before the evening ended. My shimmery, beaded shoulder purse was just big enough to hold my car key, phone, tissues, and a Beretta 21A single/double with seven rounds.

Long buffet tables lined the back wall of the first section, with round ones that could variously seat between six and ten people taking up half the rest of the area. The cake sat on a pedestal to one side. The bar occupied half the smaller central section. At the far end, a DJ had set up his equipment next to the dance floor. Soft but bouncy music emerged from several giant speakers.

Waiters circulated through the arriving crowd with trays of canapes and champagne glasses. I accepted a glass from one of the passing servers and took three careful sips to make it appear I was drinking. I walked twice around the entire room and peered into a bustling kitchen. Once I'd fixed the layout in my mind, I chose a seat at one of the round tables.

No assigned seating for this reception, which made my job easier. A sit-down dinner would've required a different strategy.

A small dais with podium stood opposite the longest buffet just beyond the cake pedestal. I was betting the toasts and welcomes would happen there. An older couple approached the table, nodded, and the woman asked if anyone had claimed the chairs next to me. I shook my head, pulling my purse closer.

"Thank you," she said, breathing an audible sigh. "Carol Mason," she identified herself. "And this is my husband, Vern. Katherine's mother is an old friend. We flew in from Chicago last night."

Katherine was the bride. Nice to know which side of the couple they belonged to. Better yet, they weren't relatives so they wouldn't know a lot of people here. "Lynn," I introduced myself, shaking hands with both. "Groom's cousin. I drove up from Raleigh this morning. I'm waiting for some other relatives, but they're running late. Stuck in traffic on 95 around Richmond." I preferred to stay with the truth where I could. Easier to keep track of. But if I had to make stuff up, I wanted it to sound realistic.

"Wasn't it a lovely wedding?" Carol asked. "Such a beautiful service."

"It was," I agreed. "The bride looked amazing!"

"Didn't she? I didn't even ask Estelle—that's Katherine's mother—how much that dress cost. It had to be a small fortune. But then she's their only daughter, and it's taken her such a long time to settle down, they were ready to go all out to make it special."

"I think it's safe to say they succeeded," I agreed. "So much work and planning went into this."

"Oh, yes. Estelle was on the phone with me almost every day. It seemed like there was some kind of crisis practically every hour. The florist couldn't get the right kind of flowers, or Katherine wasn't happy about the caterer's choices, or two of the bridesmaids' dresses looked bad on them. Always something."

It didn't take much prompting to keep Carol talking about her friendship with the bride's mother, their background, and all the preparation disasters.

"Katherine wasn't sure about the buffet menu. She worried too many things might drip and ruin guests' clothes. But she didn't want anything that seemed too...common, either. And the cake...Would you believe it cost almost a thousand dollars? Of course, with the groom's allergies to eggs and nuts, it had to be a special recipe. And Katherine ordered a special topper, and the baker had to do a custom icing thingie to incorporate it."

I managed to nod or make appropriate sounds at the right times to keep her rattling off while I scanned the room.

Twenty minutes into the conversation, a man stepped onto the dais, coughed into a microphone, and said, "Folks, if I may have your attention. Please welcome the wedding party!"

He pointed to the entrance, where bridesmaids and groomsmen sashayed into the room in couples, gathering not far from the table where I sat.

I studied each one. The eight women's gowns were all a silky, pinkish lavender hue in a variety of styles from off-the-shoulder to halter necks and every other possibility. The groomsmen wore tails with vests and cummerbunds of the same lavender shade. There were probably several pockets on their outfits where a weapon could be concealed.

The women's gowns didn't offer as many options, though any of them could have a flat blade strapped to a leg under the skirts, just as I did.

One bridesmaid tripped coming into the room and nearly fell. Distraction? I stopped watching her and looked around to check for anyone taking advantage. Almost everyone else seemed focused on the wobbly woman, but I did briefly meet the eyes of a man doing the same crowd scan I was. I gave him a quick nod and moved on. Nothing looked threatening or out of place as I finished the sweep and started another. The man whose eyes I'd met earlier had moved slightly to his left for a better view of the room, but he was surveying the area just as I was.

Who was he? Youngish, maybe early thirties, dark-haired and dark-eyed with a nice square jaw. An expensive suit hung well on his tall, lean frame. One hand held a nearly full champagne glass, while the other rested in his pocket. The way he held himself, casual in a studied way and hyper-aware of what was going on around him, reminded me of someone.

Myself. Oh heck. He wasn't just a regular wedding guest.

I turned back to watch the entrance when the DJ asked the crowd to please welcome, for the first time, Mr. Maxwell Collins and Mrs. Katherine Collins. Everyone applauded as they appeared in the doorway.

I hadn't lied earlier when I said the bride looked amazing, even if I hadn't known how true it was. She was on the short side but slender, with exquisitely dyed and styled blond hair above features that approached perfection. The creamy white dress enhanced with lace panels suited her in every way. The woman was beautiful. She knew it, and her expression...I couldn't quite read it. Happy, yes, but more. Satisfied. Almost smug.

Beside her, the groom faded into the background, he was so average. Average height, average weight, average hair color, average looks. I'd been told he had a brilliant mind and a kind heart but neither of those traits showed on first, or even second, glance. Right then he looked more stunned than anything else, though he held a solicitous arm around his bride's waist. They entered the room to more enthusiastic applause and were promptly swallowed up by the waiting crowd.

I had to stand and move to keep them in view, so I made an excuse about needing the restroom to the Masons. I moved into the crowd until I found a place where I could see both the bride and groom and Mr. Tall, Dark, and Mysterious.

I didn't like having to divide my attention, but at least I only had to shift my eyes and not my whole head to swing from the happy couple to the other intruder. Around us, servers carried chafing dishes to the buffet stations, and the aromas made my stomach rumble. I told it to shut up. Indulging my hunger would have to wait.

The groom escorted the bride to the nearest food station, where they each grabbed a plate and a few bites. The wedding party followed, then went with them to the next buffet to collect more bits. Other guests lined up behind them.

A table in the center of the room had a reserved sign on it. Two older couples, parents of the bride and groom I guessed, took seats there. The newlyweds joined them with their plates, while a pair of bridesmaids occupied the remaining two places. The rest of the guests now formed long lines at the buffets while the wedding party scattered to join other friends or relatives.

Keeping an eye on them, I went to the bar and got a glass of Chardonnay I had no intention of drinking, then moved to a corner where I could see most of the room. A couple of small groups gathered there, deep in conversation. I eavesdropped shamelessly as I watched the happy couple eat. Behind me a group of men discussed a local college football team's prospects. I tuned them out. The giggling group of young women beside me was more interesting.

"Bets on it? I give it two years, max," one young woman said, giggling at her own pun.

"I heard the prenup was pretty liberal," another stated. "Max is so besotted, he just agreed to everything Katie wanted."

"Six months," the third one added. "Max is such a stick in the mud. She won't take it any longer than that."

"You know what I heard?" Young woman number two's tone was lower and sharper, suggesting a scandalous secret about to be shared.

I was glad the noise level in the room had waned as people settled in to eat. I barely made out the words when she said, "Katie had a 'thing' with Max's cousin. *After* they got engaged."

"Which one? Lance?" Number one's faux shock gave way to amusement. "He is gorgeous."

"Lance," number two confirmed

"Hugh's not bad either. I wouldn't mind if either of them would look my way," said number three.

"But Max is rich." Apparently, number two was the most cynical of the group.

Or maybe not. "Having her cake and eating it, too?" One suggested. "That's our Katie. Speaking of eating, it looks like the line's getting shorter. I'm famished."

The party moved toward the buffet, leaving me to chew over their gossip. Lance, Hugh, and a third brother, Daniel, had been included in my briefing on the groom's family. They were first cousins on his father's side. The boys were similar in age but very different in interests and outlook, so the relationship wasn't close. But still—family. All three were serving as groomsmen.

I'd seen pictures, and I was pretty sure the young man tapping the groom on the shoulder was one of those three. Dark, handsome, and sporting a smile that dazzled even at thirty feet away, he would certainly fit the description of "gorgeous." I watched him closely, ready to spring if needed, but he did nothing more than shake his cousin's hand and say a few words before moving off to join a very young and blushing bridesmaid.

The bride's father stood and moved to the dais, holding a glass of champagne in one hand, and pulling a folded piece of paper from his pocket with the other. He coughed lightly into the microphone and asked for everyone's attention. "Good evening." He waited for the guests to quiet. "Katherine's mother and I want to welcome all of you to this celebration and thank you for coming." He went on to say how delighted they were to have Max joining the family.

I studied the bride and groom while he spoke. Max watched his new father-in-law, but also reached out a hand to clasp his bride's palm. She held her wineglass and sipped, looking almost unaware of her new husband's clasp of the other hand. To me, her attitude seemed more triumphant than in love. She glanced around the room, resting her gaze on someone for a few seconds before quirking a grin and continuing her sweep. I followed her line of sight to one of the three cousins. I wasn't sure if that was Lance or Hugh. They looked alike.

"Katherine has always been one to go after what she wanted," her father continued his talk. "Even as a girl, she was focused and driven to achieve what she wanted."

I was surprised to hear someone near me whisper, "spoiled rotten" to his companion.

"We're delighted that she settled on Max for her future," her father continued, then raised the glass as he proposed a toast to the bride and groom.

Applause and cheers broke out as everyone raised their glasses. The bride looked pleased.

I was aware of movement around me and a man approaching. Mr. Tall, Dark, and Mysterious. I watched him from the corner of my eye. Without taking his eyes off the bride and groom, he leaned toward me and whispered in my ear. "Does she look happy to you?"

I gave him a quick glance, wondering what his game was. Neither his tone nor expression suggested he meant it as a joke. "Yes. But maybe not the right kind of happy."

He looked at me sharply for a moment, as though I'd surprised him. Before either of us could say anything more, Katherine's father yielded the podium to one of the cousins. He introduced himself as Lance Collins, Max's cousin. The one who'd had a "thing" with the bride according to the gossip.

The murmurs and shifting among people present made me think the rumors were no great secret. Lance leaned on the podium, not using notes. "Since Max doesn't have any brothers to give him a hard time right now, I was recruited for the job. As cousins we didn't exactly grow up together, but we saw each other often enough. You might not believe this, but he was my favorite cousin."

A few giggled at what was obviously an inside joke, but Max himself clarified it when he spoke up. "I'm your *only* cousin."

"There's that. And I probably wasn't *your* favorite cousin." Both the groom and Lance grinned. I was confused about what appeared to be the easy relationship between Max and the cousin who'd reportedly betrayed him. I'd expected more snark and veiled hostility. But the emotions here seemed honest enough. The bride looked more puzzled, though she tried to hide it.

"But seriously, Max and I are pretty different. He was always the brilliant, nerdy, intense one, while I was the Dude. But I always respected him and was fascinated by the way he could come up with the most unusual and creative ideas to make things work. And now I get to wish him a long and happy future." He held up his glass. "To the bride and groom."

Something struck me as odd about his wording, but I couldn't place it and didn't have time to consider.

He gave way to one of the bridesmaids, who introduced herself as Katherine's closest friend while they were growing up. She was a nervous speaker, giggling as she talked about some of the capers she and the bride had pulled off as youngsters. Katherine was always the instigator, especially when they were plotting a prank to show up a teacher, parent, or other adult who had denied them something they wanted. No, she didn't phrase it exactly that way, but you didn't have to peer very hard behind the words to hear it.

As she finished with the obligatory toast, the wedding planner nudged the couple. They rose and headed for the side of the room where the cake waited. I shifted, moving forward, and squeezing past people to keep the couple in view. Mr. Tall, Dark, and Mysterious moved with me.

The sight of the long, cake-cutting knife put me on elevated alert despite the white silk ribbons tied around it and the small fake flowers woven into the bow. I scanned the crowd, saw nothing alarming, and pulled my attention back to the bridal couple, who each had both hands on the knife as it plunged into the wide bottom of the six-layer masterpiece.

Max fed Katherine a bite of cake gently, almost tenderly, while she put a small bit neatly into his mouth. Thank goodness, no stuffing in wads and smearing frosting all over faces.

As servers moved in to cut the cake and pass around slices, the wedding planner led the couple toward the dance floor, then gathered both sets of parents and took them along as well. I wandered with most of the others in that direction and found a corner where I had a decent view of the dance floor.

The DJ called for the first dance, the bridal dance with her father, the groom and his mother, and then the couples mixed it up. I spent more time surveying the guests again during this time. My counterpart, the man I thought of as "the other wedding crasher," settled near a table at the side and scanned the area as well. I took a moment to wonder who he was looking out for, since he was clearly in the same business I was.

Once the family dances finished, people pressed forward onto the floor and began to move to the music. Mostly younger guests, but not all. For now the DJ was still spinning slower tunes. The swelling crowd made it harder to keep my eye on the bride and groom.

A tap on my shoulder made me jump and turn. Mr. Tall, Dark, and Mysterious leaned forward and said, "Dance with me."

I looked back at the weaving, swaying group. "I can't."

"It's the best way to keep an eye on everyone." He held out a hand.

Dang it. He might be right. I could barely see the couple through the crowd right now. I spared a glance for my unexpected dance partner as he led me onto the floor. The rich, spicy fragrance he wore stood out in the sea of perfume, food, and sweaty aromas. Seen up close, his eyes were a very dark blue rather than the brown I'd thought. His face was more pleasant than handsome, but when he quirked a grin as I put an arm on his shoulder, a flash of dimples creased his lean cheeks. Dimples on a man were my catnip. I wished I knew what his angle was.

I couldn't afford any distraction, so I looked away, checking the crowd again. The bride and groom danced together now. Both looked stiff. Max grimaced slightly when Lance cut in, but immediately went and invited one of the bridesmaids to join him.

"The name's Jeff," my dance partner said. "You are?"

"Lynn."

"Nice to meet you, Lynn," he said as we swayed to the music. "Which one are you watching?"

"Yes."

If my non-answer bothered him, nothing in his body movement betrayed it. He was a good dancer, graceful, and easy to follow. The muscles beneath my hands were strong. He steered carefully so that at least one of us always had the bride and groom in sight. That took some maneuvering when they danced with other people. For the most part, he succeeded, regularly changing which direction each of us watched.

My feet hurt, but I was enjoying myself too much to want to stop. I didn't let that interfere with doing my job, though. I kept as careful a watch as I could in the circumstances.

My purse stayed on my shoulder, swaying in time with us. Jeff's eyebrows rose when it slapped against his side with its surprising weight. He didn't say anything about it.

I lost track of time, but I suspected it was an hour or so later when the dance music became louder and more contemporary, invoking a different rhythm and style, less conducive to being able to keep track of anyone in the process.

When they started the Electric Slide, I called a halt. My feet wouldn't take it and I couldn't keep tabs on everyone while doing it. Katherine participated, but Max had moved to the side, where he was having a conversation with the wedding planner and his parents. I noticed one of the cousins, I couldn't tell which one from behind, came up and slid something into his pocket. Since Max didn't object or act surprised, I guessed it was car keys or directions.

The wedding planner and others passed around baskets of flower petals to prepare for the couple's departure. My little container had an extra piece of paper in it. I unfolded and read the words on the back, "If Buddy's killer plays the piano, the murder weapon is the gun." That made no sense but it wasn't likely to be relevant right now.

The dance finished and the bride joined her new husband, taking the bouquet from the wedding planner. Bridesmaids and other young women clustered behind her.

Since everyone else watched her, I looked for Max.

He stood to the side now, but he looked pale, shoulders slumped, and he leaned against a table, sneezing. I shot into high alert, and raced toward him, ignoring the squeals and cries from the women waiting for the bouquet toss.

Even more alarm shot through me as I got closer and saw beads of sweat on his face and the way his chest heaved as though he had trouble breathing. "Max?" I called.

He looked my way, but he gasped and didn't seem able to speak. His eyes looked swollen and watery.

"Something's wrong?" I asked.

He nodded, then slumped toward the wall. His chest heaved, and he wheezed, struggling for breath. Jeff was beside me now and he reached to keep the man from falling to the ground. One of the cousins—Hugh, I thought—pushed to his other side.

While I ripped off Max's bowtie and tore open the top of his tuxedo shirt, something else was going on just below. Hugh appeared to reach into one of Max's pockets and extract something. He moved to stash it in his own pocket, but Jeff slashed down on his wrist and Hugh dropped what he was holding.

The metallic clink of a key ring drew my attention. The thing that hit the floor with it, shattering into crumbly bits, emitted a strong odor of—

"Peanuts." I yelled, "EpiPen." Max's face was ghostly pale, except where red spots stood out. His eyes closed. The gasping noises continued as he strained to breathe. I screamed even louder, "Does someone have an EpiPen?"

The crowd of guests surged our way, but three people pushed through to the front. Two women, one of them Max's mother, held out EpiPen tubes. A third woman knelt beside Max, saying, "I'm a doctor. Anaphylactic shock?"

"I don't know. He's allergic to peanuts," I answered.

The doctor leaned over to put an ear to his chest, listened for a moment, and checked his pulse. "Not in shock, but his airway is compromised." She took the nearest tube, extracted the injector, and slammed it into Max's thigh. A wave of relief crashed over me as she put one hand on his chest and the other at his throat. It looked like she knew what she was doing. A bit of color returned to Max's face and within moments the labored breaths grew easier.

Jeff had hold of Hugh's arm, but the pose was awkward since Max's body was between them. When Lance approached, I reached into my purse for the Beretta. I stopped when he grabbed Hugh's other arm and growled, "You idiot! What did you do?"

"Nothing. I didn't do anything," Hugh protested, struggling futilely against the two men holding him.

"The heck you didn't," I said.

Since Lance had a solid hold on his brother, Jeff let go, pulled his phone from his pocket, pressed in a number, then spoke urgently into it. After a few more quick words, he put it back in his pocket.

Katherine approached. She gasped and stared at Max for a moment, then looked at Hugh. She kept glancing between them, apparently unsure what to do next. "What's happened to him? Is he all right?"

"He's going to be," Jeff said. "No thanks to you and Hugh."

They both played innocent, claiming they had no idea what he was talking about.

Jeff turned to Max's family. "Do you want the police involved?" he asked. "An ambulance is on the way, but I didn't ask for the cops. I can change that."

"This wasn't an accident?" James Collins, Max's father, directed the question to me.

"It was not," I answered. "But we could spin it that way, if you want."

James looked at Hugh, still being firmly held by Jeff and Lance. "Him? My nephew did this? Deliberately?"

"We have reason to think so."

"What reason?"

"I saw him slip something into Max's pocket, just before he collapsed. When we went to help him, Hugh tried to retrieve and hide it, but Jeff slapped it out of his hand. Along with a car key, there was some kind of bar—power bar or granola—that had lots of nuts."

"He's allergic to them," James muttered, his tone puzzled and disturbed. "But—Why?"

"He had an affair—" Jeff started, but the ambulance screamed up to the building at that moment, and paramedics raced in.

Following a quick conversation with the doctor and taking his vitals, the paramedics decided Max was stable for the moment, but the severity of his reaction demanded a trip to the emergency room. They loaded him onto a gurney and whisked him away.

At my suggestion, his parents stayed behind for a family meeting, along with his father's brother's family and the bride's. Aside from a few curious onlookers, guests had begun to melt away, and the DJ was packing his equipment.

We retired to a small dining room off the main reception area. Jeff and I explained what we had seen while Hugh and Katherine fumed and denied. The bride's father looked at Jeff and me. "Who are you and what are you doing here?" he asked.

I spoke first. "I'm Lynn Waterstone and I'm a licensed private detective. I was hired by Max's parents to provide security. They had some doubts about the bride and her motives. They were right."

Katherine exploded. "You can't think I had anything to do with this?"

Lance stood up and stared at her. "Jeff is a former police officer who now works for a highly recommended security firm. I hired him because I really do like my cousin quite a lot. More than I like his bride and my own brother right now. I asked him to come and keep an eye on things because I knew that Hugh and Katherine have been having an affair. I overheard Hugh on the phone with her discussing how they would 'handle' the Max problem at the wedding."

"What?" Katherine screeched. "How dare you—?"

"Too late for the innocent act," Lance said. "I didn't know exactly what you and Hugh had cooked up, but I was sure it was something, and Max was caught in the middle of it."

"You can't prove anything," Hugh said.

"In a court of law, probably not," Jeff admitted. "Which is why we're here." He looked around at the group. "You probably want to get your lawyers involved."

A man I didn't recognize spoke up. "I'm the Collins family's attorney. I drew up the prenup. I admit I had a few doubts as well, so a good lawyer will find a few loopholes in it. Jeff's right that you probably don't have enough evidence for a legal case. If you want my recommendation, I'd suggest a quick annulment, which will void the prenup, and possibly a couple of restraining orders."

Jeff and I gave our names and contact information to the lawyer and left the family to further negotiations. We'd done our jobs.

As we headed for the door, Jeff said to me, "I haven't eaten since this morning and I'm famished. Want to get some dinner?"

"I'd be delighted," I answered.

FOR MORE INFORMATION about the author, please visit Karen McCullough's website: https://kmccullough.com/

Marriage, Neighbors and Best Friends: A Wally and Ollie Series

Wil A. Emerson

Once a docile town, Darby, a suburb of Philadelphia, is transforming to meet the needs of the far-reaching metropolitan crowd who want expensive coffee, designer donuts and pricey wine bars. Needs and wants aren't the same for insiders who have called this town home for many generations. Darby today is more like a bride on her wedding day. Dressed in new, old, borrowed, and blue.

Gentrification took over the north end of Main. Some residents weren't able to adapt and moved on with a little less money than they bargained for. It wouldn't surprise me if I soon got an offer to sell out, too. The Masons in the family grave wouldn't be too happy if I did.

Some of my problems, though, might be resolved if I took the bait. However, I've lived here all my life, in a home passed on by my parents. I run the Mason family business, which is located on the first level of the building I call home. The upper floors were turned into a suitable living space right after my parents were married. It's been the only home I've known and, honestly, I don't want to leave.

It's more than a place to reside. All the good things in my life have happened here. It's where I'd like to spend eternity, in one form or the other. That is, if I'm not dealt a nasty blow and forced to take my final breaths in unfamiliar, tighter surroundings. Can't say that's not a possibility considering the way I've been feeling lately. Evil deeds can land a person in jail.

For the most part, other than college days, everything I've learned has been within these plastered walls. Yes, plastered. A brick-and-mortar building, Craftsman style, held together with labor and love. The walls are thick and only need new paint occasionally. It's unusual to hear any conversations or necessary mechanical noises beyond the walls. Aromas from the family business? Unusual. I'd say almost undetectable. Unless a door or window is left open. That seldom happens. The lower-level windows are sealed per code and only the family uses the back staircases where the unsightly loading and unloading takes place. Another good reason not to relocate.

My father, who loved his business, said, 'work is work, home is home, don't be foolish and mix the two.' That's worked for me.

On occasion, though, the structure shakes a little because of these unnerving gentrification issues. Built in the thirties, well beyond horse and buggy days, the standard was to reinforce basements with solid beams and unique handmade trusses. All to a handyman's perfection. Of course, when it was constructed, there wasn't a military base close at hand with jets breaking the sound barrier. And due to recent changes, we now endure a flow of trucks and equipment of all makes and models on the main road and the building has been challenged. Rock and roll vibrations, occasionally.

I don't complain but my wife, Hillary, who's new to Darby and only been by my side for seven months, three days and two hours, late bloomers in the marriage arena, finds the street traffic to be annoying.

"Walter Mason, how can you live in such a disturbing situation? When I get your books straightened out, a change might be in order."

Problem numero uno. It's an excuse to sell out. Which in turn has caused a fracture in our newly formed bond.

She also is distracted by unfamiliar odors and repeat visitors. Problems two and three respectively. Three weighs heaviest on the problematic scale, though. Which furthers her scheme to move on. So far, I've managed to stall the decision and not reveal my true feelings. Home or wife?

The reason I want to stay, other than the aforementioned sentiments, is because the neighborhood is full of conveniences. Grocery stores, several restaurants, dentist and doctors in the same building. A good bar with live music every Friday and Saturday. Inclusive.

So much so, Hillary eagerly agreed to call the vibrant area home two weeks after we met. She's as new to the neighborhood as those big city folks knocking down walls and transforming quaint into plush.

Eventually, I said early on, she'll love the neighbors and my best friend Ollie, too. Repeated when I'm most frustrated. For the most part, I don't want to change a darn thing or give up Ollie, my best friend, or the neighbors that I love.

Ollie, Oliver Hancock, lives next door, over the hardware store of which I'm a part owner. A side business just in case the major one falls short on paying the bills. Because Ollie and I have known each other since grade school, he has a warm, safe home and when he can, he pays the rent. That being said, the other neighbors are the usual joe-steady types, mind their own business and care about the businesses they run. Respectable. Some have family members to attend to; some households are multi-generational. Those few older residents were friends of my parents. Hard to see those dear ones dependent on their offspring now. Guess that would have been my situation, too, if not for the accident that took my parents' lives.

Hillary, my wife of seven months...oh, been there. Well, I soon learned after all her bags were unpacked, she's not the neighborly let's-have-coffee type of woman. Good reason for that, she explained. Before we met, she lived a solitary existence in Southern Illinois. Raised on a farm with horses, cows, pigs. Said the animals were her real friends—never lied, cheated or gossiped. Her father ran the farm, her mother managed the daily activities of living for the tight-knit family. Even did vet service, Hillary reported, for the animals who needed sutures, enemas or dental care. Hillary did the bookkeeping. In the off season, she and the parents made wine. They were ready, she said, to branch out and sell their wine for profit.

Not having any need for daily greetings, chit chat or talk about the weather, Hillary would have continued with the lifestyle but fate dealt her cards she didn't know how to play. Fortunately for her, she'd been in the cellar to inventory its contents, study if supply met demands, when in a flash, a tornado swept away the forty-acre farmstead and every living creature on it. Save for Hillary. Contented they were, Hillary said with a mournful sigh, until that nasty sky went into a tailspin and sucked the life out from under her feet.

A sad grieving process, no place to call home and not wanting reminders of the farm she loved, she moved to the northeast. Philadelphia, the friendly city. Bookkeeping paid her bills. Farm girl adapted to that city life.

Then fate intervened again. I placed one of those ZipRecruiter ads online for a bookkeeper. In my business, numbers are not an interesting chore. Tedious. I needed help. Our initial back-and-forth chats, employer, prospective employee, went fine. Finally, face-to-face, I was smitten. A woman of her character interested in this strait-laced, no nonsense guy? No flair, standard gray suit type of guy. She responded with such zeal, why not take the big leap?

As a newlywed, and eager to form new habits, I did a quick study of Hillary. Not extravagant. Justice of the Peace wedding, no expensive white dress, sirloin steak, not fillet for the wedding dinner. Three-star hotel for our wedding night, not five.

But Hillary did have a taste for full-bodied Pinot Noirs from Oregon. So, I purchased a special cooling cabinet after the wedding. I doubted if the grapes she and her father grew in Southern Illinois tasted anything like the western fruit that turns into expensive wine, though. But it wasn't my job to judge how one acquired a taste for wine or any other brew.

This is relevant, in two ways. It brought up the subject of selling my home the first time. And because Ollie, who knows nothing about farming, grapes or wine, decided to engage in a conversation with Hillary about her beverage of choice. He got the notion that Hillary would not have acquired a taste for expensive red wine unless she'd been exposed to a similar lifestyle. Why he thought it was important to point out her preference didn't make any sense to Hillary. But it sure did create another type of storm that took on a life of its own.

Peacemaker that I am, an intervention was necessary. Knowing it helps Ollie to hear different viewpoints, I took him aside.

"Ollie," I said, "you like Snicker bars. You didn't have a taste for Snicker bars at birth. At some point you ate one and then acquired a taste for them."

"Walter Mason, don't waste your time on explanations." Hillary's keen ears picked up the conversation.

Later that evening, she said, "It's definitely time to leave the area. Your so-called friend Ollie insulted me and I expect you to exclude him from any get-togethers in your home. Whoops, our home. Remember. Married. See the ring and, don't forget, I've taken over housecleaning chores in this dusty old place."

Well, that message hit home like a dart to the bull's eye. What a sting. Hillary wasn't as *smitten* on the home front as I was and a little harsh on Ollie, at that. Felt at the time that it was a pity Hillary wasn't a woman of fewer words.

Walls didn't cave but it sure felt like a steam shovel had rolled down Main Street.

Ollie, of course, couldn't let the discussion rest. Next time he saw her, he asked when, where, how and with whom had she been living in Oregon. He's the kind that needs a discussion to play itself out. A quirk of his, so he can better understand a subject's full meaning. He'd always been like that from our early days. Always questions why or why not, what purpose does this have, I don't understand, tell me more. Done so often we have a signal between us. I put up my hand like a stop sign. That was his way and, as a somewhat mature adult, it still is.

If you grew up with Ollie, you'd understand he can't apply the same logic to situations as other people. Genetic or environmental? A debate. It's not that he's dysfunctional or a trouble maker, he's just always needed a steady hand to guide him. A big brother of sorts. And that's what I've been for him all these years. A habit that can't easily be broken.

So, when Hillary made the request, shortly into our marriage, to exclude him from our social life, I was squashed right in the middle of two tornadoes. A new wife, whom I loved and appreciated. And Ollie, my best friend, who I'd cared for in many ways since the first bologna sandwich our mothers packed for us to eat in our grade school cafeteria. How could I ignore all the bologna sandwiches shared between us? And if I threw in Hillary's suggestion to sell my home, well, it would be like putting mustard instead of mayonnaise on all those bologna sandwiches.

It was extremely difficult for me to agree to Hillary's demand that Ollie couldn't join us on occasion for dinner or have a drink together in *our* home that she didn't like one iota. And that's why I contend with this uncomfortable situation on a daily basis. Seven months, three days and four plus hours.

It makes me think about something that no man should think about doing to his wife. New, old, borrowed or blue.

SILENCE REIGNED FOR a few days after the 'no more Ollie' situation and then things seemed to go a little better.

"The best thing about a fall night is the windows can be open. Don't you agree, Walt?" Hillary smiled and nestled close.

Anticipating a romantic encounter that now included fresh air, I jumped out of bed and opened the window. Anything to please. A balmy breeze, high sixties, the sky full of stars. Luckily, I still had a disc player on the dresser from twenty years before. My valuable, extensive collection of soulful tunes would definitely enhance the experience. I dashed to press the play button. Michael Bolton suddenly crooned his smooth melody, "When a Man Loves a Woman."

I must confess, I sashayed back to bed. Hillary, all warm and inviting, music another enticement, my intentions on the rise. This was marriage at its best. Why had I waited so long?

Hillary opened her arms and I melted beside her. As I brushed aside a lock of auburn hair from her forehead, I felt her tense. So focused on her, the night, the mood the music set, the reaction didn't impact me at first.

Not until Hillary bolted upright. "What is that? How hideous? Who plays that kind of music at night?"

It was then my mind became alert to the outside environment, aware of my surroundings. The air waves carried sounds from neighbors who also opened their windows to take in the refreshing crisp autumn air. And with the waves, there came a river of music, including Ollie's boom box and his favorite heavy metal rendition of Bring Me The Horizon. At a decibel that made the windows rattle.

...bang, bang, bang, screech...screech, screech, bang...shrill, gritty, bang, bang...

"Walter Mason, stop this, make it go away. Call the police. Do something. Can't you do something?"

I made the mistake of saying, "I'll call Ollie later and ask him to turn down the volume. Don't worry, he'll do me the favor." I regained control, shifted my position to accomplish the manly mission.

"A favor? No, it's not a favor. An insane man is disrupting the quiet of the night. It's against the law. If you don't stop him, I will call the police."

"It's only nine p.m., Hillary. I don't think it's necessary to call the police." I flopped on my back.

I did call Ollie and, of course, he turned the volume down and closed his window, too. At least it seemed quieter to my not-so-sensitive ears.

Of course, the damage had been done. A cold breeze in the bedroom, metaphorically speaking. Dear Hillary swore she heard the music till four a.m. I can't attest to it. Of course, I'm accustomed to the sounds of the humdrum neighborhood I love so much. I fell soundly asleep as I had a respectable business affair to run the next day.

To my great surprise, I discovered Hillary did request a 'cease and desist' order the next day from our local precinct. They, the good fellows in blue, who also know Ollie, followed through with duty and presented him with a citation.

Theodore Robbins, the desk sergeant, called me and explained the situation. "Your pretty new wife came in this morning, Walt. All distressed. We had no choice but to help her out. Don't want her to pack up and leave you, that's for sure. We love a new pretty face on the block."

"Did Ollie take it well?"

"You know Ollie wouldn't hurt a fly. All sorry he caused a problem."

Later that day, I had coffee with my best friend. He'd just finished working on a repair project for the camera shop at the end of the block.

"Can't tell you how sorry I am that I upset Hillary. But you'd think someone her age wouldn't mind the music. A part of history, rite of passage, wouldn't you say, Walt?"

"People have likes and dislikes. And heavy metal is quite intense if you're not in that frame of mind. Maybe we've gone beyond that time in life. You, too. I do appreciate the cooperation, though, Ollie."

"Do you wonder why she's got such an intense dislike for it? Couldn't be because of her farm life, quiet and all that. I've been in your office a couple of times and she plays a jazz station. Now if you want to talk about a scatter of sounds, an explosion of notes, drums and all, I can tell you there's a lot of similarities."

"You know music, Ollie. My taste runs to a little more sedate."

"You think tonight if I play a little Knockaz Brass Band it would help me get back on her good side?"

"Knock...knock what? Never heard of them."

"They play second-line arrangements along with traditional jazz and go-go funk music. They do weddings, too. Could have used them if you and Hillary hadn't rushed to get married and left your best friend out of the wedding. Hurt my heart, Wally. Still stings I wasn't at your side. But I said all I needed to say on the card I gave you. Did you read it, Wally?"

"Sure did, Wally. Sentimental for sure."

"The back side, too, Wally? The part that said, 'If Buddy's killer was another guest's plus-one, the fireplace poker was used'? You could have waited, for you know, the actual wedding celebration."

"There is a time in one's life when love can't be postponed." I sighed.

"Knockaz might be the kind of music that bonds Hillary and me. Considering she's going to be part of us, I mean like family, for a long, long time, I'd like to make a lasting connection. Get it set firm in this early stage."

"Let's work on the good neighbor approach first, Ollie. I appreciate your offer of sharing your knock-knock music, though, but hold off for a while."

"Okay, whatever you want, Walt. I aim to please. Don't ever want to upset my best friend. Just keep me in the loop, okay? I mean, I wouldn't want you to be hurt by anything either."

I didn't have the heart to tell Ollie that my wife probably wouldn't warm up to him. Not in the near future I reasoned, due to the shaky start. The wine situation and now she'd filed a 'cease and desist.' The future? One could only hope Hillary and I had one, but the odds weren't looking good for Ollie in the picture. So, I turned the subject to something we could be open and honest about. A knack I'd learned to use with Ollie over the years so he wouldn't get the feeling he was always on the wrong side of a decision.

"Tell me about the project with Stewart's Camera Shop? Old wood needed replaced?" Ollie being a talented craftsman can make old look new and new look fashionably old when asked to do so. It's his best source of income but because he works alone, the jobs he handles aren't always high paying projects.

"Back door busted off its frame. Can you believe it? This gentrification thing is ruffling feathers. Bringing in rift raft on the work crews. See something they want, they try and take it."

"A real shame. Change can be tough. But I have faith. Things will improve. So, was it a success?"

"Oh sure, door's all set. Better than ever. I used poplar. It's stronger wood and holds up well in the rain. Should last for another thirty years."

"No, I meant was the break-in a success. Did they get in, take what they wanted? Did Stewart lose any expensive cameras?"

"Good questions. I never asked. You think I should have? Darn, Stewart probably thinks I don't care. I'll straighten it out with him, too." He laughed, "Aren't I the neighbor? Have two enemies now."

"No, Ollie, Stewart knows you concentrate on your work. He probably didn't give it a thought. But I do think it is a good reason for you to check out my back entrances. Garage and stairwell. Make sure they're secure. I've got some pricey equipment I wouldn't want to lose."

"Tell me the day and time, Walt. I'll be there."

"Tomorrow, nine in the morning. Nothing scheduled. It will be a fine day to do a little fix up and repair."

When we parted, we shared a brotherly hug and took different directions from Marie's Café. Ollie held a bag of bagels and a ham sandwich for dinner. Marie, always with an eye out for her neighbors, watched over Ollie, too. This time, though, I carried a take-out bag with two chocolate éclairs inside, an extra act of kindness for the new Mrs. Walt Mason.

"I'd like to see her in the café more often," Marie said. "Get to know the new addition to the neighborhood."

It wasn't a secret Marie had had her eye on me for several years. I surmised by inviting Hillary into her café she was trying to learn just what attracted me to the stranger from Southern Illinois. Don't get me wrong, Marie is a terrific woman and I love her like a neighbor should but there's never been anything else I wanted to do with her. Contented with friendly greetings, good coffee, and meeting Ollie for brotherly sessions suited my manly needs in the café.

"What's that you're carrying?" Hillary asked as I came through the door.

"Sweet treats, chocolate éclairs from Marie's Café. Just for you." I kissed her cheek and put the white bag on the counter. "I'd have one, too, but already had a pastry with coffee."

"I do not like chocolate éclairs, Walter Mason. Not at all. Toss'm out."

"Ah, I can't do that. It's like throwing a gift away. I'll re-gift them. Save them for Ollie."

"Whatever. Just tell that *towny woman* I don't want any of her junk food. Not my style."

"Well, let's keep it between you and me, okay? She meant well. Trying to be neighborly, that's all."

I must admit I was disappointed but then, I am extremely attracted to Hillary because of her trim body and her dedication to fitness. One's overall well-being comes first; it's a good motto for the business I'm in and marriage, too.

"I'll put them in the freezer and tell Ollie to pick them up. By the way, he's coming tomorrow morning to check out the entrance and exit doors. Add security if necessary."

"He doesn't need to be in the office, does he? I'm going over the quarterly tax statements. Privacy needed. Would rather not be disturbed at all. Especially by Ollie."

"Believe me, Ollie is not the least bit interested in tax issues. He's good with numbers, was exceptional as a kid. Always placed in advanced math classes. But, no, he has no interest." I didn't want to say 'incapable' because it would sound like Ollie had mental problems.

The truth is, he does have innate numerical skills but doesn't focus for long periods of time. And when his multiplication, subtractions and division provide results, he doesn't necessarily care about the cliff-hangers. He might ask why but usually doesn't think beyond the point. I offered him the simple task of keeping tabs on my books years ago. Making entries, expenses on one side of the ledger, income on the other. Steady employment, good benefits. He'd succeed at tallying up a column, but asset or liability didn't interest him. He'd ask, 'now what?' Of course, what further hindered his work was he might go for a run every hour or so. Or he'd stray off on something, like a google search for an unknown in his life, anything that struck his interest, and be gone for hours. Inactivity or at a desk for long periods, as incomprehensible as a foreign language.

Hillary's next comment brought me back to the present and stung, too. It made me think there was a new purpose for duct tape.

"Keep him outside or tell him to work after hours."

My morning workload was light so I made a point to spend the extra time with my friend. And it was well worth it.

"Took your advice and asked Stewart about his cameras. They stole three big ones. Worth a couple thousand, he told me. And broke into the cash box. The neighborhood is changing, he said. Looks like I'm going to have to work harder to keep us safer. Of course, I'll have to charge for the supplies but I'll do free work. Good neighbor policy."

"That's a good motto, Ollie. As far as I'm concerned, it's up to you to decide what security measures to take. Bolts, alarms, you name it. I trust your judgment."

A smile spread over Ollie's handsome face. Toothy and appreciative. Then he put his tool chest down and gave me a big bear hug.

But the warm feeling didn't last all day. After lunch, I heard a commotion in the back office and went to investigate.

"Didn't I tell you never to set a foot in this office? This is my domain. Do you know what that means?"

"Yes, Hillary. It means you work here. Do the books and keep Walt's money safe."

"Then why are you here? What business do you have in this office?"

"Sorry, Hillary. I have a job, too. Want to keep you safe. See, I fixed the window when you went to lunch. Double locks, can't be opened from the outside. Screen on inside. If they break the glass, well, the screen stops them from coming in. Plus, no one can look over your shoulder and study the numbers in your ledger. Everything is extra safe."

With best intentions, I escorted Ollie from the office.

"Let her blow off steam by herself, Ollie. Come on, let's go have a soda."

"No, not hungry now. I ate an éclair earlier from the bag that was on the back stairs. Thanks for putting it out for me. But tell me, Wally, why am

I always doing the wrong thing?"

Ollie left with a deep scowl on his face before I could explain I hadn't put the treats on the stoop. He never held a grudge long so I knew he'd be back around in no time and I could make amends. But I did feel like I'd let him down. Again.

Later that evening, I heard Ollie outside, glanced from the kitchen window and saw he had his tool box and a ladder leaning against the side of the hardware store. Good for him, I thought. Back at the job, security his main focus.

I raised the window and gave him a shout. "Thanks a lot, Ollie. I sure appreciate your help."

"Just being a good neighbor, Wally."

The next evening all was good in Darbyworld and better on the Mason front, too. Hillary and I spent a pleasant dinner together. Shared a bottle of zinfandel with pork chops, baked potatoes and green beans sautéed in olive oil delivered from Jack Levy's Steak and Chop House. They did extra favors for locals. The scratch-your-back theory. Only three doors down, they were a go-to in my bachelor days and now they'd become a mainstay of ours.

"The best part of city life is never having to cook. I think I could live like this forever."

"Is that the wine talking, my dear, or love for me and our neighborhood?" I anticipated the rest of the evening to be romantic. And relaxed over the thought she'd gotten over the urge to move.

"It is convenient. Oh, yes...love you, too. Yes." She raised her glass and tipped it to mine.

All was going so well. Then Hillary said the dark evenings of fall made her tired and suggested we go to bed early. Not much past eight p.m., but why complain. I had more than sleep on my mind. We cuddled, and I was eager to end the evening on a very positive note.

If you've ever been on a stage, in front of an audience, you'll understand what the next few minutes felt like. Full monty for me, pole dancer tossing a G-string for Hillary.

All of a sudden, the bedroom lit up. So bright, for a moment I actually fantasized we were rehearsing for a Broadway show.

"We're being invaded," Hillary shrieked. I grabbed my shirt and tied it around my waist, quickly scanned the room to confirm we were still alone. Then my eyes darted to the window but couldn't see beyond it. Deer in the headlights.

"We're being invaded," Hillary shrieked again.

"Calm down, calm down. I'll see what it is."

I ran to the spare bedroom and, even though it was as if the morning sun had illuminated the room, I could see out the window and instantly spied the new additions to the side of the hardware store next door. Spotlights. More like three runway spotlights. The kind used around airports or harbors or high crime areas. High crime area? One at each end, one directly in the middle of the building. Directly positioned toward our bedroom window. The entire space between the two buildings, as sunny as if it were high noon.

"Oh, buggers," I muttered. "Ollie's security at its best."

But would I dare tell Hillary? She would kill him this very moment if she had a chance. I quickly ran through my options. Explain or lie?

Thus far, I had been enjoying a few advantages of married life. I decided I wanted to hang on to them a little longer.

"You won't believe it. Looks like there's been a safety issue. Police protection." I pulled the draperies together, got a blanket out of the closet, stood on a chair and tucked the blanket over the drapery rod to add to the window coverage. A quick fix, more like dusk than lunch time. Back to the pleasant task at hand.

"No problem, I'll talk to the security people tomorrow," I re-enforced.

To my dismay, Hillary had put on a black sleep mask and pulled the comforter to her chin.

"I hate this neighborhood, Walt Mason. And I hate that Ollie, too. I know he put up those spotlights just to torture me. I want to kill him."

I had to stifle a laugh. Not that what she said was funny. She was upset and people make outrageous statements when they are frustrated. But I'd never seen anyone in a sleep mask with a wide-open mouth, ranting in an angry tone. It made it all so comical. Right out of the movies, I thought.

By five a.m. I'd had eight hours of solid sleep. I got up without disturbing Hillary, pulled on my jeans and walked over to have a heart-to-heart with Ollie. He'd either be up or just going to bed. His routine was as haphazard as any single man's could be.

Ollie was at the kitchen table with his computer. Games or googling. "Mind if I start a pot of coffee?"

"No problem. I'm almost done." He nodded and went back to his screen.

"What are you working on?" Curious, but also wanted to ease into the conversation about the runway spotlights. No reason to burst his bubble first thing in the morning.

"Did you know you can find out on Google where someone has lived for most of their lives?"

"Sure. But I generally just ask them."

"Of course, you do. You know the people you work with. They give you information and you settle their affair. But I mean people that you don't know well?"

"Well, in my line of business, family members seek my personal service and those in dire need can't ask for help, can they?"

"Strangers might not ask if you have something they want. They might figure out another way to get it."

An ah-ha moment. Ollie *was* concerned about break-ins. This was a great way to tie it all together but, I still couldn't rush into telling him to remove those lights as soon as possible.

"I've never had a reason to find out anything about someone I don't know, Ollie."

"My father said a long time ago, 'there comes a time in life when you have to do the right thing even if it's hard to do.' I wasn't sure what he meant. But I think that time has come, Wally."

"Your father trained you well. It's like the security job, the lights and all, you did the right thing. But they were a little misdirected, huh?" He'd given me my opening and I wouldn't embarrass him by saying it was a really bad idea to shine the lights directly in my bedroom window.

"Depends on who's looking at the lights. Have you ever met an embezzler, Wally? Ninety-five percent are women."

"Not that I know of, Ollie. Did you buy those security lamps from someone you think is an embezzler? Did they overcharge, Ollie?"

"Oh, no. I got them at the hardware store. You'll see the bill. Well, maybe Hillary will see it first since she does the books. You should keep an eye out for it, though. I've got the receipt, just in case."

"That's good of you, Ollie. I generally don't ask you for receipts. Always trust you give me accurate numbers. You're an expert at remembering numbers, Ollie. Always have been."

"Well, that's not true all the time. Sometimes I can tell when they don't add up, though. Like the ones in your ledger. Couldn't help it. The ledger was wide open. But I didn't know what to do about it. Not until I did this 'find anyone' search. It's amazing, Wally. You can find out anything about a person."

"I'll look into it if I ever have a need. Instead of ledgers, let's talk about security, okay, Ollie? The lights have to go. Today. Overkill, they flood the bedroom. A 747 could land."

"Like an airstrip, huh, Wally? But we should talk about something you should know. Just like my old man said, 'sometimes it's hard to do the right thing.'"

"Okay, agreed. You'll take the lights down?"

"Sure, no problem. But we've got to settle your embezzler problem. It starts with wine."

"It's a little early to have a glass of wine, Ollie."

"Who would even think about drinking wine this early? But expensive wine got me thinking, though. A question in the back of my mind. And no answer. You know she doesn't like our neighbors. Granted, some are hard to understand, but they're good people. Hillary isn't, Wally."

"That's a harsh statement, Ollie."

"My turn to talk, Wally. No stop signal, please."

What Ollie told me about his search didn't sadden me, it made me angry. More angry than I'd ever been in my life. And to think, I was ready to sign everything I owned over to Hillary just for her long-term security. Security. All about security.

"There's a history. Ohio, Indiana, Illinois. And then, Oregon. Wine country. You drink some and then you're hooked. But she was busted when she cooked the books at the winery there. Served two years."

I couldn't help but gasp. I looked at the screen. Same face, different name.

"Embezzlers are good at taking money and hiding it where only they can get it."

"I get the picture, Ollie." I would have cried if it weren't for the fact I felt like a fool.

How much did I have left in my savings account? Could I prove anything? My mind in a whirl.

"Divorce, she'll still get half. I've worked so hard."

"She'll sell it to those gentrification people. Make a killing," Ollie said.

"I'm so mad...I could..."

"Gotta think about your future. Security, Wally."

"I'm at a loss for words."

"Gotta think about security. Those back stairs are really shaky. Accidents happen."

Ollie and I sat with our hands around the warm coffee cups for several more minutes. He pointed to a list of newspaper articles as he scrolled through the computer. I read each one.

"You're in the right business, Wally. The kind that comes to terms with loss real fast."

Ollie took down the security lights as promised but couldn't repair the back stairs until supplies came in the following week. Jarred off their foundations by all the gentrification going on, heavy trucks, steamrolling down the street, those old rails were weak. It all worked in our favor.

Not so for Hillary, the embezzler. A shame she lost her footing, tumbled down two stories.

Neighbors all came together to grieve my loss. Good neighbors do that.

Married life? Everything good comes to an end. How many months? No more counting.

Yes, Darby changes as old and new collide, but Walter Mason's Funeral and Crematorium continues to flourish in the gentrified community. Like my father said, 'work is work, home is home.'

Ollie, he'll always be my best friend.

FOR MORE INFORMATION about the author, please visit Wil A.

Emerson's website: https://www.wilemerson.com/

The Wedding Dress in the Middle of the Road

Jack Bates

Bix gunned the engine, taking the serpentine curves at a higher speed than I felt comfortable. I slapped my hands on the dash above the glove box to brace myself, squeezed my eyes shut, and demanded he slow down. Instead, he abruptly stopped. The inertia jerked me forward in my seat. My stretched-out arms locked in the same instant the safety belt locked over my chest.

"Bix! Who taught you how to drive like that?"

"Get out."

I clearly didn't have whiplash as I could turn my head to face him.

"Is this about what I think it's about because if it is this isn't the time or the place—"

"No, Cori, you don't understand. Get out and look at the front of the car."

"Did we hit something?"

"I don't think so. Let me back up a little."

Bix dropped the gear shift into reverse, eased up on the brakes then gently stopped, putting the car in park.

"Okay. Now you can get out."

"So help me, Bix. If this is some kind of prank—"

"Cori. Go look."

I sat back and undid my safety belt. My lungs quickly responded to being freed from the tight restraint. I opened the door. Long, rutty, puddles of wet stone and mud loomed outside the car. An afternoon of showers left the washboard road a mucky mess.

"Are you getting out?" Bix asked.

I looked at my shoes. My 'wonderfully perfect for the wedding' shoes. For once my toes would not be pinched. My arches would not be punished. My dogs would not be barking at me on the dance floor.

"For a private detective, Cori, you calculate risk in a strange way. I've seen you get blood on your hands but now you're backing away from a little mud."

"You don't understand. These are Nola Abernathy pumps."

Bix capitulated. He sacrificed his own pair of nondescript, discount store loafers to retrieve the mysterious obstacle in front of the car. He bent down to pick up whatever he had stopped hard not to hit. When he stood straight, he held the item so I could see it.

He held the dress.

The dress designed by Christian Asaro exclusively for our client, Miriam Cavanaugh. The dress that had gone missing. The dress that connected the murder of Asaro's assistant, Kelly Short, to an unfortunate incident from the past. There, in the glow of the headlights, Miriam Cavanaugh's wedding dress drooped in Bix's grasp, no longer able to bask in its celebrity.

"Behold the Miriam," Bix said.

"Put it in the trunk and let's go."

"Oh, so now I can drive fast." Bix flung the verbal jab at me as he bent inside the car to lift the rear door release. He straightened the dress over the recessed spare wheel and closed the hatch.

"Sorry about your shoes," I said.

He shrugged. "I'm just glad the floormats are Rubber-Shields."

"Taking the win where you can get it, as always."

"It's the little things." He winked. "Buckle up."

Rocks and mud ricocheted and spattered against the wheel well as the rear tires spun. The car fishtailed as it dug into the rain softened road. For an instant I feared we'd be stuck, and my lovely shoes would not be seen that afternoon. Bix's skillful handling of the vehicle helped it find some traction. We were off to the Pine Shadow Country Club for the reception of the decade. Mr. Donald Bracken and Miss Miriam Cavanaugh had cordially invited friends, family, and giants in commerce and industry to celebrate their nuptials.

Bix and I were about to crash the festivities.

I'm certain more than one guest quietly shared the thought that Donald Bracken should have taken Miriam's name seeing as how her side of the aisle accused him of marrying her simply to advance his career within her father's automotive empire. Quite possibly Bracken's side of the guest list thought the same.

And someone didn't think they should be married at all.

Maybe that was the crack in the windshield, as my grandfather used to say, that shattered under the weight of so many secrets and lies.

Two days before the high-society nuptials, we were sitting in my office overlooking Old Perch Bay when Miriam Cavanaugh told me about her purloined dress. Her fiancé, Donald Bracken, held her hand, metaphorically, as Miriam explained her situation.

"My wedding gown is being held for ransom."

I can't say I was hearing that for the first time. The story had broken on social media a week before she came to see me. When the youngest daughter of a prominent Michigan automotive magnate drops an angry post on how the House of Asaro lost her gown the day before her scheduled fitting, it's going to make the news. Local, state, national news. Throw in the neighboring country of Canada and it's an international tale of woe.

All that viral coverage, of course, brought out the trolls. One more predominately than the others.

"Who is this at-the-real-ManDBQ?" I asked.

Bix laughed from the sofa by the window. "Sounds like a bad barbecue place."

Miriam Cavanaugh did not see the humor. Therefore, neither did Donald Bracken.

"Donald thinks it's his ex," Miriam said.

Bracken nodded. "Amanda Quincy. Mandy Quincy."

"What's the B stand for?" Bix asked.

"Use your imagination," Miriam said.

I decided to move us down a path of discovery. "Were you engaged before, Mr. Bracken?"

"Nothing official."

"Unofficially?"

Miriam Cavanaugh wrinkled her nose irritably at Bix for asking the follow-up question. "It was nothing. They dated for a few years through college and then some after. It was either marry or move on. They moved on."

"How long were you moving on before you proposed to Miss Cavanaugh?" I asked.

Bracken shifted in his chair. "I don't know. Almost a year."

"So, after dating Amanda Quincy for nearly a decade," I said. "You met and proposed to Miss Cavanaugh in less than twelve months?"

Miriam Cavanaugh now wrinkled her face at me. "Is this going anywhere, Miss Frost?"

"Mandy BQ's trolling seems particularly caustic. In one comment she even appears to issue a veiled threat." I put the post on my screen and read it aloud. "I'll cut you and the dress into remnants."

"It's not her," Cavanaugh proclaimed.

"You don't know Mandy," Bracken said under his breath.

"I know she lives in L.A. I know she's a producer with Los Angeles Public Broadcasting. I know she's dating a man named Ahmed Ghazzawi."

"So, you cyber-stalked your fiancé's ex," Bix said.

Before Miriam Cavanaugh could respond, I asked her, "Did you post about the gown prior to the theft?"

Miriam Cavanaugh bristled. "I set all my posts to 'friends only.'"

"Because that's effective," Bix said. "Do you have any social media accounts, Mr. Bracken?"

"No. I find the whole thing exhausting."

I didn't entirely believe him.

"Did either of you have any altercations with anyone at Asaro Gowns?"

"I had a very specific dress in mind, Miss Frost. When you wait until your mid-thirties to get married, you want what you want. I may have made several requests, but it is my dress, after all, and my father is paying for it so yes, there may have been some heated exchanges with my liaison at Asaro."

"But not Asaro himself?"

"I met with him initially. After I approved his sketches, I didn't see him again. I met primarily with this woman. Kelly Short." Cavanaugh handed me an invoice from the liaison.

Donald Bracken seemed momentarily interested. He reached for the printout Cavanaugh held. She pulled it away from him to give to me. He withdrew his hand.

"You want me to find your dress."

"I get married the day after tomorrow," Miriam said.

Bracken corrected her. "We get married—"

"Yes, of course. She knew what I meant." Miriam Cavanaugh stood. "I don't expect to be wearing the Asaro gown but I'm a Cavanaugh and I won't be taken advantage of. The dress is mine. Find the dress and who took it so I can take them to court and sue them three ways to Sunday for causing me this mental duress. Donald, let's be on our way."

I sat forward in my chair. "There's the matter of my fees—"

"Bill my father."

They left.

I leaned back in my chair. "Well, I think a ten percent increase is warranted."

Bix laughed. "She did say '*sue* them three ways to Sunday,' didn't she?"

"I don't think that's how that colloquialism goes."

"It does in her world. So, where do we go to find a pilfered wedding gown?"

"Where it all began. The House of Asaro."

I expected a glass palace with neutral, white walls, some kind of elaborate crystal chandelier, a winding spiral staircase ascending from a marble floor in the lobby to the ivory tower of inspiration high overhead.

Asaro Gowns made its home in an old tool and die factory that once stamped replacement gaskets for outboard motors. Offices were turned into private dressing rooms. The previous lobby went through a reno and became a lavish lounge complete with a full-service bar manned by a mixologist named Stephen, who should have been hawking men's underwear or cologne in a black and white TV commercial. The factory housed a runway arena and a functioning studio. Asaro could design, build, and sell all in one location.

The young woman behind the reception desk smiled as Bix and I entered.

"Good afternoon, I'm Wei Wei. Who are you here to see?"

"We don't have an appointment," I told her.

"Oh. Well, let me see if we have an agent available to discuss your wedding gown dreams." Her fingers tapped over a keyboard.

"We're not getting married," Bix said casually. "We're here to see Kelly Short about Miriam Cavanaugh's missing wedding dress."

The soft clacking of the keyboard stopped. Wei Wei looked up from the screen.

"What is she claiming now?"

"That her dress is missing."

"Look, Christian has refunded all fees for the Miriam's Dream. As far as we're all concerned that—Miss Cavanaugh is no longer a client."

"The Miriam's Dream?" Bix asked.

"Christian names all his originals after his clients. He puts the mock-up on display in our showroom." Wei Wei gestured to the area off to her right. A dozen or so headless mannequins posed inside Lucite boxes. The dresses the bash-test dummies wore were suitable for weddings or red-carpet events or black-tie formal.

"Each of those dresses has a name?" I asked.

Wei Wei suddenly remembered I was there. "Yes. It's just something Christian does. The creation remains exclusive for one year before someone else can ask for the design with minor changes."

"Do you think we could speak to Kelly Short?"

"She hasn't come in yet today. Can I take a message?"

An office door opened. A woman stepped out carrying a large portfolio in one hand and a phone that held her attention in the other.

"Wei Wei, these are Christian's sketches for the Martin-Lefler wedding. He left them with me because no one can find Kelly and Martin and Lefler are on their way in—" The woman looked up from her phone to see Bix and me standing at Wei Wei's counter. "Oh. Are you the Martin-Leflers?"

"No," I said.

"But they are here to see Miss Short, Miss Shannon."

"New clients?"

"They're actually here about Miriam's Dream."

Shannon's demeanor soured. "I thought the nightmare was over." She set the portfolio on the counter. "Olivia Shannon. How can I help?"

"We just want to know how the dress went missing," Bix said.

"And that's what we've been trying to explain to Cavanaugh's lawyers. We don't know."

"Security cameras?" I asked.

Shannon shook her head. "Nothing. No break-ins. No break outs. Nothing out of the ordinary."

"What about something out of the not so ordinary?" Bix asked.

"Such as?"

"A break in the daily routine. Any new customers the day before Miriam Cavanaugh came in for her fitting. Any delivery services picking up or dropping off packages. Anything that struck you as odd."

"Not that I can think of. Wei Wei?"

"There was that guy with the flat tire."

"Okay," I said. "Tell me about him."

Wei Wei let out a heavy breath. "Not really much to tell. He pulled in out front. Changed the tire. That's about it."

"Which tire?" Bix asked.

"Back tire. Passenger side."

"Did he come in?"

"Only long enough to use the restroom to wash his hands."

"Do you remember what he looked like?"

"I remember thinking he reminded me of the actor who played the Scarecrow in the Wizard of Oz."

"The way he looked?"

"Not so much his face as the way he moved. Exaggerated gestures. A little bounce in his step. A kind of 'everything is going to be fine' bounce. Something familiar in his movements."

Drawn into the conversation, Stephen came over from the bar. "You talking about the guy with the bad toupee?"

Wei Wei nodded. "I almost forgot about that."

"How could you forget that? It was like he put it on sideways."

Bix chuckled. "Brutal. How old would you say he was?"

"Older. Forties? Fifties? Somewhere in there."

"Anything else?"

"Yeah," Wei Wei said. "He asked if there was somewhere he could dispose of his old tire."

Bix laughed. "You mean like throw it away?"

"Yeah."

"Who throws away a wheel? You take it in to have the tire replaced."

"The thing is," Wei Wei said. "It looked like, at least to me, that he replaced the donut with a new wheel."

This information threw Bix a curve he hadn't expected. "He swapped the spare for an actual wheel?"

"Yeah," Stephen said. "I thought that was odd, too."

"What did you tell him when he asked about disposing the tire?" I asked.

"I said we had a dumpster out behind the studio. He thanked me and left. I saw him drive around to the back and a few minutes later he drove away."

"Do you remember anything about the car?"

"Old and grey," Wei Wei said.

"There was a lot of rust along the lower quarter panels," Stephen added.

"Any cameras aimed at the garbage corral?"

Olivia Shannon shook her head. "Just at the back doors. They do provide images of one of the cleaning service guys hauling bags of trash out of the shop around ten the morning before Miriam Cavanaugh came in for the fitting. The cleaners come in every morning Monday through Friday."

"What time did the Scarecrow change his flat?" Bix asked.

"About an hour after that," Wei Wei said. "I remember because I wanted to call for food delivery for my lunch."

"Can we get the name of the cleaning service?" I asked.

"Wei Wei can give you that information," Shannon said.

"We'd appreciate that."

"Anything else? I mean it. Anything. We all want this behind us."

"We need to see the video of the cleaning guy carrying out the garbage."

"Okay, but the police looked at it and didn't seem interested."

"Yeah, well, the police don't always get it right," Bix said. He hadn't learned yet that just because he didn't see anything happening, it didn't mean the police weren't looking at all possible avenues of a crime.

Wei Wei printed the information for Clark Custodial Services. She brought us around into her sanctuary and showed us the security video. The quality was better than I expected.

"Freeze it there," Bix said. "Print it, please."

The printout showed a male, early to mid-thirties, black hair with a Z cut into it. He carried three bags. Two of the bags were black with the name Clark Custodial Services printed on one side. The third bag was purple and blank.

We were only interested in the purple bag.

"I know better than to ask this," Bix said as we got in the car. "We're not going dump-digging, are we?"

"No. The dress wasn't heading to a landfill. Maybe a scrap heap or trafficked on some dark web clothing exchange. I'm betting this whole dress-napping was done purely for spite."

"Cavanaugh was pretty caustic when she came to see us."

"This is deep hate, Ted."

"You're serious."

"I'm always serious."

"No, this is, 'pay attention to what I'm saying' serious. You know how I know?"

"How do you know?"

"You called me Ted. When you say Theodore Bixby I know I messed up somehow."

"You're right, Bix. This is serious. Someone wanted to stab Miriam in the heart. Punch her in the gut. They wanted retribution."

"For what?"

"That's the missing puzzle piece."

"I can't see a salesclerk being that angry at a customer that she would sabotage her own career."

"Women fight on so many levels of mean."

"I see that. Guys just get angry and stew then have a beer and let it go."

"You don't push it down, dwell on it until it makes you snap?"

"Nope. Well, at least I don't."

I let it slide.

"I think it's time we spoke to Kelly Short."

"How do we find her?"

"Her number is on the copy of the invoice Miriam gave me at the office."

"Reverse look-up?"

"I'm already on it. It's why I have you drive."

"Oh, that's why."

Bix gunned the engine and squawked the tires.

The information the people search app provided on Kelly Short automatically linked to my maps app on my phone. Directions appeared instantly. Forty minutes later we were on the south end of Herring Creek Township, a former popular destination for commercial and recreational fishing that was already on the decline when it was sucker-punched by the pandemic lockdown in 2020. Herring Creek slowly reinvented itself with upscale lofts and art venues and interesting restaurants.

Kelly Short lived in a tiny house condo that had once been a vacation cottage getaway for bootleggers and captains of other industries. A brick wall along the back edge of the complex's parking lot still displayed bullet holes from Tommy-gun rounds one unfortunate gangster tried to escape during an attempt on his life.

Only the wall survived.

The dozen detached condos of Herring Creek Park sat back along the banks of a narrow tributary feeding into both Lower Herring Lake and Lake Michigan. We stopped at the gatehouse to tell the man inside who we were visiting. Ed, the security guard, seemed skeptical.

"She expecting you?"

"I think she knows we were on our way here," I told him. "I left messages on her phone."

"Her car hasn't left the resident lot all day. I'm thinking she might be under the weather."

"What time did you clock in?" Bix asked.

"I'm here at seven for the morning rush hour. I know. Seems funny to me, too, to hear that but they all leave around the same time for their jobs. Except Pete Rinehart. Pete flipped the old trout farm that was here into these condos. Now he's retired and lives in the only unit with a second floor."

"Who watched the gate before you?" I asked.

"Vinnie Gjocaj has it from midnight til I show up. Bunny Hopper has it in between."

"Bunny Hopper?"

"Her real name is Cheryl, but everyone calls her Bunny. I'm going to give you two visitor passes. Place this on your dash and put on these name tags. Park over there where it says visitors."

We gave Ed our names and followed his directions. He came out of his hut as we passed.

"Do me a favor," Ed said. "I've had a bad feeling all morning something isn't right at Miss Short's place. Let me know if she's okay, will ya?"

"Yeah, sure," Bix said.

"Thanks. She's a sweetheart. In the winter she sometimes brought me a hot cocoa and a croissant."

"That's nice of her," I said.

"She said it was part of her sorority mission statement. Something about adhering to some creed. Traits she said she kept beyond college. Who knew kindness had calories?" Ed laughed and patted his overhanging belly with both of his hands.

We followed the path to Unit 9. Neither of us said anything. I couldn't speak for Bix, but I had that funny, icy tickle of dread in the bottom of my belly.

A white cat sat on the inside ledge of a large picture window. The cat watched us the way a cat will watch whatever has caught its interest. Looking into a cat's eyes, it's always clear the cat is concocting some plan it must either execute with absolute conviction or abandon entirely.

Behind the cat was a comfortable and warm home. A pair of letters hung on the wall just inside the front door. Beneath the Z and M were photos. Painted above this shrine was the creed Ed said Short told him she still observed.

"Those her sorority letters?" Bix asked.

"Must be. They're over her diplomas and pictures of what looks like sorority events."

"Any idea which sorority that would be?"

"I never got into the Greek thing."

Bix tapped his phone. "Zeta. Mu. The seventh and fourteenth letters of the Greek alphabet. Dead end."

I rang the doorbell. The white cat ignored the chimes, choosing to lick its paw, stopping only to stare back at us as if to say, "How do you clean yourself after you walk through a litter box?"

A short hall extended past the kitchen. I could see three doors: One to the left, one to the right, one straight back. Bedroom, bathroom, egress. Kelly Short had to be behind one of the two side doors.

"You think Ed's got the passcode for the electronic lock?"

Bix cupped his hands over the window. "The back door looks open."

"Theodore William Bixby."

"I didn't do anything yet."

"Proactive reaction. Let's go check."

The bolt of the auto-lock hadn't found the housing properly, leaving the door slightly ajar. Bix pushed it open with his toe and called out through the house.

"Hello? Kelly Short?"

No one answered.

We pulled on plastic gloves. I opened the door behind the kitchen. A half bath with a utility closet. Otherwise, empty.

"Cori," Bix said. "Over here."

I could tell by the tone of his voice we weren't going to be speaking with Kelly Short that day or any other.

I saw what I needed to see. No matter how often it occurs or how it happens, viewing a crime scene never gets easier. Kelly Short lay on her bed, a pillow over her face.

Bix went to the guard house.

I rang the neighbor's doorbell.

Pete Rinehart stood with me outside Kelly Short's condo waiting for emergency responders to arrive.

"She's lived here about a year. Zemy moved in with her not long after Kelly arrived."

"Zemy a boyfriend?"

"Zemy is the cat in the window. Named him after her sorority. She was a Zeta Mu at Mid-Michigan University."

"Did she have a boyfriend from the college days, maybe? Girlfriend? Either. Both."

"No one I ever saw. It's quiet around here. The residents like the tranquility. I guess that's ruined, now."

"Did you see anyone here last night?"

"No, but that doesn't mean we don't have uninvited guests. The brick wall is only four feet tall, and it doesn't enclose the development. It runs for about a hundred and fifty yards in either direction with what I call bookends. Half walls that turn in off the ends, but you can easily step over them."

Sirens approached. Ed raised the gate arm and directed the responders to Kelly Short's unit. The ambulance drove along the paved path. Ed and Bix followed.

Zemy scurried out the front door as the responders entered. Ed held Zemy for comfort as a deputy sheriff took his statement. I heard him say Bunny Hopper logged in Short around six p.m. Short then went out around eight and returned around ten. She was alone each time.

When he finished with Ed, the deputy approached us. He gave his name as Deputy Sam McConkey and took our names from the identification stickers Ed asked us to wear.

"Did either of you know the deceased?"

"No."

"What was your reason for visiting Miss Short?"

"We're trying to locate a missing wedding gown."

"Your wedding gown?"

"No. It belongs to our client."

"Client?"

"Yeah, we're private investigators," Bix said. "Well, Cori is the P.I. I'm her assistant of sorts."

"Did Miss Short have the gown in her possession?"

"We don't know," I explained. "Short worked for Christian Asaro who designed the missing dress."

"Do you have a description of the dress?"

"Sweetheart neckline with a taffeta trumpet skirt and an eighteen-inch train."

"Color?"

"Seriously?"

"My sister wore red," Deputy McConkey said. He was serious. "Traditional wedding norms are being challenged if not shattered. I heard it on a podcast. The Veiled Vow."

"White," I said.

"Would your client have cause to attack the deceased?"

"She was upset," I said. "But not enough to murder."

"Do you have any idea who might have had reason to commit this homicide?"

"We're just looking for a dress, Deputy," Bix said. "We can't even ascertain what happened here is connected to the missing gown."

"But you kind of think it does, right?"

Bix nodded. "Well, yeah..."

"If we come across anything, Deputy McConkey," I said. "We'll call you."

"I'd appreciate that."

The dress wasn't there.

On our way to our car, Bix quietly asked, "She knew her killer, didn't she?"

"No forced entry. I'd say so."

"Did the visitor take the dress?"

"I don't think we can say for certain until we find the dress. She was either killed because she had it or because she didn't have it. She didn't suffocate herself."

"Dispute with a neighbor?"

"Rinehart suggested the residents are a quiet, amicable group."

"Where did she go and who did she see?"

"Get food. Meet a friend. Get a coffee. Time to check the local establishments."

The Shanty was a bastion to another era. Photos of ancient and forgotten anglers decorated the walls. It smelled of old cigarettes, stale beer, sweat. Now it advertised fifty microbrews on tap and free wifi.

◊ If Buddy's killer is one of the bride's relatives, poison was not used. ◊

Amanda, the bartender, recognized Kelly Short from the picture I showed her from Short's Job Link profile.

"She was here last night."

"Alone?"

"Yeah. Kept checking her phone. Seemed upset when she left."

Bix leaned on the bar. "Anyone follow her out?"

The bartender shook her head. "She kept to herself. Like I said, focused on her phone."

"Well," Bix said when we were back in the car. "We know she was here looking to meet someone who didn't show but was probably waiting for her at her condo."

"She lets the killer in the back door, which has no camera."

"Things get heated."

"Do they? No one hears her scream. No one says anything about raised voices."

"She didn't suffocate herself."

"The killer subdued her then held the pillow over her face."

"Over a dress Christian Asaro issued a refund. Why are we still chasing Miriam's Dream?"

"I haven't heard from the client to stop."

"Maybe she forgot about retaining you."

"If she did, I'd still like to show that I continued and completed my job so that when I take her to small claims court for breach of contract and refusal to pay, it'll be easier to sue her three ways to Sunday."

"I still don't think 'sue' is the correct word."

"Probably not."

"Where to now?"

"Home. We'll track down Z-hair tomorrow."

Clark Custodial Services took up the west end of a five-unit strip mall. An electronic bell chimed when we opened door. A young woman in a red shirt with CCS on the front came out of an office behind the counter.

"Welcome to Clark Custodial Services. Only the best to clean your mess. I'm Sarah. What's cluttering your life?"

Bix, ever impatient to get to the truth, jumped right into why we were there. "I'm Ted Bixby. This is Corinne Frost. She's a private investigator and I produce and narrate 'Frost Alert,' a podcast documenting her cases. We're looking for this guy."

Bix laid the printout on the counter in front of her.

"That's Ronny Zerilli."

"Not a recent employee of the month?"

"We dated. Now we don't."

"Best description I've heard all day."

"I'm succinct."

"You certainly are."

If I hadn't stepped in the banter might have gone on longer.

"Is Zerilli available?" I asked.

Sarah finally looked at me. "In Ronny's mind he's always available."

"I meant to talk."

Sarah sauntered over to a computer. She opened a spreadsheet. "He and Alan are on their way to clean a doctor's office. It's their only job tonight. They'll drop the van off here after they finish."

"What time will that be?"

She looked at a digital clock with ever changing numbers. "After six? Maybe? Depends on whether they stop off at the Cannery."

"The brewery on the wharf?" Bix asked.

"Unless there's another one..."

The banter tried to find a foothold. I stomped on it.

"Where's the doctor's office?"

Sarah looked from me to the computer. "Dr. Roddenberry on Yellow Bass Road."

"Thanks for the information," I said.

"One last thing," Bix said. "We'd appreciate if you didn't notify Ronny Zerilli that we're looking for him."

"No problem. I mean, why would I call him?"

"Thanks."

"Absolutely. And if you ever need any of our services, call me."

Outside I tried to shake off the cringe Sarah gave me. "I never felt so dirty coming out of a cleaner's before."

"She took a look at these guns and—"

"Please. The only reason she was flirting with you was—"

Bix hustled across the parking lot. He squatted down by the right rear tire of an old model sedan. A grey four-door with rust eating the quarter panels.

"What are you doing?" I asked.

"Look at the difference in the tread between the left tire and the right tire. The left tread is more worn down. I think this is the car that had a flat outside the House of Asaro."

"Alan have another flat?"

Bix and I turned. Sarah stood behind the store on a vape break.

"That thing is ready for the junkyard," she said, jetting a cloud of vapor.

"This is Alan's car?" Bix asked.

"Yeah. He had a slow leak in his other tire and kept having to fill it so Ronny offered to fix it for him if Alan did Ronny a favor."

"Do you know what the favor was?"

Sarah shrugged, jetted a cloud of toxic steam that quickly dissipated around her face. "Pick up a package? Maybe?"

"Do you use purple bags?" I asked.

Sarah shook her head through another cloud of vapor. "Only black with the company name on the front."

"How would you describe Alan in a DM to a friend?" Bix asked.

"Hashtag bad wig." Sarah laughed or coughed. Hard to tell.

Having absorbed enough toxins to temporarily satisfy her needs, Sarah returned to her post. Bix seemed okay with that.

"Do we wait here for Zerilli or go to the doctor's office?"

"It's Friday," I said. "We're having dinner at the Cannery. We'll find him there."

Once a fish processing plant, the facility had been re-imagined into one of the go-to destinations in Fitzgerald County. The place had all the ambience of a speakeasy themed restaurant. Dimly lit, costumed servers and actors, a jazz band.

Bix and I had our dinner. A shared dessert arrived about the same time Zerilli arrived alone. Bix slid his chair back from the table, but I caught his leg with my foot.

"We have time, Bix. Let him unwind while we eat our tiramisu."

Less than ten minutes later, Bix was at the bar.

"Ronny Zerilli."

Zerilli looked at Bix then into his IPA. "Don't know him."

"I think you have it wrong, Ronny. I know it's you."

"I don't know what—"

"Where's the dress?"

"What dress?"

"The one you stole from Christian Asaro and Miriam Cavanaugh."

"I don't know what you're talking about and I'm not talking about a dress." Ronny turned and headed for the front door. I kicked a chair into his path. Zerilli stumbled into it.

"Feel like talking about it now?" I asked as he looked down at me.

Guests near us turned to gawk. Bix returned with a fresh ale, assuring everyone everything was fine. He picked up the chair and stood there until Zerilli sat. Bix returned to his own seat. He slid the ale to our guest.

"Mr. Zerilli, I'm Corinne Frost, a private investigator. Mr. Bixby is my assistant. We were hired by Miriam Cavanaugh to find her missing wedding gown."

"Wait a second. Is this part of the show?"

"No show," I said. "This is real."

Zerilli winked like he was in on the joke. "I don't know nothing—"

Bix spun the printout of Zerilli literally holding the bag. "Let me tell you what we know. We know Miriam Cavanaugh's dress is in the purple bag. We know you left it by the dumpster so your friend Alan could retrieve it. We know Kelly Short bagged the dress so you could take it outside without raising suspicion. What we don't know is why. Why did Kelly Short hatch this elaborate dress caper? Was she mad at Miriam Cavanaugh?"

Zerilli tensed. "Why don't you ask her."

"We can't," I said. "She's dead."

His realization we weren't actors was genuine. "Wait a minute...wait...Kelly's dead?"

"Kelly? Were you seeing her?"

"We went out a few times...How did she..."

"She was murdered last night." Bix tapped the printout. "Where were you, Zerilli?"

"Cleaning an office building until midnight."

"Your partner Alan will back you up?"

"So will the app we use. Gives time, date, and location every fifteen minutes."

Bix didn't know where to go in the questioning. Sometimes he expected a tidy ending. A capper, as he called it, for the end of a podcast episode. A perfect summation that ends the episode satisfactorily. It doesn't always happen in this line of work.

"Mr. Zerilli," I said. "Do you have any idea why Kelly Short took the dress?"

"I didn't know what was in the bag. All she told me was I could make some serious cash if I helped her with something."

"That something was grand larceny."

Bix snapped his fingers. "What did Alan do with the dress?"

"Stashed it in his trunk."

"Is it still there?"

"Might be. The guy Kelly said wanted it was supposed to call us about where and when he wanted to meet for the exchange."

"What guy?"

"I don't know."

"Where is Alan?" I asked.

"He said he was going home."

"Call Alan," I said. "See if the dress is still in the trunk."

"Yeah. You mean now?"

"Yes now!" My voice rose over the din inside the Cannery. The restaurant quieted for a moment.

"Just part of the show," Bix said to the crowd. "This dirty rat owes me money."

Guests laughed and returned to their meals.

Zerilli looked at his phone. "Well, that's funny."

Bix leaned back. His impatience grew. "Care to share?"

"While we were sitting here, I got a text from Kelly."

I looked at Bix. "The killer has her phone. He knows I tried calling her this afternoon. I need to call McConkey so he can ping her phone."

"What does the text say?" Bix asked.

"It's asking what we did with the dress."

I went outside where I could make the call to the Fitzgerald County Sheriff's Department. Cars were lining up for valet parking. I walked away from the line, farther down the wharf. Couples strolled past me.

A black SUV rolled up to the valet stand. Eight men got out, all of them wearing red sweatshirts with Delta Sigma Tau on the front. One of the men was blindfolded but the mask couldn't hide who he was.

Donald Bracken was out with his old fraternity brothers the night before his wedding. Phones were raised. Images were taken. Posts were shared.

Bracken held his hands out in front reaching for the invisible before him. In one hand he held a phone. Bracken kept calling out to his DST crew who in turn led him along the wharf, inching him closer to the precipice, phones still raised for the inevitable moment he plunged into the bay.

Bracken bumped into a young woman whose boyfriend immediately shoved Bracken. The phone Bracken held tumbled into Old Perch Bay. One of the men leading the groom shoved the guy that shoved Bracken. More shoving followed until the defending DST brother got the girl's boyfriend in a headlock. The tussle became violent. Bracken removed his blindfold. It took four of his buddies to subdue the fighting between the DST guy and the gallant boyfriend. Two other fraternity brothers stopped the valet to retrieve the SUV.

The girlfriend led the boyfriend away from the stag party.

The violent DST man pulled a phone out of his pocket and showed it to Bracken. In the next instant the man pitched the phone out into the water. This made the frat boys laugh.

Bracken froze. "Miss Frost?"

I stepped toward him. "Mr. Bracken. Boys last night out?"

"You know it, sweetheart," said the violent man who tossed the phone.

"Easy, Quentin. This is the woman looking for Miriam's dress."

"I thought you said Miriam got a different one."

"She did...but you know Mimi."

"Yeah, I do."

"Ease up, brother. She's going to be your real-life sister-in-law."

"I remain optimistic that could change, Donny."

Bracken laughed uncomfortably. "Miss Frost, these are my brothers. This is Quentin, my best man and actual brother."

"Yeah. Nice meeting you. Clock is ticking, Del-Sigs. Soon the sun will rise and we will lose our brother." This brought boos. Quentin started singing to the 'Battle Hymn' tune. "Oh, we are the mighty brothers of Delta Sigma Tau..."

They continued singing their chapter song as they loaded back into the SUV.

"...on we march for glory after everything we saw/ Our little sisters praise us, that is what they're meant to do/ We love you Zeta Mu!"

The black SUV drove away.

Bix came out of the Cannery. He was alone.

"What's wrong? You look like you watched one too many video reels on social media."

"I'll tell you later. Where's Zerilli?"

"Bathroom. Stall him if he comes out. I put a tracker on Alan's car. I want to put one on Zerilli's."

"How do you know what he drives?"

"He told me. We're guys. Girls. Cars. Sports. It's all we talk about when there's nothing else to talk about. It's our thing."

"Girls-Cars-Sports. It's your thing. It bonds you like a brotherhood. Like Delta Sigma Tau."

"Who—what? I'm not following you."

"Go tag Zerilli's car. Then we need to go to the office."

The building was quiet when we got there. I searched the web for information on the Michigan chapters of Delta Sigma Tau and Zeta Mu. Bix stretched out on the leather sofa to log the two newest trackers into the app.

"Don Bracken and his brother Quentin are also fraternity brothers in Delta Sigma Tau, which is the big brother fraternity to Zeta Mu."

"The sorority Kelly Short pledged."

"Yes. They all attended Mid-Michigan University up in Pleasant Hill. Don Bracken was a senior the year his real brother, Quentin, and Kelly

Short were freshmen rushing DST and Zeta Mu."

"What are you searching?"

"Greek Life Michigan dot isp. Each chapter has an historian who logs and blogs about their activities, leadership, socials. The information they provide is public."

"Transparency."

"Not a bad plan given some things that have happened in the past."

"Such as?"

"According to the news, Quentin Bracken faced the Greek Tribunal Board for a hazing incident when he was chapter president three years after his old brother Don graduated. The tip about Quentin's role in the incident was made anonymously. Quentin Bracken was exonerated in criminal court and by the Greek Tribunal but lost in civil court to the victim's family. He was ordered to pay restitutions. The verdict also cost him an internship with a big pharma company and put DST on probation. Now guess who the president of the Zeta Mus was when older Bracken brother Don was the president of the DST."

"Amanda Quincy."

"Bingo."

"Bracken's long-term relationship until Miriam Cavanaugh provided a more desirable alternative."

"Angered, Kelly Short promises to avenge her Zeta Mu sister. This is sorority girl mean."

"Wouldn't Bracken have recognized Kelly Short from their school days?"

"Do you remember everyone you met in college?"

"So, Donald Bracken doesn't recognize Short and if she recognizes him, she doesn't say anything."

"Kelly Short calls Amanda Quincy, tells her that her ex is getting married, and wouldn't it be funny if I misplaced the dress for a few days."

"Sorority hijinks."

"Maybe. Quincy lives in Los Angeles with a new bae. What does she care about Bracken."

"Also, Zerilli said a guy would contact them about the dress. What guy?"

The name came to me out of nowhere. "Bracken."

"The groom?"

"No, the best man. When Donny Bracken reminded his younger brother he'd have a sister-in-law, Baby Bracken wasn't pleased."

"And we know there's a connection between the Brackens and Kelly Short."

"So, what if Donny B did recognize Kelly Short. He tells his brother, Quentin, and Quentin, hoping to sabotage the wedding, strong-arms Kelly Short into hijacking the gown because he suspects she knows something about the anonymous tipster that cost him a job. She owes him for not telling him."

"There is someone who might know."

"Amanda Quincy."

It took some deep digging on the web but I finally found a contact number for Amanda Quincy. I called, left a voice mail, and waited for a response I was sure I wouldn't get that night. When my phone buzzed, I was surprised. I put her on speaker so Bix could hear.

"If you hadn't mentioned the Brackens, I don't think I'd be calling back. What did the dynamic dunces do this time?"

"Not a fan?"

"Don was president of Delta Sigma Tau when I was president of Zeta Mu. Everyone assumed we were an item."

"You weren't?"

"No. Far from it. He was the kind of guy who used people like pawn pieces on a chessboard. Once he saw I didn't offer anything he could use, he moved on."

"And Quentin?"

"What a piece of work. If he didn't get his way, he wouldn't let you forget it. He'd carry a grudge to the grave."

"Did you know Don Bracken is getting married tomorrow?"

"What? Is she desperate? No wait. Let me guess. Don works for her father, right?"

"It's like you're telling me things I thought I'd be telling you. Which reminds me. I'm afraid I need to inform you that the investigation also involves the murder of Kelly Short."

"I'm sorry. Who?"

"I believe she pledged the year you were president."

"Could be. I can't say I recall her."

"She never forgot you or the creed to always be kind, help don't hurt, do what's right. It's hand painted on her living room wall beneath her Greek letters."

"You know, I seem to remember a call a while ago from a girl who said she was a Zeta Mu in her senior year at MMU asking what she should do about some hazing incident she said she had information about. I think she said it involved a Del-Sig she dated for a while. She didn't say which guy she dated but I got the idea it was Donald's little brother. I told her to go to the Greek Council and then give a statement to the police."

"She say why she called you?"

"You know how you say something like, 'if you ever need anything, just call'? She actually called."

"And that was Kelly Short?"

"I think so. Not a hundred percent positive. Sorry."

Bix dropped his laptop on my desk. He turned so I could see it.

Alan the Scarecrow was on the move deep inside the Manistee National Forest. Odd time to be driving through a national park. He got to a secluded spot and didn't move.

I ended the call with Quincy. We left immediately. I called Deputy McConkey.

We found Alan's car idling on a grassy, rutted road primarily used by rangers and emergency vehicles. A corrugated hose stretched from the exhaust pipe to the back seat window. Duct tape held the hose in place. It also sealed the window gap.

Alan was slumped in the driver's seat. The doors were locked. The car continued to run.

Bix retrieved a 5-in-1, orange emergency hammer from his glove box. He used the pointed head to smash the passenger window while I called 9-1-1. Bix opened the door, shut off the car, and dragged a groggy Alan from the front seat. He was alive.

"I didn't see his face," Alan said. "Ski mask. But he wore a red sweater under his jacket. I saw the collar."

"This is where he said to meet him?"

Alan coughed and nodded. "I opened the trunk to get the bag and he hit me with a rock from behind."

The killer had an M.O. Wait until the victim's back was turned and wham! Out go the lights.

We looked but there was no sign of the dress. We did find a confession DM on Alan's phone that Alan hadn't typed.

McConkey and an army of emergency responders arrived.

"Thought you should know Kelly Short's phone last pinged at the Cannery."

"It's in the water along the wharf. I saw the killer drop it in the bay."

"You know who the killer is?" Bix asked.

"I'll know for sure when I see him at the wedding."

"Were we invited?"

"Trust me, Bix. Miriam Cavanaugh will be happy to see us."

That brings it all back to the wedding dress in the middle of the road.

The killer ditched the gown to avoid having it found in his possession, the prank no longer funny, if it ever was. During the ceremony, Bix placed a tracker on the killer's car so we could follow his route in case he decided to book as he came out of the church and saw me, Bix, McConkey, and the Scarecrow waiting under umbrellas, throwing bird seed at the bride and groom along with the invited guests.

We reached the reception just as the killer was about to give a speech. Bix carried the dress up to the head table.

"You dropped this," Bix said. He laid it over the killer's arm, then held the microphone for McConkey as he read Quentin Bracken his rights.

The younger Bracken scoffed. "All right. Who's the funny guy?"

Bix heard the question as an invitation for an open mic night.

"You know, Mr. Real-Man-D-B-Q, taking your sister-in-law's dress was a childish prank. Killing Kelly Short for tipping off the authorities about your involvement in the hazing fiasco was just evil."

"I don't know what you're talking about."

"Amanda Quincy does."

"She's lying."

"Kelly Short's name is in the official Greek Tribunal records along with

407

a video deposition. Even if you beat that rap, there's still grand larceny along with assault and attempted murder of Alan Collins."

"He can't prove it was me who knocked him out and put him in the car."

"No one mentioned the thing about the car."

Deputy McConkey led Quentin Bracken out of the reception.

Bix got his satisfactory wrap for the podcast and once the Bracken friends and family vacated the country club, I got to dance.

Death, the Unwanted Wedding Guest
J. Aquino

Farewell, farewell! but this I tell
To thee, thou Wedding-Guest!
He prayeth well, who loveth well
Both man and bird and beast.
—Samuel Taylor Coleridge, *The Rime of the Ancient Mariner*

THE FATHER OF THE BRIDE rehearsed aloud in the limousine as it sped from the basilica to the reception. "When the stars are properly aligned, a kind of joy settles in the hearts of a man and a woman. It happens to those who are lucky and blessed because they have found each other. It sweetens the breath with honey, brightens the eyes so that they actually begin to glow, and strengthens the spine so that it can endure any adversity. Robin and Gerard have found that joy."

"That's beautiful, Dad," Lynn cheered her father on from the back seat as he rode shotgun next to the nonplussed driver. At eighty, he was frequently forgetful, but today appeared to be a good day.

As soon as he had begun his toast, Lynn's partner Jenny sank her head deeper into the backseat headrest and started to moan—until Lynn buried her elbow into Jenny's side, popping her up like toast. When Lynn's father had finished, Lynn shot Jenny a look, causing her to blurt out, "Wonderful toast, Mr. Russell!" while shifting uncomfortably in her blue bridesmaid's gown. Nearly six feet tall, a combat veteran, and presently a federal field agent, Jenny had never worn one before and kept feeling that she'd lost her legs in the blue chiffon.

Washington, D.C., was surprisingly quiet on this June morning, at least in the upper northwest part of the city. The nation's capital was still recovering from the pandemic that had crippled the nation. Robin's wedding was one of the first two-hundred-plus-guests gatherings in the city in several years, but the city's pulse still seemed tentative and timid. The stillness also represented a tension caused by world events. There were three distinct civil wars in the Middle East and armed protests in China and Russia. Congress was bitterly deadlocked. The lavish wedding reception was looked on by the elite Washington, D.C., attendees as a welcome if temporary respite from worry.

The limo pulled up to the St. Ives Hotel, the "grand dame" of the city. Mr. Russell scrambled out of the vehicle to help his wife and Robin from theirs, especially since Gerard, the groom, had exited the vehicle to join another group on the hotel steps. Lynn held Jenny back. "Tell me you're unarmed."

"And where precisely am I going to hide a gun? Besides, the security here is too tight. I even left my thigh knife and holster at home. Help me up, will you, before I strangle myself in this dress!"

Mostly mollified, Lynn felt the need to explain to her partner while extricating her from the limo. "Hey, we're on leave from the agency for the whole weekend. My sister loves you. So, let's—"

Still wrestling with the chiffon for her equilibrium, Jenny snapped, "Now why would I spoil Robin's wedding? I will be as peaceful as Mary's lamb—unless someone takes the last shrimp."

They joined up with Robin and Mr. and Mrs. Russell while Gerard Beckman, the strawberry blond but otherwise preppy, bland, and skinny groom, was urgently talking to the aged and portly Cardinal Benedetto Broccoli, who had just officiated at the wedding ceremony. There were two priests by his side who seemed more intent on watching the street than listening to what the bridegroom was saying. Gerard was handing the cardinal what looked like a substantial amount of money sticking out of a weathered envelope. The prelate shoved it into his robe's pocket and pulled away from Gerard abruptly, removing his scarlet mass from the hotel's fabled façade and leaving it briefly duller.

"We'd better go in, girls," Mr. Russell chided, indicating the need for them to catch up with the bride and groom. Since Jenny, Lynn, Robin, and the parents had spent a tumultuous but ultimately loving Thanksgiving together seven months before, the five of them had become quite close.

Watching her sister ahead of them climb the steep St. Ives Hotel's stairs while expertly maneuvering the train of her Jovani ivory, floral-embroidered wedding dress that was cascading down the steps, she remembered the time three weeks before when they were lying on Robin's bed, having finally finalized her wedding vows.

The words Robin had selected were so formal and even cold that Lynn asked her, "Do you love him?"

Robin had turned her head away and opened the latest issue of *Vogue*. "That depends on what love is."

"What do you mean?"

Robin placed her hand on her sister's and tapped it while she spoke. "Lynn, neither one of us has given them grandchildren and probably never will. Sure, they're comfortable in their surroundings at their empty-nest, disgraced-but-still-wealthy banker's Virginia estate, but," and here Robin's eyes brightened at the thought, "imagine them going to all the places they used to before the funds transfer debacle—the best balls, glittering theater premieres, and the Kennedy Center Honors. They still have their money, but this will restore their—prestige!"

"So," Lynn fretted while recalling her own neglect of her parents, "you're the sacrificial lamb."

Robin scoffed. "Hardly! Gerard's made it clear my purpose is decorative and that I'm to have my own existence. Hey, I like nice things too."

Lynn's moments of irksome recall ended when a doorman clad in a stove-top hat like Lincoln's and a cocoa cape coat like Mr. Bumble's opened and held the bulky golden door of the St. Ives with an image of a Cornish cross etched on the glass. The bride and groom, her maid of honor, one of her seven bridesmaids, and her parents trod the long, red-carpeted hallway to the grand ballroom.

Given the number of cabinet members, ambassadors, senators, and congressmen in attendance, Jenny and Lynn were not surprised that before they could enter they had to walk through metal detectors, which were binging like crazy due to the outrageous amount of jewelry, Rolexes, and gold cigarette cases passing through. Security was taking cell phones from guests and checking them like coats. Jenny saw dignitaries and their security officers led to a separate line where they were gently patted down. Those guarding the elite handed over their guns and cell phones, were hand-searched, and then given their guns and phones backs. Jenny had been in their situation and knew some of them by name.

Having cleared scrutiny, the newly married couple broke away to plunge into the welcoming throng and made a beeline for Mrs. Beckman with Robin casting a knowing backward glance at her family. Mr. Russell sighed at the ordeal that lay before them, shrugged, and held his wife's hand, acknowledging their secret mission with a nod to Jenny and Lynn.

The Beckmans were in the uppermost rung of the local social register. Grandfather Beckman had made his fortune in Texas oil, and, when those wells dried up, secured a majority interest in overseas enterprises that had paid off handsomely for his children and grandchildren. The family's current matriarch and widowed Mrs. Beckman had agreed to her son marrying Robin, but whether or not the Russells were to be invited to the innermost events of the uppermost rung was evidently to be decided by their behavior at the wedding. Robin had made their mission clear: "Don't—mess—this—up. Mingle. Smile! Be happy."

While the cost and management of a wedding traditionally was the responsibility of the bride's parents, Mrs. Beckman had insisted on inflating the guest list from one hundred to four hundred and fifty and on approving both the menu and attendees. Acknowledging there would be additional costs, she had agreed to split all expenses with the Russells, while simultaneously suggesting to those closest to her that she was paying for everything.

"Drink, mix, and mingle, or tomorrow we are banished," Mr. Russell mock-warned his family.

"It's an audition," advised Jenny, who had once been a young actress.

Lynn attempted to catch Robin's eye to wink and smile at her. But her sister seemed to actively avoid Lynn's glance. It wasn't just Jenny who had become closer to Robin over the winter and spring. But now Lynn was sensing a return of Robin's former prickliness as she flirted with becoming one of the one percent.

Her father grabbed Lynn's arm. "Alex is here. He seems to be tending bar."

Lynn's mind swirled at the idea of Robin meeting her ex-boyfriend. She carefully squeezed her way passed bulging derrieres and hands making wild gestures while holding bloody marys and came up to her sister from behind. She learned forward and whispered the information to her.

Robin tensed but continued looking ahead at Ambassador Young, a Beckman cousin who was barely disguising his contempt at his nephew marrying a disgraced banker's daughter. She nodded and slowly raised her head and moved it slightly in Lynn's direction. Her lips barely moved but pushed the words clearly toward Lynn. "Avoid him. Stay away from the bar. Don't drink."

"You too," Lynn murmured, backing away. She saw Mrs. Russell—petite, stocky, her silver hair piled high to make her appear taller, and splendidly attired in black and gold—advance like a battleship and rescue Robin from the ambassador by taking him away and chiding him for his behavior. Returning to Jenny, Lynn touched her partner's arm and muttered, "Don't drink."

Sighing, Jenny responded, "Okay. But I tell you, I was really looking forward to it."

A half hour passed, the Russells and Jenny mingled and mingled until their nerves were bleeding. Then, the other bridesmaids made extravagant signals to them that the wedding party should suggest that the other guests find their tables. Even though Jenny and Lynn were part of the wedding party, it was so large that Mrs. Russell had decided that only she and the best man were to sit at the head table with the bride and groom; the rest were assigned places at selected tables. "It's like we're goodwill ambassadors," Lynn cracked.

"Or peace negotiators." Jenny craned her head like a searchlight, looking at the various table signs that appeared to be street names while colliding with the horde of other searchers doing the same. "What's our table number?"

"No numbers," Lynn all but shouted to be heard above the clamor. "Robin and Gerard decided to name each table after a special moment in their lives. Ours is Make America Great Again Parkway. That was Gerard's. He was a Donald Trump for President supporter."

"Oh," Jenny muttered, unimpressed and trying not to show it. "Well, over there is *Muppets Most Wanted* Highway."

"That's the first movie they saw together," Lynn explained.

"Figures. I was pretty sure it wasn't *Rashōmon*. And there's Barry Bonds Boulevard."

"Gerard thinks Bonds should be in the Baseball Hall of Fame because the charge that he took steroids was a canard—his word, not mine."

"Hillary Clinton Highway—"

"That was Robin's idea."

"Excuse me," a scrawny lady with blue hair asked Jenny and Lynn with an unmistakable tone of utter exasperation, "do you know where—" she fumbled with her pince-nez glasses to read from her card, "'Roe versus Wade Highway' is?"

"I'm sorry," Jenny burped while being bumped. "I have no idea. That's the problem with not having numbers. You don't know what follows what. You have to stumble onto it."

Annoyed at the lack of the correct answer, the blue woman tried to push her way by Jenny, but the crowd around them was so tight that she bounced off Lynn and slammed into another lost soul, causing a domino effect among the guests.

"This is crazy," Jenny shouted to Lynn. "I'm surprised the fire marshal hasn't swept in. Maybe money changed hands?"

"Not so loud," Lynn hissed.

"But then you won't be able to hear me." Jenny kept searching the signs. "I keep waiting to find out there's a table named after their favorite song, the Beatles' 'Why Don't We Do It in the Road?'" Jenny's theater-trained voice projected a little farther than she had planned, and another blue-haired matron heard her and gasped at the vulgarity of Jenny's expression.

"Nice work," Lynn hissed while trying to not be toppled over by the masses and dreading that the woman's discomfort would get back to Robin.

Finally, the two of them found the Make America Great Again Parkway table and plopped down in their chairs. Already seated at the I Am Woman, Hear Me Roar table facing them were Mr. and Mrs. Russell. Lynn's father waved at Jenny and made a circling motion with his index finger at his head to indicate the wackiness of Robin and Gerard's seating plan. Jenny grinned and nodded back, remembering the sign language and special signals she had shared with her late father, which made her sad for a moment.

Wine was served—Burning Goose Cabernet Sauvignon from the Napa Valley, in keeping with the Beckmans' America First philosophy and costing at least $300 a bottle. Jenny saw in the rear of the room that the automatic dividers had—at the push of a button—finished collapsing the last temporary partition that created separate meeting areas in the 4,200 square foot ballroom. Even in this huge and now undivided space, the circular tables were jammed very tightly together. In case of fire, one couldn't walk but would instead have to jostle by tables on the way to the nearest exit. The tables were so close that Jenny, who had a sharp ear, was picking up conversations from other tables.

"I am just appalled that the Beckmans invited Cardinal Broccoli to officiate at the wedding. He's so controversial, so extreme, so conservative. I've never read any of his books, but a friend told me that he thinks women not only shouldn't be priests but should have nothing to do with church administration. He also believes that the Council of Trent was a big mistake—you know, the sixteenth century meeting that established the doctrines we grew up with."

Jenny said to herself, "Lady, you sure know your Catholic conferences," although she also noted that the woman pronounced the cardinal's last name like the vegetable rather than with the stress on the second syllable.

Another voice diagonal from them said, "You've been trying to stop this wedding for three weeks. More is at stake than you know. Just back off!"

Coming from behind them, a third voice gabbed, "And Gertrude—just now—begged me to give her all the money I had, saying she left the house without cash. I forked over a thousand dollars—making me wonder if, all appearances to the contrary, she—"

But the woman's voice was drowned out by another, exclaiming, "That's her, right over there. The one who said to her friend that they should 'do it in the road.' She's the tall brunette next to the other tall brunette."

All the while, Alex was roaming between the tables like a blond shark with a tray raised above his head serving pre-prepared martinis and bloody marys because no one was easily able to get up to the bar.

Spoons hit crystal, and the best man, a ruddy-face classmate of Gerard's, used a hand-mike to get everyone's attention. Standing behind the head table and in front of the four-piece band, he bellowed, "Welcome! Welcome to the Beckman-Russell wedding reception. I am your—host, I guess, Tony Cruise, and yes, I am as handsome as Tom, but we're not related and not even friends." He was greeted with frail laughter and responded, "Is this thing on?"

Lynn saw a flash and instinctively shouted, "Down!" at a muffled thump that could be felt at first in the sinuses and chest and heard after. Special Ambassador Young at the table next to them was flung back, crashing the chair to the floor, lying limp and dead with a spreading spot of reddish-brown on his chest. Those at his table of both sexes leapt up and screamed. Jenny triangulated the sound and the ambassador's fall with a glimpse of a figure running for the door.

"Gun! Gun!" Lots of people screamed, and at once entire tables tried to empty but were jammed in the tight space between them. Those in security pulled out their guns but were only able to wave them around because they couldn't move either. Jenny could see that the fleeing shooter was also blocked by the rushing flood of panicked guests and that the only clear path to the door was on the tables themselves. She grabbed the chiffon at her hem and ripped it up and around, baring her legs. She kicked off her shoes, jumped onto the table nearest her in one motion, and started racing towards the door, hopping from table to table. Lynn saw what Jenny was doing, ripped her own gown, leapt on the same table, and raced after her.

Smashing salads, kicking water and wine glasses, stabbed by cutlery, they kept running amid the shouts and screams. Lynn turned to see if her parents were all right and saw that Robin was at their table, covering them with her arms spread out. Gerard was cowering behind his mother's chair.

Jenny looked back too, mainly worried that one of the security officers with his gun drawn would shoot at two women rushing, however strangely, to leave. But discretion about firing in a crowded room evidently prevailed.

Turning her head forward, she could see the shooter was at the door.

Jenny reached the last table and the packed space of the panicked in front of them. She picked up a waiter's tray at her feet and jumped over heads into a small space between bodies. Using the tray to prod and batter, she yanked, pulled, and pushed people away until she, with Lynn at her back, was through the door.

Outside, as guests swarmed around her, Jenny spotted a man in a white shirt and black slacks vaulting onto a waiting Powersports-MC motorcycle with another, dressed the same, coming on behind him. About twenty feet ahead of her, the driver turned and beamed at Jenny, who instantly recognized his oval face and pointed chin and beard. Lynn blocked for her against the screaming crowd to give her room, and, with a sidearm motion, Jenny flung the tray at the passenger as she had the discus when in school. It struck him square in the back, he howled with blood shooting from his mouth, and fell back, sprawling onto the Connecticut Avenue asphalt as the driver roared away, indifferent to the loss of his companion.

Jenny started to run towards the fallen fugitive when she was seized by half a dozen armed men, screaming at her. "Don't move! Don't move!"

Jenny untensed at once and let them grab her. "Not moving. Not moving." Out of the corner of her eye, she could see they had Lynn too.

"Well, look who it is!" a familiar voice observed.

"Mitch! Is that you?" she sputtered, trying to twist to free her face to talk. "Let me explain!"

"You don't need to, Jenny," the man said wearily while looking at the twisted body in the street. "Only you would do something like that." He noticed Lynn. "You two, I mean. Rizzoli and Isles!"

JENNY AND LYNN WERE sitting on the floor just outside the suddenly deserted kitchen surrounded by Mitch and other federal agents, who were supposedly keeping eyes on them, although Mitch was the only one not on a cell phone. He was fortyish with a hangdog face and a rumpled suit.

Lynn heard one of them insisting to someone on the other end of his call, "We all protested about the size of the crowd. But someone musta had pull."

Other agents, security guards, and bodyguards were bringing guests back into the ballroom for interviews. Flat television screens showed that news of "an incident" was being broadcast, only without details. Jenny and Lynn used hotel kitchen towels to wipe their feet, which were covered with salad and scratches from the knives and forks on the tables. The bartender was moving through the agents handing them coffee in cardboard cups when he recognized Lynn and waved.

Lynn smiled up at the blond, muscled, former lifeguard and nodded. "Hi, Alex." Then she burbled to Jenny, "Believe it or not, he may be the only friend we have here."

"I do believe. I do, I do." Jenny projected up to Mitch, "We under arrest?"

"Not yet, Jenny." Mitch chuckled. "But maybe. Question is still open."

Lynn entreated, "Can I go check on my family?"

"Sure. With an escort." He gestured to one of his team to take her.

As Lynn and her shadow walked away, Jenny asked, "Still with the FBI, Mitch?"

"Yeah," he answered. "Three more years before retirement. Tell me, I understand the fact you're here because of Lynn's sister's wedding and you and Lynn are bridesmaids—"

"She's the maid of honor, I'm a bridesmaid—"

Annoyed, he snapped, "Who cares! I was asking why did you—"

"Jump on the tables?"

"Would you let me finish! I was going to say, 'get involved.'"

"Look, you got him, didn't you? If we hadn't gone after them, you wouldn't have this one. He'll be able to give you some information."

"If he lives," Mitch snorted. "He's in a coma with a fractured spine and only has a fifty-fifty chance. We're running facial recognition on him—"

"Don't bother," Jenny interrupted, again. "The driver—and shooter— was Davido Ter Arturio, and the other guy was his frequent collaborator Pasquale Sparafucile."

One of the agents heard her, hung up on his caller, and repeated the names into his cell. Mitch asked, suspiciously, "You've encountered them?"

"Oh, yeah. Hired killers. Thirty victims so far. Mostly in Europe. We've tussled—twice."

Mitch roared, "So that's it! They were settling old scores, shot at you, missed, and killed the special peace ambassador to the Middle East, creating an international incident!"

"Oh, come on, Mitch! Ter Arturio is the assassin the devil dreams of. He doesn't miss. He shot the ambassador center chest with what sounded like a suppressed FNX 45 Technical from four hundred feet! The big questions here are, how did he and Sparafucile get in and through metal detectors without detection, who hired them, and how was a motorcycle waiting for them in a building teeming with armed security inside and out?"

He started to walk away. "Tell me something I don't know."

"Look, Mitch." She stood up suddenly without asking permission. "Lynn and I have got this. You know that we have a reputation for success."

Mitch stopped his exit as if remembering. "Yeah. Like Cagney and Lacey."

Jenny took his arm and leaned in. "Here's my proposition. You're leading a patched-together unit doing the immediate steps of searching for Ter Arturio, alerting the appropriate agencies, gathering evidence, interviewing guests, and taking temporary jurisdiction from the local police. Within the hour, the whole question of jurisdiction for this will have been settled, and you'll no longer be in charge. Give us fifty minutes and a cell phone, let us gather a select group of guests together, and we will solve this for you. You'll be a hero, Mitch. Lynn and I—we're just bridesmaids."

Mitch dipped his head slightly, acknowledging that Jenny was accepting his broader, masculine terminology.

In the ballroom, Robin was leaning her floral-embroidered fanny against the wall while her mother and father remained at their table. "Well, this isn't going well."

"You're still married, Robin," her mother reminded her. "That's something."

"Sure. Anybody seen him?"

"I think he's with his mom."

Lynn, leaving her escort behind, ran up to them. "Mom and Dad! How are you?"

"We're fine, dear," her father assured her. "You two were—very impressive. Marvelously acrobatic," he said with a twinkle in his eye. "And evidently effective. The word is floating around this commune that you got 'em."

"Well, one of them."

"Proud of you both." He winked. His expression became troubled, and he summoned her with an inward flick of his hand to lean in and speak into her ear.

Lynn nodded and whispered back, "I'll tell Jenny." Lynn turned to Robin, who was still leaning against the wall. "And how are you doing, Robin?"

Her sister pushed herself off the wall and responded with a weak smile. Lynn braced herself for a bombast. It appeared to be coming. "When you two jumped on the tables, I said to myself, 'There they go again, taking charge when it's not even their party.' Running on tables! I said to myself, 'We're ruined with the Beckmans!' But then I realized—that's who you are. You take care of people. You jump in when no one else does. You take care of us. You're the good guys!"

Lynn nodded, gratified. "I saw you did a good job yourself of taking care of Mom and Dad."

"Must be in the blood." Robin moved forward and wrapped her laced arms around her sister.

Lynn squeezed her tightly but then felt tears streaming down the back of her neck. Pushing Robin back, Lynn held her sobbing face in her hands. "Robin!" She didn't think she had seen her sister cry since she was ten.

"I'm so sorry!" Robin stumbled over chair legs to embrace her mother and father in one big hug. "I'm so sorry I caused this to happen to you. I was so stupid. I should have listened to you."

Just then, Jenny rushed up. "Everybody good?" Robin turned around to her and, seeing her face, Jenny muttered, "I guess not."

"No," Lynn told her. "I think we're surprisingly okay."

"If you say so." Jenny took her arm and began budging her away. "We have to go. We're making a presentation in fifteen minutes."

"To whom?" Lynn squeaked, waving goodbye to her parents and sister while being dragged backwards.

"A bunch of people in the state ballroom."

"What's my job?"

"You're playing percussion."

THE PRESENTATION MEETING was for a select group of guests numbering fifty-nine: senators, House members, cabinet members, law enforcement and security personnel, three older women, Mrs. Beckman, Mr. and Mrs. Russell, and the bride and groom. Mitch's team was stationed outside the closed door.

The room was half the size of the main ballroom. It also had automatic dividers. But these had reduced the size of the space further to accommodate the small group lined up in three rows as well as the band equipment that was set up for an evening Rotary Club event that had been cancelled because of the shooting.

Jenny and Lynn entered, and Lynn sat at the drums while Jenny remained standing. "Hello," Jenny began, conversationally. "I wish I could say, 'Good Afternoon,' but it hasn't been, has it? I apologize for our appearance." She gestured to their bare legs and feet and wine- and food-stained gowns. "But, as I think most of you saw, we had to move quickly a while ago."

A few began to applaud, and others quickly joined in. Jenny instinctively bowed her head in response.

"We're going to try and help law enforcement close this case quickly by answering three questions. First, how did the shooter and his colleague enter an incredibly secure ballroom filled with law enforcement and get through metal detectors with a gun? Second, who hired them? And third, how was a motorcycle so easily waiting for them outside?" Winking at her, Jenny added, "Lynn, by the way, will stay at the drums and accompany me to accentuate key points."

There was a buzz of confused chatter among the group. Mitch jumped up with his political hat figuratively but firmly on. "But we want to make it clear that we are not here to embarrass or insult anyone—"

"Actually," Jenny cut him off, "while we are not here to insult anybody, we have no doubt that someone will be embarrassed. Mrs. Beckman!"

The elegantly coiffed and clad matriarch in the third and last row with her son to her left and Cardinal Broccoli to her right at the end looked up with a start. "Yes?"

"Your first name is Gertrude, isn't it?"

"I confess," she said evenly and deadpanned. "It—is. And I'm not embarrassed."

"Good! But the evening's still young," Jenny replied quickly and similarly without emotion. "How 'bout this? At the table behind us just before the shot was fired, I heard a woman say that Gertrude had borrowed $1,000 from her in cash because she had no money on her. During the interviews security conducted after the shooting, the woman was identified as Mrs. Alice Barker, and she agreed that that Gertrude was you and that the need for funds was significant given other behavior and incidents. Isn't that right, Mrs. Barker?" Jenny turned to a diminutive woman clad in black and silver seated uncomfortably in the front row.

Mrs. Barker looked back nervously at Mrs. Beckman, clearly worried about future payback, especially since the matriarch's eyes were smoldering. "Yes," she finally squawked.

"So what!" Mrs. Beckman snapped. "I left the house without money. Happens to everybody!"

"On the day of a wedding for which you had already paid out $100,000? But that's assuming you did pay that. Mr. Russell rendered his $100,000 by check in person and noticed in signing the papers that your share for the same amount was paid by wire transfer by a company that is owned by an entity in Messina, Sicily. Isn't that right, Mr. Russell?"

Lynn's father rose, stood erect, and declared clearly and overly loudly, "Yes, it is, Jenny."

"We checked, and the Messina business is controlled by Uniti Sicilia, a criminal organization. Embarrassed yet, Mrs. Beckman?" Jenny nodded to Lynn who played a rim shot on the drum.

"Young lady!" The matriarch was flustered at Jenny's discovery and was also surprised by the drums. "You clearly do not understand how transactions between large corporations are handled—"

"Perhaps not," Jenny over-spoke her, "but the Organized Crime and Gang Division of the Justice Department, the Security and Exchange Commission, and the financial editors at Bloomberg do. It didn't take them long to summarize the situation for us. Your income is dependent on your oil operations overseas, which have been negatively affected by the civil wars in the Middle East. You are in debt, no banks would loan you money, only the Uniti Sicilia. For exorbitant interest, they have been paying your bills. They even encouraged you to pay half of the cost of this wedding and agreed to cover it for you so that you could control the guest list and they could control the list through you."

Mrs. Beckman was silent and seemed to shrivel in size—slightly but noticeably, as if her soul had been taken from her.

But Jenny piled on. "In addition to the interest, which has drained all your cash, these mobsters have forced you to transfer majority ownership in your properties to them. They're picking sides in the civil wars and using their oil operations for leverage. Special Ambassador Young was in their way. And so, in answer to the question, who authorized and planned the murder, the answer is, Uniti Sicilia." Jenny nodded to Lynn, who banged a rim shot.

"I can't believe it!" Mrs. Baxter exclaimed. "The Beckmans are in debt and consort with criminals! I suspected something but not this."

Jenny provided the eulogy. "It is sad that a prominent and fabled family should not only lose its fortune but trade away its sterling reputation. The odd thing is that it wasn't the Russells marrying into the Beckmans' money but the Beckmans marrying into the Russells'. Isn't that right, Gerard?"

He turned to his mother for help, but she was still just staring ahead. "Yes," he finally muttered. "She said Robin's father's eighty and that I'd get her share soon."

"Annulment," Lynn shouted, playing another rim shot. She quickly glanced over at Robin to see if she was angry. But her sister actually appeared amused and relieved.

Mitch stood up, slowly, reluctantly. "Jenny, that's all very interesting. I'll let our organized crime division know. But are you really saying that the Beckmans were part of the plan to kill Ambassador Young?"

"No, I'm not saying that—"

"Did they have anything to do with getting the two assassins in and through security?"

Jenny smirked at the thought. "No. They wouldn't do that. At least not directly. They gave Uniti Sicilia control of the invitation list. But if the Beckmans asked any questions, I am sure they were rebuffed." Jenny started to pace, moving closer to Lynn. "Which brings us back to Gerard."

His head bobbed up, creating a flurry of red. "Me again?"

"Yes, Gerard. Sorry." Jenny grinned at his discomfort. "I forgot to mention how nice it is not to see you in a crouched position." Lynn banged another rim shot, and there was tittering from those who had seen him hiding. "Gerard, I watched you hand Cardinal Broccoli an envelope right outside the hotel."

"Ah, yeah. Sure. Mummy—I mean, my mother gave it to me to give him. It had tips for the help."

"Did it really?" Jenny walked away from Lynn and closer to the audience to look directly at Gerard with Cardinal Broccoli on his left. The prelate's red robes stood out from the lighter colored clothing around him to where it was hard on her eyes. "You see, Gerard, that was the first thing that I saw today that looked off. There was the size of the envelope. What was that? Five thousand dollars? Ten thousand? Who were you tipping? The national guard? The Mormon Tabernacle Choir! That was the interest on the loan, wasn't it, Mrs. Beckman?"

She was long past answering questions and appeared lost in herself, revisiting her moments of pride, arrogance, and blindness to the needs of others.

"And you, Your Eminence—"

The cardinal's lips formed an almost imperceptible smile at Jenny's use of the proper term of address.

"Yes, I was raised Catholic—and still am. Your Eminence, wasn't it odd that you would walk around with so much money in the pocket of your robes? Not only was it careless but improper. You are, after all, an official of the Vatican—a sovereign nation. It would have been like handing the President of France $10,000 in the middle of the Champs-Élysées. It looks bad. I've seen bishops, archbishops, and cardinals offered a lot less money by the father of the bride or the widow at a funeral whom he then instructed to give it instead to his priest-secretary. But you didn't." The old man lifted his robed arms up as if to shrug. "And by the way," she pointed to Mitch, "has anybody seen the cardinal's two priests?"

"We haven't accounted for everybody. A dozen people are still unaccounted for, including them."

"Wanna bet one is in the hospital and that you're searching for the other? Buried in the crowd, they stripped off their cassocks and let them fall, leaving them in white shirts and black pants. Your Eminence, don't you do background checks in your business?"

Again, the cardinal offered a round smiling face and extended his flapping red arms helplessly. "I did not know them," he croaked in strained English. "They were assigned to me."

"Interesting. Because the credentials with which you and the two priests were allowed to enter this country state that they were of your household. I phoned an agent I know stationed in Sicily who called in a favor from the police in Messina. They visited Cardinal Broccoli's residence and found him, the two priests who serve as his secretaries, and the rest of his household tied up in the cellar."

Lynn banged the cymbal. Everyone except Mrs. Beckman and the cardinal jumped up in disbelief. The fake prelate continued smiling.

Jenny didn't let up. "Security went easy on you because you were a priest and because you were old. They took you to a separate line with the other dignitaries and patted you down delicately and mindlessly. I can think of few better places to hide a gun with a suppressor than in the voluminous folds of a cardinal's robes."

"Bravo!" the imposter boomed out as he applauded just as loudly. His voice, now robust, apologized. "My English is little. Therefore, I will show you." The once old man rose easily. He reached to his nose and removed the putty, then stripped away the false cheeks, the fake wrinkles under his eyes and on his forehead, and finally removed his wax jowls. In an instant, he pulled his robes over his head and flung them away. He was a man in his thirties, muscular and trim, wearing an undershirt and jeans. In his hand, he held a Sig Sauer P365. "If you can hide two, you can hide three," he explained.

Mitch started to pull out his weapon, and the impostor turned it to him. "Do not. And none of you move. Not even a very little bit." Bringing his gun back so it was aimed at Jenny, he said, "I will shoot her without question and as many of you as the cartridge will allow." He saw Alex who had come in with a tray of coffee and pointed at him with his left hand. "You! Give me your uniform! The brilliant but not sufficiently prepared agent here and her boss," gesturing to Mitch with a backward nod of his head, "will walk me out."

Alex stared at the man for just a second, and it wasn't apparent if his look signaled paralyzing fear, respect for the criminal's threat, or some form of recognition.

Those in the room continued watching the man with the gun. But, gradually, their attention shifted to the handsome bartender clad in just his jockey shorts tossing his uniform over to the impostor cardinal. In that moment, Lynn, her body partially hidden by the drum set, reached down to her thigh, bare from where she had torn her dress, where she had taped, in tribute to Jenny's thigh holster, a remote-control device, which, up to that moment, had been hidden by the drum set. The wall divider to the terrorist's left swung in front of the fake cardinal, and the one behind him blocked him in from the right. "*Danare*!" he shouted and began firing at the laminated partitions, only to scream having wounded himself with a deflected bullet. Mitch and three other security guards pushed the struggling mass of walls and brought it to the ground, pinning him. The pretender prelate was flopping around like a lobster in a bamboo cage.

"And that answers the question, how they got in," Jenny called out. "That leaves the one about the motorcycle, but that's enough for now." Jenny made the gesture of dusting her hands off as Lynn banged her final cymbal clash.

The imposter cardinal was handcuffed and escorted out of the room, followed by Mrs. Beckman and her son, who, although not bound, hung their heads down as if they were. Gerard didn't even look at Robin, whose smiling attention was focused on Alex putting his uniform back on as fast as he could. Mitch answered his phone, hung up, and informed Jenny, "The task force to capture those responsible has been formed, and I am relieved of command."

"Well, when the new commander arrives you can turn those you are holding over to him. Or her?"

"Him. Of course."

"So, you're a hero."

"And Lynn and you are just bridesmaids. Still have to get Ter Arturio, though."

"Like they say, the evening's still young. I told you that the last time he left this country he utilized a commuter train, Amtrak, a Greyhound bus, a stolen car to Canada, a bus to Ottawa, a freighter to Greenland, and something else—we don't know what—to Lisbon. His pattern of escape is that he has no pattern of escape," Jenny concluded. "But, while his mission succeeded, the capture of his associates and the exposure of his client could make his survival—iffy."

As Jenny and Lynn walked down the plush red carpet of the grand staircase, they noticed that the hotel lobby was suddenly deserted and still except for the shussing sound of a vacuum and broom removing the debris left by temporarily imprisoned wedding guests and law enforcement who didn't believe in recycling. Suspects and key witnesses had been carted off. Wedding guests who were not registered at the hotel and even most of those who were had fled the scene as soon as they were released for home, plane, or train. Non-wedding hotel guests had not been allowed to register and, consequently, decided to find shelter elsewhere. There were still a few federal agents around in the ballroom, which was sealed off with yellow tape. But compared to early afternoon, the place seemed empty of people.

Jenny and Lynn walked to the registration desk where the manager was minding the store after the storm. His blue suit was pressed and dressed to sparkle, and his Poirot mustache waxed to tusk-point perfection. "Are you still in business?" Jenny joked, mostly.

The manager took no offense. "As much as possible."

Lynn assumed command. "We're with the Russell wedding party. We were scheduled to stay overnight. Do we still have rooms?"

"You do!" He tapped at the computer to print out keys. "You have been upgraded to suites, and there will be no charge for your stay. We know what you did today and appreciate it. If you had not, we would be closed a week rather than opening tomorrow—as soon as the police finish their work in the ballroom. As it is, our advance business is doing well—murder scenes do that."

"I admire your business approach," Jenny said.

"There are two complimentary suites—your parents in one, you two and the bride in the other. She wasn't planning on staying, of course, but her plans have clearly changed. Meals are included and will be served in your suite since our restaurant is closed until breakfast. It shouldn't surprise you that your dinner will consist of the food from the wedding dinner. What remains after guests are served will go to the poor."

"Good plan!"

He handed Jenny the room access card and turned to Lynn. "Oh, and, Miss Russell, I told your father about the complicated situation. The authorities are reclaiming the one hundred thousand dollars that Mrs. Beckman had transferred to us from Sicily. I regretfully informed Mr. Russell that he would be liable for the total amount. And he informed us—"

"That he would not be held responsible for the cost of a wedding reception that did not take place, citing the doctrine of impossibility that prevents the contract from being fulfilled. Sounds like my dad."

"Which is what our lawyer told us he would say. They advised us to return his check." The manager shrugged and smiled. "The way it goes."

Lynn and Jenny ambled to the elevator. "Good for Dad! He's the only one who came out ahead today."

"And Mitch and the District of Columbia food kitchens."

"Yeah, and we get to room with Robin!"

"Swell." Jenny sighed. "Girls' night in."

"Excuse me, Lynn?" They turned to see Alex seeming timid and uncertain of what to say. "I—I—ah—just want to thank you—thank you both—for saving my life today."

"Well." Lynn shrugged it off. "It never got that bad. But it could have. You're welcome. Take care of yourself."

The elevator door opened, and Lynn started to move to it. But Alex hadn't finished. "I'd also like to make a confession."

"Well," said Jenny. "Since a fraudulent cardinal performed a wedding today, I guess two women could hear a confession."

"After Robin dumped me, I was really hurt and mad. I was playing basketball at the YMCA on Rhode Island Avenue with a guy who was staying there, and I began mouthing off about her, her family, the wedding, being just a bartender. He got very interested in Robin's family and the St. Ives and bought me a drink."

"I see." Jenny was already ahead of him. "Did he have an oval face, and a pointed beard?"

"Yeah. And he played lousy."

"He doesn't have time to practice. Did he ask you if there was a place to park a motorcycle where no one would see it to steal?"

"Yeah, as a matter of fact, he did. And I showed him this recessed place in the shadows of the hotel building. After what happened today, I realized who he was—"

"And that's how they hid the motorcycle," Jenny crowed. "Questions answered. Over and done. Lynn, please call Mitch and tell him Ter Arturio may be hiding in plain sight at the YMCA—where he has a room and is a familiar face."

As Lynn turned away, Jenny said to Alex, "Thank you. That could be a big help. Hey, why don't you have dinner with the family upstairs in our suites—"

Alex almost jumped back he was so alarmed. "No! I don't think so! I wouldn't want to do that. I'm sure Robin wouldn't want it either. And—even if she did—" He panted in his effort to explain, gave up and said, as simply as he could put it, "Like I said, she really hurt me. And I can't forget it." He took several steps back and then spun around and away.

Lynn returned laughing at her call with Mitch. "He's done his press conference with the new commander and was preparing for a television interview on CBS about his great capture this afternoon. But now he's postponed it to rush to the YMCA and possibly have another bit of breaking news." She caught the look of sadness on Jenny's face. "What happened? Are we fired?"

Jenny's answer was to walk over and hug her. "I was just thinking of how lucky and blessed your folks and people like them are in their relationships."

Lynn thought she understood but didn't know about Alex. "I'm sorry for Robin too. Oh, she'll laugh it off. But she didn't feel she could marry Alex, jumped into Gerard's greedy and unloving little arms, and ended up in a mess. Relationships are hard—and elusive. Shakespeare had Romeo say, 'Love is heavy and light, bright and dark, hot and cold, sick and healthy, asleep and awake—everything except what it is.'"

"And what did another old man say, that true love 'sweetens the breath with honey, brightens the eyes so that they actually begin to glow, and strengthens the spine so that it can endure any adversity'?" Jenny suddenly remembered something. "You know what! I just realized from what I said to Alex about confession! We don't need to get Robin an annulment."

"Why?"

"The priest at her wedding was a fake, so she's not married, just humiliated. Come on, we'll sit up with her, watch rom coms on cable TV, and eat wedding cake while sitting on the floor. We may have to take a more active role in her romances."

"Yeah," Lynn agreed. "I hope it has lousy job security." They renewed their path to the elevator. "You know, death was the surprise wedding guest today. Bad for Ambassador Young, of course. But unexpectedly good for Robin. Maybe next time, the surprise guest at her wedding will be—love."

We Haven't Had Cake
Sharyn Kolberg

Earlier in the evening, standing at the altar in front of friends and family members, the bride and groom had made promises to each other. But that was hours ago, and things had changed since then. Now here they sat, still enrobed in their wedding finery, thinking about what the future might hold, wondering if the whole evening had been a mistake.

The bride had realized after everything that had happened at the wedding that she didn't really know the groom at all. Where had he come from? He had appeared in her life out of the blue and taken her by surprise. She hadn't been looking for love—although realistically, wasn't everyone looking for love? When he showed up, however, there was love, knocking her over with a one-two punch. She had fallen quick and hard.

If she had been knocked over, he had been gently shoved. It had taken him a while to recognize love's impact, but when he did, he rushed in with his typical all-or-nothing action-oriented bull-in-a-china-shop style and they were married within three months of his proposal.

It was a beautiful wedding. Much nicer than his first, the one he had neglected to mention to his bride-to-be. It was the kind of thing that was difficult to bring up if you didn't confess to it at the get-go. He didn't think he was being dark or devious by not saying anything. He thought he was being kind.

"I SUPPOSE WE SHOULD talk about it," he said, breaking their silence.

"Ya think?"

"She made a heck of an entrance, didn't she?" he said. "After all these years."

"She certainly knows how to garner attention," she said, looking him straight in the eye. "Why didn't you ever tell me you were married before? And to *her*, of all people."

"*Garner attention*? Who says garner attention? What are you, a dictionary?" He grinned, hoping to relieve her uneasiness. He knew how much she loved to play word games, how she prided herself on her vocabulary even if it did sometimes make her sound old-fashioned or erudite, a word he could barely pronounce. He never let a moment of pretentiousness pass by without calling her out on it later. It was a game they played and one of the little things that surprisingly brought them together.

She resisted the snarky retort she had at the tip of her tongue and instead closed her eyes and sighed. "I'm not in the mood for your little games right now," she said. "I just meant that she knew how to make an entrance, she and her clone shining like disco balls. Not to mention that she came in spouting lines like she was still on the set of that stupid soap opera."

"*Thunder and Lightning*. She played Raven Thunder."

"And that's who you were married to? Raven Thunder?"

"She wasn't Raven Thunder when I married her. She was Ginny Jacobs. She signed her soap contract and our divorce papers the same day. She never told me about the kid."

The 'kid' looked to be about 12 years old. She was the spitting image of her mom, especially dressed alike as they were—silver lamé gowns, matching kitten heels and a parade of diamond studs in each ear. They hadn't been invited, but they had sparkled their way into the ballroom like two Disney princesses out of time and out of place.

The bride was shocked; the groom embarrassed. They had been in the middle of the YMCA dance when the soap star and her mini-me stormed in. The soap star signaled to the DJ to cut off the music, which left the newlyweds and their guests standing on the dance floor like a Studio 54 museum exhibit, arms extended high in the "Y" position.

As the dancers scurried back to their seats, the soap star began shouting.

"Where is he? Let the scoundrel show his face!"

'The scoundrel' and the bride had lowered their arms, but remained on the dance floor while Thunder kept up with her rant.

"You!" she screeched, staring at the groom. "You're nothing but a lousy deadbeat dad. Have you ever paid a single penny in child support? Ever?"

"Child support? I never even knew I had a child!"

"Well, here she is in the flesh," she said, grabbing the girl by the shoulders and pushing her in the groom's direction. The girl, now standing under a ballroom chandelier that illuminated her many-studded ears and supplied her with a flattering but eerie halo effect, pointed her phone in the groom's direction. In fact, everyone in the room—family, friends, and wait staff—had pulled their phones out of their pockets or purses. The party planner pulled her phone from out of her cleavage, dropping some tissues and a copy of the evening's menu in the process, on the back of which was written "If Buddy's killer was on his payroll, the knife was used." Everyone was now holding their phone aloft, hurriedly pressing record.

The startled bride was doing her best to take control of this sudden turn of events. "Please get out," she begged. "Go away. Go home. It's my wedding. We haven't even had cake."

The groom continued to argue that it was impossible for him to have contributed to a child's upkeep when he hadn't known she existed. The soap star seemed to think that was a minor detail. The groom was getting louder with every passing moment, yelling at the intruders to leave him the heck alone as they were ruining his wedding and his life. He used a tone of voice the bride had never heard before. She didn't like it at all, even if she agreed with his sentiments. She stayed in the background, weeping and hiccupping.

The soap star grabbed her daughter's hand and dragged her out, dramatically declaring to the bride and groom and everyone within earshot that they hadn't heard the last of her.

AT HOME LATER THAT evening, the bride was still wearing her

blush-colored corseted wedding dress and sole-killing heels. The groom was in his tux, his hand-crafted Spanish patent leather lace-ups just the slightest bit snug. They were both uncomfortable in oh, so many ways, but neither wanted to talk about it.

They yawned, simultaneously. She giggled. He grinned. They'd both had too much to drink, even though the wedding had ended earlier than planned. She was too tired to even think about the night's events. She let her husband—a word that was foreign to her ears—answer the doorbell when it rang.

The soap star and her daughter were still dressed in their silver splendor.

"Come on in, you two," he said, leading them into the living room where the sleepy bride sat. She woke up.

He turned toward the soap star. "Did it work?" he asked.

She laughed. "Just like we planned," she said, grabbing her daughter's hand. "Right, Baby? I knew it wouldn't take long for everyone at the wedding to send their videos to everyone they know. And now..."

Her daughter interrupted and boasted, "It's going viral!" Her mood changed as she turned to look at her mother. "I asked you not to call me Baby anymore. My name is Blue."

"Okay, Blue. I'll try and remember," she said as she plucked her phone out of her pocket. "Let's watch this thing."

The young girl, the groom and the soap star huddled around Thunder's phone. The bride stood in the background, trying to make sense of what was happening. The soap star and the girl had ruined her wedding and the groom had known it was going to happen? How could he have done this to her?

"Why?" she said to the trio staring at the video, laughing and clapping. She looked at her husband. "Why would you play such a nasty trick on me?"

The soap star answered, "Don't you get it? This thing is going to go all over the world. I'll be back in the spotlight. Blue will become an influencer. I can see it all ahead of us, clear as day."

Thunder and Blue weren't the only ones hoping for a big payout. The groom had been promised a steady income stream from the soap star when she and her daughter started raking in the money from sponsors and affiliates. The groom wasn't exactly sure how this was supposed to work, but Blue assured them she knew what she was doing.

The groom explained to his bride that he had been reluctant to go along with the scheme, especially when he, Blue and Thunder had decided not to let her in on the plan until after the wedding. She wasn't a very good actress—or liar—and would probably have given the whole thing away. He knew she'd be angry about being left out of the loop but he also knew she'd get over it when she heard about the big money payoff.

All four watched the video again. Blue and her mother laughed loudly. The bride turned toward Thunder. "How does this help us?" she asked. "You seem a little crazy, it's true, but it makes us look like the bad guys. I look like a total wimp and he comes off like a jerk and a reprobate."

"I'm not a reprobate, Miss Dictionary Head."

"What are you, twelve? No offense, Blue."

"That's okay," said Blue. "What's a reprobate?"

"A bum who leaves his family in the lurch," said Thunder. "Like your real dad."

"Wait. What?" said the bride, staring at her husband. "You're not really her father?"

He had the decency to blush. "Um, no."

"I can't believe this!" she said. "I can't believe I married such a blockhead."

"You mean me?"

"No, I mean George Clooney. I'm not like you—I've told you about everyone else I've married. Which is no one, you idiot!"

"Okay, okay, everybody calm down," said the soap star. "Listen to this. It's only been a couple of hours and we've already gotten more than 25,000 hits. You and I are gonna get rich from this, Blue, I can feel it."

"And famous," Blue added.

"And famous."

"You and Blue are gonna get rich and famous? What about me and Hubby? We're gonna end up in the stupid people's meme hall of fame. But right now, I'm too tired and too drunk to take any more of this. I'm going to bed." The bride stomped off and slammed the bedroom door behind her.

"That went well," said the groom.

Blue turned to the groom, handed him Thunder's phone and pointed at the video. "She just doesn't understand social media. When this vid plays out, we'll make another one and another one and everyone will follow us to see what we do next. We're all gonna be Kardashian rich. Mom promised."

"Well, if she promised..."

The soap star laughed. "I don't know about Kardashian rich, but we'll be a lot better off than we are now. And I'll be on a soap again in no time. Raven Thunder will be back on top!"

"Not if she's dead, she won't." They all turned their heads in the bride's direction as she stumbled in from the bedroom, a silver pistol in her hand. "Raven Thunder was killed off once. Now I can get rid of Ginny Jacobs. Then I guess you'll leave us alone." She knew she wasn't making any sense, but she didn't care. Which decision was worse—the one to marry someone she barely knew or the one she was about to make with a gun in her hand?

The groom was shocked to see his bride standing there, wedding dress all askew, brandishing a gun he didn't know she had. Maybe it was a mistake, he thought, to marry a woman he barely knew. He'd thought she would love the whole viral video idea, but apparently not. Apparently, she was going to kill them all. This whole plan was turning out to be a disastrous decision. He moved toward his bride, hoping to bridge both the physical and mental gap between them.

"Don't do it," he said, and held up the phone. "Look. We've now got almost 40,000 hits."

"Well, here's one more," said the bride as she shot the phone out of his hand. The groom howled in pain and rushed to the bathroom to look for bandages. The bride threw down the gun, laid down on the rug and cried and cried, her mascara bleeding black lines down her cheeks.

IN AN UNUSUAL MOVE, Ginny Jacobs knelt down to try and comfort the bride, while Blue wondered if the groom had been smart enough to hit record before the phone blew up.

To Have and To Scold
Becky Clark

Charlee Russo's eyes darted around the posh restaurant. She elbowed her best friend, AmyJo McFarland, seated next to her, whispering, "What in the world are we doing here?"

"I assume I'm here because Allegra thinks we're still joined at the hip, like in college." AmyJo studiously compared two forks at her place setting. "These look the same to me. Which am I supposed to use for my shrimp cocktail?"

"Just use your fingers." Charlee plucked one of the shrimps by its tail, dangled it above her mouth and took a big bite.

The mother of the bride suddenly loomed between them.

At her withering gaze, Charlee wanted to slide under the well-draped table.

"First of all, that's not shrimp cocktail, dear," she said disdainfully to AmyJo. "That's *cocktail di gamberetti*." From her exaggerated accent, it was clear to Charlee that she'd learned Italian from Mario Kart. "And second, use your seafood fork." She shook her head and pursed her lips. "Do try to fit in. This is only the rehearsal dinner. As Allegra's bridesmaids, you have much responsibility." She sashayed away, greeting people with air kisses on both cheeks.

All Charlee and AmyJo got was a haughty little sniff.

"Responsibility? Egads. I can't believe I said yes when Allegra asked me to be in her wedding," Charlee said.

"Why wouldn't you?"

"For starters, I've barely heard from her since we graduated."

"You haven't?" AmyJo asked. "I thought you'd kept in touch. I assumed you told her you wouldn't do it without me."

Charlee gaped at her friend. "I thought she asked me because *you* told her you wouldn't do it without *me*!"

They stared at each other for a beat, then turned their gaze to Allegra, the bride-to-be.

"She must have needed two more female bodies. And we were both already in Colorado, within driving distance of Aspen. I also said yes because I thought there might be other people from college and we'd get to have a mini-reunion. Remember how popular Allegra was? I wonder what happened," Charlee said.

AmyJo glanced around the restaurant. "Are we the only bridesmaids?"

"Oh, geez, I hope not!"

"She looks so bored." AmyJo gestured toward Allegra. She was standing off to the side of the room, staring at her phone.

"I guess when you grow up with money, you're not impressed with *cocktail di gamberetti*." Charlee mangled the Italian too.

"For the record, I'm not impressed either." AmyJo picked up the tiny, barely visible cocktail fork, using it to make useless incursions upon the shrimp. She cut her eyes at the strangers sitting around their table. When it was obvious nobody was paying them the slightest attention, AmyJo picked up a shrimp with her fingers then impaled it upon the fork.

As AmyJo chewed triumphantly, Charlee whispered again, "What are we *doing* here?"

THEY FINISHED EATING, then decided to mingle and make sure they weren't the only bridesmaids. But in case they were, they resolved to play rock-paper-scissors to see who had to be maid of honor. Neither thought it would be much of an honor. Allegra hadn't even spoken to them yet, and it seemed no rehearsal was imminent. They'd have to guess at their responsibilities—or maybe invent some—because they couldn't find Allegra anywhere.

They did see Liam, the groom, standing next to a young woman. They assumed he was the groom, anyway, since earlier they'd seen Allegra kiss him behind the tall ficus plant near the restrooms.

"Let's go introduce ourselves," Charlee said. "Find out if we're the only bridesmaids."

As they approached, the groom's eyes grew wide then darted around the room. Before they reached him, he bolted. He moved so fast Charlee didn't even have time to call after him.

She and AmyJo reached the woman he'd been chatting with. "What was that all about?" Charlee asked.

The woman glanced after him. "Guess he's shy."

"He was talking to you," AmyJo pointed out.

"Yeah, I guess he was," she said. She began searching the area around them.

"Did you lose something?" Charlee asked.

"What?"

"Are you looking for something?"

"My glasses."

"Those?" Charlee pointed to the top of her head.

The woman pulled them from her head and stared at them like she'd never seen them before. After a bit she said, "Thanks," and walked away.

"Do you know where Allegra is?" Charlee called.

The woman didn't stop, so Charlee hurried after her, tapping her on the shoulder.

Charlee repeated her question.

She frowned. "What?"

"I'm Charlee and this is AmyJo. We're bridesmaids."

"I'm Ellory." She walked away, stowing her glasses on top of her head again.

Charlee and AmyJo raised eyebrows at each other.

"Doesn't your brother always call you Space Case?"

Charlee nodded.

"I think you've got competition."

Charlee stared after Ellory. "What do you think they were talking about when we walked up. They were standing awfully close and he sure ran away fast."

"You don't think they—"

"I'm being ridiculous. My imagination is working overtime." But Charlee wasn't so sure.

A server walked by with a tray holding tiny glasses of Amaretto. They each accepted one and stood sipping, watching the crowd. Allegra was nowhere. The rehearsal dinner was elegant, but not much fun. Most of the guests appeared to be friends of Allegra's parents, and the younger ones didn't appear to want to cut loose and dance to a string quartet playing Mozart. The actual rehearsal never happened.

"Do you think we can leave yet?" AmyJo said.

"We've presented ourselves for rehearsal and dinner, so I think our obligations as bridesmaids have been met. But let's go that way." Charlee pointed to an inconspicuous side door.

They stepped through the doorway and almost ran into two women about their age who had their heads together, whispering. They stopped immediately, but not before Charlee heard one of them say, "Allegra's car."

The women stared at Charlee and AmyJo as they passed. At the end of the hall, Charlee glanced over her shoulder. They were still staring.

"This is gearing up to be a great weekend," Charlee muttered.

THE WEDDING DIDN'T begin until four o'clock the next afternoon, but Allegra's mother had emailed, texted, and hand-delivered the precise schedule for the day. Charlee found it had been slid under the door of the room she and AmyJo shared at the exquisite inn rented out just for the bridal party. The groomsmen had their own posh digs at the other end of Aspen, closer to the ski slopes, although skiing was off the menu in June.

AmyJo padded out to the living area of their room, squinting at her phone. "Who texts this early?" she grumbled.

"Allegra's mom. It's in writing for easy reference, too. Our entire day planned out to the microsecond." Charlee handed AmyJo the paper. "Heads up, though. No mention of when we're allowed bathroom breaks or our one free phone call."

AmyJo plopped on the couch and began reading the schedule. "Group yoga. Mimosas and muffins. Presentation of bridesmaids' gifts."

"We were supposed to buy her gifts? Because we're her bridesmaids?" Charlee rubbed her temples with her fingertips.

"I think she bought gifts for us, to thank us for being bridesmaids. Maybe you need coffee?" AmyJo said gently. She continued reading. "Arrange gifts for photos. Mud masks. Shower. Hair. Makeup. Morning stroll while Allegra writes her vows."

"After we're all made up?"

AmyJo shrugged. "Rich people don't sweat."

"Is food anywhere on that list? I won't make it to the reception on just mimosas and muffins."

AmyJo shook the paper at her. "Luncheon," AmyJo dragged out the word, "is after the stroll. Then Photographs while dressing."

"*While* dressing? Kinky."

"Get this. Then we each sit down for an interview."

"With who?" Charlee asked.

"Whom." Again, AmyJo affected a tone and drew the word out. "Some political reporter guy."

"Weird. An interview? With a politics guy?"

"Dunno. Maybe he got demoted to puff pieces. Then, it's the First Look with bridesmaids, bride's family photographs then—Wait." AmyJo's eyes widened. "Did that say group yoga?" She reread the schedule and groaned.

"I'm sure it's not mandatory."

AmyJo pointed at the heading on the schedule. "Mandatory activities."

CHARLEE AND AMYJO HEADED toward the grassy area near the pool where a group had gathered. Charlee recognized the two whispering women from the hallway, as well as Ellory and the groom, again, standing close together. There were also four older women, and two more men. They all wore yoga clothes.

Luckily Charlee slept in yoga pants and a t-shirt so she wore that.

AmyJo slept in Hello Kitty boxers and a sports bra. So she wore that.

"Perfect. We've been waiting for you two. Let's get started." The perky yoga instructor handed them each a yoga mat, two foam blocks, and a water bottle, all branded with the bride and groom's name.

AmyJo said, "I've gotta tell you I've never—"

"Okay, everyone. Let's meet in Down Dog."

"—done yoga before."

Charlee and AmyJo had barely rolled out their mats by the time the rest of the class was well into their Sun Salutations. As usual when late for a yoga class, the only space open was directly in front of the instructor. They followed along the best they could, struggling through the class for thirty minutes before collapsing in a heap on their mats.

Charlee glanced behind them and saw the men and the older women had disappeared. The two whispering women from the hallway last night were whispering again. The one who mentioned Allegra's car sat on her mat rubbing her ankle. The other one held her low back. Two more yoga casualties.

Charlee guzzled water while fanning herself with her ponytail. AmyJo dumped her water directly over her head, soaking her sports bra in the process. At Charlee's judgy look she defiantly grabbed her ample breasts. "Steamy girls are dreamy girls."

Charlee snorted.

The instructor finally realized she was the only one still in vinyasa flow. Her voice trailed off. Flustered, she gathered up her bag and hurried away.

The class groaned on their mats, trying to recover. As everyone collected themselves and their gear, Charlee heard the whisperer say, "I think I really hurt my ankle. I'm not sure I'll be able to walk down the aisle later." Her friend helped her hobble away.

Charlee and AmyJo veered away from the group to return to their room.

"Where are you going? All six bridesmaids this way!" Ellory called after them, waving the schedule. "We're three minutes late to Mimosas and Muffins. C'mon!"

"Three minutes, oh no," AmyJo said sarcastically under her breath.

But they turned and followed her to the lounge.

Allegra was already there and greeted them with tall champagne flutes of mimosas. "Nice outfit," she said to AmyJo with a good-natured laugh.

"You should wear that to the ceremony." AmyJo laughed. "I'm serious. All eyes would be on you."

Charlee took a sip. "Peach. Yum."

AmyJo coughed. "And strong."

"Help yourself to the muffins." Allegra waved toward a table and Charlee made a beeline for it.

Surprised to find only a dozen blueberry mini-muffins in a grocery store plastic clamshell, she simply stared. When AmyJo joined her, Charlee whispered, "That's only two for each bridesmaid. And none for Allegra."

As she placed her allotted mini-muffins on a napkin, AmyJo said, "Maybe they won't want any."

"We can only hope." Charlee plucked her two muffins, popping one in her mouth immediately. "These will not hold me until lunch. I'll end up fainting during the wedding. You'll catch me, right?"

"Not if I faint first."

"That's fair. Last one standing does the catching."

They mingled over mimosas, getting the opportunity to meet the other bridesmaids.

Fiona and Bianca were the whisperers. They made no effort to move from the couch, but introduced themselves as cousins.

"It must have been nice for Allegra to grow up with cousins her own age," AmyJo said.

Fiona pointed at herself and then at Bianca. "*We're* cousins."

"How do you know Allegra?" Bianca didn't look up. She had a bag of ice on her ankle. Fiona sat next to her, punching a pillow and squirming around, trying to get comfortable. It seemed to Charlee Bianca didn't care about her question; she'd simply asked out of politeness.

"She and AmyJo and I went to college together," Charlee said.

Allegra returned with more mimosas, eyes popping wide. "Bianca! Are you okay? What happened?"

Bianca waved away her concern. "Just twisted my ankle during yoga. I'll be okay."

"Was the class too strenuous? I'm sorry I didn't get there in time."

"No worries. I just surrendered into the pose a little too much."

AmyJo rolled her shoulders. "I had trouble smiling through my collarbone."

"Goodness. I hope everyone is okay for the wedding." Allegra handed around the mimosas then tucked the empty tray under her arm. "Fiona, can you please help me with something?" The two of them walked away.

Bianca returned her attention to her ankle.

Charlee and AmyJo took the hint and walked over to Ellory standing in front of the table staring at the muffins.

"Don't stuff yourself," Charlee said.

She jumped. "What? I didn't—"

"Sorry. I was just kidding." Charlee leaned in conspiratorially. "Kinda thought there'd be a more lavish spread after that dinner last night." She gestured toward AmyJo. "We've already had our quota, so you go ahead."

Ellory stared at the bare table. "I could have sworn I ordered full-sized muffins. I meant to, anyway. And fruit. And a cheese plate." She plucked a mini-muffin and took four bites to eat it.

Charlee filed this away to use as a character trait in one of the mysteries she wrote.

"How do you know Allegra? We went to college with her." AmyJo eyed the muffins.

"Our mothers are friends."

Fiona bustled toward them carrying yet another tray of mimosas. "Bottoms up, ladies!"

They finished their mimosas and exchanged full ones for the empties. Fiona swooshed away, delivering cocktails to the others.

AmyJo took a sip. "Wow. Even stronger."

Ellory had wandered away, but they remained near the table, both eyeing the muffins.

Suddenly Charlee picked up the clamshell and began offering muffins around the room to the other bridesmaids. She returned to the table and AmyJo. "No takers. I say we can have another."

"How decadent." AmyJo plucked another muffin and ate it in one bite.

Charlee attempted four bites, but only made it to two.

"I met the other bridesmaid." Charlee pointed.

"The yoga instructor who tried to kill us? She's a bridesmaid?"

"Her name is Decolletage."

"Decolletage?"

"Decolletage. I made her spell it for me. No accent."

"Oh my gosh!" AmyJo guffawed. "I just realized Allegra alphabetized her bridesmaids. AmyJo, Bianca, Charlee, Decolletage, Ellory, and Fiona."

"That's crazy!"

Fiona came by with fresh mimosas.

"Are you trying to get us drunk?" Charlee laughed, but drained her drink and took another. "Hey. Are the groomsmen's names alphabetical too?"

"What are you talking about?"

AmyJo pointed at each bridesmaid alphabetically and said their name.

Fiona shrugged and continued delivering mimosas.

Allegra stuck her head in the lounge and Charlee called her over.

"What are the groomsmen's names? Did you do that on purpose or was it just luck? I'm dying to know."

Allegra looked perplexed. "I have no clue." Bianca called to her and she hurried away.

Charlee and AmyJo sipped their drinks.

Finally, Charlee tipped her chin in Allegra's direction. "No clue what their names are, or no clue if it was just luck?"

"Or just no clue what we're talking about. She does have other things on her mind, after all." AmyJo laughed. "It would be hilarious if she had no idea who the guys in her wedding were." She looked at Charlee. "Do you know all of Ozzi's friends?"

"How in the world am I supposed to know that? It's like asking someone why they didn't get your email."

"Or if the refrigerator light stays on when the door is closed."

"Or if you decide to be indecisive, are you?"

"Or if you have fun wasting time, is it wasted time?"

"Who knew we were so cerebral?" Charlee blinked hard. "I can't decide if we've had too much to drink, or not enough."

"Definitely not enough." Fiona appeared and poured champagne into the flutes they already held. When they tried to protest, she said, "It's Allegra's wedding day! Anything goes!"

Charlee glanced around. "Where'd Allegra go?"

"No idea." Fiona swigged right out of the bottle then clinked the bottle against their glasses. "Happy wedding!"

She topped off the other glasses and Charlee noticed that the undiluted champagne had a direct effect on the volume in the room.

Someone turned on some music. Charlee helped herself to another mini-muffin and began to dance with AmyJo.

After they killed a couple more bottles, Allegra returned to present each bridesmaid with an envelope of assorted gift cards. Mostly coffee places and fast food.

Charlee and AmyJo high-fived. "Score!"

The other women seemed not to know exactly what they held in their hands.

"Rich people, amirite?" AmyJo said a tad too loudly to Charlee.

Allegra gathered everyone around to place the gift cards in some sort of creative display for the photographer.

To Charlee it looked like a scattering of gift cards on a table, but Allegra had a more discerning eye. She nudged a corner, rearranged slightly overlapping cards, and otherwise worked artistic sorcery on them. While she worked, the bridesmaids gathered around, Bianca leaning on Fiona. Everyone got into the spirit, clapping in rhythm and chanting, "Brides! Maids! Gift! Cards!" When Allegra stepped aside and offered the masterpiece with a flourish, the lounge erupted in cheers. "My mother will love this!"

The photographer was snapping away when Allegra's mother came in. "What is this?"

"Brides! Maids! Gift! Cards!" all the bridesmaids shouted.

"Are you ladies...drunk?"

"Don't be silly, Mummy! You wanted photos of the bridesmaids' gifts and we got good ones for your album!" At her raised eyebrows, the photographer nodded. Allegra scooped up the gift cards and handed them around, herding her bridesmaids from the room in front of her.

Charlee was the last. Allegra pulled her aside. "I'm relying on you to get everyone to the spa for mud masks. My mom was *adamant* about spa time. There's a car waiting out front. Here's the address." She pressed a piece of paper into Charlee's hand then disappeared.

Allegra's mother turned her attention to the bridesmaids in the hallway and clapped twice. "Mud mask time, ladies. You want to look your best for photos."

"Under control ma'am." Charlee wobbled and tried not to slur. "C'mon, ladies. Follow me to the mud." She turned and waved to Allegra's mother who gave her a terse nod in return.

THEY WERE HOPELESSLY late for their hair and makeup appointments after returning from the spa and showering. The spa had no record of any appointments being made for a bridal party. When Charlee called Allegra to tell her, she asked to speak to the person in charge. Charlee handed the phone over, apologizing with her eyes for what she expected to be a Bridezilla dressing down. But the owner of the spa listened to Allegra with a smile. "I'll take care of everything. Thank you." She handed back Charlee's phone and ushered them to a quiet room where she plied them with more champagne and readied them for full-body mineral mud wraps. By the time their mud was plastered on, none of them cared what time it was.

As they chatted, while being powerfully detoxified, exfoliated, and rejuvenated—something Charlee hadn't even known she needed—she found out that none of the bridesmaids were very close to Allegra. They all seemed as surprised as Charlee and AmyJo at being asked to be bridesmaids. Charlee couldn't help but feel sorry for Allegra. How had she gone from having a zillion friends in college to barely having any acquaintances just ten years later? And why did she want such a large bridal party? Six bridesmaids and six groomsmen were a lot.

Allegra's mother was waiting in the driveway of the inn when their car dropped them off. Her face was pinched and her lips practically invisible. "Where have you been?" She took one look at the somewhat muddy bridesmaids tumbling and stumbling from the car and accosted the driver instead, repeating, "Where have you been?"

The driver pointed at Charlee. "I went to the address she gave me," he said and quickly sped away.

Charlee shrugged. "Mud masks were on the schedule, but they upgraded us." She performed a woozy full-body gesture. "To unitards."

"That was supposed to be done onsite," she fumed.

Oh, that was the snafu, Charlee thought. Allegra must have smoothed everything over with the spa, protecting them from the wrath of her mother.

THE HAIR AND MAKEUP gals were in a tizzy by the time everyone staggered in, bridesmaids dresses askew. The bland apricot color made their complexions appear even more washed out than the alcohol had.

Charlee overheard one of the hairdressers whisper to another, "This wedding is cursed. I've never seen such a disorganized mess. It's like someone is sabotaging it."

While they waited their turn for beautifying, less pickled now, Charlee told AmyJo what she'd heard.

AmyJo thought it over. "Decolletage *did* try to kill us with yoga."

"And Fiona got us drunk," Charlee said. "And Ellory tried starving us to death."

"And you kidnapped us to the spa." At Charlee's panicked look, AmyJo quickly added, "According to Allegra's mother, anyway."

"Are you *kidding* me?" one of the hairdressers screeched. "I was promised they'd be here! What am I supposed to do now?"

"What's the matter?" Charlee asked.

"The tiaras. Nobody can find the tiaras!"

"Take a breath. We're on it!" Charlee pulled AmyJo's arm. "We'll find them."

They hurried from the room.

"Should we call Allegra?" AmyJo asked.

"She has enough to worry about. They've got to be around here some place. And I need to redeem myself for the spa."

Charlee and AmyJo tore apart the adjoining dressing room but didn't find them.

"Maybe they're in her car and she just forgot to bring them inside,"

Charlee said. She stuck her head in the doorway and called, "Does anyone know which rental car is Allegra's?"

Nobody said anything. Charlee asked again, louder this time.

"I think it's a red SUV," Decolletage said.

Bianca shot her a dirty look.

"Sheesh, Bianca, I'm not going to steal it!" Charlee executed an overzealous eye roll that hurt her neck. She and AmyJo hurried to the inn's small parking lot.

Charlee cupped her hands around her eyes to peer in the windows of the only red SUV around. "There's sure a lot of stuff in here."

"It's probably already packed for her honeymoon. No reason to haul everything out only to have to repack it."

Charlee pulled on the hatch. She was surprised it opened. Maybe Bianca was right to be worried about car theft. She hoped if Allegra caught them snooping in her car they'd be forgiven. But probably only if they found the tiaras.

They stood at the back of the SUV and began rooting through bags and boxes.

Charlee found one filled with a dozen rolls of toilet paper. "They're going camping for their honeymoon. For a long time, by the looks of things." Or one of them has a medical condition, she thought. She suddenly felt guilty prying into Allegra's life and was about to stop when her hand touched on something that felt tiara-like. She pulled out six tiaras and AmyJo whooped. They slammed the hatch and hurried back to the hair and makeup room.

They heard the caterwauling as soon as they opened the outside door. Took the stairs two at a time. Charlee waved the tiaras in the air and shouted, "I have them! They're here!" She skidded to a stop when she saw it was Allegra's mother doing the shrieking, and not Allegra.

AmyJo crashed into Charlee's back.

Charlee looked at Allegra, who stared numbly at her shrieking mother. She hurried to Allegra and pressed the tiaras into her hands. "Everything's fine. They're right here, shiny and perfect."

Allegra's mother stomped and stormed around the room, tearing into every pile and bag in sight.

Charlee stepped backward to the doorway. "What's going on?" she whispered to the hairdresser.

She leaned close. "The wedding dress has been stolen. The bride said she hung it right over there this morning, but now it's gone."

"Oh no!" Charlee's hand fluttered to her mouth.

"Who would steal a wedding dress?" AmyJo asked.

Charlee pulled AmyJo by the arm out of the room. "Nobody. You said yourself Allegra had a lot on her mind. She probably forgot her dress in her car just like she forgot the tiaras. C'mon, before she blows a gasket."

"At least Allegra is calm," AmyJo said.

"She's not calm, she's in shock."

They bunched fistfuls of dress, racing back to Allegra's car. This time they ransacked it, AmyJo from the back seat and Charlee from the rear hatch.

"I found it!" AmyJo shouted. "It was stuffed under the back seat."

They both carried it, hurrying awkwardly back to the bride's room. Everyone had disappeared except for Allegra and her mother who apparently hadn't stopped raving the entire time.

Allegra sat, a blank look on her face. "I tried to tell you," she said quietly. Her mother didn't respond, probably hadn't heard over her own wailing.

Charlee handed the wrinkled pile of wedding dress to Allegra's mother then dropped to one knee next to Allegra and whispered, "We'll figure out who did this."

Allegra didn't respond.

"I know it's hard to wrap your head around someone you know trying to sabotage your wedding, but I swear to you, we'll get to the bottom of it." Charlee gave Allegra a one-armed squeeze around her shoulders then again pulled AmyJo from the room.

AmyJo went the opposite direction. "I still need my hair done."

Charlee followed her to the hair and makeup room. "There's no time! We have to figure out what's going on."

"What are you talking about?"

"AmyJo, that was no accident. That dress was stuffed in there on purpose. No bride treats her wedding dress that way."

"Somebody is purposely trying to wreck Allegra's wedding? Who?

Why?"

Charlee put a finger to her lips while pulling AmyJo down the hall, away from everyone. "For starters," Charlee said quietly, "Bianca. Did you see that look she gave me when I said we'd go look for the tiaras in Allegra's car? She didn't want us near that car." She looked meaningfully at AmyJo. "Perhaps so we wouldn't find the tiaras or the dress."

AmyJo leaned in. "Why would she hide them in Allegra's own car, though?"

Charlee thought for a minute. "I don't know, but let's go find out."

"Charlee, this wedding starts in less than an hour."

"Then we better hurry!"

THEY RACED AROUND THE inn, searching for Bianca, finally locating her in the kitchen. She sat on the floor in the corner. Her right ankle was iced, resting on top of her left thigh, her dress puddling around her like a melted orange Creamsicle.

Charlee and AmyJo stood over her, moving closer and closer as the kitchen staff bustled around behind them.

◊ If Buddy's killer is a blood relative of his, poison was not used. ◊

"Is the wedding starting?" Bianca asked worriedly.

"Would that bother you?" Charlee asked pointedly.

She shifted the ice. "What are you talking about?"

"Why didn't you want me to go to look in Allegra's car for the tiaras?" Charlee stared straight down at her.

Bianca stared straight up. "If you must know, I didn't want you to find the decorations Fiona and I were going to use on the car. We stashed them there for convenience's sake after hearing Allegra tell Liam it was unlocked. And now we probably won't even have time to decorate it since you led us on that wild goose chase to the spa."

Charlee scrunched up her forehead, thinking. "The rolls of toilet paper?"

Bianca sucked in a breath. "Did you decorate the car without us?"

"Of course not! We were looking for the tiaras. Which you didn't want us to find."

"Why wouldn't I want you to find them?" Bianca patted the sparkly tiara nestled in her hairdo. "I look fantastic." She smoothed the bodice of her dress and floofed the skirt around her on the floor. "Now, if only I could walk."

Charlee frowned. "You're telling me the only reason you didn't want us near the car was because you were afraid we'd TP the car without you?"

"Why else?"

"Ohferpetes—Where's Fiona?" Charlee asked.

"How should I know?"

Charlee and AmyJo bolted from the kitchen and almost crashed into Fiona carrying a long stick. She pointed the weapon at them. They flinched and backed away.

"Have you guys seen Bianca? I can't find her anywhere." Fiona shook the stick at them. "I tried to find her a cane, but this was the best I could do."

AmyJo pointed at the kitchen door.

"Wait." Charlee grabbed Fiona's arm. "Were you and Bianca going to cover Allegra's car in toilet paper?"

"Yeah! Hilarious, right?"

"Seems wasteful," AmyJo said with a disapproving shake of her head.

"Why were you trying to get everyone drunk this morning?" Charlee asked Fiona.

"Allegra told me to! She said everything was so boring and insipid." AmyJo started to say something, but Fiona quickly added, "Her words. Not mine. She made me promise to keep pouring mimosas to liven the party up."

"Did you hide all the food too?" AmyJo asked.

"I wish I had, then I could go get some. I'm starving." Fiona practiced using the stick as a cane while entering the kitchen.

Charlee and AmyJo watched her go, then looked at each other. In unison they said, "Ellory."

They saw her in the middle of the area where the staff was setting up chairs for the ceremony around her. She appeared to be searching for something on the floor.

When Charlee and AmyJo reached her, she looked up. "Have you guys seen my—"

AmyJo pointed to the top of her head.

"Oh, cheese and rice!" Ellory disentangled her glasses from her tiara and placed them on her face.

"Ellory," Charlee said, "did you know Allegra was trying to get everyone drunk? Is that why you didn't order any food?"

"I did order food. I can prove it. I have an emailed receipt." She patted all the nonexistent pockets in her bridesmaid dress until AmyJo pointed at the phone in her hand. She clicked and scrolled then stepped close to them. "Here it is. Everyone thinks I'm ditzy because my memory sucks, so I wasn't sure myself until I went to find the receipt. See? I ordered a ton of food! Fruit, cheese, pastries, all kinds of stuff."

"Then where was it?" AmyJo quirked one eyebrow.

"That's what's so weird. After I found the receipt, I called the restaurant to complain, and they told me I cancelled the order."

"You did?"

"No!" She paused. "I don't think so, anyway." She glanced at her phone then patted her glasses. "I mean, why would I?"

"Because you're in love with Allegra's groom and wanted to ruin the wedding?" Charlee said. "We saw you canoodling—"

"Canoodling?"

"Yeah, you know, kissy face and stuff." AmyJo struck a pose.

"No, more like this." Charlee struck a sexier pose.

"Oh," Ellory said, nodding. "Canoodling."

"Yes. With Liam—"

"Who's Liam?"

"The groom."

"Oh. I thought his name was Leo. Never met him until yesterday." Ellory wandered away from them and Charlee couldn't think of a reason to call her back.

They both stared after her.

"Excellent liar, or complete ditz?" AmyJo asked.

"Let's go find the groom and ask."

Charlee and AmyJo hiked up their dresses again and scurried across the parking lot from the main part of the inn to the smaller building where the groomsmen were getting ready. As she pulled open the door to the building, a glint of sunlight on metal flashed. She turned toward the direction it came from and saw Liam closing Allegra's car door. Charlee called his name. He looked directly at them, then took off in the opposite direction.

Charlee and AmyJo again grabbed handfuls of taffeta and finally chased him down near the swimming pool. Charlee was ready to throw him in if necessary.

He wasn't wearing his tuxedo jacket yet so Charlee grabbed him by the back of his cummerbund and yanked him to a stop.

AmyJo bent over, placed her hands on knees, panting.

Charlee kept her grip on him and tried to catch her breath. "We saw you...canoodling...with Ellory."

"Canoodling? What are you talking about?"

AmyJo straightened up and struck her canoodling pose. "Canoodling. You know."

"I know what canoodling is. I'm not an idiot. But what does it have to do with Ellory?"

"You and she were standing awfully close yesterday at the—" Charlee said.

"You mean like you and I are now?" he asked sarcastically. "Are *we* canoodling now?"

Charlee dropped her grip on his cummerbund and took a step backward.

Liam brushed himself off and straightened his clothes. "Ellory is hard of hearing so she tends to stand a little too close to people."

Charlee and AmyJo shared a quick *that's legit* look.

"Why do you dart away every time we come near?" Charlee asked him.

"You're a mystery writer. YOU figure it out!" Liam darted across the lawn.

Charlee needed a moment to think. She pointed to a glider and AmyJo nodded. They sat, staring toward the parking lot.

"AmyJo, what if he was tampering with Allegra's car somehow because he and Ellory are in love and going to run off, maybe even leaving her at the altar?" Charlee gasped. "Or what if he's only marrying her for her money and *then* he'll run off with Ellory?"

"That would be terrible!"

"Even more terrible if he messed with her car somehow. Not a divorce...maybe a fatal car crash!" Charlee helped AmyJo extricate herself from the glider and they hurried to the car, tossing looks over their shoulders as they went.

Allegra's car was still unlocked. AmyJo opened the driver's door. "Get in," she whispered to Charlee. "We can't leave the doors hanging open. Someone might see."

"Good point." Charlee brushed a maple leaf from the driver's seat and sat, searching the console and dash for anything that seemed out of place.

AmyJo was on hands and knees in the back seat, dress up over her butt, rooting through everything she could reach.

"What do you think I'm looking for up here?" Charlee asked.

"No idea." AmyJo's response was muffled, since her head was fully immersed in a Neiman Marcus bag.

Charlee wrangled her dress so she could kneel and look over the driver's seat at AmyJo. "Nothing seems weird up here. Are you finding anything?"

"Lots of things. None of which seem to explain anything."

"I'll try in back." Charlee squirmed from the front seat and closed the door quietly before opening the hatch. She pushed bags and boxes out of the way to make room so she could heave herself inside. She scooted backward, then closed the hatch. "It's dark back here." She was systematic about her search, but her system consisted solely of dumping the contents from each bag, then tossing it over her head behind her.

"There's nothing in here!" Charlee howled, pounding her fists on a small carryon suitcase. "What are we doing?"

AmyJo popped up over the back seat. "We're looking for something—anything—in this car that shows Liam has any nefarious plans. This whole affair has been fishy from the minute we got here. We're not leaving until Allegra and Liam are happily ever aftering!"

Charlee sighed deeply. "AmyJo, we have been over this entire car. There's nothing here." She bent all the way over and rested her forehead forlornly on the suitcase.

"What's in that?"

Charlee didn't lift up her head. "In what?"

"Your pillow there."

Charlee straightened up. "I'm not going through Allegra's luggage."

"Why not? We've gone through everything else."

Charlee dropped her head again.

"We're running out of time, Charlee. Just open it."

Charlee heaved herself up as if she weighed seven hundred pounds. She unzipped the suitcase and flopped it open, revealing skimpy camisoles, barely-there nightgowns, and a lot of black lace.

AmyJo grabbed one of the camisoles, dislodging the whole bunch. "This is beautiful," she marveled, holding it to her torso. "I'd need two of them to cover the girls, of course, but—"

"Look what you did! Now she'll—" Something caught Charlee's eye. She swept aside the rest of the lingerie. "Look at this!"

AmyJo dropped the cami and leaned over the seat. She tried to see what Charlee was holding. "What is it?"

Slowly, Charlee turned the small framed photo so AmyJo could see.

AmyJo squinted. "Is that...Allegra and Liam? At a wedding?"

"Not any wedding. *Their* wedding!" Charlee pointed. "They're in the center of the picture. And look at those bridesmaids!"

"All of Allegra's friends from college!" AmyJo pointed and named each one.

Charlee dug through the suitcase. A small box with the top of a wedding cake inside. A pretty bouquet in a box. Charlee looked at the photo again. The same bouquet Allegra held in the picture. A pair of white sneakers on which someone had written in puff paint *Here comes the bride* on one, and a big heart with *Taos 2023* on the other. Charlee pulled a piece of paper from a large envelope. She held it up and pointed to the curlicue words at the top. Marriage Certificate.

"They got married last week in Taos, New Mexico."

"That's impossible! They're both inside there, getting ready to get married." AmyJo studied the certificate. "Allegra must have been married before. This is a guy named Pierpont William Summersby." AmyJo's smile evaporated. "What if it's this Pierpont guy trying to sabotage this wedding?

We've gotta go warn Allegra!"

Charlee showed her the date, just last week.

AmyJo frowned, trying to piece the puzzle together. "Dates can be forged."

Charlee held up the photo. "That's them, though."

AmyJo squinted again. "Is it?"

Charlee studied it closer. "Now I'm not sure." Suddenly her eyes widened. "What if it's Allegra who is planning on doing something to Liam so she can be with this Pierpont guy?"

AmyJo's eyes matched Charlee's. "Like what?"

"I don't know, but we need to stop this wedding!" Charlee shoved the marriage certificate back in the envelope and tried to disengage herself from the wreckage she'd made in the car. She was tangled in yards of slippery dress fabric. Any direction she turned, something stopped her progress to open the hatch.

AmyJo had vacated the back seat, so Charlee threw the envelope in AmyJo's direction, then executed a tactical somersault worthy of an Army Ranger, landing directly on the seat.

AmyJo helped her out of the car. They balled their dresses in both hands and sprinted toward the inn.

Two ushers in tuxedos opened the doors and they rushed through. The orchestra played Pachelbel's Canon. Bianca was almost to her place near the wedding arch. Fiona was halfway to her spot next to Bianca. Decolletage was just beginning her step-pause-step, following Fiona. Liam and his groomsmen were waiting nervously, expectantly, facing the crowd.

Charlee and AmyJo flew up the back stairs and down the hallway. The long train of Allegra's wedding dress was peeking out from the top of the landing of the spiral staircase. They screeched up to her and saw the surprised face of Allegra's father, standing next to her.

"It's about time you showed up! Perfect timing, but you almost ruined my fancy wedding! We couldn't have that now, could we?" Allegra said.

Charlee and AmyJo both started talking at once.

Allegra raised one hand. "Why are you both breathing so hard?"

Charlee pulled the marriage certificate from the envelope. "Why are you sabotaging your own wedding?" She didn't know what she expected, but it wasn't a grin from Allegra.

The orchestra launched into "Here Comes the Bride." Allegra linked arms with Charlee on one side and AmyJo on the other. "It's show time!" She stepped aside, pulling them with her. "You go first, Dad."

He did, perplexed by this change of plan.

Allegra watched him go. Hidden from view on the landing, they heard the crowd start mumbling in low voices. Charlee heard Allegra's mother say in a shrill voice, "Where's Allegra? You were supposed to escort her down!"

Allegra and her two confused hostages began the slow step-by-step descent of the spiral staircase. The chattering of the crowd stopped as they came into view. At the first turn, the staircase narrowed and the three women had to squeeze close together. At the second turn, it narrowed a bit more.

Charlee and AmyJo were practically in Allegra's wedding dress with her.

Allegra stopped, overlooking the huge crowd. She released AmyJo and Charlee, waving her arms until only one wavering cello note remained.

"I just wanted to say, thank you all for coming to my mother's wedding. I don't know any of you, but I can only assume my father's campaign coffers are full to the brim now!" Allegra spoke brightly. "But I have an announcement. This is all a sham. I'm already married!" Allegra pulled a necklace from inside her dress. A ring dangled from it. She held it up, showing the crowd gaping up at the scene on the stairs.

Allegra's mother stood and shouted up at her. "To whom?"

Allegra didn't answer, simply crooked her finger at someone.

Charlee looked at the marriage certificate in her hand. "Pierpont William Summersby," she muttered. "Liam. Short for William. Duh."

"Duh." AmyJo slapped her forehead.

"Duh." Allegra looked back at them with a grin.

She shooed them down the stairs and Liam joined her.

Charlee and AmyJo grabbed the nearest chairs to watch the rest of this show.

Allegra's mother blustered toward the staircase, clearly intending to storm the castle until she remembered a ballroom of people stared at her. She stopped in the center of the room and placed her hands angrily on her hips. "What is all this about, young lady? We have bent over backward to give you the wedding of your dreams!"

Allegra and Liam joined hands. "First, I'm not all that young. Second, this is the wedding of *your* dreams. I told you I wanted a small wedding with a few friends and family. A DJ with dance tunes, not a thirty-piece orchestra. Mexican buffet, not a five-course dinner."

"And a margarita station." Liam nudged Allegra. "Don't forget the margarita station."

"A Mexican buffet and margaritas?" Allegra's mother turned toward the guests. "I would never have subjected you to that!"

Someone in the crowd shouted, "I love Mexican food! All that guacamole and cheese..."

Someone else shouted, "Big fan of margaritas! Can I get one?"

Allegra's mother whipped around toward the voice. "Of course not." Her voice dripped with disdain.

"Too bad!"

"Yeah, too bad!"

Allegra's mother turned back to the staircase. "You said this was all fine with you! You are an ungrateful child!"

"I knew this would happen, so I came prepared." Allegra dug into a hidden pocket in her wedding dress and pulled out a phone.

"She has pockets!" AmyJo nudged Charlee.

Allegra motioned for the crowd to be quiet, then clicked on an audio file and held it outstretched in front of her. Her recorded voice said, "We just want a small wedding. Mexican food, margaritas. Real simple."

"What'd she say?" a voice in the back called.

The message was relayed in waves across the room. Allegra paused the recording until a hand waved in the furthest corner of the room.

She pressed play. Her mother's tinny voice said, "This is our chance to fleece a bunch of donors. And if we're paying, we have final say."

The words again traveled in waves across the room, along with some gasps and at least one, "Well, I never!"

The rest of the recording went the same way.

"Then keep your money. We'll pay for our wedding ourselves."

"Don't be ridiculous."

"Okay, fine."

"See?" Allegra's mother turned to the crowd. "She said fine!"

By then, half the crowd was heading for the exit. Most everyone made a special detour, however, to call up their good wishes to Allegra and Liam on the spiral staircase on their way out.

Allegra's parents had disappeared. When the crowd thinned, Charlee and AmyJo climbed the stairs toward Allegra and Liam.

Charlee leaned on the railing a few steps below the happy couple. "So, neither of you were trying to kill the other. You were trying to get back at your mother, so you gave me wrong directions to the spa."

Allegra giggled. "That was inspired. It was only supposed to be masks onsite. But when I saw they did full-body wraps, I knew that would take up a ton of time."

"You cancelled Ellory's breakfast order. You told Decolletage we all were good at yoga. You told Fiona to get us drunk."

"Yep. We barely got through half of Mom's itinerary. I had more planned, until you stole my thunder." Allegra pointed at the certificate. "What were you doing in my car, anyhow? In my suitcase in my car, to be precise."

"We saw Liam messing around and got worried. What were *you* doing in there?" Charlee asked him.

"Leaving Allegra a love note."

"There was no love note in that car," AmyJo said.

"A maple leaf? On the seat?" he said. "It was code."

Charlee laughed. "I brushed that off. Sorry."

"Wait," Allegra said. "You thought he was trying to kill me? Why?"

"Because every time we saw him, he'd run away. Very suspish." Charlee narrowed her eyes at him. "Why'd you do that, anyway?"

Liam reddened. "I would have spoiled Allegra's plan. I have no poker face."

"That's putting it mildly!" AmyJo said.

"But why such a big scheme?" Charlee asked.

Allegra wrinkled her nose. "I had to take a stand. My mother ignores me until she wants to use me to get campaign donations. She's done this my whole life."

"I hope you find a way back to each other. My mom is the most important person in my life." Charlee turned toward AmyJo. "Don't tell Ozzi."

They glanced down and saw Fiona and Bianca speak to the conductor. As they walked away, Bianca aided by the stick, the orchestra struck up some Lady Gaga.

"Let's dance!" Allegra shouted.

The bridal party met on the dance floor and boogied to pop songs played in sumptuous orchestration.

Bianca and Fiona disappeared after a few songs but returned with the catering staff carrying trays of tacos and pitchers of margaritas.

An hour later Charlee looked toward a far corner of the room where Allegra stood with her parents, talking. Charlee nudged AmyJo.

When Allegra and her mother hugged, they both got puppy dog eyes and said, "Aww!"

The orchestra packed up and Charlee and AmyJo headed to their room. Charlee pointed across the parking lot.

Every bit of Allegra's car was wrapped in toilet paper.

FOR MORE INFORMATION about the author, please visit Becky Clark's website: https://beckyclarkbooks.com/

Whodunit?

NOSY NEWS NETWORK
Official Press Release
For Immediate Publication

● ● ●

Those of us here at Nosy News Network are frantic to catch the late Buddy Bill Corey's killer. Have you been collecting the Wedding Whodunit clues? We certainly hope so!

If you've figured out who the killer is and what weapon they used to murder the unfortunate Buddy Bill Corey on his wedding day, don't forget to input the answer by December 31, 2025 in the format of "Killer/Weapon" (ex. "Tiger Corey/knife") on this webpage: https://marlabradeen.blogspot.com/p/malice.html If you're correct, you'll receive a free ebook download filled with fun extras such as recipes, alternative endings, character profiles, author interviews, bonus stories, and more.

A list of suspects and clues is included with our original press release located at the beginning of the book.

Thank you for taking on the case! We're eager for justice to be served and we know you are too.

Acknowledgments

To our readers, thank you for picking up our stories! If you enjoyed this collection, please consider leaving a review on your favorite online retailer and/or review site. Even a short review will be invaluable in helping us to connect with new readers.

To our Kickstarter backers, thank you so much for making this anthology possible! Your support made it possible for us to bring this collection to life. We would especially like to extend our gratitude to the following backers and believers: **Tammy Barker, Joyce Corey, Francelia Belton, Kristi Amick, Wil A. Emerson, Anonymous Reader, Ada Bell, Barb Goffman, Laura Rose, The Freeman Family, Rosie Pease, Laura Greg, Dr. Paula Stamp, James Bernier, Jr., Jill Hoover, Steven M. Smith, Jimmie Raymond, Maura Abbott, Jennifer Schindler, John Idlor, Mary Jo Rabe, Becky B, A, Jerrie the filkferengi, Betty Van Dyke, Kellye Garrett, Brooke Craig, Jackie Kripas, Olive Pollak, Dwayne Keller, Karen Fonville, Shannon Molloy, Suzanne Baginskie, Abigail, David H. Hendrickson, Gillian McDunn, Audrea Martin, Teresa Inge,** and **Karina Krogh**.

About the Authors

JOSLYN CHASE (https://joslynchase.com/) is an award-winning author of mysteries and thrillers. Any day she can send readers to the edge of their seats, chewing their fingernails to the nub and prickling with suspense, is a good day in her book. Joslyn's story, "Cold Hands, Warm Heart," was chosen by Amor Towles as one of the Best Mystery Stories of the Year 2023. Her stories have appeared in *Alfred Hitchcock's Mystery Magazine*, *Fiction River Magazine, Mystery, Crime, and Mayhem*, and *Mystery Magazine*, among others.

CHARLOTTE MORGANTI (https://charlottemorganti.com/) is a Canadian writer of crime fiction. She has been a burger flipper, beer slinger and a corporate finance/mining lawyer. Charlotte writes novels and short stories, ranging from gritty investigations to lighter capers. She usually sets her stories in small towns that miraculously harbour both villains (often cunning, occasionally inept) and the sleuths who pursue them. Charlotte and her husband live in a small town on the Sunshine Coast of British Columbia.

P.M. RAYMOND (http://www.pmraymond.com/) hails from New Orleans but currently lives on the East Coast with 27 cookbooks and an imaginary dog named Walter. You can find her enjoying a café au lait and indulging in the storytelling mastery of Shirley Jackson, M.R. James, Joe Hill, Tananarive Due, and manga maestro, Junji Ito. Her work has appeared in *Flash Fiction Magazine, Kings River Life Magazine, Dark Fire Fiction, Pyre Magazine, The Furious Gazelle*, and *Dark Yonder*. She is named to the 150 Black Women in Horror.

PAIGE SLEUTH (https://www.marlabradeen.com/) is a pseudonym for mystery author Marla Bradeen. She is the author of over forty novels and novellas, including the Cozy Cat Caper Mystery series set in the fictional small town of Cherry Hills, Washington.

TERESA INGE (http://www.teresainge.com/) is an author in the Mutt Mysteries series, Virginia is for Mysteries series, *50 Shades of Cabernet, Coastal Crimes: Mysteries by the Sea*, and *Murder by the Glass*. She is president of the Sisters in Crime, Mystery by the Sea chapter, and a member of the Hampton Roads Writers, and Short Mystery Fiction Society. Combining her love of reading mysteries and writing professional articles led to her writing short fiction. She can be reached on all social media.

SALLY MILLIKEN (http://www.sallymillikenauthor.com/) writes contemporary and historical mysteries and crime fiction. In January 2023, her first short story called 'Trailblazer' was published in *Hook, Line, and Sinker: the 7th Guppy Anthology* from the Guppy Chapter of Sisters in Crime. Sally is working on her first novel, a story set in 1882 and based in the coastal area of Massachusetts where she lives with her family. Sally is a member of SinC, SinC NE, SinC Guppy Chapter, and the Short Mystery Fiction Society.

REBECCA OLMSTEAD (https://www.rebeccaolmstead.com/) is an award-winning author of short stories, mysteries, and non-fiction. Her work has appeared in multiple periodicals, and she has published four books. The debut of her Gabrielle Dorian Mystery series will release in October, 2023.

NIKKI KNIGHT (https://kathleenmarplekalb.com/nikki-knight) describes herself as an Author/Anchor/Mom...not in that order. An award-winning weekend anchor at New York City's 1010 WINS Radio, she writes short stories and novels including the upcoming Grace the Hit Mom Mystery *Wrong Poison* (July 2023, Charade Media). Her stories appear in magazines including *Alfred Hitchcock's Mystery Magazine*, online, and in anthologies. She, her husband, and son live in a Connecticut house owned by their cat.

SHARI HELD (http://www.shariheld.com/) is an Indianapolis-based, award-winning fiction author who spins tales of mystery/crime, horror, romance, and fantasy. Her short stories have been published in dozens of magazines and anthologies, including *White Cat Publications*, *Hoosier Noir*, *Yellow Mama*, *Asinine Assassins*, *The Big Fang*, and *Murder 20/20*, for which she served as co-editor.

BARBARA HOWARD (http://www.authorbarbarahoward.com/) is a mystery and YA author of over a dozen books, including the trilogy, Finding Home Mystery Series; *Final Harvest*, *Charlotte's Revenge*, and *Milo's Journey*. She is a first generation tech geek turned master gardener. She returned to her Midwestern hometown after an extensive career as a Department of Defense Project Manager at the Pentagon and spends most of her time treasure hunting, spoiling her fur-babies, growing veggies, and plotting whodunits.

ASHLEY-RUTH M. BERNIER'S (http://ashleyruthbernier.com/) short fiction has appeared or is forthcoming in *Ellery Queen Mystery Magazine*, *Black Cat Weekly*, *Stone's Throw*, and *The Best American Mystery and Suspense 2023*. Originally from St. Thomas, Virgin Islands, she is an emerging writer of Caribbean mysteries. Ashley-Ruth lives with her husband and 4 children in North Carolina, where she teaches first grade and finds very few things more valuable than uninterrupted writing time.

KD SHERRINFORD (http://www.kdsherrinford.co.uk/) was born in Preston Lancashire in the UK. She now lives on The Fylde Coast with her husband and their children. An avid reader from an early age KD was fascinated by the stories of Agatha Christie and Sir Arthur Conan Doyle. She gained inspiration to start work on her debut novel *Song for Someone* after a visit to The Sherlock Holmes museum in 2019. The first two books in The Sherlock Holmes and Irene Adler Mystery series were published last year by Extasy Books.

STEPHEN D. ROGERS (http://www.StephenDRogers.com/) is the author of *Shot to Death* and more than 800 shorter works. His website includes a list of new and upcoming titles as well as other timely information.

ELAINE TOGNERI (http://www.elainetogneri.com/) has over forty published short stories in markets ranging from webzines and anthologies (*Malice Domestic 15: Murder Most Theatrical*) to major magazines (*Woman's World*). Her story "Genius" appeared in 2021's MWA Anthology: *When a Stranger Comes to Town*. She is a member of Mystery Writers of America and Sisters in Crime. Elaine holds an MA in English from Rutgers University and is the founder of the Sisters in Crime—NJ Chapter. Webpage—elainetogneri.com @ElaineTogneri

LYNN HESSE (https://www.lynnhesse.com/) is an award-winning author of the novels: *Well of Rage, Murder in Mobile, A Matter of Respect, Murder in Mobile, Book 2, Another Kind of Hero*, and *The Forty Knots Burn*. Onyx Publications published "Shrewd Women" in 2022. "Bitter Love" appeared in *Crimeucopia, The I's Have It* by Murderous Ink Press, 2021, United Kingdom. As a modern ballet dancer and former law enforcement officer, she writes and lives with her husband and his rescue cats near Atlanta, Georgia.

MARGARET S. HAMILTON (https://margaretshamilton. wordpress.com/) has published over twenty short stories in anthologies and online publications, including "Black Market Baby" in *Masthead: Best New England Crime Stories*, and "Dealing at the Dump" in *Cozy Villages of Death*. Margaret is querying her first traditional amateur sleuth mystery, *Curtains for the Corpse*, set in a small Ohio college town. She lives in Cincinnati and is a member of Sisters in Crime and MWA. Margaret blogs monthly on the Writers Who Kill blog.

BRITISH NIGERIAN AUTHOR STELLA ONI (https:// stellaonithewriter.com/), enriches her crime fiction with insights from her dual-cultural background. Her debut, *Deadly Sacrifice*, the first in her police procedural, the Toks Ade series, was a SI Leeds Literary Prize finalist. "The Black Widow of Oshogbo," featured in the anthology *Midnight Hour*, is part of her Lara's Detective Agency series—a work in progress. She's also putting the finishing touches to the first of her new edgy cozy, The London House Mystery series.

ROBERT PETYO IS A DERRINGER award finalist whose stories have appeared in small press magazines and anthologies. He writes primarily mysteries, but also SF, fantasy and horror and an occasional mainstream piece. He lives in Northeastern Pennsylvania, is happily married, and is recently retired from the Postal Service, which allows him more time to read and write. Unfortunately, there never seems to be enough time to read and write.

PAMELA KYEL (http://pamelakyel.com/) is Baltimore (pronounced "Bawlmer"), Maryland, born and raised. Life has taken her from Maryland to Montana to Italy and points in between, courtesy of the US Air Force. Being a military spouse, she has a front-row seat to the workings of the military, and she uses that in her book, *Charm City Crab Puff*. She is a member of Mystery Writers of America and Sisters in Crime.

KAREN MCCULLOUGH (https://kmccullough.com/) has authored dozens of published novels and stories in the mystery, romance, suspense and fantasy genres, including the Market Center Mysteries Series, originally published by Five Star/Cengage and reprinted by Harlequin Worldwide Mystery Library, and three books in the No Brides Club series. A member of Mystery Writers of America, Sisters in Crime, and the Short Mystery Fiction Society, she is also past president of the Southeast chapter of MWA and served on the national board.

WIL A. EMERSON (https://www.wilemerson.com/), a registered nurse turned full time author, always had a desire to write. Her love for the unknown, solving mysteries led to the publication of her first novel. She's acquired a long list of short story publications with leading anthologies.

"Unexpected Reunion," a top five finalist in the 2022 Derringer Award, "Unfurled" published in India, and Murderous Ink Press, London, featured two of her deadly engaging stories. The Wally and Ollie series is a humorous, murderous collection.

JACK BATES IS AN AWARD winning writer of short fiction, screenplays, and stage plays. His most recent play, *The Sketch Show*, premiered with the Bunbury Theatre troupe in upstate New York.

J. AQUINO IS AN ATTORNEY, retired journalist, and author. His fiction has appeared in *A Matter of Crime Vol. 2*, *Shakespearean Whodunnits*, *More Shakespearean Whodunnits*, and *Royal Whodunnits*. He is a member of the Mystery Writers of America and the National Press Club.

GHOSTWRITER OF MORE than 20 non-fiction best-sellers, SHARYN KOLBERG has moved into fiction, with short stories appearing in *Ellery Queen Mystery Magazine*, *Mystery Magazine*, *Black Cat Weekly*, *Literal Latte*, *Mensa Bulletin Fiction Issue* and Akashic Books "Mondays are Murder."

AWARD-WINNING AUTHOR BECKY CLARK (https:// beckyclarkbooks.com/) is seventh of eight kids, which explains both her insatiable need for attention and her atrocious table manners. She likes to read funny books so it felt natural to write them. She surrounds herself with quirky people and pets who end up as characters in her novels. She writes several cozy mystery series, and *Eight Weeks to a Complete Novel—Write Faster, Write Better, Be More Organized*. Visit https://beckyclarkbooks. com/ for your "Becky Clark Starter Kit" of free books.

Milton Keynes UK
Ingram Content Group UK Ltd.
UKHW040603130923
428584UK00001B/52